Wartime Brisbane ma
Pinney. Too young fo...
tographic colourist, munitions worker, ambulance
driver, and finally nursing to the end of WWII.
Twenty odd years later found her on M.V. Ocean
Spray co-authoring the historical novel of Cape
York, *Too Many Spears* with husband-writer, the
late Peter Pinney. Today she lives in Queensland.

Time Out for Living

Estelle Pinney

Pan Macmillan Australia

First published 1995 in Pan by Pan Macmillan Australia Pty Limited
St. Martin's Tower, 31 Market Street, Sydney

In association with
Selwa Anthony

Copyright © Estelle Runcie-Pinney 1995

All rights reserved. No part of this book may be reproduced or
transmitted in any form or by any means, electronic or mechanical,
including photocopying, recording or by any information storage
and retrieval system, without prior permission in writing from
the publisher.

National Library of Australia
cataloguing-in-publication data:
Pinney, Estelle.
Time out for living
ISBN 0 330 356 57 7.
I. Title.
A823.3

Typeset in 10½/13½ Sabon by Midland Typesetters, Maryborough, Victoria
Printed in Australia by McPherson's Printing Group

This book is dedicated to my dear companion and husband of so many wonderful years, author Peter Pinney. Thank you, Peter.

Acknowledgements

The author would like to thank family and friends for their loving support and encouragement. Special thanks to Cousin Rita for her sharp-eyed vigilance; patient and willing typist Patricia Allen; good and true editor Barbara Ker Wilson; Val Hesterman who was often on hand to 'boil up the billy' and Curley Meath who knew all about larrikin sailors.

This book was written with the financial assistance of the Queensland Office of the Arts and Cultural Development—*Arts Queensland*.

1

*I*T'S NOT EVERY day in the week that a girl from Muckadilla joins the Navy.

Destiny caught up with Lulla Riddel the day Chas, ex-yardman of the Royal Arms, charged into the bar in navy rig. Pulling beers had little to do with the war effort and Lulla had often dreamed of 'something better' ... someday. But a steady job, and her own small room at the Arms, was a voucher for security; a commodity she had rarely enjoyed. It was Chas, jaunty in uniform and a newfound self-esteem, who set the pace. So she counted her pennies, kissed the regulars good-bye, and caught the night train to Brisbane.

'Medically unfit!' Lulla could not believe her ears. 'What do you mean, "medically unfit"? I'm as strong as Riley's bull.'

The naval doctor's gaze remained impassive. 'I'm sorry, Miss Riddel.'

There had to be a mix-up. Someone else with her results. That other girl—the one with legs like a sparrow. But Sparrow-legs had flown. Accepted. She had marched off with the others under the trained eye of the petty officer.

What had they uncovered with their testing and their poking? T.B.? Something awful that she knew nothing about? Alarm bells clanged.

'Well, what is wrong with me? Tell me. I can take it.'

The doctor's lips twitched a fraction. 'Not as bad as all that. You are just myopic.'

'My—what?' It sounded like a dog's disease.

'Short-sighted. You need glasses.'

'Is that all ...' Her legs trembled with relief. She'd known that for years. Long ago the problem had been solved by learning to move closer. Friends had learned not to be offended if she passed them by without a sign of recognition.

'Well, that's easily fixed, isn't it? If I have to wear glasses—so be it.'

'I'm afraid it's not as easy as all that. You must understand—may I call you Lulla?' She noted the familiar gleam in his eye and an approval that had nothing to do with ships or the sea. She was used to that. 'However,' the naval officer continued, 'the Navy insists that recruits must have 20-20 vision. Without glasses.' His sympathy was genuine. 'Again, I'm sorry.'

He tapped his teeth with a pencil, and the gleam

returned. 'Er—you wouldn't care to—?' She knew what was coming. 'Dinner, perhaps?'

'No. No thank you.' He had one foot in the grave anyway ...

'H'm, pity.' He studied her, head on one side. 'You're certain?'

'Quite.'

The petty officer who had marched away with the recruits now returned.

'Tucked 'em up safely, sir.' Lulla was ignored. 'That the lot?'

'I'd say so.' The official facade slipped back into place and the doctor, with a brief nod of dismissal, motioned for Lulla to be shown the door.

'Good luck, Miss Riddel.'

Already the intruder, Lulla took one last look at the whitewashed buildings of H.M.A.S. Moreton. High-flying flags snapped at an errant breeze, and suntanned matelots, tramping across the gravelled square, whistled low as they crunched by. Not an hour ago she had walked through the gates, so confident, the idea of rejection—if she'd even thought of it—laughable.

Now what to do?

It was only a short walk to the river and the Gardens. A place to think things out. Poinciana trees shaded a path that followed the river's bend where lunch-time office girls and servicemen sauntered along the blossom-stippled path.

The Navy had suggested that she might try the Army. 'They're not so fussy.' Damn it, it was the

Navy she'd burned her bridges for. Not the bloody Army ... or the Airforce, for that matter. There was always bar work, of course. Once a barmaid, always a barmaid, as the saying goes. But that was finished with. For good.

Lulla absorbed the chatter and studied their style as girls passed her by; so carefree, so smart ... so *employed*. If only she could type! Shopwork? Now that was a thought! Not a bad idea: and the end to beer-sodden fingers and the inevitable throbbing whitlows.

'Hello there!' A young bombardier blocked her path. He stood as tall as she did, grinning wide under the slouch hat.

She was not in the mood for casual pick-ups. 'On your way, soldier. Can't you see I'm busy?' But it was said with a smile as she stepped aside to let him pass.

He made no move. 'Look, just a bit of a walk, eh? And there's the kiosk over there.' His eagerness touched her. 'We could have an ice-cream or something. Wouldn't take long. Wouldn't take up much of your time.' His gaze held hers, half-pleading.

A lemon tinge beneath the tan betrayed him. He was dosed up with atebrine. On leave from New Guinea? Or just going. Lulla felt herself weaken. The boy sensed it. 'Come on. The unit's leaving tonight, and I haven't spoken to a girl—especially a looker—for weeks.'

Definitely not. There was a job to be found, then a room somewhere or tonight she'd be sleeping under the stars. 'Sorry, mate—but I meant what I said.'

He shrugged, giving in. 'Can't blame a fella for trying ...'

A few paces on, she paused and turned. He was still there, looking very much alone. 'We—ll, all right. I could do with a cuppa anyway. It's been quite a morning. But'—she shook a warning finger—'we'll make it a Dutch treat, okay?'

'You little beauty!'

He was beside her in a flash and, falling in step they walked briskly to the kiosk.

Lulla's head was spinning. Things had happened too fast. Here she was standing outside MacIntyre's Light Metal Works, helpless in the face of actualities. If she had guessed how the day would end, there and then she would have caught the first train back to Muckadilla.

Lulla had left the boy-soldier back in the kiosk and had found Brisbane's Queen Street, torpid after its lunch-hour rush. It dozed. Surely, down that long thoroughfare of department stores, newsagencies, ironmongers and chain stores, work could be found to suit her style.

Allan & Stark thought so, and would have placed her that very afternoon behind Soaps and Perfumery. But A&S had little to say in the matter. Now if Manpower would release her, well ....

The Manpower Committee! She hadn't given it a thought. Muckadilla never had one. To Lulla, Manpower meant the faceless wartime bureaucrats who without fear or favour, could snatch a girl out of one job and shove her into another. Or a man, for that matter. Man and Woman power, she thought resentfully.

The story was the same wherever she went. Manpower had the first pick of the single girls, and the last say. Eventually she found herself in a dreary government office where a humourless soul entered her name in a ledger, handed over forms to be filled in and then directed her to MacIntyre's on the other side of the river.

The galvanised gates were shut tight, but the sound of machinery screeching and whining, clattering and banging, told her that MacIntyre's was hard at it. She wondered if her knocks could be heard above the din. Then a narrow door, a mere slit in the long iron fence, opened.

'Yes?' A man, too old for soldiering, squinted her over, then beckoned her to step inside.

'I was told—*ordered*—to report here.'

The man sniggered, holding out a hand for Lulla's papers. 'They're roping 'em in today. You're the third.'

The more she saw of MacIntyre's, the less she liked it. Trapped! Jesus wept ... what a dump! She recalled the boozy comfort of the Royal's bar room.

This was like a prison.

Everything in sight was made of roofing iron: fences, walls, partitions. Sheets and sheets of it: battleship grey if newly erected; rusting and gaping in the older sections. To the right of the gates a shed had been converted into an office. Across the yard and to the left was a two-storeyed structure of fibreboard and sheeting iron. A sign on the top landing read WOMEN'S CHANGE ROOM.

A small group of women in overalls left the room and clattered down the stairs. It amazed her that they found anything to be cheerful about, but they beamed a friendly greeting as they passed close by. The women entered a building squatting fatly beside what appeared to be the main machine-shop. There was a covered breezeway that joined the two, with crates stacked shoulder-high against one of the walls.

The gatekeeper handed back her papers and pointed over to the office.

'Ask for Mrs Daniels.' He gave her bottom a friendly squeeze, ignoring Lulla's glare. 'We'll be seeing you.'

Not if I see you first, you randy old coot!

A woman appeared at the office door, and stood there waiting. Not quite fifty, Lulla guessed, but smartly dressed, with her hair pressed neatly into puce-tinted finger waves. She took the proffered forms without a word. It had to be the Daniels woman.

'H'm, a barmaid. Well, it cannot be helped, I suppose.'

Pardon me for living ... The heated asphalt burned through the soles of Lulla's shoes, and rivulets of sweat tickled her neck. How long was she expected to stand in the sun? As if in answer, Mrs Daniels looked up, frowning.

'Can you begin right away?'

'You mean now? This very minute?'

'Isn't that what I said?'

'Yes—well, no! I only arrived this morning. I was going to enlist, but—'

Mrs Daniels' expression signalled a distaste for barmaids wishing to enlist.

'Besides,' Lulla gabbled on, 'I haven't the right sort of clothes.'

'We supply overalls, of course.'

Overalls! Instead of smart and snappy navy whites. Lulla could have wept. What a blob!

'But Mrs Daniels,' she countered desperately, 'I've got to find lodgings. For tonight.'

As the factory could not provide accommodation, Mrs Daniels had to let the matter rest. 'Oh, very well then. Begin tomorrow at seven sharp,' she said shortly. 'Now come along and meet your shift. That will save some time.' She stalked ahead, calling over her shoulder: 'You're consigned to the lacquer room. The annexe.'

It was the smaller building. Here it was quiet. Large push-out windows overlooked the river. It seemed as if the annexe had been an afterthought, without fencing, and with a park flush against the building's outer wall.

Not a lathe in sight, but shallow crates like those stacked in the breezeway covered most of the central floor space. Like grey metal eggs snug in straw nests, the boxes held rows of newly moulded hand grenades. Benches lined the walls and the women

Lulla had seen leaving the change room were busily occupied. In spite of the open windows the air reeked with the smell of varnish: not surprising, as large pots of the stuff were placed within easy reach of each woman's paintbrush.

Mrs Daniels inspected a varnished grenade inside and out. 'You see, it's all quite easy.' She was the schoolmarm lecturing a not-so-bright pupil. 'And over here'—one pale hand indicated an area partitioned off with cyclone wire—'is the finishing or drying room. It speaks for itself. We call it the cage.' Lulla could see two of the team busy screwing in bases, attaching levers and pins to the shellac-bright hand bombs.

There was another barricade of wire dividing the cage from what Mrs Daniels called the holding room. From where they stood it was easy to see the tiers upon tiers of completed grenades. Crate upon crate. Silent, sinister rows, high enough to block out light from the squares of glass set into the sloping iron roof. It was a brooding fortress of weaponry; a backdrop for death. Lulla shivered and marvelled that a handful of women could tackle so cheerfully what seemed a gigantic and lethal task.

'Those women have done all that?' She had already assumed that the grenades were made in the main shop.

'There are two shifts, day and night,' said Mrs Daniels.

'Any chance of the whole lot blowing up?'

Mrs Daniels snorted at such ignorance. 'They're

not filled with explosives, naturally. That is handled elsewhere. You need not know about it. *Security*.' She rolled the word 'security' around her mouth, enjoying the flavour of it.

A chunky lad appeared through a side door. He carried a bucket brimming with shellac. Sighting Mrs Daniels, he froze; but a nod from one of the women encouraged him to step inside. He did the rounds topping up the pots, careful not to spill a drop. He carried his head down and to the side, not daring to meet the women's gaze.

'That's the boy Micky,' Mrs Daniels said in undertones. 'He does most of the lifting.' Her eyes followed his every move. 'He also has a nose problem ... among other things.' There was a handkerchief pinned to the bib of Micky's overalls, and as he came closer Lulla realised that he was more than a boy. He was a man approaching his middle years. He hurried past, averting his eyes, and slopping varnish into the last remaining pot he scuttled through the door.

All the while they had been in the annexe, not one head had been raised in greeting—nor curiosity. Mrs Daniels obviously applauded such dedication to the war effort. She was even smiling.

'Ah, yes—Janet.' A small, slim brunette was beckoned over. She had the look of the Irish, her delicate complexion flecked here and there by the sun, and small lines plucked at lips innocent of lipstick. Already Lulla was prescribing cold cream.

Mrs Daniels took hold of Janet's arm. 'You were

looking for someone to share your flat, I'm told.'

It was easy to guess that this was news to Janet. The girl flushed pink. 'No, Mrs D, I—'

'Your husband's at sea again. Is he not?'

'That's not the point at all.'

'Of course it is. You cannot live there alone.'

'I can, Mrs D. And I intend to.'

'It *is* West End after all.'

'Nothing wrong with West End,' Janet challenged.

'I wouldn't say that. Now Riddel, here—'

'Thank you, but no, Mrs Daniels!' Janet's pink was turning bright.

Lulla stood by, feeling helpless; all she could do was listen, speechless as a washerwoman sucking pegs. The fight had gone out of her.

But the girl, Janet, was standing her dig. Here was the sparrow trouncing the crow. Mrs Daniels retreated by consulting her watch. 'Well, please yourself. I'll leave Riddel with you. She begins in the morning.'

Lulla pulled a face behind the disappearing back. '*Miss* Riddel to you, old cock.' She gave a fair imitation of the woman's strangled vowels. 'Now be good girls, and play nicely together. Jee-sus ... talk about bossy britches! Is she always like that?'

Together, they burst out laughing and Janet held out her hand. 'Most of the time, yes. Then after all that, she forgets to introduce us. I'm Janet Hope.'

'And I'm Lulla. As in Lullaby. And by the way— I can find my own bed and breakfast.'

At that moment an older woman came into the

annexe. She had a tally sheet and board tucked under her arm. 'Hoo—we didna' make it. We'll—' She caught sight of Lulla. 'Hello, who have we here?'

'Reinforcements coming up, Andy,' Janet said. 'Lulla, meet our forewoman, Mrs Anderson.'

'Call me Andy. They all do.' She was a Scot with a burr to match. Her pale eyes behind pebble glasses assessed the new recruit. She took a quick look at Lulla's ringless fingers, and gave a small grunt of satisfaction. 'Not married, lass. That's something. Ye'll be here for a good wee while then. Now come with us to the change room. I'll find you a locker.'

Just then a whistle shrilled and the day shift came to an end. Brushes were downed; the night shift was already waiting outside.

'They're keen,' said Lulla, excusing herself past them.

'Aye. We all are.'

The factory was now brisk with workers on collision course; the day shift eager to be gone, the night shift anxious to start. As the three women crossed the yard, Andy voiced her relief that another hand would swell the ranks. But not for long, she said, for the two walking ahead of them, sisters, would be leaving soon. Manpower had released them.

Lulla's mood took an upward swing. 'So you can get off the hook?'

'It's possible.' Andy pursed her lips, giving the matter some thought. 'There's ways and means; especially if the auld man is an M.P.'—nodding towards the two in front—'or a lawyer, or something like that. Now if your dad's one of those—or if you're married, well, then.' She was unperturbed by Lulla's disappointment. 'Cheer up, lass, it's not all that bad. Give it a chance.'

A trolley, pushed by a darkly handsome man, clattered towards them. About the same age as herself, Lulla guessed, and as the trolley drew level she found herself staring into a pair of black and merry eyes.

'Well, now ...' His glance flicked over her, like the quick lick of a tongue; but his grin made mock of his bold appreciation. 'Who have we here? Daryl Missim's the name, and remember, I saw you first. Apart from that, what are we doing tonight?'

'Give the lass a chance!' Andy gave him a friendly push. 'Just ignore him, love. By the way, Daryl, what's it feel like to be engaged, eh?'

Feigning innocent surprise, Daryl took a backward step. 'Fair go, Andy, the nuptials haven't started yet.' He threw Lulla a wink. 'Well, not quite, anyway.'

It was easy to tell that Daryl, for all his cheek, was tolerated and liked by the forewoman of the annexe. She sniffed. 'He's a bit of a lad, this one, Lulla, and I'd ignore him if I were you.' But she was smiling as she walked off to the change room.

But Lulla had no intention of ignoring the best thing that had happened in a day of disasters. Her saucy look matched Daryl's for pure cheek. 'Ask me another time.'

'How about tomorrow, then?'

'Aren't you the fast worker!'

'Gotta be quick ... How does the Cremorne Theatre

sound?' He produced two tickets from his overalls pocket and waved them under her nose. 'Happen to have these just in case. Vaudeville. Like it?'

'Try me out.' Lulla finished the sentence with a little soft-shoe shuffle.

'That's settled then. We'll start off with a slap-up feed at Nick's. Then a night of song and dance.' He twirled a moustache that wasn't there, giving her another broad wink. 'And who knows what else might be on the menu?'

'Nothing for you to nibble on.' Harmless enough, she judged, but he promised to be a ton of fun. He gave her a salute, the trolley a hefty push and rattled off whistling.

Janet was waiting at the bottom of the stairs; Andy had disappeared into the change room. Lulla wondered if the forewoman might think her too fast, but Janet laughed, shaking her head, and assured her that Andy was 'all right'.

'Is that chap Daryl really engaged?' Lulla asked as they walked up the stairs.

Janet shrugged. 'Could be a rumour, no one knows for sure. Anyway, it's said she's only a kid, still a schoolgirl.'

'Crikey! Never too young, eh?'

Janet smiled. 'That's those desert sheikhs for you. He's one of the Missim clothing factory tribe, you know.'

As they reached the top landing, Janet stopped and on impulse squeezed Lulla's hand. 'I'm real glad you're with us. I know you'll fit in. And by the way—

you can stay with me until you find a place that suits you.' She gave a wistful smile and admitted that Mrs Daniels had come close to the mark. 'I do get lonely. It's awful when Kirk's away. Not knowing where he is. Wondering if ... But that's what war's all about, isn't it.' She sighed, then brightened up. 'Hey! Do you like crumbed chops and chips?'

'One of my favourites.'

Life was loaded with ups, Lulla had to admit, swinging behind Janet into the change room. One minute you're ready to cut your throat, and the next ...? A bed to sleep in, crumbed chops for tea, and good times ahead—starting tomorrow night.

What more could a girl ask for!

'You *must* have some bobby pins, Mr Mostyn. Not even one packet?' Lulla's red-tipped fingers measured out a dainty half-inch. 'Not even a teensy-weensy packet?'

But the chemist had developed, over the months, an immunity to practised blandishments. 'Miss Riddel, remember there *is* a war on.'

'As if I'm allowed to forget.' He could be so bloody prim.

'Now let me finish, Miss Riddel. Hairpins are made of metal, you know. And metal—'

'Is needed for bullets and guns. As you've mentioned a hundred times already. Come on, Mosie,' she wheedled, 'I know you've got them.'

'You had three cards last week. What do you do with them?'

It was none of his business that every night she spiralled her hair into pin-curls—over a hundred, when she bothered to count them—and now she was doing Janet's as well. You could lose a whole slew of them in a night's jitterbugging at the Troc. Not counting a session with a bloke who wouldn't take no for an answer!

'Very well.' Her tone was suddenly brisk. 'I'll have some Cure-em-Quicks. Ah … let me see. Hair tonic! Now that's been gathering dust since fat Nellie was a chick. Dust it off and I'll take one.'

Beaming, the chemist reached for the tonic, gave it a rub with his shirt sleeve, and, mildly triumphant, placed it on the counter. She grinned back. It was a game they often played.

'I'll clear you out of that old stock yet,' she promised. 'Now, how about those pins? And Modess. Let's not forget the Modess—that's one thing our fighting lads won't be needing.'

'Miss Riddel!' He dived under the counter just as she heard footsteps coming into the shop.

It was Janet, her shoulder weighed down with a bulging string bag. She dumped the bag on a chair and massaged a sore spot. 'Ready?' she asked.

At the sound of her voice, the chemist reappeared with a neatly tied brown paper parcel, and the pins. 'Mrs Hope. How nice.' Almost furtively he pushed the package towards Lulla. 'There, Miss Riddel,' he whispered. As Lulla rammed the Modess into her own string bag, she could not help thinking that the chemist would be more comfortable dealing in groceries—Bushells tea and Iced Vo-Vos would have suited him well.

He was relieved that all Janet needed was toothpaste. 'That fine sailor husband of yours …?' He looked around as if Japanese spies were white-anting the walls. 'Home soon?'

'I'm afraid not. I don't know really.'

She sounded weary and dispirited. Lulla's heart went out to her. Poor kid. The irony of it. Janet had come from Cairns to be with Kirk, who had been based in Brisbane. He had warned her, Janet had admitted to Lulla, to stay where she was. He could be shipped off to anywhere at any time. But the longing to be near him had overcome her usual caution. No sooner had she arrived than Kirk had been shipped north. To Cairns. But he had ordered her to stay where she was. The North, he told her was no fit place for a woman; overrun by troops and threatened by invasion.

An exodus had begun. The North was funnelling its population south.

2

THE CITIZENS OF Cairns had abandoned their customary Sunday night stroll around 'The Block'. They lined the Esplanade hoping to confirm or dismiss the truth of rumours that had peppered the town all day.

As Hilda Scott studied the spasmodic flaring on the far horizon, just on the edge of sight, she felt betrayed. For all her forty years Hilda had believed that anywhere north of Townsville was the safest place on earth to raise her girls. Wherever Alf's pipe-dreams had dumped them, from tin mine to goldfield, the most harm they'd ever met was the time Peggy tripped over a carpet snake and broke her arm. Even when their pitiful attempts at growing tobacco failed, they hadn't quite starved to death.

'Tobacco,' Alf had enthused, 'you can't go wrong.'

But go wrong they did; and after that final, bitter bust-up, all that Alf had left behind were Eveleen and Peggy, and a tin shack furnished with butter-boxes and hessian. But no real grief had come of it. Hilda had the girls and that was all that really mattered.

Now the North cried danger: the Pacific war, cyclonic in its terrifying destruction, was bearing down on the coastline with speed. Bale-fire licked at the horizon, lighting up the under-belly of storm clouds. Men looking out to sea argued the cause of it.

'There it goes again. Can't you hear it? Gunfire.'

'Be blowed. Thunder, more like it.'

Hilda moved closer to listen. Men were expert about such things. The night sky flared again.

'What do y'call that, ay? I'm tellin' you—'

'It's lightning. Sheet lightning.'

'Funny bloody lightnin'. Didn't you see them Catalinas go out? I reckon something big's happening out there. And it's not a bloody bushfire.'

There and then, Hilda Scott made up her mind.

Lightning, gunfire, or someone letting off crackers; if nothing else, it was a warning. Ugly stories were seeping down through the islands on the fate of those enmeshed in the Japanese invasion.

It was time she and the girls packed up and cleared out.

As if they could be snatched from her at any minute, there came a sudden need to see that all was well. Peggy and Eveleen were in the minuscule park across the road; phantom lights beyond the reef were outclassed by the strident brass of the United States

Naval Base Band. The girls had stayed behind to listen.

As Hilda hurried across the street, she heard a clarinet scaling the final peaks of *Golden Wedding*, and arrived in time to see Evie up there with the band, caught fast in a seabee's arms. Without missing a beat, the sailor tossed her from one hip to the other, swished her down through his legs, spinning and twirling in a smooth performance of flashing, tanned thighs topped by bright pink panties. The whooping, cheering locals had never seen anything like it—and already, Hilda guessed, the gossips had relayed Evie's latest escapade far and wide. Where and when had Evie picked up such a routine? Had she been hanging around that naval base again? And where was Peggy?

Flushed and jubilant, Eveleen took the sailor's arm and marched down the steps. At first, she gave no sign that Hilda was standing close, and would have passed on, if Hilda had not prevented it. 'Where do you think you're going?'

'To the Beehive for an ice-cream.' Evie's eyes defied her mother to remonstrate in front of the crowd. 'Oh, and this is Paul.'

The boy smiled and asked politely, 'You Evie's Mom?'

'That's right.' She tried to relax and returned his smile. He looked a nice enough lad. 'But we have to go, Paul. School tomorrow. You understand, don't you.'

The sailor backed off. 'Sorry, ma'am. School! Evie didn't say ...'

'She wouldn't. Goodnight, Paul.' The crowd made way for mother and daughter, grinning as one.

When they reached the deepest shade of the weeping figs, Eveleen wrenched her arm free. 'I'll hate you forever!'

'Never mind about that, where's Peggy?'

'Home. She wouldn't stay.'

'I'm not surprised.'

Peggy Scott could not remember a time when her mother did not have a boarder in the house 'to make ends meet'. Teamed up with her father's 'you can't go wrong' (before he disappeared) it was a formula for living. The hackneyed sayings seemed eternally bonded, like Siamese twins.

So when Hilda rented the tuckshop opposite the school, Peggy found with satisfaction that living in such cramped quarters had its compensations. Lodgers were out of the question. The little shop put on a brave front facing the street, but the rabbit-hutch rooms at the rear could not be stretched to meet the needs of strangers.

Evening hours were the best part of the day. Just the three of them. Evie and her homework at one end of the table, Hilda rolling pastry at the other. The room cosy with the smell of herbs simmering in the mince pot for the next day's meat pies, the smell of vanilla icing, and on the counter, only steps away, the temptation of rasberry drops and aniseed balls and Texas Chews laid out for the picking. To mull over the day's events and talk about the refrigerator soon to be installed was a time to be cherished.

They'd be able to make their own ice-cream, and Icy Thrills—the new taste craze sweeping the school. That would push up the takings; what with her own job at Woolies, and the tuckshop making its way, ends were meeting very well indeed. And now her mother was standing there with talk of moving on.

'But *why*, Mum?'

'I've struggled too long and too hard keeping us together, Peg. And I'm not standing for a swarm of slope-eyes breaking us up.'

'It's not that bad, is it?'

'Bad enough. If you'd both been with me down at the Esplanade you might have learnt something. People are worried. I'm worried. If they take Port Moresby, that's it. We've had it.'

'Aw, come on, Mum. What about the Army?'

'And what about *their* Navy? Singapore's gone, they could be anywhere. Well, we're not staying to find out. We're going to Brisbane. Further, if we must. The shop goes up for sale tomorrow.'

It shocked Peggy to see her mother so frightened. So scared. Ready to cave in without a fight. But it gave room to an idea that had niggled her for weeks. An idea that had occasionally been taken out and dusted.

'I'll be eighteen soon.' She hesitated, not having the knack of explaining things. 'If we sell out, I may as well join up.' It sounded like a threat. But she plunged on. 'The Land Army. Wouldn't mind that.'

'Haven't you had enough of the land?' Hilda's

startled gaze met eyes as deeply grey as her own. 'Do you want to slog out the best years of your life on another farm? It broke your father's heart, and God knows it aged me fifty years.'

'Mum, let's face it: Dad was no farmer. And that was no farm,' said Peggy flatly. 'It was a rotten, clapped-out piece of dirt.' She shook her head in mock despair. 'And don't stick up for him, neither.'

'All right, all right! You've said it all before. But let's get south first, before you think about joining up.'

Peggy did not walk—she stomped; and now she stomped off to the tiny kitchen to bang pots and slam cupboard doors. Onions had to be peeled and diced for tomorrow's mince pies. Hilda drew in a long breath. They managed to hurt each other at times ... but meanwhile, there was Evie and the business in the park to clear up.

Eveleen was sulking in the cane chair where she had hurled herself on arriving back at the shop. Sensing that she was now centre-stage, she glared a direct challenge. 'I'm not going south.' Tears were gathering for one of her frequent storms. 'No one cares how I feel, or if I want to go.' Hilda braced herself as they began to flow. 'We're always shifting,' Evie wailed. 'What about my friends—and what about school?'

'Last week you were begging to leave. Besides, there's talk that all coastal schools could close down for the duration. Another good reason for leaving.

Now, don't cry, love. It's all for the best. You'll see.'

Eveleen jerked away from her mother's conciliatory touch. 'I can't leave Paul. We love each other. Madly. I'll die if you take me away from him!'

She hid her face under a wild tangle of sun-streaked hair. Sobs and gulps embroidered a tantrum of operatic intensity. It wasn't the first time Hilda had found herself coping with Evie's romances. It had always been so. Going right back to a day when she had dragged Eveleen out from under a mulberry tree, not five years old, and a small boy had been sent home with a smarting backside. Trying to contain Evie, without actually chaining her to a post, was like staying ripe fruit from popping seeds. Peg was a babe in arms compared to her nubile youngest. And there was now a Yankee naval base down at Smith's Creek, and an army camp not ten minutes bike ride from their front door!

'Evie, look at me. This Paul ... where did you meet him? And what's more important, when?'

The girl darted her a glance, lips clamped tight. Before a hand could stop her, she sprang out of the chair and slammed through the back door. There came a slight rattle of a bicycle chain, and tyres whispered over gravel. By the time Hilda had reached the yard, Eveleen was pedalling fast down the road.

Just as well they were moving south. Too much to do battle with here.

Hilda went back inside to get pennies for a phone call. 'I won't be long, Peg, there's still time to ring through an ad for tomorrow's *Post*. The sooner we sell the place, the better.'

'Want me to come?'

But Hilda had already left.

The night air was sweetened by the frangipanni tree at the corner, its petals clustered ivory against the green dark of the leaves. Hilda breathed deeply of its perfume and wondered if frangipannis grew in Brisbane. There was much she loved about this tropic town; the quarrel of flying foxes on hot, still nights, the incessant chatter of mynah birds by day; buffalo grass coarse and springy beneath bare feet, and monsoon rain that hammered tin roofs for weeks on end. She would miss it all.

Cane toads flopped a step in front of her on their nightly migrations to the street, to hold mute and solemn council in pools of lamplight. She kicked one out of the way. As she walked by houses silent in sleep, there came the sound of motors in the distance. Looking back, she saw the dimmed headlights of a truck heading towards the town. She realised that it was one of many, as vehicle after vehicle drew close, and went by in a convoy of gigantic proportions.

Exhaust fumes doused the scent of night blossoms. Like flies around dead meat, motorcycles farted and spluttered, and darted up and down the continuous line. The noise brought people out of their beds to watch the grim parade. Never had so many machines rolled along that wide, straight road which led into the heart of Cairns. A few blocks further on, the trucks turned left and then went north. As the last tail-light disappeared, Hilda was convinced that the right decision had been made.

Let the men who would defend it have the place to themselves. Give them room to build their airstrips, mend their ships and train their fighting men. Much better that she and the girls move on and leave them to it.

Dawn light filtered through the smoke grime of carriage windows and touched the line of sleeping forms carpeting the corridors. Another comfortless night over.

Peggy threw off her blanket and sat up, stretching and arching life back into cramped limbs. The swaying, jerking floor of a train was a poor substitute for a good horsehair mattress, her aching back complained.

Drowsily she studied the inert bodies as they lay, head to toe, some wrapped in army greatcoats; the lucky ones under blankets as grubby as her own. The airman whose stockinged feet had used her head as a footrest for half the night, stirred and shivered. He had no covering at all, only the shorts and shirt he slept in. He snored, mouth agape, oblivious to the cinders swirling in from an open window. She herself had opened it in self-defence against the airman's socks and the reasty night.

Evie, cocoon-wrapped in a flannel sheet, was still asleep, unaware that a seaman had dumped his duffle bag at her feet, adding another link to the slumbering and fitful chain.

For four days and three nights they had been travelling on the Southern Mail, now fifteen hours overdue at Brisbane. There had been delays at sidings, stops at crossings, interminable waits at stations in deference to the packed troop trains hooting their way north. Theirs was a train of abnormal length with a hodgepodge of carriages, most shanghaied from honourable retirement. The compartment where Hilda slept was plushly curlicued with Edwardian extravagance, and two troopers had commandeered the overhead luggage racks for their makeshift beds.

Peggy wished that she had thought of it first.

Hilda dozed in her corner seat; she had refused the space that the girls had kept for her on the floor. 'You'll be able to stretch out at least,' they had urged her. But Hilda had been adamant, vaguely shy of sleeping cheek by jowl—or tip to toe, she had corrected herself—with complete strangers. Now she yawned and massaged a nagging hip, her first thought to see how the girls had managed through the night.

Peggy, camped close to the door, beckoned and pointed in the direction of the W.C. 'Come on, Mum, let's get there before the mob does.' Her cheeks were creased with sleep and heavy chestnut hair swung loose about her face. Hilda felt the warmth of her morning smile.

'What about Evie?' she asked.

'I've been prodding her for the last five minutes. Not a stir.' Peggy scrambled to her feet, and began folding the blanket. 'You know what she's like.'

They picked a careful path between the bodies to the lavatory door. Although shut tight, it could not contain the acrid reek of overuse. Peggy's grimace underlined her disgust. 'Stinks worse than a cattle duffers' dunny. Hope there's enough water.' She thrust her head through a nearby window and spat. 'Phew! You go first. In case there isn't.'

Others were now stirring. Again Peggy leaned out the window as far as she could, breathing in the fresh, gusting air. They were passing through countryside lushly green and pungent with lantana. It reminded her a bit of home. Sugarcane and long rows of bananas and pawpaw trees stopped short at an escarpment to the east, glazed by the morning sun. A few houses and a siding were snatched out of sight as the train gathered speed. There seemed a sudden need to dump its noisome load onto the platform at Roma Street station. How far, she wondered, was Brisbane now?

Someone jiggled her elbow. It was Evie, hair combed up into a tight roll, and wearing Hilda's lipstick.

'Hey!' Eyes glistening, eager bright. 'Did you get a load of that sailor?'

'I saw him. What are you doing with Mum's lipstick on? And her rouge. You haven't even washed yet.'

'Who cares.' Eveleen ran a tongue over her teeth, and wet a finger to wipe the sleep and soot from her eyes.

'There! Satisfied?'

No use saying anything. Peggy shrugged. Boy-mad, that was Evie ... She studied the long line of men, scratching itchy chins, pulling on boots, and more than one of them eyeing Evie with interest. All heading south. Soldier, sailor, beggar-man, thief and hardly a woman in sight. Poor Mum.

Already Evie was licking her lips at the idea of Brisbane.

3

*L*ULLA AND JANET had to agree that the suburb of West End served them well. Only twopence tram fare from the city's heart, and its cluster of shops—not flash, but handy to the flat—attended to all their needs. Timbered houses lined the streets and were rented out to working families, widows, and a sprinkling of Mediterraneans comfortable with close-knit and compacted living. It was left to the once elegant stuccos to house the drifters, the lonely, and old Diggers from the Great War reminiscing on tall front steps.

Although Lulla sometimes missed the small crises, the unexpected, that could turn mundane bar work into an eventful day, she conceded that assembling hand grenades was better than pandering to a daily swarm of bar flies and maudlin drunks. She was forced to admit that the past months had treated her lightly, and that working for MacIntyre's wasn't all that bad.

With overtime she was earning close to men's wages, and she shared three comfortable rooms and a bathroom with an obliging workmate who, if pressed, could run up a dress in an afternoon. From that first night she and Janet had clicked, and had decided that sharing food, rent and ration coupons was the way to go.

'There's only one problem,' Janet worried the next day. 'What happens when Kirk's in port?' Blushing, she was far too modest to mention the double bed screened off from the front room by nothing more substantial than a pull-back curtain. It did little for privacy.

'Yeah,' drawled Lulla, 'I see what you mean …'

They approached the landlord, Mr Hickey; the flat across the hall was vacant. But the landlord's wife would not have a bar of it. They didn't rent out to single girls, and neither were they keen on the idea of two young women sharing, even if one was married. Of course, there was a war, and things had changed. Anyway, the Hickeys had told them, the other flat was spoken for.

Surprisingly, however, they did suggest that Lulla could use the room 'up the back' when Mr Hope was home on leave. Five shillings a week, Mrs Hickey said, furnished and all. 'Up the back' at the end of a path which skirted Janet's flat was a shed, its entrance concealed by a tumble of boisterous poinsettias. Once the living quarters for a gardener, the minuscule dwelling struggled to house a cast-iron bed and a dressing-table—enough, Lulla found, for the brief hours Kirk had managed to be with Janet.

Lulla turned the corner for home. As always, Franklin Street caused her much pleasure. There was something neat and cosy about the way the cottages, side to side, bravely fronted the road leading up and over the hill. There was a park up there, which made a Sunday afternoon stroll worthwhile.

Palms and shade trees softened the cubes of timber. In the late afternoon, children and happy dogs often played on the footpath, making light of the gathering dusk. It was a place where people talked over front-yard fences.

But it was their own handsome dwelling, one of three "sisters", as Janet called them, that gave her the keenest pleasure. Three elegant ladies on their side of the street, so alike that the same romantic must have built them all. They were the gingerbread houses of childhood. The first two, in their faded gardens, wore tattered iron lace and matching cobwebs, and attic windows slept beneath sloping roofs. Their quaint design had been created by a dreamer to withstand the weight of snow that would never come.

Their own spick-and-span frontage filled Lulla with pride of possession, even if she and Janet only rented a small part of it. The roof wore many coats of post-office red, the timbered walls had been stuccoed and painted cream, a foil for phlox and nasturtiums encrusting the base of the house with brightness, beside emerald lawns. The low concrete fence was spiked with cypress pines trimmed into submission. In all, Lulla decided, congratulating herself on her luck, a most suitable place; a cool refuge from the grid-iron austerity of the munition works.

Today it had been Lulla's turn to do the shopping. Potatoes and onions were mentally ticked off the list, bread—butter, not a hope; but the prize, three tins of sardines. Almond Rocca and ciggies from the Yanks, bless 'em, was easy. But sardines? The Aussie Army obliged now and then, but at the moment Lulla was fresh out of Aussie-army types.

Two houses away she smelt a rib roast cooking. At the front gate, it was strong enough to picture spuds and pumpkin in a dish of sizzling dripping. At the front steps, Lulla was certain that Janet had splurged a fortnight's meat coupons to perdition and merry hell. Kirk must be home!

Lulla took the steps two at a time. 'You old son-of-a-gun!' she yelled, and flung open the door, thrilled for Janet.

It was a blessing to see him safe and sound: a sunlit, golden man who seemed to fill the small front room with his presence. Kirk pointed to his out-thrust chin. 'Plant one there,' he ordered, then opened his arms wide.

The bear hug blocked out her view of a stranger who sat by the window. He rose to his feet as Janet came from the kitchen, pink and warm from the oven's heat. She set a vase of jonquils on the table.

'They're lovely, Spanner. Has Kirk introduced you to Lulla yet?'

'Just about to, Jan,' said Kirk, putting an arm over the man's shoulder. 'Lulla, meet Spanner Larkin. Old shipmate from way back, and the best pal a man could wish for.'

Spanner Larkin had already left port when looks had been distributed; and by the wandering flattened nose, Lulla guessed that it was not only the enemy he had done battle with. A bit of a lair by the cut of his rig; and she knew enough about the Navy to realise that the fit of his uniform was due to a George Street tailor. No regulation issue for this seafaring dandy—bell-bottoms extravagantly flared, and the neat bow on his jacket hung a foot beyond good taste.

Be careful of this one, Lulla Riddel, she warned herself as she proffered a welcoming hand.

As for Janet, Lulla found cause for self-congratulation. Talking Janet into a nightly ritual had not been easy, but the time spent in creaming the delicate skin had paid off. Smooth as a baby's bum; and her hair, coaxed into submission by a chainmail of pins, now hung shoulder-length in a glossy pageboy. Would Kirk notice the difference?

Lulla felt a rare stab of envy. Janet would soon be in the arms of that golden man, loved and cosseted. Snug in that lovely big bed.

Better than a slap and tickle in the park, on a cold winter's night.

She caught Spanner's eye. He was lounging against the archway leading into the bedroom, and somehow she was certain he knew exactly what was going through her mind. She flushed like some mawky kid caught out reading *Man Magazine*.

Janet, back in the kitchen, called out that dinner was ready and could Lulla help to dish up....

Dinner waited.

At the last minute the men had left to buy lemonade to go with the port wine Spanner had brought with him. Standing by the kitchen window (their flat overlooked the street), the two women kept watch, ready to bring plates hot to the table.

'Well, what do you think of him?' Janet wanted to know.

'Kirk? I'd snatch him right from under your nose, given half the chance. Gorgeous brute.'

'Don't hedge. You know who I mean.'

'Oh'—all innocent blue eyes—'you mean Spanner.'

Lulla stalled, lost in reverie, trying to analyse the lazy speculation of Spanner's gaze when they had been introduced. But her thoughts were distracted by a returning vision of lean hips, and the muscular backside emphasised by those snug-fitting bell-bottoms.

'Well, as I said to m'self first go, be careful.'

'Careful of Spanner!' Janet sounded hurt. 'That's a funny thing to say. Kirk and Spanner are the best of mates. Kirk would trust him with his life. He already has.'

'Jan, we're talking about *men*. Don't you know

that good mates can be absolute no-hopers where women are concerned? My old Dad had mates who would die for him. They told him so every day in the pub. Mum wasn't impressed, but. As for Larkin ...' She captured one of her hundred Betty Grable curls and wound it around her finger. 'I dunno ... Would I save the last dance for him, eh?'

Janet crossed over to the stove and took a peek into the oven, looking concerned. 'Hope it's not drying out.'

Lulla joined her. 'Looks all right to me.' Quickly she broke off a piece of fat, transparent as amber, blew on it and popped it in her mouth. 'Gawd, I'm hungry.'

They took up their post, back at the window.

'Lulla, don't you want a regular boyfriend?'

'And lose a bit more of my heart every time he went off again? Not on your life. Free, white and twenty-one, that's me. Give us time, Jan. Let me live a bit.'

'And what do you mean by that?'

'I'll spell it out. Everything's changing. Fast. Even you must know that. Don't you feel it? See it?' The gleam of a convert shone from Lulla's eyes. 'After this mess is over we'll be able to do anything. Oh, I don't know what exactly. But we'll be doing it. That's something we can thank this bloody war for, anyway.'

'Lulla! That's an awful thing to say.' Whether Janet was shocked by Lulla's sentiments or her swearing was hard to tell.

But Lulla was out to prove a point. 'It's true.

You've just got to poke your nose inside MacIntyre's to know that much. Listen to the girls talking. Look what we're doing. Men's work—perhaps not so much in the annexe, I'll admit, but men'd be doing it if we weren't.' She gave the wary Janet a poke on the chest. 'Something else, if you haven't noticed ... We're finding out that husband, home and a bunch of kids is not the be-all and end-all to a girl's ambition.'

Surprised by her own eloquence, Lulla gave an embarrassed giggle. 'Gawd, listen to me spouting off.' To escape Janet's half-accusing stare she leaned out the window on the lookout for Spanner and Kirk. 'Not a sign of them yet.'

By now the street was darkening; the houses opposite had lost all detail, blocked in by a wintry indigo sky. A front light in the flat across the hall came on. It enamelled the lawn, twin to theirs, yellow bright.

'Oh, I forgot to mention.' Janet, standing beside her, squeezed Lulla's arm to show that all was forgiven. 'We have new neighbours. A woman and two girls. Daughters, I suppose. They seem nice enough. They—' then her face lit up. 'Here they come!'

The front gate squeaked open, followed up by Kirk's special whistle. Janet flew to the stove and handed over two hot and loaded plates to Lulla. 'Quick, the gravy's in the saucepan.'

They hardly spoke through the roast beef and baked potatoes, and not until an apple-pie, bisque-crusted, as smooth as a pebble, was placed on the table and the tea poured, did speech fully return.

Lulla moved her chair, unsure if the pressure from Spanner's knee was deliberate. The small round table was a tight squeeze for four. Her first impression of him had altered slightly; the predatory air and the mocking half-smile had mellowed under the influence of Janet's cooking. Talk turned to ships and war.

Kirk pushed his cup over to be refilled. 'By the way—' his tone was casual '—me and Spanner will be calling in here more than usual.'

Janet tensed, teapot held midway, not believing it. 'Here? In Brisbane?'

'That's what I said, old girl. Ask Spanner.' Slowly, Janet placed the teapot back on the stand; it was Kirk who prised her fingers, one by one, off the handle. He began pouring his own tea, and topped up Janet's cup. 'Go on, Spanner. Convince her. Tell her all about it.'

All Spanner did was growl that it might be all right for married blokes, but playing at milkman wasn't his idea of winning a fight. He then went on to enlighten them. 'A flamin' milk run is all you can call it. We're going Merchant Navy, that's what. And a Pommy ship at that.'

'Why the grouch?' Lulla helped herself to more apple-pie.

'Well, it's sort of wasting a man's time, isn't it.'

'Is it?' She reached for the custard.

'Best pair of gunners in the Navy—'

'Don't be a bull-merchant, Larkin,' Kirk broke in.

'As I was saying,' Spanner complained, 'the best gunners in the Navy, and we're told to man one of their toys. Pop gun! Shove a man-sized cannon on the deck and she'd sink clear to the bottom.'

'Will you be in convoys and things?' At once Lulla regretted the question; it was common knowledge that merchant ships were more vulnerable than most. She stole a glance at Janet, sitting quietly pale, while the two men nattered on unthinkingly about ships and guns and war. Lulla could have knocked their heads together.

Janet spoke at last. 'Can you say or hint ... say where you're going? If you expect ...' Her eyes implored Kirk to tell.

'We'll be lucky to see the outside of the Reef, old girl. Ever heard of T.I.?'

Janet nodded, partly mollified.

'Where's that?' Lulla butted in.

'Up north.' Kirk gave a wry grin. 'Don't think the war's lost by telling. It's a speck near the tip of Cape York. Look it up on the map sometime. As Spanner said, we're on a milk run. No more than that.' He tweaked Janet's nose. 'So look out, love, I'll be home so much, you'll be begging the Navy to put me back on the *Canberra*.'

'Never!'

A knock at the door postponed Janet's intention of kissing Kirk's cheek. 'Who is it?' she called.

The door opened and a young girl stood there with a cup in her hand. There was a quick intake of breath as she walked towards them. Faded khaki shorts and an old tennis shirt only heightened the effect of rich curves and smooth limbs. Her hair had been freshly washed, and a cascade of curls tumbled around her shoulders. She was sun-ripened fruit ready to be enjoyed, and in those few short steps she managed to convey that she was more than ready to be plucked.

It was her eyes that held them silent. Jewel eyes of aquamarine; more green than blue, more blue-green than grey. The cold touch of the sea was in their depths and sent shivers down Lulla's spine.

'Mum wants to know if you can spare a cup of sugar.' The drama of her being there was dimmed a little by the banal request. 'I'm Evie Scott. We shifted in today.' By now she was close to the table, and had put the cup in Janet's hand.

'Ta,' she murmured. Not an inch away from Spanner's elbow, her attention was focused on Kirk. 'You in the Navy, Mr Hope?'

Janet came from the kitchen with the sugar. Old Hickey would have supplied their name to the girl. 'Here you are, Evie.'

Eveleen ignored the cup, and Janet felt those enormous eyes flick over her. She heard herself gabbling, 'Would you like a slice of apple-pie?'

Her hand holding the cake knife shook slightly. Why so nervous? She put it down to Kirk's surprise announcement. In spite of his assurances, a dread engulfed her that all was not as simple as he made it sound. She realised that no one was talking. Lulla seemed to be fascinated with the pattern in the tablecloth, while Kirk looked downright uncomfortable; as for Spanner, his hungry gaze latched onto Evie had nothing to do with second helpings of roast beef.

Blast the girl. For lack of something better to say, Janet asked again. 'Sure you wouldn't like a piece, Evie?'

'No thanks. We've had our tea.' Eveleen looked as if she'd rather take a large bite of Kirk. 'We're from Cairns, you know. There was lots of sailors on the train. One of them was the spitting image of you, Mr Hope.'

'Not me.' Kirk sounded relieved, turning to Spanner for some kind of support. 'We're not landlubbers.'

Eveleen's eyelids drooped a fraction; the look could have been perfected in front of a mirror. 'We all had to sleep on the floor.' Visions of a trainload of copulating salamanders. The child was a witch, and she showed no intention of leaving.

'Evie?'

A woman stood at the open door. There was no mistaking the relationship. The close-cropped ringlets still held traces of the yellow that gilded the daughter's hair. While Eveleen's grace held the lush promise of youth, the woman's frame had been pared down to the austere lines of a battler. Her face was tanned, cross-hatched and weathered by hard times and a tropic sun.

'Evie!' The woman did not hide her exasperation. 'What do you think you're doing?'

'Just getting some sugar.'

'Who said we—' She bit back the words. 'Oh,

never mind. Go and give Peggy a hand with the dishes.'

The siren, now a schoolgirl, flounced from the room.

Apologising for the intrusion, the woman introduced herself as Hilda Scott. Refusing an offer of a cup of tea, she apologised again before leaving.

'Evie left her sugar behind,' Spanner commented drily.

'Whew!' Lulla fanned herself with a hand. 'That's trouble, if ever I saw it.'

Spanner Larkin grinned. 'If that's trouble, just lead me to it!'

4

*J*ANET WAITED FOR Lulla by the annexe door.
'Coming?' she called.

It was not like Lulla to dawdle when the lunch whistle blew. Usually she was first off the floor, often critical of the meagre time allotted for meal breaks.

'You need that long to get to the change room, let alone the twink,' she had protested to Andy. 'No wonder some of us have overalls dropping down to our knees by the time we get there.' She had exploded when warned that leaving the bench between legal breaks was frowned upon. 'What if I'm busting for a pee?' she'd demanded.

Andy tried to look severe. 'In that case you get my permission, and if I'm not around, you must ask Mrs Daniels.'

'You're having me on.'

'It's the rules.'

'Well then—without meaning to offend, Andy—here's one girl who'll go when she damn well pleases. So tell that to the old bat; with luck it might get me the shove!'

Janet remembered that day well. The first time that anyone cocked a snoot at the management. After Lulla's outburst, when Nature called, Lulla went; as did the rest of the shift from then on. In spite of Mrs Daniels' pursed lips, nothing was said, and no one got the sack.

Today, though, Lulla gave the impression of being fused to the workbench. It was hard to understand.

'Hey! Wake up, Australia—lunch time!'

Lulla gave no indication of hearing Janet, apparently absorbed in shellacing grenades. Then an unmistakable sound broke the silence. A snuffle. Janet could not believe her ears, or her eyes, as she witnessed Lulla take out a handkerchief to blow her nose.

'You're crying!' She was by Lulla's side in an instant, already feeling guilty. Had she been too immersed in her own affairs to notice that Lulla was going through a bad patch? In the past weeks no one but Kirk had existed for Janet. True to his word, the ship had docked in Brisbane at regular and frequent intervals, culminating in two weeks leave.

Had Lulla, banished to the back room, felt out of it? She dismissed the idea at once. Lulla wasn't like that. But Janet was convinced that whatever troubled her flatmate, she was somehow to blame for it.

'Have I—we—done something to hurt you?'

The hand bomb, given its final touch, was put down to dry. Only then did Lulla turn and reward Janet's persistence with a watery smile.

'You've done nothing. Just leave things alone for a bit, eh? Maybe I'm not feeling so good. Now please, Jan, go!' Firm hands bundled her out into the breezeway. Lulla managed to laugh at herself. 'Talk about the blubbers ... The others will be back soon, and I need to put on a fresh face. Go and eat a sandwich. Scoot! And thanks for worrying!'

Near to tears herself, Janet did as she was told.

It was bad enough that Janet had caught her out. She had managed to stay dry-eyed all morning. And yesterday. And the day before that. But now, everything had caught up with her, and only God knew what could be done about it.

Her troubles began the night that Evie Scott, making like Lana Turner, had shimmied into the flat.

Cup of sugar, my eye! They had all agreed on that.

But Evie's appearance had managed to wreck a pleasant and cosy evening. She had left them all feeling restless and disturbed, and when Janet began to clear the table, it could have been construed as an act of dismissal. Easygoing Kirk had turned morose, then made it clear that he and Janet had homework to catch up on.

Which was fair enough.

It had been up to Lulla to see Spanner down the front stairs. She should have left him then and there with a 'Goodnight, nice meeting you', and shut the gate behind him. But what did she do? Only look at her watch (feeling sorry for the poor coot, him standing there) and say, 'It's just after eight, and the night's only a pup ...'

Spanner had looked hopeful. 'Any suggestions?'

It was an innocent enough remark, and Lulla thought of the Institute Dance Hall. She could tell by his walk that he must be a knockout on the dance floor. But Spanner was broke. The Purple Para port and the jonquils had skinned him out.

'I'll shout, I'm feeling generous,' she offered airily.

But Spanner wasn't the sort to let a girl pay.

'Well,' she said, 'there's always the Hill. Not exactly the Seven Wonders, but nice enough. Jan and I often take a walk up there. Interested?'

Spanner gave an extravagant sweep of his arm. 'Not only is she beautiful—she has brains as well. Lead on!'

Lulla gave a bob. 'Only doin' me bit, sir.'

Halfway up Highgate Hill he took her arm, tucking it into his. She felt the warmth of him through his winter serge, and was grateful, for the night was chill enough. The top of the Hill was an open space of nobbled grass, bushes and tall gum trees, barely large enough to accommodate a dainty rotunda topping the crest like a single cherry on a cake. It seemed the right thing to do, to walk inside it and around it and admire the view.

'They used to have a compass thing in here once,' Lulla told him, 'but they've put it away for the duration. Can't let the Japs know which direction Sydney is.' She chuckled. 'Or Coolangatta, either. Never prise them away from it, I bet. That's if they could get this far.' Suddenly anxious. 'Will they?'

'Not a hope in hell, Princess.'

Princess? She let it pass with no more than a sidelong glance. They left the bandstand to sit on a park bench and gaze down on the lights of Brisbane sprinkled through the crisp night air. Stars overhead echoed the lights below, and Spanner sat in silence for some time before making comment.

'They're not real serious about the blackout, are they.'

'Brownout it's called.'

'Well, with all that blinkin' and winkin' down there, a man's pretty safe lighting up, I reckon.' He offered her a cigarette, and she wondered where a threepenny bit could hide, let alone his cigarettes and matches. His uniform fitted like the skin of an eel. She refused the cigarette, but asked where on earth he kept them.

'Inside the cap, Princess.' He slipped an arm around her shoulder as if smoking was the last thing on his mind.

'I thought you wanted to light up.'

'After.'

'After what?'

For an answer he took her hand. His calloused palm was reassuring while he gently stroked the soft skin between her fingers. 'You have nice hands, Lulla.' He ran a thumb over one immaculate nail.

'And in munitions, too. How do you manage?'

'With difficulty. I'm down to my last skerrick of remover. It's crazy, y'know.' She freed her hand and held it up admiring the smooth painted ovals under starlight. 'There's plenty of polish around, if you search. But remover?' She shrugged. 'No can do.'

A hint of a breeze stirred the treetops. It came from the west, an icy promise that tomorrow would be cold and crystal bright. Lulla shivered, tucking her skirt tight around her knees, and allowed herself to be hugged close for a minute. He was so warm; then remembered the warning she had given herself back at the flat. *Be careful of this one, Lulla Riddel ...*

It was time to move.

'Better get back, Spanner.' She could feel his disapointment as he let her go.

'Must we?'

All businesslike now, she brushed herself down. ''Fraid so. Early start tomorrow.'

'Sad ...'

She should have recognised the signals, and shot through. Before she knew it, he was on his feet drawing her close, and she wasn't prepared for the strength of his arms or the urgent pressure of his mouth.

Damn it! Why must they spoil everything? It had been so nice; so comfy just chatting—and one little hug. Her own stupid fault! Twisting her face aside, chin smarting, eyes watering, arms clamped tight, hips pinned firmly in his grip, she found that she couldn't move.

'Hey! We only came to view the sights.' Joshing sometimes helped.

All he did was tighten his hold, and his body in those damn bell-bottoms semaphored the old familiar message—strong enough to win on points. Kirk and his trusted friends! With her thoughts on the boil, she deemed it wiser to let him nuzzle her throat, nibble an ear, while she waited for the right moment. When it came, she sagged heavily in his arms, her full weight catching him off-balance. She broke free, and all that was needed was a push to send him flying.

'Thanks for spoiling a lovely night, Spanner Larkin.'

He smacked the dirt with a thud, then scrambled to his feet, rubbing his backside. He shot her a lopsided, rueful grin.

'Smart trick ...'

'And there's more where that came from!' She was on her way then, high heels tapping out her moral indignation.

Spanner rammed his cap firmly back on his head and followed. 'Lulla, square dinkum. I didn't mean—'

'Not much you didn't.'

Her stride lengthened as she hit the steep downward slope at a furious pace.

Spanner broke into a trot to catch up. 'Look, I apologise.'

'So that makes everything all right, does it?'

Spanner discovered he had a ringside view of

Lulla's rounded hips. They jiggled with every thump of her three-inch stilts and he dared not imagine what her knockers were doing up front. If only she knew it, he considered in admiration, that walk of hers would have a monk begging to be dismantled. *Down boy*, he urged, drawing level with her. But he was getting nowhere. Obviously, with a girl like Lulla, a walk meant just that, a bloody walk; if he was to see her again he'd have to change tack. Pronto!

He reckoned she could be a hard one to gauge; not like Kirk's missus, as sweet and docile as they came. But this one ...? He took a quick look as they passed beneath the half-shaded street light. A strawberry blonde for true; great blue eyes spiked with lashes, a beauty spot, teamed with lips that dared a man to act like Clark-bloody-Gable. Shove a walking stick down her back, and she'd be a ringer for one of them kewpie dolls you can buy at a country show. But far from dumb—and a bit too rangy to tussle with. By now they were halfway down the Hill. He'd take a punt.

'Hold on,' he grabbed her arm, 'race you to the bottom. Down to the tram stop.' For a few seconds she studied him with narrowed, warning eyes. Then suddenly, snatched off her shoes, taking up the challenge.

'You're on!'

Lulla sprang into action, faster and faster, just keeping in front. The sailor, boots pounding, inched ahead. Not far to go. She caught up, hair flying, pins scattering, but with a surge of extra speed he reached the tram stop first, turning suddenly holding his arms wide. Impossible to avoid him. Breathless and laughing, he gave her a quick squeeze, then let her go.

'Give you a silver for that, Princess.'

'Best runner in the school, didn't y'know.'

He stepped back, eyebrows questioning. 'Friends again?'

'H'm, we'll see.'

He left her answer dangling between them without further comment, and on the short walk home there was enough fresh air between them to revive a drowning man.

The next afternoon he showed up again. He must have borrowed the cash, for he gave her flowers and carried a bottle. Not gin, as she first thought.

'Here,' he said, 'this should last you a while. It's acetone. Not real bad for taking that nail polish off.'

She hadn't the heart to mention that acetone was laid on by the gallon at work, nor that fingernails ended up like soapflakes if you were silly enough to use it. The fact that he'd remembered a stray remark touched her, and that night she went with him to see *Mrs Miniver*.

After that, it was the Coconut Grove, or the City Hall. His foxtrot made the back of her legs tingle. He certainly knew how to hold a girl! Every night, but for one, they danced; that one night—freezing cold, it was—he'd steered her up the side of the house in a sort of erotic manoeuvre, his body guiding her with persuasive strength, kissing away her protests and excuses.

Warm in bed. Dark. Secluded. Safe, and him so smooth and lean; rhythmic and controlled as his dancing had been.

Sad, stupid fool that you are Lulla Riddel ...

Lulla jabbed the loaded brush onto the grenade. Her monthlys were overdue, and Spanner was somewhere between Cairns and Thursday Island. Not, she told herself grimly, that he could do anything about it.

He'd done enough already!

She blew her nose hard, left the bench and took a quick look in a mirror someone had tacked to an upright. She applied fresh lipstick, licked her finger and smoothed down already immaculate eyebrows. She felt the gaze of someone behind her, and turned. It was the pot boy. Distress puckered his face.

'Luthy? You crying?'

'Nah ...' she sniffed a smile. 'Something in my eye.'

Micky did not believe her, and his eyes filled in sympathy. She dug into a hip pocket and produced a packet of Spearmint chewing gum and a packet of Lucky Strikes. 'Chuck said these were for you.'

Micky blinked and remembered to blow his nose. Not for the first time she wondered what afflicted him. Poor little bugger; such an overflow of mucus that it clogged not only his nose, but his ears as well. She regretted that he had witnessed her moping—he was a gentle little man. He wandered off, forgetting there were pots to be filled before the shift returned.

Then another voice called out to her. 'Hey, Lulla! Been looking for you.'

Daryl Missim was the last person she wanted to see. He came into the lacquer room, eyes snapping with good humour, glancing over his shoulder as if expecting to be followed.

'About that little item we discussed.'

'What little item?' She was not in the mood for deals.

'How could you forget. I'm talking about that French georgette. Beaud-i-ful.' He kissed the tips of his fingers. 'And for you, special price.' He tapped the side of his nose, and reminded her that he also waited on the Lucky Strikes that Chuck had promised. It was a game they played, half in jest, half in secret. Since his family's business' Missims' Creations, had turned to making army greatcoats, Daryl occasionally managed to produce what he called a remnant.

'Some remnant,' Janet had once remarked, 'at least four yards of it, and pure silk!' And had run up a dress in record time for her first date with Chuck O'Neil. Chuck—head supremo of a generous P.X. canteen. Between Chuck and Daryl, the cupboards were full. Often.

'Well,' Daryl's voice nudged her, 'do you want it?'

When would she be able to wear French georgette again? How could she have tossed good sense out of the window, and let Spanner Larkin come in? French georgette—what a joke!

'Sorry, Daryl. I know I said I'd take it, but no. Not now.'

He hunched his shoulders. 'You're the loser, friend.' She knew he would get twice as much as she had offered, on the 'black'.

He made one more effort to catch her interest. 'I've tickets for *Mrs Miniver*. Best seats. Same place? Same time?'

'Sorry, I've seen it.' The refusal sounded too abrupt. She wished he would go. She felt ill, and Daryl's shrewd appraisal filled her with terror. Did he guess? Nothing much escaped Daryl. But the sound of the whistle put a full stop to his speculation. With relief, Lulla picked up another grenade. 'You'd better go.'

'What about tomorrow night?'

'No!'

Not tomorrow, Missim. Or the day after that. Good times were over, perhaps ... But there was one last chance; something remembered from the old days when girls got together. Some girls, anyway. A bottle of gin and a near-boiling bath did wonders for bringing on 'the curse'. Old Mrs Kel—the monthlies—call her what you like, it didn't matter. As long as she came!

Gin, and a hot bath. Gawd, make it work! There was enough gin hiding in the back room to drown in it. Tomorrow she'd plead a sickie. It had to work—it *must* work, or she was a goner.

It was a case of do or die—or be double damned.

5

THE FLAT REEKED of gin.

Janet had her first whiff of it on the front steps. And where was Lulla? She followed her nose to the bathroom, and heard the sound of gushing water. When she opened the door, the gin-laden steam sent her reeling.

'Lulla! Good grief, what are you doing?'

If the implications were not so alarming, the sight of Lulla coming to a slow boil in a near-full bathtub would have paralysed her with laughter. An unopened bottle of Gilbey's had been placed by the bath in easy reach; a half-consumed bottle was in her hand.

'Mus'—mus' get rid—mus' lose it, Shan.' A limp hand waved Janet away. 'Wobble off, 's good girl.'

Janet made a snatch for the bottle, but Lulla hugged it close. 'Bug off, Ducks. Mos' appreciative.

But ... bug off.' She burst into soggy tears. 'Oh, Gawd!'

The gas heater throbbed and roared, threatening to explode. Blistering water spurted and spluttered out of the tap. Janet turned both gas and water off.

'Lulla, get out! You'll kill yourself. If you don't drown first.'

'S'marvellous idea.' She giggled wretchedly. Sweat and even more tears oozed down mascara-clotted cheeks.

'Please,' Janet begged. 'Get up. Here, give me your hand.'

Lulla's eyes, bovine with despair, drifted out of focus and swivelled completely out of sight as she slowly subsided, bottle and all, beneath the water.

Janet screamed. She grabbed a hank of floating hair, pulling hard. Lulla popped up, wild-eyed and gasping. Janet held on fast.

'I won't let go until you're out!' She used both hands to keep her flatmate's head afloat. Steam ribboned through the open door, making it easier to breathe.

Sobbing, coughing, conceding defeat, Lulla tried to rise, but her legs refused to obey. 'Can't. Better—jus' leave me drown.' Flopping back in a splash-drenching wave.

Janet held on grimly. 'Hold on to the edge, damn you,' she panted. 'Hold on tight!' She plunged her hand deep into the tub, but withdrew it quickly. The water was almost scalding. She tried again, groping hurriedly for the plug, found it and pulled hard.

Water gurgled, fast disappearing as Janet tried to still her galloping heart.

With the crisis over, Lulla lay there pink and pulsating as an overwrought squid. It was all too much for Janet. She gave one shriek of hysterical mirth and sank to her knees in the bathroom slop, helpless with laughter. 'Let's get you out of there.'

Janet sat beside the bed, waiting, gently stroking damp hair away from Lulla's sleeping face. Eyes flickered open.

'Feeling better?' she whispered, 'you've been out for quite a while. Like a cup of something?'

'Thanks, no. Ugh!' Shuddering. 'I feel terrible.'

'Do you wonder?' Janet lifted Lulla's head and turned the pillow. 'You could have killed yourself. And why didn't you tell me?'

'I was hoping and praying I'd have to tell no one. Especially you.'

'For God's sake, why?'

'You're so—so ...' Lulla gave up trying to explain.

Janet blinked back hurt. 'I'm so what, Lulla? Come on, tell me.'

'Decent, for a start. Good. You must know what I mean. Do you think I want to admit—oh, hell ...' Lulla struggled to sit up, pulling the sheet around her. 'Anyway, I didn't want to worry you. Not yet.'

'Worry me!' Janet announced to the ceiling. 'Did you hear that? She didn't want to worry me. Oh, Lulla, I thought you knew me better than that.' Now brisk, she tucked the sheet more firmly around the miserable Lulla's shoulders. 'How far—I mean, how long is it?'

'I'm over two weeks. Two whole weeks. Me!'

Janet's sympathy and concern vanished in astonishment. 'You've gone through all that just because you're two weeks overdue? That's nothing. I'm as erratic as a broken-down clock.'

'Not this chick. Never was. You could set Big Ben by me.'

'Is it …?' This time Janet hesitated, realising that in part Lulla spoke the truth: understanding her reluctance to confide. Such intimacies were rarely, if ever, discussed between friends. Girls, single girls, might find themselves pregnant—even to herself she stumbled over the word—but no one wanted to know the details of how it happened. Not really …

She took a deep breath. 'I know Chuck's fond of you, I—'

'Chuck? Come off it, Jan. Dear old Chuck's about as exciting as a side of mutton. No, not Chuck. Take another guess.'

'Not Daryl!' Janet failed to hide her shocked dismay. Daryl was a spiv. Everyone knew he worked for Mac's solely to avoid the call-up. He waxed fat while Kirk and men like him risked their lives every day in the week. 'Not Daryl,' she whispered.

'Don't judge too hastily, Jan.' Lulla felt an obligation to speak up for him. 'Daryl's all right. Anyway, it's not him.'

'Then who?'

Lulla's face wore the ravages of self-incrimination,

eyelids mere slits from too many tears. 'I suppose you had to find out sometime, and Kirk might already know. God knows what men talk about at sea.'

'You think he knows?'

'Randy bastard. Him and his rotten acetone.'

'Kirk? You're talking about my Kirk?'

In spite of her woes, Lulla had to stifle a giggle. 'Idiot. I'm talking about Spanner. Spanner-bloody-Larkin.'

'Spanner! But you hardly know him.'

'I know him, all right.' Irony overlaid the regret. 'If I'd been stepping out with Tojo himself you wouldn't have noticed. Can't blame you for that with Kirk around.'

'I can't believe it. Oh, yes I can,' Janet hastily amended. 'Spanner's a charmer if ever I saw one. But, Lulla—'

'I know, I'm crazy ...' Lulla's sigh came up from her red-painted toenails. 'But what's a girl supposed to do? You tell me. You meet a fellow. You hit it off. If there's time you might get to know each other better. Do a bit of courting—pre-war, like. But there isn't time, is there? A dance or two, a film, maybe, then they're off to God knows where; and just like the line he's spun you, it happens to him. Boom-boom! Gone-finish ... And not even knowing what hit him. Jesus, what can a girl do?'

She became aware of the stricken horror on Janet's face: the picture had been too clearly drawn. Boom-boom! Gone-finish. *Kirk*. But who could imagine him dead? 'Gee, I'm sorry love. Why can't I shut my big mouth. He'll be okay. What does he call it? A milk-run. Thursday Island and back. As he says, a piece of cake.' She squeezed Janet's arm. 'I'm just making excuses for my own weak stupidity.' Then she thumped the bed with her fist. 'After all I said about kids and husbands. A new sort of life for us females. Hell! What's the use. A woman can't win.' The pillow was thrashed into submission before Lulla slumped back on it. 'But I'll tell you one thing. If I come out of this, if that gin does the trick, I swear on a stack of bibles—never again. Fingers crossed, legs crossed, and never the twain shall meet.'

'Amen to that,' said Janet fervently.

A week dragged by with Lulla alternating between threats of going bush, or hurling herself under the nearest pie cart. Recalling hearsay, she told Andy of her predicament, and after much persuasion, the forewoman admitted to having a friend, who knew a woman who had a friend who 'fixed things up'. She gave Lulla a phone number, and closed her ears to further questions.

Lulla phoned, and made arrangements.

Janet was appalled and said it was a ticket to hell; apart from that, she said, Lulla could find herself six feet under. She could not understand her stubborn refusal to write to Spanner, and could not comprehend that love had not come into it.

'Spanner doesn't love me, and I don't particularly care for him.'

Sacrilegious words; nearly as shocking as Lulla's

determination to go ahead with the abortion. Janet's only contribution to the illicit plan was to light extra candles at Benediction and pray for Lulla's soul.

Later, Janet swore that her prayers had been answered. Lulla swore that it was the gin and being boiled like a raw prawn; but one morning she woke up to a familiar, dull cramp inching down her thighs. It was like a visit from an old and dear friend. With whoops of wild hope, she threw back the sheets, and rushed off to the bathroom.

'Lordy, lordy! It's happened!' Her happy noise woke Janet up. 'Holy joy, and I've been saved forty quid!'

Her eyes sparkled, her hair came alive with an exuberance of its own. 'Come on! Get up, and I'll even go to church with you and light a couple of candles for good measure.'

'Quiet, for heaven's sake! You'll wake the whole house.'

'Who gives a hoot? I live again!'

After things had settled down and they were into their second cup of tea, there came a knock at their front door. Janet sprang from the chair, her heart lurching. *He's dead. Missing. Dear God—why else a summons at such an early hour?* She asked Lulla to see who it was—her own trembling fingers refused to turn the latch key. Hilda Scott stood in the hallway. The relief was a physical pain.

Hilda gave a small, apologetic smile. 'Sorry to disturb you like this, I knew you were up'—she gave Lulla an oblique glance—'but I'll come straight to the point. I know you both work in munitions, and I wanted to catch you before you left ... you being on morning shift, and that.' Again the apologetic smile. She hesitated, not getting to the point at all, as if embarrassed at what was to follow. 'Ah—I was wondering if there's something down there I could do. If you know of anything, that is.'

As Janet seemed incapable of answering, Lulla gave Hilda a friendly grin of reassurance. 'There's a job going in the annexe. Two, in fact. Your Peggy might be interested too.'

It was surprising that Peggy had not already been manpowered into something, somewhere. Janet, coming to life, gave a nod of agreement. They had done little over the weeks, she felt, to help the Scotts settle in. Here was the chance to make up for it. She stepped inside, inviting Hilda in.

'We're having a cuppa. Bit of a rush, but—' An idea struck her and she changed course in mid-sentence. 'Better still, come down to the factory with us. We'll introduce you to Mrs Daniels. She's a bit of a dragon—'

'And for cor' sake,' swooped in Lulla, 'Don't mention that you want to work in the annexe. She'd know we put you up to it, and she'd pack you off to the machinery shop just to nark us. The old bat hates having her mind made up for her.'

6

DARYL MISSIM AND Lulla sat beneath the slow-moving fans of the Greek Club. It was not the first time they had been there. Not long after the Scotts had joined the grenade team, Daryl and Lulla were in the breezeway hosing down newly moulded grenades, when out of the blue he'd asked, 'How do you like Greek food?' He'd had to raise his voice above the jetting hose and the clamour of the nearby machine shop.

'Not bad,' Lulla had yelled back. 'There's a Red Rose Cafe in Roma. Used to go there sometimes after Saturday's closing.' She smiled at the memory. 'We'd pile into someone's truck, whoop it down to Roma, have a feed and more than likely end up "round the Burri log" for a singsong. Watch the sunrise. Nice.' She held a grenade up to the light, inspecting it for flaws. 'Yair—you could say I like Greek food. And so?'

'Not talking steak and eggs with a slice of beetroot. I'm talking about real food.'

'Pardon me for being a bushie. But I happen to like steak and eggs. Fish 'n chips too, with a splash of the good old Holbrooks to liven it up. Any objections?'

Daryl had turned off the hose. Taking Lulla by the elbow, he gazed deeply into her eyes. 'Ah, my lovely ... come with me to the Greek Club, and I'll feast you on yaprakia and baklava.' He twirled his invisible moustache. 'We'll sip Greco coffee as black as sin and sweeter even than your kisses.'

'You're about as seductive as a garden rake, Daryl Missim. But you've talked me into it.'

Now, looking about her, Lulla decided that the Greek Club was the best place for eating out (as the Yanks called it) in Brisbane. Romantic. Different.

Two storeys high, with white plaster peeling, it stood well back from the footpath; the minute and graceful portico was screened from busy commerce by a palm or two, azalea shrubs, and a rampant flush of morning glory.

Old men played backgammon here, and she quietly enjoyed their surreptitious glances of approval. A gramophone standing by the stairs played a record she had heard so many times over that now she could hum the tune, tapping her feet to its syncopated beat. And never, for the life of her, would she forget the night when the old men danced. Men holding hands! Dancing without women ... so solemn, so serious as they followed the rhythm in a series of complicated steps. All new to Lulla and as outlandish as the beads they click-clacked through their fingers. She grinned to herself.

What a dumb-cluck she had been.

There was one more good reason for liking the Greek Club. An absence of uniforms, especially the clean-cut lines of the Americans', who were swiftly taking over the town. Sometimes Daryl, in civvies, caught up against a background of khaki and royal blue, pricked Lulla with a mild sense of guilt. But here, amongst the old men, although he was not a Greek himself, somehow he fitted in.

'You're quiet tonight, Princess.' Spanner's name for her; it seemed an intrusion.

'No—just taking it all in. You know how I love it here. It sure beats the Royal at Muckadilla.'

Daryl beamed, well satisfied with the answer. He tucked his thumbs into his waistcoat, his back braced against the chair. 'Just stick by me, Princess—we've only skimmed the surface of this old burg.' He studied her closely, the humour fading from his eyes. 'Kirk's in town, isn't he?' They all knew the sleeping arrangements when Kirk had shore leave. Daryl leaned closer, anxious to catch her reply.

'He's home,' she answered matter-of-factly.

'Jan must be pleased, eh?' The tone casual. She knew what he was driving at. Kirk was home all right; and where, she wondered, was Spanner? The few times he had been around she had made excuses not to be there. Lately, so Janet had told her, Spanner had been playing the field.

Well, good luck to him.

Suddenly Lulla's keen enjoyment of the club had lost its zest. Blast Spanner Larkin and his quirky, lopsided grin. She let Daryl wait as she took out a compact and lipstick from her handbag. He watched every move as she outlined her lips and pressed them together, carefully examining the result before Daryl's steady gaze.

'Ready for coffee?' The crimson lips parted invitingly. 'At my place?'

'I'd like that.' He called for the bill, impatient to leave.

Lulla reckoned that an old-fashioned smooching would do her the world of good. It was weeks since her hair had been mussed-up by a handsome man. She had managed to keep them all at arm's length, so to speak. She was wondering if she had panicked unnecessarily. But one big fright was enough, thanks very much. (Well, two, she admitted in secret to herself.)

Cuddles and kisses would go down well tonight, and without a qualm, she judged that Daryl would fit the bill nicely. He was easy to handle without inviting too much trouble. A mention of his young fiancée, she had discovered, and Daryl cooled off very quickly.

'Well, Blue Eyes, do we make a move?'

Gallantly he pulled out her chair. *Always does the right thing, does Daryl*, she thought, and felt a rush of tenderness towards him. She was starting to feel reckless. A dangerous sign: especially when compounded with a surge of desire for the good-looking man taking her arm. Daryl was generous and never spared a penny when they hit the town. He deserved a break, she decided, giving his arm an extra squeeze.

They were halfway across the floor when Daryl came to a dead halt, his attention attracted by a man who sat alone.

'Just the johnny I want to see.' He made his excuses. 'Won't be long, sweet'—tapping the side of his nose—'business is business.'

He left her stranded by a vacant chair. She didn't know whether she should laugh, or walk out on him. It was one time she could have done with a pair of glasses, to see more clearly what they were up to. She edged her chair closer.

She could see enough that they spoke earnestly together, once darting a quick look in her direction. What did *that* mean? She guessed that like Daryl, the stranger wallowed in the black market. Well, she wanted no part of it. A diamond flashed from the stranger's little finger. Daryl had tried wearing one, once, when he called for her. But only once. 'Not when you're out with me,' she'd snapped. Somehow, diamonds on a man were too foreign. Too racy, even for her; an affront to those who laid their lives on the line for six bob a day.

Daryl returned, his eyes gleaming with satisfaction. 'It pays to know the right people,' was all he said.

'Yeah,' she answered drily. 'I bet it does.' She

made no effort to conceal her irritation.

Everything moved smoothly for Daryl, it seemed, like the taxi already outside waiting for them. Not even a Yank could hustle one up as quickly. Daryl even had his own transport on tap. As he ushered her protectively into the back seat, she vowed that if he mentioned once again that it paid to know the right people, she'd clobber him one!

He sensed her displeasure and accepted the aloof silence as a penalty for deserting her at the club. He would never guess that she was suddenly ashamed of all the favours she had taken from him as her due. Tickets to the best seats, lavish dinners at Princes and the top hotels. While she wore shot taffeta and French lace, girls yearned for a piece of parachute silk to sew up a wedding dress. She cringed over the blatant bartering that went on between them, backed up by Chuck's P.X. larder. Why, she was no better than Daryl himself!

What's the female gender of black marketeer? She asked herself. Black marketress? Well, no bloody more!

Daryl shrugged when she made it clear that the night ended at the front gate.

Her mood was sour as she made her way around the side of the flats and along the path to the back room. Skirting the poinsettia bushes, she thought she heard movement behind the closed door.

Possums?

Lately they'd been playing cricket on the roof. A

huddle of them occupied a mango tree in the adjoining yard. There came a scuffling sound, and she wished she had a torch. She went over to press her ear close to the wall. Was that whispering?

'Who's that?'

No answer. Her heart gave a jolt. Burglars! She suppressed a scream as the door flew open. A girl sprang outside, slamming it shut behind her.

'Evie! Evie Scott! What the hell are you doing here?'

'Nothing.'

'What sort of answer is that? Have you been ratting around my—'

'It was hot in the flat. I—I thought it might be cooler up here. To sleep.'

'In *my* room? You've got a bloody hide.'

'Didn't know you were using it, anyway.' Evie's tone was sullen, her back still pressed against the door.'

'That's a funny one, that is. You know damn well that Kirk's home,' Lulla hissed. 'You've done nothing but give him the glad eye all week. How Janet puts up with it—but never mind. Just move!' She grabbed the girl's shoulder. 'Are you going to shift?'

Someone—something moved inside the room. Evie stiffened, refusing to budge. With both hands Lulla heaved her aside. Evie stumbled and fell. In seconds Lulla was through the door, switching on the light.

'Hey! Come back here!' She dived for a muscular

leg as it vanished through an open window; and missed. Using her bedroom as a cat house. She'd skin the little bugger alive!

Outside, Evie lay where she had fallen, pinned fast in a patch of light. She sprawled in a confusion of snapped twigs and branches and poinsettia leaves, wearing nothing more than a swami petticoat.

Lulla seethed. 'Are you going to lie there all night? Get up! Oh Gawd ... just look at that bush. Old Hickey'll have a fit.' Quickly she turned off the light and wondered if she was too late. Even now, the landlord could be viewing it all from an upstairs window.

Evie made no attempt to move. 'Are you going to tell Mum?' was all she said, her voice surprisingly calm for a girl caught literally with her pants down. Lulla could have smacked her cheeks, for once made speechless by the girl's shameless behaviour.

'I said, are you going to tell Mum?'

Lulla found her voice. 'I'll tell her all right,' she hissed. 'Get up, I said. And keep quiet! Before Old Hickey comes down. He'll blame me for this as sure as eggs. Could even think I put you up to it.' With an effort she dragged the girl to her feet.

Night failed to hide Evie's smirk. 'Mum and Peggy's at the pictures. So we've got a bit of a wait. That's if,' she mocked, 'you're game to tell her.'

'And what does that mean?'

Evie gave a soft laugh, as if shrewdly guessing that Lulla was loath to confront Hilda with a half-naked daughter. She gave herself a small shake and brushed away fragments of crushed flowers and twigs. 'Now if you don't mind, I'll go and get my dress and shoes.'

'You bloody well will not.' Lulla blocked the entrance. 'Just you stay where you are.' Unwilling to turn the light on again, she groped in the darkness and located Evie's dress on the floor. 'Here,' tossing it over to her, 'make yourself decent.'

Evie was prodded step by step to the back landing. Tinted glass framed the door and a hall light threw harlequin patterns of rose and chartreuse over her face, its beauty smooth and detached as a celluloid doll. Before she went inside, she turned, facing the older girl.

'I wouldn't say too much to Mum if I were you, and by the way ... that *was* Kirkland Hope on the train. You just tell Jan that.' She was sly and knowing, as if the two of them shared some secret.

How did the little witch find out Kirk's full name? Jan never used it. And if he was on the train, so what? But Evie could turn a casual encounter on a crowded train into a full-blown love affair. After all, Lulla reasoned, what husband would ever admit to meeting her? Even by chance.

She bundled the girl into the hall. It was quiet there. No sound of the Hickeys from above them. 'If ever,' Lulla gritted, 'and I mean ever—I catch you within coo-ee of that room again, day or night, I'll strip the hide off you myself.' She gave the girl a shake. 'I mean it, Evie.'

'You're not telling Mum, but. Are you?'

'Shut up! I've had a gutful of your cheek!'

Incipient triumph mocked her. "'night, Lulla. And frankly, I don't give a toss if you tell Mum or not.'

At the sight of her bed, Lulla's anger went into overload. 'I'll kill her!'

The sheets were crumpled; the starched and carefully ironed pillow-cases were creased and smeared with lipstick. She sniffed. Yankee fags! Had Evie discovered her cache under the bed and helped herself? Nothing would surprise her, after this. Evie's sandals lay where they had been kicked off, panties left beside them. Lulla's first reaction was to hurl them outside, but she thought better of it. She was amazed that the girl should take such brazen risks. Maybe it was just like she said—she didn't give a toss.

The clear young voice still teased her brain. 'That *was* Kirkland Hope on the train.' It could mean anything. But the implied illicit encounter had chilled Lulla through. The little wretch had her over a barrel. Janet had enough to cope with. Hilda too, for that matter.

She began ripping off bedclothes, accusing herself for a coward, knowing in her heart that Hilda should be told.

'Damn and blast, the little trollop,' she said aloud, pitching soiled sheets and pillow-slips into a corner. 'I'll murder her! So help me, I'll murder her!'

7

*H*ALF-PAST FIVE early morning: in flat No. 2, the smooth routine of women preparing for the day's work ahead and a seven o'clock start was in full swing. Sandwiches Peggy had cut the previous night were cool in the ice-chest; breakfast, to Hilda's satisfaction, was on the table by six; while Evie, eyes tightly shut, stayed in bed pretending sleep.

For Eveleen, each morning was a progression of hateful sounds that climaxed in an abrupt departure from the security of bed. It always began with the whistle of the boiling kettle—to her a detested alarm clock—which preceded the audible stirring of porridge and subdued voices offsetting the clatter of cutlery. How she loathed the all-pervading smell of breakfast cooking! She pulled the blanket over her face and ears to block out the morning, waiting for Peggy's third and final call.

'Ev-vie! I'm coming in there at the count of three.' Eveleen burrowed deeper into the bed. Peggy's counting scratched on nerves like the persistent buzzing of a fly too stupid to know there's clear glass between it and the outside world. *How she hated that voice first thing in the morning.*

'THREE!' she heard, 'I'm on my way!'

Any second now, and the sheet and blanket would be snatched off, no quarter given. Eveleen clenched her teeth, clutching the bedclothes, anchoring herself to the bedhead. 'I'll get out when I'm good and ready!'

Peggy grabbed a leg. 'Well, breakfast's ready, Mum's ready and so am I. It's about time you were OUT!'

It took only one solid tug and Evie was dumped, kicking and furious, on the floor.

'I'll kill you one day, Peggy Scott. Just wait. You're a bitch and I hate you!' But soft enough for Hilda not to hear.

Peggy grinned. 'Hate me now, love me later—what's the diff. But that bed's got to be aired before it's made up. You know that. Them's the rules and it's your turn to do it, before you go.' She held out a hand to help Evie up. The offer was ignored.

Hilda bustled in with a school uniform over her arm. 'Here, love, I've pressed it.' She swished the dividing curtain across the room. 'Now get dressed, or you'll be eating breakfast by yourself.'

'Who wants breakfast?' Evie had it worked out that if she dawdled in the shower she'd miss having to eat with them altogether. It would still leave her sitting at the table, everything looking normal—she hoped—when finally they had to leave for work. Hilda liked to see her dressed and ready for school before they went. All she had to do was wait. She had her own plans for the day, and school wasn't part of them.

They left Evie in her dressing-gown picking at toast. Hilda dropped a hand on her shoulder. 'Hate leaving you to eat alone, love. We should all sit at table together, like a family. Nothing but rush in the morning ...'

Evie shrugged. 'I don't mind.'

Peggy reminded her again that it was her day for cleaning up, and said Lulla had given them some chocolate and her share was with the sandwiches in the ice-chest. In silence, Evie waited for the door to close on them. She heard her mother greeting Lulla and Janet in the hall and as their footsteps hurried down the concrete path, she thought it a good idea to wave them off. She opened the outside venetian blind, and pushed her hand between the wooden slats. 'Bye, Mum! Peggy!' And had to smile at the pleasure on Hilda's face and the surprised look on her sister's.

Now they were gone. Good! She surveyed the table with distaste. Plates creamed with drying egg yolk; butter peppered with toast crumbs. 'Enough to make you puke,' she said aloud. She picked up the plates and dumped them in the kitchen sink.

She then went to the ice-chest for the remains of

last night's jelly—and the chocolate. She removed the sandwiches, took off the greasproof paper, then flushed them out of sight and mind down the toilet. Not finished yet, she rumpled her school uniform just enough to indicate use and a day spent in safeguarding nubile curves. Then, snitching a cigarette from Hilda's supply, she waltzed back to the breakfast table to smoke in a delicious peace sweetened by jelly and chocolate.

Evie bounced through the Pig & Whistle's door intoxicated by a bouquet of fresh milk, malt, vanilla and strawberry essence. FRAPPES—ALL FLAVOURS—*with* FRESH CREAM, the sign behind the counter said, and the heady whirring of the milkshake mixer welcomed her in.

Her eyes had already appraised the first of the early birds. One, a mere boy in bedraggled army greens, putties askew, gulped down milk as if he'd spent a week under the desert's sun. Her gaze slid over him and on to the next, a lone American soldier who did not raise a heartbeat as far as she was concerned.

She ordered an ice-cream soda and gave the American one long steady look; a dress rehearsal for when the right one came along. But before he could make a move, she lowered her lashes, scarlet lips pouting over the drinking straw and turned her back on him. The lad in army uniform ordered another glass of milk and, braver than his counterpart, ventured to speak.

'Nice morning, I reckon.'

She snubbed him, her look coolly dismissive. He tried again. 'You're here early—I'm too late.' He studied his crumpled clothes, sadly shaking his head.

She couldn't help herself. 'Late for what?' It was easy to tell he was slightly drunk, in spite of the early hour.

Encouraged, he stepped closer—she increased the distance between them. 'For everything,' he said, giving a vague wave of his hand. His gesture included the other soldier. 'For bugle call—that's what the Yanks say, don't they? For breakfast. And too late for a girl, y'know? They won't have us now. Back too late ...' His voice trailed away, but was picked up by a shrug. 'Don't suppose—' He studied her, calculating his chances; his gaze rested for a moment on the neatly dressed G.I. then came back to Evie again. 'Nah!' He shook his head. 'Not a hope in hell.' Swaying slightly, he emptied the glass and, drawing a kind of dignity about him, left. He looked back only once to deliver Evie the salute of a rejuvenated stoic.

Evie took long, gratifying pulls at her straw. It seemed that the Pig & Whistle was in for a quiet morning. No one came. The American, having long finished his drink and failing to score either with Evie or the girl who had served him a double malted, disappeared—still on the loose and on the prowl.

Evie had just enough change to invest in another ice-cream soda. She thought it over and wondered if the cafe down the next block was a better prospect. She was saved from making a decision by the sudden and boisterous entry of a carefree group. She didn't have to turn around to see who they were. It wasn't only the twang in their voices: they carried in with them the sweet, sharp tang of P.X. shaving lotion, and the distinct pungency of Havana cigars.

Not a cold shoulder in sight as they clustered around the girl; fresh as a flower, hair tied back with a ribbon to match the blue of her sleekly clinging crepe dress.

'Chocolate frappes coming up,' was Evie's happy but unspoken comment.

Bill was his name and Evie had culled him from the pack before ten minutes had gone by. Bill the marine; six foot three inches in army boots, bronzed of face, newly arrived. He was near to bursting his trouser seams with robust health and splendid muscles enriched by generous helpings of army chow, gruelling pack drills and day-long hikes. The mutual attraction between them was instantaneous, and after one chocolate frappe apiece, they found themselves walking hand-in-hand down George Street.

'Gee,' Bill squeezed Evie's hand. 'What a break meeting a sweet chick, first time around.' His thoughts, never too far away from food at any time of the day or night, made him ask where a guy could pick up a hamburger.

Evie, blissful as Bill over her luck in their encounter, was eager to please. 'Sometimes there's a pie cart down at the Gardens. He sells hotdogs too, but I don't want one, thanks.'

Bill slapped a magnificent thigh. 'Well, cut mah legs off, an' call me Shorty! Hotdogs! Just lead me to him, baby.'

Evie was willing to lead her Titan anywhere. Completely in tune with the bright, sunny day, the girl giggled at every compliment Bill uttered. They strolled by a flower shop—no more than an alcove opening onto the footpath.

'Stay here, Evie'—he chucked her under the chin—'don't go away now,' and he stepped inside the blossom-filled cubicle. She could see him picking over the blooms with special care and was delighted when he chose an orchid of a rich and regal hue. She had seen many like it in the North, in gardens and rain-forests, but the idea of having one specially chosen for her to wear was novelty enough to impress the girls back at school.

She allowed him to pin the purple extravagance on her, and if his hand brushed her breast, by accident or design, she hardly noticed, or cared.

Piecart Benny was already there when they arrived and Bill ordered his hotdog. 'Sure you don't want one?' But when Evie saw the vulgar red of it, glistening and swollen with hidden fats, she decided that she was hungry after all. Piecart Benny slathered tomato sauce down the centre of Evie's roll, and was about to do the same for the marine when Bill gave a sudden sign for him to stop.

'No ketchup for me, buddy. Make mine mustard.'

Benny looked hurt. 'There's Holbrooks (black sauce, to some). Tomato. But no mustard. This ain't

Lennons, mate.' Bill gave a good-natured shrug and said that ketchup would do just fine. Piecart Benny gave his usual measure of sauce and charged the marine twice the going price.

They took the path that followed the river. The slow, broad stream made small impression on a girl used to the sparkling cascades and clean gravel beds of the northern rivers. There was still resentment simmering inside her at being snatched away from the delights of Sunday swims and picnics. She missed the jungle shade where a day could be spent beneath vines that hung like curtains, trysting places of warm, red earth beneath a pelt of emerald grass.

Restraint or guilt had never bothered Evie's conscience, nor had fear kept tight rein on over-zealous passions. Something told her that there was little to worry over: much to the satisfaction of a nameless boy who had been a love-mate since the day Evie had turned fourteen.

They sat on the sloping bank, and fed breadcrumbs to sparrows homing in for early lunch. He told her that back home he fooled around with motor engines, but admitted that mostly his time was spent in serving customers at the pumps, with gas. 'Wiping windscreens and that, most of the time.'

Evie obliged by telling that she supported a 'delicate' mother, and that her father (for once she told the truth) had left them when she was a little girl. Nothing but sympathy from Bill, who shook his head over a man deserting wife and child in their hour of need. There was no mention of Peggy.

Evie lay back on the grass, shading her eyes, stretching in a way that made Bill's heart do backflips in his chest. Resting on an elbow, he bent over her. 'You must be one of the prettiest girls around. We were told how pretty you Aussie girls are. Haven't had that much time to notice. Only flew in yesterday.'

His eyes roved over the length of her, returning always to the full mounds of her breasts. He looked about him; the park appeared near empty, and the slope of the bank hid them from view. Evie's eyes reflected the green of the leaves about them and she seemed to be waiting, with parted lips, for his kiss. As their lips touched he wondered just how far he could go. Nerves flared as Evie's tongue flicked over his own, so quickly that he wondered if it had been imagination. He surfaced for breath and by her lazy smile knew that the day was far from over. A grunt escaped him as he eased his trousers to accommodate the turn of events.

He looked down at the girl lying there, eyes half-closed, distrusting the obvious signals she was sending up—was she too easy? He remembered his sergeant's grim warnings; clear instructions before they'd even set foot to ground: 'These gals are easy on the eye. Some even speak good English, and most have the morals of an alley cat.' As he spoke he'd doled out rubber sheaths. They were told to be sure to use them. 'The place is riddled with the clap and crawling with crabs the size of one of them copper pennies. I'm tellin' ya!'

Bill found all that hard to believe as he looked down on this lovely girl, prettier than any movie star, practically begging for him to take her. She smelt wonderful and so far she hadn't asked for a red cent. He came to the conclusion that his sergeant must have been a mite over-cautious.

He fell on her again, pressing closer, feeling the arched response and wishing to hell that the sun would suddenly disappear.

Evie tried squirming away from him. 'Someone might see us.'

He could only agree.

'I don't like kissing in public,' she whispered.

His face was buried so deep into her flesh, that he could barely speak. 'What can we do?' he asked. Although it hurt, he was fully prepared—he even expected—to delay what had been started until the sun went down. He never doubted that something could be arranged. What she suggested next made his vitals lurch in an explosion of lusty excitement.

'No one will see us ...' she was saying and went on to tell him of a stand of trees further along. 'Big trees,' she told him, 'wait till you see them.'

He was willing to take her word for it and they wasted no time, except to snatch kisses, to reach the promised, sequestered place.

She stopped at a spot where the tended path crumbled away to shale and river mud. He suspected that at high tide the bank would be completely covered by water.

'See, up there.' She was pointing out a leafy colony

of a species that was new to him. A canopy of glossy foliage flowed from tall branches, cascading right to the ground. The thought of being sheltered there, out of sight, bedded hard and strong inside her, belted his nerve centre with the impact of a baseball bat. He didn't know if he could climb the small rise without making a fool of himself. He wanted to throw her on the ground, then and there, where they stood; his bursting impatience was nearly more than he could bear. He wondered if she was feeling the same way as he followed her towards the trees.

Without hesitation she took his hand and, as if knowing of some secret door, led him into a silent space, its lovely filtered light gilding her face. Silent space: green and gold. For such cool shade, the grass and fallen leaves were dry, he noticed as he sat beside her. She lay down, raising both arms ready to receive him. Smiling. Waiting. He was the one to lift her skirt, the petticoat; pull down her briefs; feverish and frantic that he'd be too late.

Her turn now. He knelt between her legs. 'Undo me, honey. Come on, quick!'

She gave a low and teasing laugh, eyes glazed by green sunlight. 'Undo yourself, soldier.' While he struggled she placed a hand between his thigh, palm up as if she needed to weigh his manhood. Through the thick army cloth he was aware of every stroke and movement before she slowly drew her hand away. He unbuckled his belt, hastily pulled his trousers down as far as necessary, and with a groan fell on her. Pushing and bucking, his eyes tightly closed, not daring to look at her. She lay there in the lucent green waiting for him to finish.

'I have to go now.'

She held Hilda's wristwatch up to the light. There was only an hour left—a little more if her mother decided to shop on the way home. Not forgetting Lulla and Janet. That was the trouble with Franklin Street, too many stickybeaks to keep an eye on her every move. Now the day was nearly over as far as she was concerned, and the goblins of uncertainty were nipping at the edge of confidence. Had she entirely disposed of that cigarette? Dirty dishes still in the kitchen sink. Suddenly, Evie was in a desperate hurry to get back to Franklin Street. She scrambled to her feet. 'I'll be late for work. Are you coming?'

'Sure, sure ...!' But he still lay at her feet, appearing reluctant to move.

'Evie?'

'Yair?' She busied herself brushing off twigs and bits of grass. She examined her dress for stains and creases. 'You want to ask me something?'

'Ah' He got to his feet to hold her again. *There wasn't time for that.* 'Did you enjoy it, baby?' He seemed anxious.

'It was nice.' She could see that it was not the answer he wanted. 'Well, not too bad.'

He couldn't know that the enjoyment for Evie was the chase, the capture, but not the conquest. There was the thrill of her power to stir; to tease. What came after was all right. It was the getting there Evie found irresistible.

He asked her if they could meet again—'same time, same place'. He was referring to the Pig & Whistle. 'We could take in a movie, and maybe after ...'

'I'll see.'

'Maybe you could bring a girl. My buddy—he's kinda shy.'

'I'll see about that, too.'

Evie was not sure just how many days she could wag school without being found out. One more day maybe—at the most two.

He had to be satisfied with her half-promise to meet him the next day.

'Well, I'll see you home, we'll—'

'No! I live too far out of town. Anyway, I'm going straight to work.'

'Well, I'll take you there then,' he offered.

Evie's eyes flashed. 'I said no! I mean it! Just leave me in Queen Street—that's good enough.' She glared at him tight-lipped; a different girl from the breathless beauty who had led him by the hand to the cloister of trees. Startled, he raised both hands to ward off her growing anger.

'Okay, okay! Just as you want, honey. But you will see me tomorrow—promise?'

She said once again that she would if she could. He had to be content with that.

Outside the tall iron gates of the Gardens a taxi cruised by. Bill hailed it. 'At least take the cab, sugar.'

He touched the orchid on her shoulder. 'I'll get a Slipper for you tomorrow—if I can find one—to match your eyes. A slipper orchid for a Cinderella baby.'

She was thankful for the ride. She'd be home in tons of time now. Time to do the dishes. Time for a shower to scrub out the smell of him. As the taxi crossed the bridge, she unpinned the orchid and tossed it out the window. Curiosity made her turn around to see where it had landed. It lay on the tramline. Royal purple and gold, with the tram to Bulimba bearing down on it.

The Hickeys had seen her leave in the morning. They watched as the taxi cab brought her home. They wondered if they should inform the mother. In the back flat adjoining the Scotts, the woman paid to keep one eye on her was busy entertaining a lady friend. Pouring ersatz coffee and slicing homemade Kuchen Brot, she was too busy to worry over a brat with the eyes and manners of a witch.

'I have tried,' she complained to her friend. 'Believe it ... you must believe it.'

Evie, not caring what anyone thought and shrewdly aware of people's inherent dislike of meddling in family affairs, was pretty sure she was safe enough. Take Lulla, she assured herself. Apart from dirty looks, Lulla had kept her mouth shut.

By the time Hilda arrived home she was sitting at the table surrounded by pads and books. The sight was enough to raise a smile on Hilda's face.

'How did it go today, love?'

'Pretty good.' Then, feigning interest, 'Where's Peggy?'

'With the girls.' Hilda kicked off her shoes and sitting down, tenderly rubbed a bunion, drawing in her breath at the hurt of it.

Evie looked up from the book she was reading. 'Mum, my uniform's torn. Sorry, and that. Must have been a nail, or something. Think you can mend it by tomorrow?'

Her smile eased some of the tiredness from Hilda's body. 'Of course, love. Anything else happen apart from that?'

'Just the same old thing. Nothing much. Oh—and I've done the vegies.'

'Good girl.'

She went back to her studies as Hilda watched for a while, almost absently, rubbing her foot. She sighed and stretched tired muscles. 'You're not a bad kid, Evie.' Her lips lifted in a slightly ironical smile. 'That is when you want to be.'

'I try ...' said her daughter cheerfully.

8

*L*ULLA SPUN AROUND the annexe, snatching Hilda up on the way, giving her a whirl before going on to Janet and pivoting her expertly across the floor.

'They're wonderful! Marvellous!' she sang blithely, sending Janet off with an extra spin.

'Mad as a hatter!' Janet laughed, collapsing against the bench while the team looked on. Lulla was in one of her moods. 'Anyway,' Janet wanted to know, 'who's marvellous?'

'The Yanks. Who do you think? The goddamn, wonderful, crazy Yanks.'

'Does that include Chuck?'

'You can forget about him.'

Andy's eyes glinted with sly humour. 'And what's happened to the Dutch laddie?'

'That was last week. Anyway, I found out he's married, the dirty rat ...' Lulla, grinning, rested against one of the uprights. 'As for the American lads, it's the manners of 'em. So polite it hurts. 'Light your cigarette, ma'am.' 'Orchids to match that cute outfit, ma'am.' 'Your chair, honey.' As for last night, oh Mumma mia ...' She hugged herself. 'He was really something.'

'Don't like Yanks,' Peggy broke in, 'too flash for me.'

The day shift was at lunch. They had voted to stay in the lacquer room; the low-ceilinged change room was too hot to bear in a heat that felt more like summer than autumn. Peggy had said it was a good idea, for the night shift had beaten yesterday's tally; they could catch up.

'Eat as we go along,' she urged.

But her enthusiasm had been howled down by the others, with Hilda protesting that Peggy was no daughter of hers. 'They're getting enough blood out of this old stone. I'll take my full time, if you don't mind.'

None of the other women—homebodies like Hilda and Janet—could test the claims that Lulla made of the Americans' grace and generosity. Even Peggy seemed content with a night at a picture show in the company of Hilda and Evie. But if not quite approving of Lulla's defection to the opposite camp, they were always keen to hear first-hand of encounters from an expert.

'What I'd like to know,' said a new girl who matched Lulla curl for curl, and wore an engagement ring tied around her neck with a piece of string, 'do they really talk like they do at the pictures? Or are they putting it on?'

'They surely do. Take the bloke last night. Gary Cooper to a T. Ask Peggy. She heard him when he called for me, eh, Peg?'

'Never bothered to listen. Told you, don't like Yanks.'

'Now don't be sassy, kid.' There was an unfamiliar twang in Lulla's voice, as, unperturbed, she rummaged through her duffle bag. 'Look what I've got for afters, girls.' She held high a block of chocolate.

Hilda's eyes widened. 'It's as big as a brick!' She held out a hand. 'And I'm not too proud. Thanks very much, and ta.'

Micky trotted in with his lacquer pots, and began filling-up. Lulla shoved a packet of Camels down the bib of his overalls.

'Don't flash 'em around,' she warned, 'there's some light-fingered wallys out there.'

The newly installed siren sounded, its metallic shriek demanding an instant return to the workbench. Lulla pulled a face. 'Makes the old whistle sound almost friendly.'

'Yair,' said Peggy, 'but they reckon it wasn't loud enough. Made some of us late for work.' She went on to remind the team they were two crates behind the morning quota, and the night shift's score was going to be hard to beat.

'Who cares,' said the new girl, ignoring Peggy's scowl. 'Blast the night shift, I say …'

In spite of themselves, the team was loath to be beaten. Everyone knew that Management encouraged rivalry between the shifts and between machine shop and annexe; not a man or woman made a move without checking the scoreboard nailed inside the main gate.

It became a race to beat the clock.

Hilda, Lulla and Janet varnished without pause, while Andy and the rest screwed bases into the rows of dried grenades. Peggy, because she was the strongest, teamed up with Micky to stack the completed crates in the holding room, keeping up the pace and counting as she went.

'One hundred more to go,' she crowed. 'We'll do it easy.' Sweating and panting, she surveyed the near-empty benches. 'But we need some more in here—I could help outside with the hosing.'

'You're a slavedriver, lass, but go to it!'

Now the boy joined up with Andy, screwing in bases. Eyes blinking, face crimson, his stubby fingers flew over the crates.

Why do we do it, Lulla wondered. *Why do we keep on raising the ante? Only makes it hard for ourselves. And they'll top us tonight, sure as eggs.* The boy was snuffling beside her. Poor little bugger, flat-out. She nudged him. 'Where's your hankie, love?' He gave her a sheepish grin and gave a quick swipe at his nose. She noticed that Hilda had removed her gloves again. Lacquer stained everything it touched; already Hilda's nails were brown and brittle as onion peel. She'd never learn—it would be whitlows next ...

'Mum!'

It was Peggy. She stood by the annexe door, a worried frown buckling her forehead. A dainty young woman stood at her elbow.

'Mum,' Peggy called out again, 'someone wants you.'

Hilda's brush, suspended in mid-air, dripped shellac. Nerve ends flared as she recognised the English teacher, Miss Lacey, from Eveleen's school. What now? Why here? Ignoring the furtive glances of her workmates, she hurried outside.

'Mrs Scott, I apologise for the intrusion. But the Headmaster insists that you come with me to the school.'

'Right now?'

'I'm afraid so.'

'She's not hurt, is she?' The question was only a formality. Hilda had already half-guessed the answer.

'No, no of course not. The Headmaster—' Miss Lacey, uncomfortable in her role as messenger, searched for the right words. 'I suggest we wait until we get to the school. My car's outside.'

'Is it that bad?'

'Please. Headmaster will explain.'

Through her numbness, Hilda felt her shoulder gently squeezed. She had forgotten all about Peggy standing there. 'I'll come with you, Mum.'

'No, you won't.' She knew she sounded too abrupt. Too harsh.

'But, Mum—'

'For God's sake, Peg. Do as you're told!' She

gentled her voice, trying to cushion the rebuff. 'It's better you stay out of it. Go home with Janet and Lulla while I sort this out.'

Her handbag was on a shelf under the workbench. She excused herself and hurried back to collect it. As she joined Miss Lacey, waiting outside, she heard Peggy say, flatly matter-of-fact: 'I don't know about you lot, but I'm packing it up for the day.'

No chance now of topping the night shift.

The Headmaster's office held no surprises. She had seen enough of them. Maps pinned to the walls, cupboards of varnished pine, an umbrella stand sprouting a flush of bamboo canes. The man behind the desk rose to his feet.

'Ah—Mrs Scott.'

His handclasp was cool and dry in contrast to her own stained and sticky fingers. 'Please take a chair.'

She was grateful for it.

Without preamble: 'Eveleen has not attended school for more than a week.'

She could only sit there, remaining silent.

'At first,' he said, 'we gave her the benefit of the doubt. She could be ill. But of course, we discovered that was not the case.' Soberly, he held her gaze. 'You're not aware of this?'

'Of course not,' she whispered.

He nodded, satisfied. 'However,' he went on, 'Eveleen was seen at school today. Unfortunately, she did not return to attend classes.'

'Oh?'

During the lunch break, he told her, Eveleen had been seen talking to friends at the far end of the school grounds. Hilda could not take her eyes off him, watching as he tapped his cheeks with light fingers, looking over her shoulder as if Eveleen was in his sights.

'That's not the end of it, I'm afraid.'

It was also observed that two men in uniform were waiting for her on the other side of the street. Not only did she join them, but she took a companion with her.

Evie, Evie. God in heaven—what's going to happen to you?

'Mrs Scott? I'm afraid the time has come—'

'But she's always home when me and Peggy—' Hilda licked dry lips, the words refusing to flow. Where was Evie now? Home, as usual? 'She's always there,' she said desperately, 'always. Even doing her homework.' Cunning Evie ....

'Ah, yes. You work in munitions, I believe.' His eyes took in the stained overalls, the sweat-blackened leather belt, the workman-like boots. 'If you stayed at home, perhaps ...'

'That's impossible.'

'Your husband approves? He doesn't resent you working?'

'My husband has nothing to do with it. We're separated.'

Now it was out and she braced herself against the usual reaction, the entrenched disapproval. Abruptly, the Headmaster pushed back his chair to cross the room and gaze out the window. Hilda's face burned. She knew exactly what he was thinking. Like mother, like daughter. Wasn't that what they all said? She should have lied and said that Alf was away fighting the war. Doing his bit. That was the catch-cry now.

The Headmaster returned to his chair and sat down, tapping out secret codes on his cheekbone. 'That does alter things a great deal, Mrs Scott.'

Surprisingly, the official mask of authority had slipped. 'I had no idea. Not easy to be both mother and father, eh? I know well enough.' He paused, his thoughts drifting. 'My own dear wife died two years ago.' He carried on, ignoring her murmur of sympathy. 'You must have surmised by now that Eveleen faces expulsion. But I'll review the matter and see what can be done.' He gave her a fleeting smile. 'One cannot deny that Eveleen is a high-spirited child.'

You can say that again, agreed Hilda silently.

Evie was already home when Hilda arrived. As usual she lay on the couch reading a magazine, schoolbooks stacked on the floor within easy reach.

''Lo, Mum.'

'How was school today?'

'Same as usual.' She kept on reading.

Quick strides brought Hilda to the couch. She ripped the book from Eveleen's hands, hurling it across the room. 'Look at me when I speak to you!' She gripped the girl's jaw, forcing her startled eyes to meet her own. 'Now tell me. What *did* happen today? The truth!'

A different Hilda now, as she glared down at the daughter. Face mottled with anger: no softness there. Evie knew that she was in deep trouble.

'Well, Eveleen, I'm waiting.'

Excuses, denials, raced through the girl's head. There was no escaping the accusing voice or the fingers digging deep into her cheeks, making it difficult to speak.

'Come on, girl, out with it.'

With a grunt of pain, Evie wrenched herself free. 'What's the point? You know already.'

'All I know is, that you haven't seen the inside of a schoolroom for days. You've been seen in the company of soldiers, and worse still, talked one of your mates into going with you. Are you out of your mind? Tell me, for Christ's sake—what have you been up to!'

'Nothing.'

'Don't lie to me!' The mother bent low, her breath anger-hot, close to Evie's face. Quickly the girl twisted over and burrowed deep into the pillow. She gave a smothered denial that no one could believe, including Evie herself. Now was the time for tears and fervid declarations that no one loved or cared; injustice was a mantle of thorns to be endured. It usually worked. Evie tasted blood where soft skin had been pressed too hard against her teeth.

But the mother's fury was spent as suddenly as it had erupted. It left in its aftermath a cold determination to punish. To hurt. To teach, where so far she had failed. There was nothing else to do.

Evie never moved. Too late for tears now. In the awful quiet, she heard the sound of her mother's belt sliding through the keepers of heavy cloth and knew that she was in for it. She braced herself.

THWACK!

They heard it across the hall. It was Janet who held Peggy back. 'Stay with us,' she cautioned, 'you must leave them alone.' Only when they heard Hilda's raised voice had they realised that Evie was already home. It seemed as if the house had stopped breathing as it counted the measured blows of Hilda's fury.

The sound went on and on, and when at last it stopped, the house sighed.

Gently the two friends released their hold on the younger girl—Janet had one arm around Peggy's shoulder, Lulla gripped Peggy's hand. Poor Hilda. Poor Evie. The two friends exchanged knowing looks. It didn't take a bucket of brains to guess why Hilda had been summoned to the school. Evie had been born with her nappy on fire! Not for the first time, Lulla wondered if Hilda should have been told about Evie's foray into the back room. Would it have made any difference?

Janet went off to the kitchen to make tea; Lulla felt as if her mouth had been swabbed out with alum. She wet her lips and remembered the bottle of Scotch stashed away for emergencies. They could all do with a good slug.

Peggy tensed at the sound of footsteps crossing the hallway. 'Peggy, you there?'

'I'm coming, Mum.' Already she was halfway across the room, as Janet, bearing a steaming teapot, came from the kitchen. Peggy paused and turned. Tears welled in her eyes and she smiled through them. 'Thanks,' she whispered. Then, without warning, she rushed Janet with smothering hugs and favoured Lulla with the same. 'You're a pair of rippers, honest. I mean it!'

The flat seemed unnaturally empty after Peggy had gone.

'Well, that's that,' said Janet, mopping up spilt tea.

Lulla wondered again if she should speak to Hilda. *Wait and see what happens*, she advised herself. A damn good belting sometimes saved a lot of breath.

9

They blinked in the harsh sunlight of afternoon, mildly surprised to find Albert Street going about its usual workday affairs. The reality of *Cover Girl*, now eclipsed by the Metro Theatre's velvet drapes, still held them in its thrall.

'That Gene Kelly—' The thought of the dancer's muscular thighs shivered all the way down Lulla's spine. 'G-rr, I could have him for breakfast.'

'Yeah, he's a bit of all right.' Coming from Peggy, that was praise indeed.

'Glad you came along?' Lulla prodded.

'I suppose.'

Not one for idle conversation, our Peg, Lulla mused. Far too serious for a kid, but straight as a die. As straight as that damn hair of hers. She'd given up trying to persuade Peggy to go to the hairdresser down the street.

'You get a permanent, and I'll show you how to pin it.'

'What do I need pins for, if I get one of them waves?'

'So you can roll it up.'

'What for?'

No point in saying that hair, innocent of rolls, curls, or bangs, was as stylish as Aunt Fanny's bloomers.

'Well—to be smart, I suppose.'

'Huh!' After that, they had let the matter rest.

Straight or curly—if she only realised it—Peggy was as attractive as that sister of hers. Lulla had said as much often enough. Not beautiful, as she'd once told Janet, but different. Different in a way that stopped men in their stride; but one steady look from those clear grey eyes kept them moving on. Lulla despaired. Did the girl even sense the admiring glances coming her way? Collectable like stamps they were, for the hard and lonely times. But then a girl'd have to be buck-toothed and hairy as a goat if she didn't score at least one wolf-whistle a day. Lulla smiled complacently; her own share of whistles was on target.

Brisbane had changed dramatically since that first day Lulla had tried to join the Navy. Service uniforms had been in abundance then, but over the months they had multiplied like the air-raid shelters cluttering the streets from the Quay to the Valley.

Civilians stepped aside to give service men and women right of way. They marched five, sometimes six abreast along the city footpaths, ready for any devilment their linked arms might ensnare.

Lulla loved it all. High adventure was only a tram-fare away. She revelled in the tensions and charged excitement of a war kept at bay by those who occupied, if only briefly, the once sedate and rustic streets of Brisbane. History was on stage, served by a diversity of nations that poured their personnel into the Southland before disgorging them to all points north and east of Brisbane. Australians, Americans, British and Dutch; men from Hong Kong, Poland, sailors from France. A horde of strangers who came from the North; black and white, cream and cinnamon, turban-swathed heads and Bombay bloomers. A parade of ribbons and badges, patches, pips and braid—a kaleidoscope of merit worn by the men and women who roamed the city streets.

Strange odours permeated the air: the smell of foreign tobacco, of aftershave lotion. Rich coffee harvested from P.X. stores percolated in suburban kitchens, and housewives tried their hand at chicken Maryland, chow mein and nasi goreng.

Lulla joked and flirted, her choice of partners as varied as they were plentiful. She dined out more than once a week, and danced the other nights away. The Trocadero, the Upadian, the Institute, she favoured the lot. Tonight, she decided she'd try her luck at the City Hall. A good mixture of uniforms there. She wondered if Peggy would like to go along.

Peggy walked stolidly beside her; if she heard the

'Hello Toots' from a lad in airforce garb, she gave no sign of it.

Lulla nudged her. 'He made a pass at you.'

'I heard him.'

'Nice-looking, too.'

'Wouldn't know about that.' Peggy looked straight ahead. 'Don't care about being called Toots.'

'Well, he doesn't know your name, does he? And he looks a nice enough kid. As lonely as all get-out, I'm betting.'

Peggy quickened her stride. 'Well, you have him.'

'Bit young for me, kid.' But feeling sorry for him, Lulla tossed a wink over her shoulder as he dropped behind.

By now they had reached the corner and Peggy checked her watch. She said it was too early to go home, and what she'd like was afternoon tea.

'I mean proper afternoon tea,' she said eagerly, her face lighting up at the idea. 'You know, in a proper cafe.'

'Well, there's the Shingle Inn, or Rowe's.'

'Rowe's!' Peggy's enthusiasm was catching. 'Well, what are we waiting for? Come on.'

She hurried off as if expecting Rowe's Cafe to slam the door in her face for being late.

In Peggy's eyes, Brisbane's smartest cafe was worth every penny it cost. It was a bit of a giggle the way Lulla's finger curled up like a question mark with every sip of tea. Posh or not, she wouldn't come into that! But Lulla was all right; and she'd made a nice job of her. Peggy's eyes watered with the mess of soot and vaseline Lulla had insisted she use on her lashes, and the wartime lipstick tasted like suet. But when the final result had been examined in the mirror, Peggy had been astonished.

'There,' Lulla had announced, pleased as punch, 'what d'yer think?'

Now Peggy's scalp was itching like mad from the sugared water that stiffened her hair like a picket fence. But Lulla had insisted on that too. 'We're fresh out of hair lacquer and it's the only way to make it stay put,' she'd said, combing it through Peggy's hair, 'and stay put it will, when you're wearing one of my hats.'

Peggy was grateful for the hat, for hardly a woman there was without one and most of them wore gloves. Many, in the company of be-ribboned officers, wore their shoulder posies like a badge to the same exclusive club: they nibbled on iced cakes and ate ribbon sandwiches with a knife and fork. And how did they make those patty cakes last? Two decent bites of hers and nothing left but crumbs on the plate. They were nearly as good as the ones Mum used to make for the tuckshop. The tuckshop ... and dear old Cairns. She'd never get back now, even if she wanted to. Had to have a good reason and a Government pass. Who said it was a free country? But she liked Brisbane now, and Lulla and Janet were good friends. Even Evie had seemed more of a pal lately. The whopping Mum gave her must have done some good ...

But the memory of Evie's belting was on Peggy's

forget list. Like Dad—where was he now? And Robbie. Would he ever make it back? Singapore was a real shemozz. Him with his 'Goodbye Toots' and that one kiss. Even then he missed, and got tangled up in her hair. Yair, forget about Robbie.

Did Lulla have a forget list? Sometimes Peggy envied Lulla. She always seemed so carefree, so full of fun. Always on the go; boyfriends and friendly boys, as she liked to call them, were in good supply. Aussies, Yanks, they were all the same to her, and Franklin Street never forgot the day she arrived home with a Chinese boy in tow. Not a word of English between the two of them, but somehow Lulla managed.

'Give 'em all a treat, and a square-cooked meal never harmed anyone,' she had said as airy as you like. When the landlord objected, Lulla's defence was solid enough to send him scurrying to the bastion of the upstairs flat.

'A merchant seaman, Mr Hickey—a mere lad.' (Peggy and Hilda admitted that Lulla could bung it on when she wanted to.) 'A *boy* you're fussing about. To offer hospitality is our patriotic duty, and you could do with a little of it yourself, sir!'

'That's Lulla,' was all the annexe said when they heard about it next day.

Mr Hickey never complained again about the strays Lulla and Janet brought in for a free feed, and Peggy and Hilda had applauded the landlord's rout with much satisfaction. *Yair, Lulla's all right ...*

The plinking and tinkling of silver teaspoons on

genteel china matched Lulla's polite invitation to finish up the last cupcake. Peggy shook her head, and copying her companion, dabbed her lips with a serviette.

'No, thanks. Full as a tick. Will we go now?'

'Why the hurry?' Lulla took a compact from her handbag and checked on the damage wrought by pikelets, jam and whipped cream. 'A few running repairs—and by the way'— she eyed Peggy over the top of the compact—'I'm going to the City Hall tonight. Like to come?'

Already Peggy was shaking her head. 'Can't—early shift tomorrow.'

'Early shift! Just turned eighteen and she talks like an old woman. You never go out at nights, Peg.' A finger waggled under the girl's nose. 'And don't call that fleapit you go to with Hilda a night out. That's punishment.'

'Good enough for Mum and me.'

Feeling piqued, Lulla drew on her gloves. It wasn't the first time Peggy had knocked back an invitation to go dancing. An afternoon matinee with Lulla Riddel was one thing—but when the sun went down …

Peggy's features were settling into sulky mode. She could have been Evie in one of her moods; lips set into a tight line, scowling. 'If you really want to know,' she challenged Lulla, 'I can't dance.' She sniffed, haughtily for her. 'And that's the truth of it.'

Lulla waved aside her relief. 'Is that all? A few nights at Sandy Robertson's—'

'I'm not going to no dance studio unless I can dance.'

Ignoring such quaint logic, Lulla beamed. 'Well, I'll teach you.'

Hope bloomed, brightening the girl's face. 'Could y'teach me the pride of Erin, and that?'

'Sure. And the gypsy tap, *and* the foxtrot—the lot!' She was delighted to have found a chink in Peggy's armour. 'Learn a few basic steps and you'll be on the floor in no time. The Institute, first …'

'What if I trip? Stand on someone's toes?' Peggy's eyes were wide in growing panic.

'Not to worry.' Lulla, full of confidence, laughed away the idea. 'Those army clod-hoppers—and most of 'em there are Army—you can tramp all over them and the poor loves wouldn't feel a thing. In fact, you're doing your bit by dragging them around the floor.' Lulla patted Peggy's hand. 'Just leave it to me, love. You'll be all right.'

'Do Yanks go there?'

'Purely Aussie territory. Anyway—'

'Good! Don't like—'

'So you've told me a dozen times.' A passing waitress placed a small silver dish beside Lulla's elbow. Lulla gave it a glance. 'Four-and-six each, and fix me up later.' She dropped a ten shilling note onto the dish. 'Ready to go? Let's get home, and we'll start those lessons straightaway.' She pushed back her chair.

Peggy hesitated, uncertain. 'We going to wait for the change?'

'In a joint like this, kiddo, a lady always leaves a tip.'

Outside Rowe's the air vibrated with charged excitement. They felt the impact like a blow as men in uniforms hurried by, some running, others shouting to comrades on the opposite side of the road. Airforce and Army pushed and shouldered a pathway through shoppers and workers homeward bound. While the two girls had been playing ladies, more than a peak-hour rush had set the streets abuzz.

It took only seconds for Lulla to wake up. 'It's a brawl!' she whooped. 'Quick! Up there!'

They joined the jostling, rowdy mob until they reached the corner shop. Their view was blocked by *aficionados* who hurled ribald advice from the safety of the pavement. The girls found a toehold on a crowded stairwell between a milliner's and a paper shop, and for the first time they had a clear view of the fracas.

'Take a look at that!' Lulla had good reason for sounding impressed.

Festering rivalry had erupted in Queen Street. For weeks, spasmodic scrapping between Airforce and Army had ignited in dance halls, flared up and down the narrow staircase of the Upadian, threatened a race meeting at the Park, while under the bleak eye of the military police, bar room spats had been sorted out in lavatories and hotel corridors.

From where they stood and as far as the eye could see, men punched and kicked, grappled and lunged, a heaving restless tide that bellowed and laughed, cursed and jeered. Most joined in for the fun of it, a few with murder in their hearts.

Trams were at a standstill. One had been overturned. Frustrated trammies, grumbling threats, stood helpless as the ebb and flow of battle eroded peak-hour schedules. 'Where's the M.P.'s?' they wanted to know.

Lulla squeezed Peggy's arm. 'Never thought I'd see the day. The R.A.A.F., in an all-out blue. Supposed to be the pick of the crop.' She hollowed her cheeks, raising one eyebrow. 'The creme-de-la-creme, you might say.' Then, doubling up: 'Curdled a bit now, I reckon.'

Peggy winced, her attention caught by a capering pair not many yards off. '*O-ooh*, look—that must've hurt. Fair and square on the kisser! There he goes again! *O-ooh!*'

'Nice bit of footwork, but.' The girls strained on tiptoe to take in more.

A carefree drunk had commandeered the upturned tram, an ancient wooden trolley open-sided to the weather. He urged someone, anyone, to take him on, and those who tried he kept at bay by stamping on their fingers and pelting them with prawn heads from a paper bag clutched to his chest. Swaying and giggling, he scattered the last of his shot among the mob and then there was nothing left to do but lose his footing and tumble through an open window out of sight.

Peggy shrieked, while Lulla wiped away the tears.

'Nothing like it since the Ringers had a ball. What a stoush!'

'They're mad. That's what. Can't bear to watch.' But Peggy gave a running commentary between widespread fingers. 'Look,' she yelped, 'three against one. The bullies!'

'He'll match 'em. He's finished two off, already. What a king-hit! Right up from the boots. One to go. Ha ha! That's my boy.'

'And you're just as bad as the lot of them.'

'Nuts ... they're enjoying every minute of it.'

A civilian close by was elbowed by another. He threw a punch, and was flattened for his trouble. They were no more than an arm's length from the girls. Lulla looked around with a barmaid's practised eye. 'The natives are getting restless. Time you and I went.'

What happened next took them by surprise. A new contingent had arrived unseen. Whistles sliced their warning through the uproar. Batons prodded and whacked unprotected heads. Word quickly spread through the confusion.

'It's the bulls! The M.P.'s!'

'Fuckin' Yanks—not ours!'

Now the fighting, previously a half-laconic and sometimes humorous contest, changed direction. Army and Airforce closed ranks and the few Americans who had cheered and jeered from the sidelines escaped while they could. Their own law enforcers had a mean reputation.

There came a sound of smashing glass. Wildly

swinging fists and batons were coming dangerously close.

'Oh, Gawd. Peg, hang on to me. Try and get further up the stairs.' But the press of bodies from behind gradually edged them from their vantage point into the hurly-burly of the footpath. For a few moments they were separated. Lulla squawked. Heavy boots crunched down on peep-toe shoes.

'Get off me foot! You great lug!' She gave the offender a hefty push. Peggy reappeared, bare-headed and desperate.

'... hat! It's gone! I can't find it.'

'Never mind the hat. Let's scoot!'

Vigorously they shoved and elbowed their way through the melee, dodging blows and reeling bodies; then breaking free and running down a narrow lane. There, where an off-shoot of the Queen Street riot was reduced to a few half-hearted scuffles, they paused to catch their breath.

'I should go back and get it,' said Peggy.

'Get what?'

'Your hat.' Peering back along the lane. 'It's not so bad now. With the M.P.'s—'

'Those mongrels. You stay right here with me.'

'But it's your second-best.' Peggy looked stricken.

'So I'll get a new one.'

Elizabeth Street was quieter, and the fight was losing impetus. They could tell from the occasional police whistle that punctuated the yells and shouts of a battle running out of steam. Brawlers and stragglers, escaping long batons, took off into side streets with dishevelled clothes, bleeding wounds and swollen bruises already growing dark.

Clanging bells and the clatter of wheels announced that trams were on the move again. Even so, they decided it would be quicker to make their own way across the river and home. Still the refugees from Queen Street passed them by, some melting into crowded bars. They had to dodge a new-sprung challenge as Army and Airforce fronted the Navy outside Nick's Cafe.

Peggy hopped out of their way. 'They're mad, I'm telling you.'

'They're men!' Lulla quipped, laughing all over again.

10

THEY WERE NOT alone crossing the bridge. Workers streamed by, a few running for dear life to catch suburban trains full-steam to go, ignorant of the up-ended confusion on the other side of the river. Peggy hurried along, avid to test Lulla's new role as dance instructor and her own ability to follow. Halfway over, someone tapped her on the shoulder. She gave a small jump and turned.

'Excuse me, ma'am ... I reckon this belongs to you.'

A tall young man, an officer of the American Navy, held out Lulla's battered leghorn. Peggy wished her hair was not a swirl of sugar rolls. Instinct told her that he would prefer it straight and shining-loose.

'It's not mine,' she said, filled with confusion.

'Oh, I could've bet ...' The American hesitated, puzzled.

'Well, yes,' she muffed, 'you're right. I was wearing it. But it's—it's hers.' She waited for Lulla to speak up. But Lulla had strolled further on, and was now leaning against the railings as if utterly fascinated by the river traffic nudging at the current. *Why wasn't she here, helping out?*

The American studied her, trying not to smile. 'Well now. Do I give it back to your friend? Or you?'

She all but snatched it from him. 'Ta.'

It looked a sorry thing. Mortified, Peggy hid it behind her back. She concentrated on the American's slim, tanned hand, and a signet ring that matched the gold banding on his sleeve.

'Allow me to introduce myself.' *Talks posh for a Yankee.* 'Julian Ludwig. Ensign Julian Ludwig, USS *Tulsa*.' Pride tinged his voice as he touched the braided cap sitting squarely on his head. It was close enough to a salute to be embarrassing. 'And your name, Miss?'

'Peggy Scott.' Her mind scrabbled for the right words to keep him there. 'Lulla!' she called out in desperation, 'Come here.'

Lulla sashayed over, giving the impression that she had arranged the whole meeting. Peggy flapped the leghorn at her.

'This is Julian.' Her head was full of fairy floss, as if all that sugar had seeped through and softened her brain. 'And—what's your second name again?'

'Ludwig, Peggy.' She'd never heard her name sound so attractive. Unusual, even. But Ludwig …? Her head suddenly cleared, and she looked him straight in the eye. 'Ludwig. You German, or something?'

'My folks are, Peggy.' *He sounds proud of it!* But her heart flipped again, and Lulla was holding out her hand, a smile her guarantee of approval.

'How-de-do. I'm Lulla Riddel. So kind of you to rescue our hat.'

There she goes again. Bunging it on. But Lulla's easy manner encouraged him to ask if he could walk them across the bridge; Lulla giving regal consent, of course. No point in protesting as Julian stationed himself between them and anchored Peggy's arm firmly through his own.

She heard him explain that his ship was in drydock, and that ship's repairs were nearing completion. In a day or two, the *Tulsa* would put to sea again. Her sense of incipient loss was no more surprising than the pleasure she felt with his arm cradling hers. For once she envied Lulla's light and careless chatter, admitting sadly to herself that Julian and Lulla made a lovely couple.

All too soon, they had reached the southern bank. What now? Was that the end of it? But Julian was saying something wonderful—although most of what he said was engulfed by the rattling of an outbound tram. Bells clanging, it cornered Stanley Street with reckless flair as Julian raised his voice.

'Tonight!' he yelled, then flushed as a gap in traffic noise gave unwonted energy to the word.

Was he asking them out? Both of them?

But Lulla was shaking her head. 'Count me out,

Julian. Sorry.' She gave a wicked grin. 'You're free, aren't you, Peg?'

'I—I don't—'

'Well, that's settled then.'

Already Julian was busy explaining that first, someone had to be found to take over his watch. Lulla was writing down their telephone number. Another tram shot by.

'There's my trolley. Have to go!' He snatched the note from Lulla's hand and jumped the footpath, racing across the street.

Peggy remembered that she had a voice. 'I'm not—' But Julian was waving goodbye, clinging for dear life on the running board, looking very pleased with himself.

'Lulla Riddel!' Outraged. Hands clamped on her hips. 'What did you do that for?'

'Why not? He couldn't take his eyes off you.'

'Didn't seem like that to me.' Not to be placated, Peggy began walking fast.

Lulla caught up. 'How would you know?' Lulla scoffed, 'you never lifted yours above ground level. C'mon, Peg, give yourself a break.' She took her hat from Peggy's grip and shoved it determinedly into a nearby litter bin. 'You can wear the one with the roses next time.'

'There won't be a next time.'

They side-stepped a starburst of vomit outside the Trocadero's closed doors and ignored the drunk lying prone beside it.

'As I was saying,' Lulla wheedled, 'you'll be doing

yourself a favour. He's top-drawer, for sure, and the poor boy could be at the bottom of the sea in a week. Go on, do your bit, and have some fun.'

'You reckon?' There came a subtle shift in Peggy's voice. 'And if I do, will you come too?'

'I don't play gooseberry, Peg. You know that.'

'Well, I'm not going. And that's that.'

'Gawd Aggie ... all right.'

'If he phones, that is.' Peggy sounded almost wistful.

'Want a bet on it?' Lulla whistling *All the Nice Girls Love a Sailor*.

They met outside Lennon's Hotel, and Julian's eyes lit up when he saw her.

'Say, Peggy, you look just grand.'

And who wouldn't, in this get-up, Peggy told herself. Another time she would have confessed to her borrowed plumes, but the pressure of Lulla's elbow warned her to keep it quiet.

True to his word, Julian had brought not one, but three fellow officers as partners for Lulla. Ribboned and polished to sartorial perfection, they saluted the girls, obviously approving of Julian's taste in women. Lulla glowed in the warmth of their wit and banter as they tilted for the privilege of escorting her into the hotel. Her pleasure cooled a little when she happened to sight Spanner Larkin, flanked by two bright and pretty girls, crossing the street.

Carefully she watched his approach; although he gave no sign that he'd seen her, there was a touch of bravado in his swagger and the way he clutched the girls tightly to him. *Never does things by halves, does Spanner*, Lulla thought as the sailor drew close.

Bearing down on them, Spanner plotted a dangerous course and veering just in time to avoid collision, threw a wink. 'Atta girl, Princess ... in the big league, are we?'

She could have smacked both sides of his silly face. Who was he to talk? One night and one stupid slip were enough to cop his snide remarks for all time. Had Peggy noticed?

But Peggy and Julian were already through the doors. Lulla felt cool fingers on her elbow. It was the one with the good looks of the Irish.

'And Princess you are, me darlin'. It must be my lucky day!'

Lulla tossed him a dazzling smile as she accepted the offer of an outstretched arm. *And nuts to you, Spanner Larkin!*

Even the elegance of Rowe's Cafe could not compare with the sumptuous glamour of Lennon's Hotel lobby. Jardinieres of exotic blooms stood sentinel by the entrance, marbled pillars soared to support a ceiling glittering with chandeliers. Peggy remembered Lulla's tip and tried not to appear as outclassed as she was feeling. Her own *Evening in Paris* was swamped by Coty's *l'Origan* and *Emeraude*, while the damp breath of the cocktail lounge exuded a bouquet of beer, bourbon and Gordon's gin.

As Lulla caught up, Peggy whispered, 'Lulla, I'm scared. I'll do it all wrong.'

Lulla grinned to herself—Peggy would surely pass out if she had realised that General Macarthur himself ruled the roost upstairs. Few people in Brisbane were unaware that here was the Allied Command Headquarters for the Pacific War. 'Sh-h,' she whispered to Peggy, 'just do what I do.'

Bellboys marched at a clip with the authority of full-blown generals, seemingly unimpressed by the colonels, the admirals, the captains of ships and 'planes who had made the grand hotel their personal club.

Julian was leading the way into the lounge. It was alive with the buzz of tongues, the clink of glasses and laughter; and on the floor above them there were men who, with deadly intent, played a game of war.

They all squeezed into an alcove. Already Lulla looked as if she owned the place. Peggy glimpsed herself in one of the mirrored columns that repeated over and over the restless gaiety of the room. She liked what she saw. Beneath a bobbing pink rose of a hat, a radiant, happy face smiled back at her. Hers!

And sitting close, the most handsome and dear man she could ever wish to meet. No one need tell her that this mingling as an equal with the battle's elite was only war's happenchance. It was pretend; the miracle of Julian, while it lasted, would forever be a cherished memory. As Peggy took an experimental sip of the Manhattan Julian had ordered, she gave herself a talking-to.

'Make the most of it, Peggy Scott. Tomorrow it's back to the salt mines, as Mum would say ... He'll go away, and there's a horribly huge chance you'll never see him again.' She settled back into red leather and helped herself to a dish of pretzels and devilled almonds. She grinned at the circle of attentive and admiring naval officers. Lulla was right. Have fun! Have a ball! She raised her glass.

'Bottoms up,' she said cheerfully, and wondered why they laughed.

11

'FOR A GIRL who thumps around like a five-legged bandicoot, you're not doing real bad.'

'Thanks for the compliment, friend.' Peggy held out her arms to Lulla. 'Come on, we've wasted five minutes already.'

'Pardon me if I finish a sandwich. Anyway, you don't need me to try that gypsy tap again. A-one, two, three. Go to it! And don't look down at your feet! How many times—' But Peggy was away. Lulla swallowed bread, tried to whistle *Margie*, and failed.

Peggy skidded over concrete, between stacked crates of hand grenades. They towered overhead as solid as city blocks, blotting out sunshine from the banked skylights. Not long after Julian had finally said goodbye, Peggy stopped moping and had challenged Lulla to begin the dance lessons as promised.

'And none of that jitterbug stuff, either. Not built for it.'

At first they had tried out in the Scotts' flat. Easier to swing a cat in the confined space than swing into a waltz. The hallway next, but that was aborted after the first round. Mrs Hickey, squawking threats, said they could pay for new lino if so much as a scuff appeared.

'So what do we do now?' Peggy had asked.

Lulla had suggested once again that they try Sandy Robertson's Dance Studio.

But Peggy dug her toes in. 'Like I said before, I'm not going—'

'All right. So let's drop the whole idea.' But Peggy's eyes had betrayed her disappointment and Lulla, with a 'Gawd Aggie,' caved in: the onus was on Peggy to find them a place to suit their needs.

It was Hilda's suggestion that they use the holding room. 'It's quiet enough in the lunch break, and who's to stop you?'

Peggy proved a quick learner with a natural rhythm which made teaching a pleasure. She also had a sweet, clear whistle that accompanied Lulla's humming. Now she acknowledged Lulla's approval with a hint of complacency and a few fancy steps of her own.

'Not bad, eh?' She slid to a stop and waited for praise.

'Good enough to make your debut at the Institute. How about tonight?'

'Maybe ...' Suddenly Peggy cocked her head to one side, listening. 'Did you hear anything?'

'Like what?'

'Like—I dunno. I heard it once before.' Peggy shook her head, vaguely puzzled. 'It's stopped now. Sounded something like a mouth organ.'

'That was me singing, dill-pot.' Lulla pointed to the girl's unopened packet of sandwiches. 'You eating? All that dancing and no potatoes makes for a skinny girl.'

Peggy peered inside the bag, sniffed, and pulled a face. 'Soggy spaghetti. Anyway, I'm not hungry.'

She never felt hungry lately. Not since Julian had left with a promise to write. There had been a week of blissful outings: of pictures; and picnics, long walks by the river. But now, the lump of desolation that resided in her chest left little room for food. She prayed for letters, and the postman's whistle would start a fever of longing that could hardly be endured. Letters arrived. But none for her.

Oh, Julian, please write … please.

Peggy leaned back against the crates, resting. It was peaceful in the deserted annexe. Cool. Nearly cold. The hum of idling machinery in the factory could have been the humming of bees. Lulla opened a fresh packet of Chesterfields, expertly flicked up a single cigarette and offered it. 'Want one?'

'You know I don't smoke.'

'You should try. It helps sometimes.'

'And what does that mean?'

'Nothing really.' Lulla put the cigarette to her own lips and lit up, concentrating on the first deep draw. 'It's a companionable sort of thing,' she said, 'you and your fella smoking at peace. Not saying much. It sort of goes with the silences.' There came a fleeting memory of Spanner Larkin's jawline and crooked nose as a match flared in the night, which Lulla put promptly aside. 'By the way ... when do you see Julian again? Any idea?'

Peggy took her time to remove a spot of lacquer off a fingernail. 'How should I know. He hasn't written, has he.'

'He will. He's mad about you.'

'Y'reckon?'

A bleakness sat strangely on Peggy's face as Lulla asked: 'How long now since he's gone?'

'Weeks.' Peggy targeted a streak of shellac on her arm, picking at it. 'Maybe he was married, and felt lonely,' she said, chewing her lips in thought. 'Yair ... he could be married. The nice ones usually are. But even the nice ones will lie and kid you along to get what they want. Eh?'

She looked so despairing, so abandoned, that Lulla wondered if Julian had done it with her. *Made her*, as the saying went. Lulla longed to ask; to be of help, but realised the futility of questions. For what decent girl would admit to it? Not Peg, for one. It was a secret not to be shared, even with your best mate. Lulla concluded sadly that Peggy would have to work out her own heartaches and fears by herself. That was the way of things. *And we all pretend that life's a bowl of cherries*. She dropped the spent cigarette butt and ground it into the cement, pressing a smile onto her face.

'Hey!' she punched Peggy lightly on the arm. 'We've got ten minutes left. What do you want to do? Sit outside for a bit?'

Peggy came up smiling. 'Who wants to sit?' she said briskly. 'Didn't you mention the Institute? Come on, I'll be the man this time. Let's dance!' She began whistling in three-four time.

They romped down the corridors of boxes, colliding and bumping, laughing and apologising to the silent, grim-storeyed crates. They swayed along walkways as narrow as goat tracks, until Peggy pulled up short.

'There it goes again. Hear it?'

'You're right. It *is* a mouth organ.'

Peggy whistled a few bars of *Daisy Daisy*. 'Now listen,' she said softly. They heard the simple melody repeated, then made splendid with trills and slides and the curlicues of a virtuoso. It ended in a flourish of arpeggios. Then silence.

'Who is it?' Peggy called.

A short, stocky figure appeared from behind one of the far stacks. The busy trot was unmistakable. He tapped the spittle from the instrument, placed it back to his lips, and rippled off another arpeggio.

'Micky!' Lulla let out a whoop of surprise. 'You cunning fox,' she declared as the little man marched towards them, still playing.

Peggy thumped Micky on the shoulder.

'You never told us you're a bloomin' genius.'

'Nobody arth me.'

Just to prove that it was not a fluke, Micky

plunged into *Colonel Bogey*. Marching on the spot, stubby fingers waving like banners, his bright monkey eyes gleamed in answer to the girls' obvious delight. And as the factory whistle gave a blast, Micky led the way through the maze of grenades, high-stepping into the annexe as the rest of the team returned to the benches.

It took only moments to feel the undercurrents and tensions which kept the women tight-lipped and silent. Work usually began with a litany—not to be taken seriously—of complaints laced with ironic humour. It helped ease the team into the tedium of the assembly line. Micky, always sensitive to mood, grabbed up his pot, tripped over his feet and sprayed the floor with shellac. He earned a glare from Andy.

'Canna' ye do something right for once,' she snapped, '—and who are you gawping at, Lulla Riddel?'

'Hey! Hold on a minute, Andy.'

'Och, I didna' mean it.' The forewoman handed a rag to the pot boy. 'It's all right, lad. Just wipe it up before we're all glued to the floor.' She motioned to the others to begin. 'Come on, girls. Get busy. We might be fashed by the latest piece of news but there's a quota to meet.' Even as she spoke Andy had worked halfway through the crate in front of her. Brown-glazed and shining wet, the Mills bombs stood by in military formation; without gunpowder or priming as lethal as chocolate eggs.

Lulla fronted Andy, hands on hips. 'What's up? What's happened? I'll not lift a brush until I find out.'

'Ye haven't heard the latest, then.'

'No. Peg and I—'

'Anyway, it's most likely just a rumour.'

'An-dee, c'mon, spit it out!'

Rumours were as much a part of MacIntyre's as the steel filings that peppered the floor and the water slopping underfoot. But occasionally, one was stamped with the hallmark of authenticity and refused to be ignored. And it took a lot to upset Andy.

'Well, there's talk of the factory slowing down.' The forewoman peered through a grenade and blew out a shower of metal dust. 'Perhaps closing down altogether.'

'It's a joke! In wartime?' Dawning hope eclipsed Lulla's disbelief. 'It can't be true!' She spun around on her heel, joy splitting her face in a grin. 'Well, here's one who'll not be sorry. Glory be! I've heard the Yanks are looking for locals. All sorts of jobs. And the pay'd make your eyes bug.'

'Not so fast, lass.' Andy put down her brush and took a cloth from her pocket to wipe her hands. She motioned to Micky to refill her pot. Watching her sombre expression, the grin slowly disappeared from Lulla's face.

'What else?'

'Manpower won't let you go that easy. It seems those Yankees you're so fond of have put a proposition to our lot—the politicians—and they're listening.'

'Ah, yes. The God-damned Yanks,' Lulla half-teased, 'and what are they up to now?'

'They'd like to turn us into cooks and seamstresses, that's what. *They* supply the guns and ammunitions (och, we're not clever enough for that), and *we* produce the bully beef and navy biscuits—not forgettin' the army coats and boots 'n such. Lend Lease, they're calling it. I'd like to lend-lease them just where it hurts!' Andy's brush viciously attacked the innards of another bomb. 'And tha's the nub of it, lass.'

For the first time Hilda Scott spoke up. 'If it's true—and I pray it's not—we all know what that means.'

It meant a return to women's wages. The team most likely split up between clothing factory and cannery. Yeah ... they all knew what that meant.

Isabel, a new addition to the annexe, sniffed. The annexe knew that at any second, Isabel would start crying. She often did. Manpower had impounded her from one of Queen Street's better stores. She had tried hard to settle in, and was only just succeeding. At first, she had been consigned to a lathe in the machine shop, but the constant damp and oil, and the heavy boots she had been advised to wear, caused blisters which festered into an eruption of boils. She had been sent to the annexe. The annexe, although sympathetic, lay bets on how long she would last. Her tears began to fall. 'It's all quite terrible. Just as I was getting used to things ... a clothing factory! Oh, no! I couldn't bear it.'

Numbly, almost absentmindedly, Lulla took her place beside Andy. To Lulla, the idea of a clothing factory made the annexe and MacIntyre's a place of sweet refuge. Everyone knew what conditions were like in most of them. Sweatshops; and all flat-out. Fingers stitched together more than once before you reached top-peak efficiency. Stitching tents, even worse: and a bonus in nosebleeds if you happened to be the bunny waterproofing. For her own sake, Lulla tried to laugh spectres out of sight.

'Arrh! Rumours. The place is infected with 'em like fleas in a boarding house sofa. Furphies; take my word for it. We're stuck here for the duration—worse luck!'

But no amount of joshing could lighten the team's spirits and the afternoon dragged on without relief. Minutes before the crossover to night shift began, Peggy did her usual count of the day's results.

'Three crates down, Andy. Old Daniels will skin us alive.' Shamefaced, as if the fault was all her own, she handed over the tally sheets.

'It's been a muckle of an afternoon. I'm not surprised.' Andy studied the sheets, her lips pursed. 'Anyway, I'll tackle Mrs Daniels when I take these over. Closing down, indeed! We should be told the truth of the matter, and I'll—' The knock-off whistle interrupted, bringing the day shift to its end, and the women wasted little time in quitting the annexe.

Lulla spotted Daryl Missim on the way to the change room. For the first time in weeks she waved, and beckoned him over. Daryl was bound to know what was going on. He had his ear to the ground, and she had heard mention that Missims had won a contract with the Americans. Gossip had it that father and son would be millionaires before the war was over. It could be the reason for Daryl's renewed and frantic attempts to be released from munitions, a standing joke in the main shop.

'Hey, Daryl! Come here.'

Daryl staggered in pretended shock, and by the time he had reached her, she was laughing.

'You're a fool, Missim.'

'To be favoured again by the glorious Lulla, I give thanks.' He touched his forehead and chest in obeisance, 'As does my father and grandfather before him.'

'Shut up, you silly goat. This is important. I want to ask you something.'

'Ask away.'

'Have you heard that Mac's is closing down, and some of us might be shoved into anywhere?' Her oblique glance was more speculative than sly. 'Clothing, for instance?'

'Come on, Lulla, how would I know?'

'Because you don't miss a trick, Missim.'

''Fraid the answer's no.'

'Fair dinkum?'

He placed his hand over his heart in the way she remembered; half-mocking, self-deprecating. 'Would I lie?'

'We won't go into that.'

In spite of his denials, there was something else that Daryl was holding back. Some news that would make headlines between them; a secret that scratched to be let out. Intuition was vindicated when he brushed her ear with a whisper.

'But there *is* some small thing to tell.'

Her curiosity allowed him to shepherd her away from the bustle of the change room stairs. They were watched, but she didn't mind as he guided her behind a disused and sagging shed.

'This better be good, Daryl.'

He then told her of a certain Manpower official whose daughter was soon to be married: an affair that warranted top billing in the Sunday papers. Word had filtered down that the father would be happy to exchange favours for a length of embossed satin and a bolt of taffeta.

'Piece of cake,' Daryl told Lulla, tapping his nose, 'I just happen to know where to put my hands on the goods and we do the deed tonight.'

'Yeah? Go careful on that one. Wouldn't trust any of the sods.'

'He's all right. We've done business before. Frank Ingram. Heard of him?'

'No, and I don't want to.' She wondered how he could be so confident. 'Just be careful, that's all.' The idea of Daryl tangling with Manpower made her uneasy.

'Not to worry, Princess.' He stood not two inches away from her. 'And nice of you to care.'

She could smell the cologne he used; an affectation picked up from the Americans, and one that she approved of. It made a heady brew mingling with the sweat of a hot afternoon's toil. He ran a finger down the full length of her arm, gently stroking the inside of her wrist.

'It's been a long time, Lulla ... you and me.'

'Uh-huh.' Body glowing warm and swelling with unusual tenderness for him.

Daryl, for all his bravado, could be as gullible as a two-year-old; but it was the grown man who caused the unfurling, the quiet seduction of her most intimate and hidden parts. Encouraged by her quiescence, he rested his arms loosely on her hips. 'I've missed you. You're the only girl I can really mesh with, you know. Understand what I mean?' He tightened his grip.

'Uh-huh.' Already, the other side of her was planning what to wear when he got around to making a date. The Greek Club again? She tried to ignore the pulsing that was taking over her loins. Baklava. Sweet and sticky ...

'Lulla?'

'H'mm?'

'How about tonight?' His fingers massaged her spine.

'What do you think?' She'd start purring any second ...

'By the way,' he said matter-of-factly, 'how's old Chuck? Seen him lately?'

She broke away from him, furious with herself that she had so readily responded to that persuasive touch. Even considered taking up the threads once more.

'Always on the make! Don't you ever give up, Daryl? Using people? It's sickening!'

He stepped back, looking stunned. 'What's wrong? What have I done now?'

Lulla backed off, despising him; hating herself. 'I'll tell you what's wrong. Ever since I dumped you, you've—'

'Fair go, Lulla.' He stood there, eyebrows questioning, upraised hands cupped to catch the words she hurled at him.

'Doesn't matter a toss who ended it, anyway. But there's one thing I'm sure of: from the day you lost contact with me, and with old Chuck, as you call him, you've missed out. No Chesterfields,' she began ticking off with her fingers, 'no Lucky Strikes. And no Scotch—that must have hurt.' She knew she was being unfair, for every transaction had been a profitable three-way arrangement. 'And remember that night at the Greek Club? While I sat there like a dummy, you busied yourself with that—that Arab trader hatching another miserable coup. "It pays to know the right people",' she mimicked cruelly, tapping her nose. 'But I woke up to myself. And now this. Five minutes of sweet talk and you must bring Chuck, the P.X. man, into it. Well, for your information I dropped him the night I dropped you. Finish! Kaput! Understand?'

He waited until she had run out of breath, anger staining his cheeks.

'Is that all?'

Without warning he grabbed her arm, pulling her

roughly back to him. 'So you were upset that night, were you? How long did you have to wait? Five minutes? Ten? You wouldn't know the half of it.'

She gave a grunt, twisting from his grasp. Rubbing where it hurt. 'I hope to God you get that damned clearance, Daryl Missim. With you around, it reminds me of what I'm capable of.'

He watched her going with the realisation that he had botched it—maybe for all time. Lulla was some girl. Desirable, salty, and much too honest for her own good. A shame. They'd made a great team for a while there. Never mind.

Then Lulla did a strange thing. Before she disappeared around the corner of the shed, she stopped and turned, shading her eyes against the afternoon light. Looking back at him. To see if he was still standing there? He raised his hand to give a laconic salute.

She shrugged, almost with regret, before turning the corner out of sight.

12

DARYL MISSIM GAVE the Hillman's bonnet an affectionate pat, congratulating himself on his good luck. Nice little job, the Hillman, a bargain at half the price. Widows were a walkover when it came to selling—getting rid of the old man's stuff; and like most women, this one hadn't known a front-end from a whore's backside.

He chuckled. Low mileage and light on fuel. Not that petrol was a problem; not when you knew ... Daryl pulled up short, hearing Lulla's voice. Mocking him. Contemptuous. Backing away from him as if he had the clap.

I hope to God you get your damned clearance, Daryl Missim. Christ, she could hurt a man. Well, piss on her. And piss on that new-found conscience of hers.

He slammed the door of the Hillman, locked up

and pocketed the key. A bloke was liable to turn soft if he listened to Lulla. Miss out on opportunities that in wartime hung like rosy plums, ripe for the plucking. Thinking of opportunities, he peered through the rear window of the car and his mood lifted at the sight of two brown-paper parcels wedged behind the driver's seat.

There lay his ticket to freedom!

He turned to inspect the grounds behind ornate double gates, half-expecting Ingram to be waiting there. But that was not the arrangement—and he was early. At the end of the driveway, half-hidden by a smother of foliage, stood a large weatherboard house. Manpower had moved to the edge of the city. As more clerks and scribes were enfolded into its bureaucratic arms, the town office could no longer contain its own workforce.

Manpower had commandeered one of Brisbane's oldest homesteads: but even this was not enough to house the documents, the files, the paraphernalia of officialdom. Under the weeping figs, nestled close to venerable azaleas, fibro huts had sprouted like toadstools.

In the quickening dusk, lights from open doors and windows challenged the gloom and a sprinkling of men and women still sat at their desks. Daryl felt his pulse quicken: something was wrong. According to Ingram, all the office staff should have left twenty minutes ago. Ingram had assured him there'd be no trouble delivering the stuff to his office in the main house. But then, Daryl reminded himself, he *was* early. Too anxious. And that could be a mistake.

Yet a sixth sense, fine-tuned by ancestral traders who had filtered down from the Old Silk Road via the covered stalls of Istanbul, could not be ignored. He hurried back to the car, removed the packages, and slipped into the shadows just inside the gates.

Banked oleanders surfed over a high wooden fence that concealed a rubble of neglected garden beds. He followed the line of shrubs until well clear of the driveway. Lights in several huts were winking out; by the sound of it, things were at last winding down for the day. For long minutes he waited concealed by sombre greenery, making sure the grounds were finally deserted before shoving his parcels deep into the oleander bushes. If there was to be a hitch with Ingram, he'd collect them on the way out and no harm done.

Although he felt more confident now, he kept to the grass at the side of the driveway, avoiding the crunch of gravel. Elation swamped him; a Manpower release at long last! The family of Missim, with him in charge, was ready to go full bore ahead!

Ingram, his bald pate glazed in lamplight, was in full view. He sat at a desk in his office, with double French windows open to the veranda. Daryl shook his head. The man had no idea; too much space around him, too much exposure for a night of honest horse-trading. He felt justified in having left the cloth in hiding. Still, why should Ingram show caution? What was there to worry about? Ingram was only giving a bloke a licence to quit his job. That's what

Manpower was all about, wasn't it?

At the sound of footsteps on the veranda, Ingram looked up from the small task of filling a fountain pen. 'Ah! Come in, Mr Missim, come in.' Daryl was waved into a chair.

Ingram's appearance always came as a slight shock. He looked hardly the sort to sanction under-counter deals, and his mild manner belied the absolute power he had over the lives of people like Daryl Missim and Lulla Riddel. To Daryl, he could have been your friendly family chemist ready to dispense a cure-all for every woe.

Ingram wiped the gold nib of his pen while mulling over the sheaf of papers stacked before him. Daryl recognised them as the many applications he had bombarded Manpower with; the evidence of his unflagging persistence.

On one of the sheets Ingram crossed out a comma, and wrote in the margin.

'So,' he said at length, smiling, 'you wish to rejoin the family business.' He referred again to the letter before him. 'Army greatcoats, eh?'

'And tents.' Daryl could not resist adding the probable. 'That's if we can keep up production.' Concern etched his forehead. 'But the old fellow—my father—can't do it alone. The workload. The problems. Unskilled labour, absenteeism ...' Daryl shifted his chair closer to the desk. Leaning forward, he faced Ingram full-on. 'It all takes its toll.'

The Manpower officer nodded gravely. 'I understand.'

Daryl touched his chest, eyes hazed with blatant grief. 'It's his heart, I'm afraid.'

'I sympathise,' Ingram murmured, right on cue.

He returned to scrutinise the papers once more, leafing through each page. Taking notes. The younger man watched every move. Interpreting a raised eyebrow, a nod of the shining head. He began to wonder. Why no mention of the bridal satin—the other half of the deal? Why was he acting so coy? Did he want more? Something for the wife, perhaps? Well, that could be arranged. No problem. He jumped as Ingram abruptly pushed back his chair, standing up.

'I see no reason why we should not approve of this.' He picked up Daryl's recent letter. 'No reason at all.'

It was an effort not to show relief; not to leap up and pump Ingram's hand. Even as the thought flashed through his mind, the man had crossed the room, opening a door. It should have led to a hallway, but instead revealed a glimpse of a large office with vacant desks and silent telephones.

'We'll get someone to type out the necessary papers. Won't keep you.' Ingram paused; 'I assume you have the material with you. The *goods*,' he said almost playfully.

'For sure. But there were people about, and you said—'

'An unexpected assignment the town office couldn't handle.' Ingram frowned over the laxity of city clerks, then, with a nod hinting of conspiracy, closed the door behind him with a discrete click.

The vacuum left by Ingram's sudden departure dismayed Daryl. Why the delay? He became aware of the steadily rising beat of his pulse, and sought to discipline his nerves. All this cloak-and-dagger stuff for a miserable scrap of paper! But he had to do it. The factory—the family depended on him. Depended on him for his flair in getting things done; for his contacts and know-how. Here was Missims, teetering on the brink of undreamed-of expansion, while he hosed grenades in a back alley with a bunch of women.

But wasn't that what you wanted, Missim? he accused himself. Come on, admit it. Admit for once in your life that the idea of war—a real Jehad—had you scared shitless. You jumped into munitions before you could say 'shoot'. So don't run away now. Crawl through crap if you have to. But get that clearance!

Nervous, for something better to do he left his chair to prowl the room. There was little to see except for a filing cabinet and a portrait of Queen Victoria hanging above a bricked-in fireplace. She smirked at his discomfort, as if there was some secret shared with the absent Ingram. Out of the corner of one eye he saw a woman flit by the French windows. By the time he turned, she was gone. Who else might be around? There could be an army of pen-pushers busy behind closed doors and portable cubbyholes.

He looked at his watch. How long does it take to write so many lines? Thirty minutes had gone by since he'd first walked down the drive. Thirty minutes! He should have been clear of the place in less than ten. High heels tapped across bare boards, and stopped outside the inner door. He half-expected to see it open—a friendly face would be welcome—but the door remained closed and the footsteps moved on.

What the hell was Ingram up to? Something was on the nose, and it wasn't mullet gut! Forget about the deal. Get out of here ... fast!

As he skirted around Ingram's desk, two men strolled across the veranda, their combined bulk blocking his escape. There was no mistaking the walk; the hats; suits matching as if they shared the same tailor. Eyes reflecting the same impersonal contempt that blitzed his spine with slivers of ice.

The demons! The police!

'Leaving, Missim?' one asked. *They knew his name!*

Daryl marvelled that the hammering in his chest could pass unnoticed. He could smell his own glue-sweat, his armpits and groin tacky with fright. He fought back the urge to wipe his face. The detective spoke again.

'Just a few questions that need to be answered.'

'Fire away.'

'Cocky young shit, aren't you?'

'Takes one to know one.' *Christ, what was he saying?*

Without warning, and moving swiftly for all his size, the detective closed in, his face inches away, breath brassy with suppressed rage. Daryl tensed. Which soft part of him would take the blow? Those fists meant business! But the policeman drew back. Daryl noticed a small jagged scar stitching a thin line beneath his eye.

'Careful, Missim,' he warned.

Relief coursed through to every nerve end. Daryl Missim might be a shit to them, but the family name still held good in the right places. But how good? Checks and balances made a mish-mash of clear thinking. Stay calm, he advised himself. Act cool, and you might get out of this.

The detective's voice, softer now: 'Just tell us. What are you doing here, Missim?'

'I had an appointment.' He tried to sound surprised at such a query.

'Oh, yes ... who with?'

'Frank Ingram.'

'Why?' The questions hit with the speed of bullets.

'A clearance.' He forced his hands to stay close by his sides. 'That's all I'm here for.'

The detective's eyes narrowed, disbelieving. 'That's all, eh?'

'That's all.'

'It's not what Ingram says.' So they knew Ingram. Had already spoken to him. Weeping Jesus ... what had the man said? The bastard! Of course they had to know him.

'I asked you, Missim. Is that all?'

Daryl kept his lips closed, the question left suspended between them. The second man—he could have been a younger brother, so alike in build and style—had perched himself on the corner of the desk. He riffled through Daryl's papers, one leg swinging, snapping a rubber band against his thumb. The sound held the menace of a cracking whip. He spoke for the first time.

'Ingram says you've got something for him. Right?'

'What could I have?'

'That's for you to tell us.' He flicked a glance towards his partner. 'Right, Harris?'

Harris! Doyle and Harris! The names exploded in his gut. The other *had* to be Doyle. They were a pair. Detested and feared by the petty miscreants who hovered on the fringes of serious crime, and pity the poor sod who tangled with them. Oh, yes. He'd heard of Harris and Doyle. Damn—if he only knew what Ingram had told them! Could they be bluffing? *Just hold on. It's Ingram's word against yours.* Daryl looked the policeman straight in the eye.

'What would I have for him?' he repeated, shrugging. 'I'm here for a Manpower release. Nothing else.'

In the silence that followed, the rubber band snapped and Doyle eased away from the desk. 'So. No special arrangements. No fair exchanges. Come on, Missim. What's between you and Ingram?'

'Nothing. I—'

'You knew him before this. Right?' Doyle's voice gained momentum, his face swelling with compressed tension. 'Come on, we've had a bead on you for some time. Now! What's between you and Ingram?'

'Nothing, I tell you. Nothing.'

'You're lying.'

The questioning continued, with Harris joining in. It was like a well-rehearsed play; one taking up when the other let go. They circled like hungry dogs, ready to pounce at the first slip.

But the family name of Missim held them at bay.

'We'll say it once more. There was a deal. Your release in exchange for goods. Rationed goods. That carries a heavy sentence. It can be lightened—or it can go on for a long, long time.'

'And I'm saying there was no deal.' The knots in his stomach were a physical ache. How much could a body sweat? Thank God he didn't have the stuff with him!

'What about your old man?' Doyle asked. 'What does he know about it, eh?'

'Leave him out of it. He doesn't know—'

'So it's stolen goods as well, is it.' Doyle's lips thinned into a tight smile. 'It takes a slimy shit to thieve from his own father.'

'I didn't steal—'

'He knows about it, then.'

'He knows nothing. I know nothing. There's no deal. There never was!' He was losing control; his voice too shrill.

'You're a snot liar, Missim. A little dago twerp from way back,' Doyle mouthed softly. Then his palm smacked down hard on the desk. Daryl flinched, conscious of sweat trickling and stinging.

With a nod from Harris, the detectives moved in. Each took an arm; they were close enough for Daryl to feel the threat of taut, hard muscles straining against their coat sleeves. Stale body stink from Doyle, and when he spoke his voice was even quieter than before.

'We'll just take a look inside the Hillman. New, isn't it?' His tone was friendly, casual. Daryl's tongue was too dry for speech.

Together, they trundled him down the stairs. The brightly lit office was now a haven against the pitch-black of the deserted grounds; here, only the shrubs thick between the silent huts would be witness to a pummelling that was bound to happen. Harris and Doyle had a reputation.

Daryl could not believe his luck as the two men kept up a brisk pace along the drive. The oleanders were passed by without so much as a glance. Those packages were as snug as bugs in a rug. He was congratulating himself as they marched through the double gates.

The sight of a uniformed policeman standing beside the Hillman was like the jab of a cattle prod. Shocked, he wondered how many more of them were about. Had the grounds been searched after all? Torchlight swept across his face as he heard Harris ask, 'Anything in the car?'

'It's locked.'

'So what?' Harris turned to Daryl. 'Open it,' he ordered.

With a hand miraculously steady, Daryl inserted

the key into the lock. His heart no longer pounded to the point of suffocation. Obligingly, he switched on the overhead light.

Harris himself searched the car. He covered every inch of leather, the floor, behind the dashboard, the seats, cursing and grunting, finding nothing. He straightened, panting heavily. 'The boot. Open the bloody boot!'

Almost smiling, Daryl did as he was told. The empty boot vindicated his claim to innocence. It drove Harris wild. A vicious push sent Daryl staggering. Harris attacked the interior of the car again, thrusting his body between the steering wheel and the seat, prodding and poking without result. A floor mat spun through the air as Harris pushed another door open. He began working on the front seat.

'Get off your arse, Doyle, and help,' he bellowed, 'pull the fuckin' thing apart. It's somewhere. I know it.'

Together he and Doyle wrenched at the front seat, forcing it away from the framework, ramming it hard under the steering wheel. Torchlight splayed over and around the confined space, revealing smooth, grey leather, not so much as a thread of cotton.

Harris turned to the policeman still searching the boot. 'Leave it. Did you search the grounds?'

'As much as I could. Jeeze, Alec, I'm here to guard the car. You'd need the whole bloody force in there to make a job of it.'

Harris grunted, chewing his lip. Reluctant to leave go, murderous in defeat. Doyle mooched around the

Hillman giving the tyres experimental kicks; he seemed to be losing interest in the whole procedure. He knelt down, peering without enthusiasm under the chassis.

Daryl lowered his eyes, not trusting the darkness to hide his glee. A suspicion that had begun during their walk down the drive now hardened into a solid core of triumph. They had blown it! Pounced too early. No goods, no charge. Let them pull the car apart bit by bit, if it made them happy. The game was over. Doyle and Harris. What a mug pair! He could have laughed aloud.

The sound of an approaching motor directed their attention to the road. A covered van pulled up, and with the engine still running, a constable eased himself out from behind the wheel. He waited beside the van as the three policemen went over to meet him. 'Just stay where you are, Missim,' Harris ordered.

Daryl saw Harris shrug as they conferred in whispers. He wondered if they would take him in after all. They could do anything if they really wanted to. Four against one. But it was only Harris who returned.

'This time lucky, Missim. But we've not given up on you. Not yet.' Two hard fingers jabbed Daryl's chest. 'Think you're fuckin' smart. But not half as smart as Doyle and me. As for that Manpower clearance, forget it.' His fingers prodded again. Hurting. 'You haven't a hope in hell!'

Harris took a few paces towards the police van,

then stopped in mid-stride, coming back. 'By the way—you can tell that red-headed floosie of yours that it's not clever to mix with shit like you.' His hand dropped heavily on Daryl's shoulder, the steel of his fingers biting deep into flesh. 'Warn her, 'Missim. There's a good lad.'

He watched them drive away.

Warn her Missim. Fear for Lulla tightened his gullet. Holy devil. Why bring her into it? How long had they been onto him—and her? Once the bastards sank their fangs in they never let go. They meant business. She must be told. Fast! He wondered if she was home. The luminous hands of his watch pointed to twenty minutes after eight. Was that all? If someone had asked him he would have sworn it was closer to ten. Still early enough to see her.

But first things first.

Leaning casually against the car, he extracted a cigar from his vest pocket, taking time to light it. Listening. Not sure that they had done with him; maybe they'd left someone behind to spy him out. Where was Ingram now? Snuck out the back way most likely, the slippery turd!

He rolled the cigar around his lips, chewed on it, taking satisfaction from the moist, aromatic leaf. Anyone watching would understand the delay in driving off. Calming his nerves, they'd think. The shrilling of night crickets confirmed that he was alone. Even so he waited another ten minutes before venturing back inside the gates.

The perfume of oleander blossoms was nearly too

sweet as he cautiously approached the spot where the packages were hidden. He bent down to retrieve them, in a fever to be gone. He felt around. Nothing there. Down on hands and knees, he crawled deeper into foliage damp with moisture, keeping the fence at finger-tip distance. In complete darkness he made wide circles with his arms, way beyond the point where the parcels might possibly be.

Cobwebs snared him, insects lay in ambush to sting and nip. Broken glass stabbed his shin, twigs teased his ears and threatened to poke out an eye. Past all reason of success, he began inching his way back to the starting point, unwilling to admit that he'd been tricked. It had to be Ingram. Or did the cop guarding the Hillman find the stuff after all? It'd bring him a packet on the black.

All bastard crooks, the lot of them. His shin began to throb and the insect underworld crawled and burrowed happily down his shirt. He'd had enough!

Body trembling with fatigue, he hobbled back to the car, and opened the door.

'Damn!'

It had slipped his mind that the front seat was still wedged beneath the steering wheel. He gripped it with hands slippery in sudden sweat and levered it back into place. Thankfully, he slumped into comforting leather, turned on the ignition and gave the starter a pull. There was no response from the engine. He tried again, then his eyes widened catching sight of the petrol gauge. Empty! A full tank when he started out. Some prick had milked him dry!

No other option but to leave the Hillman where it stood, and just as Doyle had previously vented his frustration, Daryl circled the car, kicking rubber before slamming all four doors in disgust. With nothing better to do, he began limping down the street towards the city.

Piss on the world. Piss on Harris and Doyle. And double-piss on Ingram!

13

*P*EGGY HAD AT last run out of excuses. It was on the way home from work that she had to admit to Lulla that her quickstep and swing waltz would pass muster. 'But,' she hedged, 'you're going out with Daryl, aren't you?'

'What makes you say that?'

'I saw you two sneak behind the shed.'

'All I did was ask him if he's heard anything. About Mac's closing down. You know that!' Showing irritation with Peggy turned a battle into a rout, so Lulla changed tactics and did her persuasive best. 'C'mon, love. A night's dancing will cheer us both up. You'll have a good time, I promise you. And with all that teaching'—she paused letting it sink in—'it's time you made a start. True?'

Peggy nudged a tobacco tin on the footpath with her toe, then gave it a kick hard enough to send it spinning and clattering across the road. "Spose you're right,' she said moodily. 'Okay.'

'Well ... don't knock me down in the rush to get there!'

About the time the police had Daryl Missim cornered in the Manpower office, Lulla was outside the Scotts' flat, a blouse swinging off one finger. She rapped lightly on the door before entering.

'Here it is, ironed and ready.' She pulled up at the sight of Peggy seated at the table. 'Hey! What's this? You're still in overalls.'

'I'm not going. Sorry, Lulla.'

'You're *what*?'

Peggy held up a letter, joy illuminating her face. A torn envelope lay discarded on the carpet. 'It was here on the table. Mum must've—'

'It has to be from Julian!' Congratulations wreathed Lulla's face. 'And about time too. Tonight we celebrate. What a beaut excuse for us to trip the light fantastic!'

'I don't want to go, Lulla, I said ...'

Lulla stopped her dipping and diving. The white blouse, still dangling from her hand, drooped and signalled defeat. Her colour heightened, the smile faded. 'Why not?'

'You don't really mind, do you?'

Lulla did mind; the disappointment had caught her off-guard. 'You're letting the side down, Peg.'

'Aw, come off it, Lulla.' Peggy's glow subsided a fraction as she tried to shrug away Lulla's obvious hurt. 'What difference does it make if I go or not?'

'You'd be surprised. Quite a lot.' Lulla could have added that most of the girls and women she knew, like Janet, were married or about to be. They were content to stay at home knitting socks and baking Anzac biscuits and fruit cake for their men at war. It would be an admission that she might be lonely for female company; that she was fed-up with walking alone into a dance hall.

'Anyway,' Peggy said at her stubborn best, 'who's to say I won't prop up the wall all night?'

'That was your excuse last time.'

Peggy had a hundred to fall back on, and now Julian's letter was added to the list. But the young girl made a conciliatory plea. 'Don't get snarly with me.' She clutched the flimsy airmail pages as if she was afraid they would blow away.

'Well I am snarly, damn it. You can take my word for it.' Looking down at Peggy, Lulla knew that whatever she said, the girl would be staying home. Dreamily folding the letter, she slipped it down her front; out of sight, keeping her hand pressed there as if the very essence of Julian lay between her breasts. 'I can't go, I've got a date with Julian.'

'That's a funny way of putting it,' Lulla snapped. Then she exploded. 'Gawd Aggie, Peg, it's only two pages long. You could read the thing fifty times over before we leave.'

'That's right. And I'll want to read it fifty times again. A hundred and fifty times again. Just to touch it. To feel—feel where his dear, darling hand has touched it.' She closed her eyes for a second, then opened them. 'And you know what, Lulla? The ink's blurred in some places. It's hot up there where he is, and sweat could've done that. His sweat.'

Lulla broke out in gooseflesh. She had to acknowledge this was a Peggy she knew nothing about. A voluptuous happiness flowed from the girl, almost tangible in its intensity. Shadows of envy washed over Lulla. When had she last felt like that?—Come on, she found herself arguing, who wants it? Forget about that richness surging when everything feels so good; so sweet, and strong. Then look out, Lulla! She tried ignoring the tingle of memory that Peggy's bliss inspired. Appraising her young friend, she acknowledged that whatever flowed between man and woman, it was worth the hurt and heartache, which more often than not was bound to happen.

Peggy picked the envelope up from the floor, smoothing out creases. 'He loves me, you know,' she said softly. 'He says so. And I thought ... I thought ... never mind. I thought wrong.' She turned her gaze full on the older woman, appealing for her to understand. 'Would you go out dancing, honest—if you were me? Without him, that is.'

'You win, kid. So I go it alone.'

'Not for long, Lulla. You're never alone.'

'If you say so ...' Lulla studied the blouse still hanging from her fingers. 'Well, you won't be needing this, I guess.'

Peggy tried hard to appear contrite. 'Reckon not. But thanks for ironing it, anyway.'

Like a well-oiled wheel, the progressive barn dance circled easily around the floor, its regimented steps permitting thoughts to wander.

Not a bad turnout, Lulla mused, and Peggy should be here. Just the right sort of crowd to cut her teeth on. A sixty-forty hop with familiar tunes and not much competition, looking at the girls. Peg would have had every dance.

er bore a vague resemblance to Daryl, and she regretted her snide remarks and anger of the afternoon. Daryl's self-esteem was easily lanced, and she suspected she had made a good job of it! Maybe she'd been too hard on him, too ready to jump at conclusions at the mention of Chuck. She'd keep her eye out for him tomorrow and show the old olive branch.

h the change of partners, she automatically adjusted rhythm and stride to accommodate the man swaying towards her. Would Daryl crack it for a release, she wondered. He'd seemed so sure of himself. Well, she sent over a silent message, wishing him luck. Someone had to get the breaks.

Another change, another parting in the waltzing chain, and this time an army sergeant; before he had touched her hand she had judged him. Neat on his feet and as interesting as a paper bag. Sweaty, too. More than most.

Lulla finger-tipped a wet shoulder. They plodded through the motions while the orchestra doggedly thumped out *Lily of Laguna*. The circle steamed and melted; a hothouse of sodden khaki, humid serge, limp cotton dresses. The soldier spoke: 'Last dance booked?'

'Not yet.'

'How about it, then? Live far?' Right to the point this one; but then you don't wast time in the old Progressive. She pretended not to hear as she swung away from him, her arms at the ready for a new partner. The dancers moved back, then surged forward. Always in time, almost tidal, in obedience to *Laguna*'s tune.

Back and forth. Separate. On to the next one.

'Well, if it isn't the Princess herself!'

A wild stab of recognition jolted Lulla back to life. Spanner Larkin! Standing there, arms open wide!

She felt herself clamped tightly to him as Spanner broke the circle and headed for the centre in a series of pivots that had Lulla laughing and protesting, demanding they should stop. In answer, the pace quickened until the outer ring—a carousel of rainbow colours—spiralled and whirled around them. Overhead lights spun at a dizzy speed and she would have fallen had she not been fused to his shape. When he did release her, she staggered. He caught her.

'Out of practice, Princess,' the voice teased. 'And who thought those Yanks could dance.' He kept a firm hold on her, nearly too close and too long for dance hall protocol. 'Want to sit out the rest of it?'

Head reeling, Lulla refused an offered arm. 'You do what you like, but I'm finishing the set.' But the orchestra conspired with Spanner and brought *Lily of Laguna* to a drum-rolling end. Ignoring the sustained clapping, the leader announced a fifteen-minute break. Spanner grinned his approval as he led her off the floor.

'It's time that you and I had a good, long talk, Riddel ...'

They sat atop Highgate Hill again, on the same park bench as before. Now, the stubble of winter's grass had gone; underfoot was thick with clover and jumping jacks. In the night glow, nasturtiums humped and scattered and ran unfettered down the slope, their scent touching the river breeze with sweetness.

Lulla had allowed the sailor to steer her away from the dance hall, only once raising pale objections that she had promised someone the next foxtrot. Spanner's answer had been to 'forget it'.

A good long talk had been the excuse. But there had been little talk since they'd left the Institute. The walk to the Hill had been punctuated with kisses. Embraces in shadows. Hard, hungry mouthings, each one more arrogant, more thrilling than the last as she had curved into him.

And they weren't talking much now, Lulla confessed to a tripping heart, nerve ends firing where his fingers touched. She had to acknowledge her weakened state. If footpaths had been feather beds she would have been out for a duck.

But on the summit the breeze cooled her burning skin, ushering in caution.

Spanner indicated the tangled weeds and clover. 'Why not down there. It's much softer. Sweeter, too. Come on,' he coaxed. As if he expected it, he did not seem to mind her silence as he lightly stroked her thigh. 'Strong legs, Lulla. Wonderful legs.' He continued the gentle caress.

She made no attempt to stop him. So easy to sit there. Not moving, feeling the long length of her muscle from knee to crutch responding. Tensing. Not moving as his hand cupped her knee. So gentle. Tender.

She sat there. Eyes closed; sorry for the moment when she must take his hand away. Just one minute more. That's all ...

Suddenly, without warning, he thrust his hand deeply between her legs, half-leaning across her. Drawing breath from her parted lips. Flesh and belly ached to keep him there, but she slipped away, gasping. 'Cut it out!' Hating herself for saying it.

'Christ! Why not? What did all that mean back there, under the trees? I thought you couldn't wait to get here. You liked it enough then—or was it all an act?' He lunged at her again. His hands were everywhere, demanding surrender.

She pushed him off. 'You know damned well it wasn't an act!' Her anger and frustration matched his. She tried to control her breathing, one hand on Spanner's shoulder keeping them apart.

'Of course I like it, as you so crudely put it. Too

much! I wish the kisses and petting could go on for ever. But you've got to know when to stop, Spanner. Can't understand that? It's what comes after that causes the trouble. Only for me, though.' She allowed herself a pause, gauging his reaction. 'Only for me. Not for you, not for the man. And you know it.'

'So we'll be careful.' So carelessly uttered, his assumption that her concern could be so easily disposed of. As if the matter was settled, he placed his arm around her, ready to begin where he had left off.

Lulla knocked it aside. '*We'll* be careful,' she echoed bitterly. '*We*! Aren't you taking a lot for granted? As for careful, that's a laugh. Who'll be careful? You? Me? Like the last time, no doubt.'

'Nothing happened, did it?'

'No ... nothing happened.'

She adjusted her rucked-up skirt. It seemed a prudish and over-fussy thing to do. Knees together, ankles crossed, just as mother ordered: but give credit where it's due, Spanner made—if reluctantly—space between them; his gaze focused somewhere down the hillside while shared tensions simmered down. He gave a small grunt of rueful acceptance, then fished inside his cap for cigarettes.

'And I thought you and I made for a great team, Lulla. Silly, eh?'

'Not silly, Spanner. We just went too far, that's all.'

'You reckon.' He struck a match to light up.

'I—I ...' Lulla's throat seized, not trusting herself to say more: allowing him time to take quiet enjoyment in his smoking. Before he had finished, she held up two fingers. 'Want to share?'

'You! Smoking ... since when?' But he handed over the packet.

She gave a shaky laugh. 'Since a while. Something to do with my hands, I suppose.'

'I know what I'd like to do with mine.'

'You never give up, do you?'

'Why should I?' He dared to give her a lopsided grin. 'Anyway—it's all part of the fun.'

The few lights that sparkled the dark spread of the city blurred and splintered. Why was she crying? There was nothing to cry about. To her annoyance she could not stifle a small hiccough and a sob escaping from the well of unshed tears inside her. It had a startling effect on Spanner. His half-smoked Capstan was tossed away as he turned to look at her.

'Why the tears, Lulla? That's not like you.'

She took a quick, hard drag on her cigarette. It was a nervous gesture more than anything else. 'A fit of the blues, Spanner, I guess,' was all she could say.

Carefully he removed the cigarette from her fingers, dropping it, grinding it out with his heel. 'Not good enough, Princess. Don't care to see my favourite girl like this, eh?'

She had never seen him so solicitous, so concerned. There were no demands now as he drew her close to him, arms around her. Stroking her hair; murmuring words of comfort. No attempts to kiss her. He only offered to see her through a bad spell. So unexpected—so different from the carefree, likeable larrikin she knew.

She gave way to heavier tears, sobs that racked her body, while he held her tightly, saying a good howl was just the thing for the blues, or whatever was hurting her so.

She couldn't have given him a reason, a sensible answer, if he'd put a hundred quid in her hand, she told him—keeping to herself that perhaps it was over a baby she thought he'd given her not long after they'd met ... and hadn't! Her mistake; recalling the fiasco of the hot gin bath. Perhaps it was just over the whole, bloody, rotten mess that the world found itself in. Men coming and going, most never to be seen again. Girls like poor Janet, with husbands like Kirk—every day a bonus if they managed to stay alive.

She didn't know why the hell she was crying! But she appreciated the arms about her, and his stillness as he waited for the tears to dry. She gave a few gulps, searched her purse for a hanky and blew her nose hard. He was right. She did feel better after a good howl; empty almost, and very grateful for a pal like Spanner Larkin.

'Come on,' he said after a while, 'I'll take you back to the flat.' He got to his feet, hands outstretched to pull her up.

They strolled down the hill towards Vulture Street. Houses dark and quiet; dark shadows beneath the spread of trees. He spoke of the night they had raced to the tramstop. Their first night. 'Thought you were going to beat me there, for a while.' He chuckled, remembering.

Lulla gave him a quick nudge. 'Huh! What made you think you really won, Larkin? I could beat you any day—or night.'

That stopped him in his tracks. 'You hinting that you let me win? Y'kidding.'

'Am I?' She was taking off her shoes. 'Want a second try?'

'We'll do it fair, this time.' He, too, began removing his navy boots.

Barefoot, they stood in line, poised, ready to go.

'One,' he called.

'Two!' she echoed.

'Three—' and then, together: 'GO!'

They were off. Straining. Legs pumping to get the lead. They were well matched and halfway down, not an inch gained and no quarter given as they pounded down the hushed street. Neither could shake the other off, both were nearly toppling with the impetus of the race and the steepness of the slope; bitumen and gravel bit into the soles of their feet.

But the race was brought to a sudden halt. Around the corner at the base of the hill, two army trucks lumbered into view. Spanner had no desire to be pinned, without boots, in the headlights of the approaching vehicles. He drew back into the shadows of the trees, Lulla with him. Breathing fast, they waited until the trucks passed by.

Spanner was the first to speak. 'Well, that puts paid to that!'

'And lucky for you, Larkin.'

'No contest, Riddel. No comment!'

Under the royal spread of the weeping figs, they grinned in mateship, appraising each other, their smiles gradually fading. Spanner took hold of Lulla's wrist bringing her close. 'Seems as if this was how we started on the way up,' he had to quip. Lulla nodded, feeling glad there was a second chance to start all over again.

Something had happened there, up on the hill. His concern over her distress had shown a different man, a more tender one, and she moved towards him, ready to give him her lips. She put her arms around his neck melding into him.

They kissed under the trees, passions rising, a strong need between them to strengthen a memory of that one and only night they had loved together, months ago. It had been winter then, it was summer now, and, as Spanner folded her in his arms, the smell of her enriched the perfume of frangipanni flowers in gardens close by, drifting in the moist, heated air.

'I want you, Lulla. No man needed a woman as much as I need you now.'

'I know. I understand ...'

No one saw them walk up the path or enter the back room. No one saw how her hand trembled as she unlocked the door. It seemed to Lulla as if it was the first time for her. Something precious was about to happen and there was no reason for words between them.

Inside, they kept to darkness, enough starlight filtering through the window to make out shape. They undressed and lay on the bed side by side. A pact had been made.

They had all the time in the world, all the night. She was the first to make a move, but only to trace her fingers along the line of his crooked nose, feeling the outline of his lips. He lay there, not moving. Her hands glided down his neck pausing to note the rise and fall of his chest, the matted hair; her own passion rising. She felt the ridge of hipbone; the hollow beneath. She would kiss there later. Not now. There was a strange and delicate bond between them: desire; deep friendship; an urgent need to give the best to each other—to please. To enjoy.

Now his groin; feeling the hard length of him, she allowed her hand to rest there. Not moving. It was the signal for Spanner to slowly, carefully, roll over, taking the weight on his elbows. Taking his time. No need to hurry.

Penetration ...

As on the dance floor they were partners, each responding to the other's touch. In unison, moving together. For the first time since entering the room, the sailor spoke.

'Happy, Princess?'

'Yes, oh yes. But be still awhile.' Her breath came faster. He obeyed, his weight coming to rest on her. Time now to kiss her cheeks, still salty with tears;

that long and lovely neck. Kisses deliberately gentle. He waited. Then ...

'Lulla girl, you're not making it easy.'

Her arms around his tightened. She was stirring.

'Now?' His voice husky, already quickening his rhythm. No stopping now. Not wanting to. She keeping up with him. They moved to a sweet, wild tune that scaled and flamed the heights. And through the night wild music touched them again. And again ... No questions asked. No promises given.

They made memories that night. Memories enough to warm a woman's heart in lonely times and to companion a sailor's solitary watch at sea.

14

*I*T WAS HOT afternoon. Sunshafts pierced heavy overalls through to the skin. Not one in the queue complained. No one complained on payday.

Sweat scalded a heat rash which had plagued Peggy for days. Like savage mites, it nipped her backside and she longed to scratch. Better not, she cautioned, too many men around for that. They could scratch like dogs and not a word said. Look at old Hickey. Embarrassing it was, sometimes.

The queue behind her grew. But the pay-out hatch, like a lazy eyelid, remained half-shut. She called out to Lulla, six bodies away and closer to the front. 'What's going on? You're the closest. Have a look.'

As the pay clerk's cubbyhole was a mere appendage to the main office, Lulla, ignoring the hatch, went over to peer short-sightedly through one of the larger windows. She then sauntered back, linking into Peggy's arm.

'Well?' Peggy asked, 'What's the hold-up? If you can see that far.'

'Don't be sassy.' Lulla gave her a light pinch. 'The pay's there, all right—and I don't need glasses. Not yet!' She squinted up at the sun bombarding them. 'Jeez—it's hot! They've no right making us wait this long. Yak-yakking under the fan while we blister out here.'

'Who's yakking?' The younger girl was getting impatient.

'Him.' Lulla nodded towards the pay office. 'And that old bat Daniels.' She unbuckled overall straps, flapping the bib, making a breeze. 'Gawd knows what they're on about.' She missed the fleeting frown on Peggy's face as the girl lowered her voice to a whisper.

'Mr Simpson and Mrs Daniels?' Worrying, Peggy made a small meal of her fingers. 'Think they might be talking about us? You know …?'

'You're a worryguts, Peg.'

Although the annexe had heard nothing more about the transfer of female labour to other factories, the rumour persisted that MacIntyre's could close down; that the plant could shift *en masse* to Moorooka. Anything hinting of change squeezed the heart with unease.

Lulla plucked a damp blouse away from wet skin. 'I'm sopping.' Still complaining, she moved back to her place in the line.

Peggy burned and itched, trying not to scratch. They shouldn't have to wait around like this. Why not get paid in groups, the way Lulla had once suggested? 'In *our* time for a change.'

Always one for bucking the system, was Lulla. Like the morning Mrs D had walked into the annexe. 'No more talking during working hours,' she said. Talking held up production. Talking hampered the war effort. She was always nagging—Peggy gave a surreptious rub—always on about something. And it didn't go down real good with Lulla either.

'No one confers in the main workshop,' Mrs D had told them, all smug and superior, 'and I see no reason why—'

'How can they,' Lulla had railed, 'they're nailed down and glued fast to those rotten machines. And there's all that damned racket—'

'Language, Riddel!'

'*Miss* Riddel, thank you very much'—game as you like.

In spite of the heat, the sun, the waiting, laughter bubbled as Peggy recalled the morning. Hammer and tongs they were going, with Mrs D demanding that someone find the forewoman. Then Andy appeared with Micky trotting behind her. They had been taking stock in the drying room.

Andy had held up her hand. 'I've heard part of it.' Her Scottish burr was thicker than cold porridge as she faced up to Mrs D. 'Now ... if you can prove there's a slowdown over a wee bit of talking, I'll put a stop to it. Right now. But we both know production is up. Take a look in there.' She had pointed to the drying and holding rooms where bombs were stacked high; some of the rows close to the roof. 'If they don't go soon, we'll not fit a wee mouse in there. Let alone another crate.'

'An exaggeration, Mrs Andrews.'

'When are the soldier lads coming to collect? They've not been here for more than a fortnight.'

The annexe could only guess what happened to the grenades once they left the factory. Army trucks arrived as the night shift clocked off, and morning would find the holding room empty, looking hugely bare. Some thought that the hand bombs were taken to be filled and primed behind the old night-soil pits south of Rocklea. Others laid bets they were flown straight out to New Guinea and the islands, to be completed there.

'Well?' Andy had demanded, 'when will they go? You'll have young Micky asking for danger money just to have smoko in there.'

Andy's careful words and her steady gaze distorted behind pebble glasses had repelled further carping. With a sniff for an answer, Mrs Daniels had swept out of sight, to everyone's relief.

Now, sweltering under the sun, Peggy grinned as she remembered the rout. One up for Andy and the annexe: not so for Lulla.

'Be careful, lass,' Andy had warned her, 'ye're heading for trouble.' Everyone knew that Lulla was on a collision course with Mrs D; and that meant Old Man MacIntyre as well.

All Lulla did was point out that MacIntyre's were stuck with her for the duration. 'So they can go jump in the lake. I'll say my piece when I want to.'

'They could shift you to the machine shop,' Andy persisted. 'Break up the best team in the plant.'

'Then I'll cut my throat!'

Peggy slipped a hand into a side pocket, freeing her thighs of swami panties sticking to angry pustules like Clag. Heat-drugged she waited, willing the pay clerk to appear; wondering if today the postman had been kind. Surely he had left a letter. He was the only link she had with Julian. Julian's first letter—and so far the last—she already knew by heart. 'My sweet Peggy. My own girl, dearest lover ...' Just one more, Julian, she silently begged of him. Please—just one more.

By now, the men up front were losing patience. They began rapping the counter, voicing irritation.

'C'mon, there.'

'Open up!'

'Bush week's over, Simpson.' The yammering grew more assertive, bordering on the belligerent until the hatch slammed up and Simpson's face, peevish with annoyance, glared at them.

'All right, all right!' he sniped back. 'Name?'

The line commenced its clockwork progress.

Peggy noticed Lulla, pay in hand, frowning down at her unopened packet. As if expecting something to spring out, cautiously she slid a thumb under the flap. She removed the pound and ten shilling notes, carefully counting, and checked over the few remaining coins.

'Hey, Mr Simpson!' Her face thrust close to the hatch. 'There's some mistake here.'

'I don't make mistakes, Miss Riddel.'

'Yeah? Well, take a look at that.' Lulla pushed the envelope, and contents back to the pay clerk. 'Five bob short. And there's overtime.'

'Included.'

'Like hell it is! By my reckoning, there should be nearly eight quid there.'

The challenge could be heard clear down the line.

'Not so.' Simpson sounded wary: even uncomfortable. He took a pencil from behind his ear and made a few notations on a pad near at hand. It was a delaying action that did little to allay Lulla's growing concern. He kept on writing, not lifting his eyes. 'Mrs Daniels has not spoken to your forewoman, then?'

'About what?' Lulla snapped back.

'You've no idea? That is unfortunate.'

Peggy, now alert, strained to hear what Simpson had to say. When a superior—and in Peggy's book, a pay clerk was all of that—began mouthing in such a precise and careful manner, it was time to look over your shoulder for sharp knives.

Simpson, by way of an answer, stuffed the money back into the envelope and tossed it across the counter. Peggy felt the temper of the queue building up at the delay; they were all restive and, like her, boiling in the heat. When Simpson finally spoke it was to say that Lulla and Mrs Anderson should go to the office. Lulla's neck, already pink with sunburn, turned to a dull red. Peggy, familiar with the signs, waited for the explosion.

'Andy's not here. She never collects on payday—and you know it!'

'You're holding up proceedings, Miss Riddel.'

'Bugger proceedings! You tell me what's going on. You're the pay clerk, aren't you?' Lulla spun around to face the jibes of 'we're not here for the duration', and 'get off the pot, Lulla'.

'Pipe down, will you!' she yelled back. 'There's something wrong here.' But her voice was lost among the catcalls and whistles; helpless against the derision of her workmates, she dismissed them all in disgust and strode over to the office. 'Always had to fight my own battles, anyway,' she called.

With the redhead out of the way, Simpson went back to work. 'Next!'

In turn, Peggy stepped forward, heart beating and anxious. She studied the neat figures on her pay packet. Lulla was not the only one to be short-changed—three-and-six, at a quick count. She should front up to the office as Lulla was doing. Ashamed and miserable, she had to admit that the thought of locking horns with Mrs Daniels was too awful to contemplate. It was with relief she saw Hilda leaving the change room and waved her over. Mum would know what to do.

Hilda, as always, was dressed for the walk through the huddle of West End shops to Franklin Street. She rarely passed through the factory gates without stockings, hat and gloves. 'Never know who you'll bump into,' she asserted when the girls teased her. The memory of her discomfort in the headmaster's office still stung.

She hurried over. 'What's wrong? You look upset. And where's Lulla?' She looked up and down the line.

Peggy nodded towards the office. 'She's in there. It's to do with our pay. We're short.'

'Both of you?'

Before her daughter could speak, Lulla's voice, magnified by anger and frustration, erupted through the door. 'What do you mean, women's wages? That's all we ever get. Never was the same as the men, and well you know it!'

'You get the award.' Mrs Daniels' voice.

'Not this week. Look at it—five bob short if it's a penny. You call that the award?'

'You work in the annexe. Quite different from the factory, the machine shop. Quite different.'

'Since when?' Lulla was losing ground.

'Since this week. MacIntyre's have been more than generous in the past. It never was mandatory to pay "floor" wages to those working in the annexe.'

'I don't believe it.'

'You had better believe it.' They were neat phrases glossed and chewed over with relish.

'Well, it won't end here, Mrs Daniels. I'll speak to the union. I'll—'

'Do so by all means. Now is that all, Riddel?'

'*Miss* Riddel, to you!'

Peggy winced. By now Lulla's eyes would be snapping sapphire chips, her freckles standing out like rust spots. She gave her mother a nudge. 'You going in there?'

Hilda shook her head in sympathy; but that was all. 'Not now. Andy is the right one—with our support—to sort this out. Lulla's overstepping the mark.'

'Mum! That's not true. She has every right—' But now, they could hear Lulla demanding to see Mr MacIntyre himself. Peggy caught her breath, dismayed by Lulla's audacity. The whole queue listened. Deadly quiet.

'I want to see him. Right this minute!'

'Impossible!' Mrs Daniels shrilled above the factory clangour. '*Miss* Riddel, if you don't leave this office at once, I'll get someone to remove you. Bodily. Do you understand?' The Scotts realised that Mrs D in her rage, had spat the plum right out of her mouth. She sounded just like anyone else. 'Well, Riddel, are you going?'

Lulla's exit came up to expectations. She flew outside, pistols blazing. Her next move stunned them all. Silver and copper coins were hurled back through the office door.

'Here, take the lot. They're not worth having!' One by one, the banknotes were tossed into the air, and, as they fluttered down about her, she burst into tears. Gulping and bawling, she ran past the astonished factory hands and fled across the yard, charging up the change room steps two at a time.

Only the men dared to laugh.

A few of the women left the queue and headed towards the change room. They clustered at the foot of the stairs, uncertain of their next move.

Hilda, with Peggy standing by, retrieved the scattered notes and the one penny that had fallen short of the office. When Lulla cooled off, they reasoned, she might regret her spendthrift defiance.

15

*L*ULLA'S RAGE OVER the pay cut lasted all the way back to the flat. Threatening mayhem and muttering maledictions she headed straight for the bathroom and the panacea for all vexations, a shower and shampoo.

Let Mac's do their damnedest, she fumed, savaging a face washer with soap. We'll strike. Go slow. Anything to make them sit up! Anger and hurt dissipated in a flurry of soapsuds and although she was still determined to confront management in the morning, reason advised a cool and cautious head.

First things first—get Janet on side.

No trouble there, she decided, scrubbing arms and legs. Janet had been the first to console, just as hostile over MacIntyre's grudging handouts. 'Without fair warning too,' she'd protested, compounding the injustice of it all.

Lulla heard Janet's return to the flat. She had volunteered to do the shopping, checking coupons before she went, saying that a nice piece of rump would cheer them up no end, without a mention of saving coupons for Kirk's next leave. Janet was a sport.

Lulla turned the shower off. The towel roughed her skin to rose and she was more than generous with the baby talc. After tea, they'd go next door and persuade Hilda and Peggy to take a stand with them. Four out of the annexe was a good start. The rest of the team were bound to follow. Or were they? Who could she really depend on? The new girl? Andy? No, not Andy. A couple of men on the team would be handy: they'd never put up with the tripe that was dished out to women. She thought of Daryl Missim as she wrapped a towel around herself. Even his presence would have lent some weight to the cause. But Daryl was more than two weeks gone. The deal with Ingram must have been a success. Lucky Daryl.

Kitchen noises could be heard as Janet put the stores away. She heard the lid of the cake tin jiggled and slapped back into place, and hoped that Janet had brought home a honey roll. She could do with a sweet thing.

'Bathroom's all yours, Jan,' she called out. 'I'll start on the spuds.'

Peeling potatoes, and planning stratagems to bring Mrs Daniels to heel, Lulla missed the sound of the front door opening. She jumped as Kirk Hope bounced into the kitchen bringing with him the smell of hot chips and Abbotts Lager, a huge grin splashed across his face. One arm anchored a parcel of fish and chips to his side; the bottles were wedged tightly under the other. Equally at home, following close behind, was Spanner Larkin, clutching his own share of packets and bottles. It looked as if they intended making a night of it.

Kirk planted a malty kiss on both cheeks. Spanner blew her one.

'Later, Princess, later!' he offered cheerfully.

Lulla felt a fool standing there, hair in pins, and nothing more between the three of them than a bath towel. Fazed by their blatant appreciation and Spanner's silent whistle, she shouldered past them and made a dive for the bedroom.

Blotto; the pair of them.

The flat vibrated with male exuberance and bantering nonsense. Janet, who never engaged the eccentricities of the bathroom shower without wearing a bathing cap, would not have heard them. As Lulla slipped into her silk kimono she decided against warning her. Let it come as a surprise.

Kirk had dumped the fish on the table. Pieces of mullet, crumbed and glistening, slid from their wrappings and stained the pine-topped table with grease.

'You great clunk,' scolded Lulla, 'I only scrubbed that this morning.'

Unabashed, Kirk popped chips into his mouth. 'Where's the missus?' He winked at Spanner; they could all hear the gas heater pulsing steadily in the bathroom. Kirk's smile broadened. 'Now that's what I call good timing,' he said, rubbing his hands together. 'Keep the fish hot, love—the beer cold. This won't take verr-ry long.'

There was purpose in his stride as he left the kitchen. They heard the squeal of Janet's happy remonstrations cut short by the slamming door.

Lulla's hand itched to slap the smirk off Spanner's face. 'You're pickled!' she bristled.

'Not yet. But I'm working on it!'

'Orr-ah!'

As she lit the oven and made room for bottles in the ice-chest, she could feel Spanner's amusement at Kirk's lusty exit. Trust Larkin to find it all so funny! The gas heater throbbed with steady rhythm. She tried to douse speculation by banging the oven door, rattling cutlery, and playing dumb to Kirk's rumbling laughter ... and Janet's silence, after the first delighted squeal.

Bloody men!

Were they actually under the shower together? IN THE RAW? *Gawd Aggie* ...

She just hoped old Hickey wasn't sniffing around; sidling along the path, spying beneath the window, listening for all his worth, and later complaining loudly about disgusting behaviour. Dirty old devil: the tap turned on so hard and fast that the lettuce she was rinsing was torn to shreds. She prickled as a curl, still damp, was gently moved aside. Spanner tested his luck by blowing lightly on the spot where the curl had rested.

'I'd say it's the back room for you tonight, girl.'

His suggestion was shrugged off and when she turned to face him, he was looking down at her as if she was a particularly juicy mango.

'None of your business, Larkin.'

She reached for a cutting board on a shelf above the sink, slapped it down hard on the table and attacked a tomato. It was nearly impossible to make a salad with him blowing down her neck.

Spanner moved in, all innocent. 'Have I said something wrong?'

'Oh, shut up!' He had the nerve of a spiked-up bullock! A stifled gasp was heard by both of them. That was Janet. Spanner raised an eyebrow. Lulla panicked. She burned all over. 'Bread,' she said frantically, 'we're out of it.' It was difficult to breathe. 'And vinegar. Can't have fish without vinegar.' The corner shop was still open. Any excuse to escape those hungry eyes, and the audible high jinks going on just a few feet away.

In a dash to quit the kitchen they collided, shoulder against shoulder. The sailor's hands steadied her, before sliding down the cool silk to her hips.

'Gotcha!' He kissed her. Just once. Then let her go with a slap on the backside. 'Go and put a dress on, before I do you a mischief ...'

The old camaraderie the four used to share had returned. The space beneath the circular table was comfortably congested. Nothing was left of the fish and chips, and only a handful remained of the prawns. Spanner nipped the head off one, tailed it, and with the speed of long practice removed the shell in one piece. A thumbnail gouged out the sandtrack before handing it over, pinkly naked and perfect, to Lulla.

'There. Wrap your pretty lips around that. But keep talking. I'm interested.'

Lulla accepted the offering with delicate fingers. She felt the pressure of Spanner's knee and let it be. His close attention to her row with MacIntyre's had been more than flattering. She leaned back in her chair, arms crossed. 'Well, you've heard it. What do you think?'

'Notta so good.'

Kirk spoke up, addressing Janet. 'You didn't say anything about this, Jan.' It seemed as if he doubted Lulla's word.

'Hardly had time,' Lulla snapped back, then could have bitten off her tongue.

Why bring that up! Not a reference had been made to Kirk and Janet's absence before the fish and chips had appeared on the table.

Unperturbed, Kirk gave a lazy smile. 'Yeah ... you could say that.' He tweaked Janet's cheek. 'She was a bit on the busy side,' he drawled, exuding a complacency bolstered up by Janet's compliance.

Lulla ignored him and turned to Spanner. 'I'm waiting, Larkin. What's your opinion?'

'About what?' Teasing. Exchanging glances with his shipmate. Lulla's clamped lips refused to fuel their needling. Even so, Spanner's expression changed as he sipped beer. He looked thoughtful. Lulla settled back, well satisfied. No flies on Spanner Larkin. There was a fair chance he could talk Janet around to her way of thinking. Janet had proved a disappointment. She was getting cold feet; her anger over the pay cut was fading fast.

Spanner reached for a toothpick and cleared his thumbnail of prawn meat. 'So y'did your lolly. Not surprising.' He took another gulp of beer, rolling it around his mouth, taking his time to swallow, and gave her a steady look, slowly shaking his head. 'Wrong thing to do, Princess. Wrong move to make.'

'I can't believe this.' Stunned, she sat there, feeling betrayal all over again. He had seemed to understand. To be tuned in to her way of thinking. 'Are you telling me that we—that I should have copped that treatment? Not say a word? You're mad!'

'Now hang on a minute.' The sailor held up a hand. 'There is a right way of doing things.'

'Oh—so I'm to blame. Me!' Lulla cast around the table for support.

Spanner remained calm, studying her, his look almost tender. 'I didn't say that. Now listen to me.'

'All right. I'm listening.'

'For a start, there's your shop steward.'

'Hah!' Lulla's resentment was eclipsed by a surge of triumph. 'I was waiting for that,' she crowed. 'There's no shop steward. Mac's won't have a bar of one. Ask Janet.'

Janet nodded, but said nothing, giving the impression she would rather be in the kitchen making tea.

Lulla pushed her glass over to Kirk to be refilled. 'When I started—it seems like forever ago—there was a sort of shop steward. He organised a meeting. In the street, just outside the gates. You can guess what happened.'

'Do tell.'

'They brought in the police to break it up. A couple of fellows were arrested for cluttering the streets—that's a joke, you could've fired a shotgun down there and be lucky to hit a mynah bird between the eyes. Anyway, the shop steward disappeared. Never saw him again.'

Spanner's eyes were hard to read behind a self-imposed screen of tobacco smoke, although Lulla thought she caught a look that signified he knew all about clashes with exasperated authority. She knew that before he joined up, Spanner had been a Kalgoorlie miner.

'So don't talk to me about shop stewards,' she carried on. 'You fight your own battles out there ...' Her voice trailed into silence, brooding over the humiliation and perfidy of workmates; hearing the catcalls that had forced her from the queue. Oh, yes—the women had made suitable noises after it was all over, but their readiness to let sleeping dogs lie had offended her sense of justice. Even the Scotts had been off-side.

Kirk refilled her glass. The chilled beer tasted good, and she felt a little drunk. Janet, looking owly-eyed, belched behind polite fingers as she presented Kirk with her near-empty tumbler. 'Me too,' she said.

Kirk, about to pour, paused, then placed the bottle back on the table. 'Steady, old girl,' he cautioned, 'who in this family is a two-pot screamer. Eh?'

'Not any more, sailor.' Janet giggled and blew him a kiss. 'Pretty please?'

Kirk shrugged: not happy, but giving in. 'By the way,' he said, 'what is this fuss with MacIntyre's? You never talk much about the factory, do you.'

'Didn't think you'd be interested,' said Janet.

'Well, you're dead wrong.'

Lulla mulled over that one. As far as she could recall, Kirk had never troubled his head over the factory. Was Golden Boy counting Janet's pennies? Pay cut or not, the pennies were never counted when Kirk was ashore.

Spanner spoke up. 'What you need is advice from your working sisters over in West Aussie. That right, China?' Addressing Kirk.

'Whoa, there! Hold on. You might give them ideas.' Kirk distanced himself with upraised hands. 'They're stirrers all right, over there. Must be all that sand.'

Spanner had the devil's gleam in his eye. 'Ever heard about the day,' he asked them, 'when your sisters held up a train in a bid for natural justice and industrial harmony?' He half-rose, looking about him. 'Where's the soap-box?'

They laughed and told him to get on with it.

Spanner reported that the women of Western Australia had no trouble slipping into the boots of their absent menfolk. Easily as keys into well-oiled locks, he told them. 'A tough bunch of ladies,' he said in admiration.

'And what have we here?' Lulla mourned. 'A bagfull of jelly babies. But go on, we're all ears.'

Spanner spoke of a new Government foundry sited on the outskirts of Perth. 'My sister works there. She reckons it has the lot: canteen, decent change rooms, showers, hot and cold running dunnies ... you want it'—he snapped his fingers—'you've got it. Only one problem, but.'

The girls were fascinated.

'Every can of cream has its flies,' Janet hiccupped, wagging a finger.

Transport was the problem, Spanner told them, and erratic rail services. Workers on late shift waited too long between trains. Few had cars, and pay could be docked because of a train's late arrival. Night shifts were shifts of terror for women stranded on lonely blacked-out stations.

'Like all women, they got their way in the end.' Spanner's eyes puckered up. He made them wait while he rolled a makings, taking his time to wax the end of it.

'Come on, sailor, out with it!' Janet demanded.

'She mus' be drunk,' Lulla murmured. 'She's beginning to sound like me.'

Spanner obliged. 'Now here comes the best bit. Those gutsy ladies—after months of complaining, and getting nowhere—boarded the train. There must have been a mob of 'em. They went as far as East Perth station, jumped off there, and from then on they walked. Walked in front of that bloody engine all the way through to City bloody Central. Can you beat it!'

Lulla sparked at the thought. 'Hope y'not making this up, Larkin.'

'Ridgy-didge. And what a sight it was! News of it crackled around the town like a bushfire gone mad. Tools downed, washing left in the tubs, even some of the shopkeepers went down to the tracks to cheer them on. Bloody lovely, it was. And me on leave, lucky to see it.'

The sailor paid homage to the women of his home state with an upraised glass. 'To the ladies!'

Lulla wished with all heart that she could have been there to march with them. What a giggle! 'Can you imagine that happening with this lot? In Queensland?' She shafted a swift look at Janet. 'Think you'd have the—' she corrected herself—'*we'd* have the guts, the nerve to do something like that? Do you, Janet?'

Janet was making careful rings on the tabletop with her glass. 'I know what you're getting at, Lulla. And believe me,' she said earnestly, 'I'm just as wild—'

'Enough to support me tomorrow? To have another go at them?'

'I don't know ... shouldn't Andy—'

'Forget Andy. She's there to see the job gets done. Not held up. No, it's up to us.'

They spoke to each other as if the two men had ceased to exist. Lulla flipped open her cigarette case, and finding it empty slapped it back on the table. Spanner slid over his makings. She gave him brief acknowledgment, before going on. 'As for Hilda and Peggy,' she said, teasing out tobacco strands with long fingers, 'what a cop-out.'

'You must be fair, Lulla,' Janet protested. 'To those two, holding up the works is tantamount to treason.'

'Balls!'

'Lulla!'

Spanner softly cheered. Kirk remained silent, not approving. Janet, now quite sober, became persuasive. 'Hilda and Peggy aren't letting down the side. None of the girls are. They're just scared. Scared that their jobs might disappear overnight. Scared that Manpower might shove them into something else, far worse than MacIntyre's could ever be.'

'Nothing but rumours. Maybe Mac's stirred the pot themselves. They're a tricky lot. Do anything to keep our noses glued to the lacquer can.'

'Perhaps.'

'Think about it,' Lulla said emphatically. She scrutinised her attempts at rolling together paper and tobacco. Disgusted with the lumpy mess, she pushed the tin and papers back to Spanner. 'Roll us one, will you?'

She could not shake off her conviction that more was to come besides reduced wages. But what? Longer hours? They were long enough now at six straight days a week, with no public holidays, as well as talk of the unthinkable—no time off for Christmas and Easter. What was the world coming to? War or no war.

A stop-work meeting was out of the question. Jan was right. The women were scared shitless. But something in our own time ...

'Jan, how about—'

'Sorry. Count me out.'

'Gawd Aggie! I'm not asking you to blow up the joint.'

Lulla slumped back, taking savage drags on the cigarette that Spanner had obliged her with. In the silent room, in the silent house, the clock striking nine in the City Hall tower was clearly heard. The street had closed down for an early night.

Kirk shifted in his chair, made uneasy by the approaching squall that teased the edges of his content; this feisty brunette drinking by his side, sparring with her red-headed flatmate, seemed to have usurped the malleable sweetheart he had married. Between them they could louse up a promising night. It was clear to him that Lulla's cave-in was a temporary ploy to give her time, time to amass further arguments that would place victory in her hands and Janet's head on MacIntyre's chopping block; maybe even risk of a jail term.

Janet spoke up, determined to justify herself to Lulla. 'If there *is* going to be a partial shutdown, I want to be one of the last to go. I've no desire to can fruit salad or sew tents behind one of Missims' machines.'

Kirk's smile was easy. 'Now, girls, how about a

bit of hush.' He gave his wife's hand a pat and her cheek a peck. 'Anyway, love, I can see this turning into a lo-ong night. Right, Spanner?' He stretched lazily in the chair. 'Not a bad idea for you two girls to hit the sack. Early shift tomorrow, isn't it?'

Janet remained seated, granite-eyed, silently challenging him as Lulla attacked his unguarded flank with an elbow.

'Hey, there, sailor boy, leave me out of this. The night's just a pup.' She turned on Spanner. 'And what do you have to say about it all. Time for the cot?'

She could have meant anything, and Spanner's lips twitched.

'No comment.' He ducked, one arm upraised as if expecting a poke from Lulla's sharp elbow, and sighed in mock relief as the telephone in the hallway rang. 'Saved by the bell!'

'You'll keep, Larkin. You'll keep!'

16

A PHONE CALL IN Franklin Street was never taken for granted; even the men tensed at its strident demand. It could mean a summons back to the ship. That had happened before.

They heard the Scotts' door open and someone take a slide across the hall.

'I'll answer!' Peggy called out. Blatantly they eavesdropped to catch what was said. They heard Peggy shriek. She squealed again, followed by a gabble of ecstatic excitement. Janet and Lulla beamed at each other, grievances put aside. Julian Ludwig and *Tulsa* had to be in port. This was confirmed by Peggy hurling herself into their flat, arms semaphoring wild joy.

'He's back! Here! He's waiting at Lennons for me!'

The women bounded up to hug her: each safe

return of friend or lover was always cause for celebration. Julian was instantly forgiven for his one and only letter; who could deny Peggy her rapturous relief?

'Get those 'jamas off and get prettied up. Quickly!' Lulla ordered, pushing her towards the wide-open door.

'And yell, if there's anything you need,' said Janet.

But Peggy held back and shot a worried look across the space between the two flats.

'I dunno. You see, Mum's not home yet. It's her euchre night at Andy's place.'

'So what?' Lulla knew exactly what she meant, and as she spoke, Eveleen Scott sauntered into view. It was a marvel, Lulla noted sourly, how Evie, in boy's pyjamas matching Peggy's stripe for stripe, could manage to look as seductive as a houri belly dancer. It wasn't fair! The younger sister placed an arm loosely across Peggy's shoulder.

'Why not tell them, Sis, what the problem is.' There was little pleasure in watching her smile, and already the joy had disappeared from Peggy's face. 'Tell them I'm the problem—go on ...' Now she invited them all to pass judgement. 'She doesn't trust me.'

'Of course I do, you silly goat.'

Eveleen's full gaze was on Lulla. 'You tell her, Lulla. I can be trusted, can't I?'

Trusted to foul things up. An instant flashback of Evie sprawling over bruised poinsettias. It was beyond Lulla's understanding why the girl should rekindle the memory. She assessed Kirk—nothing there, except mild amusement; Spanner looked intrigued, and Janet distinctly hostile. Evie was now easing her way into the room.

'H'mm ... the Navy's back in town. 'Lo, Spanner. And *hello* 'Kirk. Long time no see.' The air crackled when Evie was around. 'Don't worry, Sis. Plenty to keep an eye on me here.' Her own sea-green eyes fixed steadily on the men; one could drown in them.

Peggy moved quickly, placing herself between the girl and the sailors. 'You can't butt in like this,' she whispered.

'Not for you to say.'

'Better do what big sister tells you,' Kirk drawled.

Darts of hatred glanced off Kirk's indifference. Evie, spiteful and spitting, backed off. 'That's right. Push me out. But keep an eye on me anyway. Pigs! That's what you all are. Pigs!' She ran back to the Scotts' flat.

There was a droop to Peggy's shoulders. 'Don't know what's wrong with her. Been funny all the week, and it's not funny ha-ha. She seems to hate me.' She sighed.

Lulla patted the girl's cheek. It was almost a motherly gesture. 'We all know Evie. Now don't let it spoil everything. We'll keep watch over her, promise.'

'Well, Mum shouldn't be that long. Sure it's okay?'

'Scoot!' And Peggy was already gone.

A bowl of olives and one of salted peanuts had

replaced the prawn shells and vinegar, with Janet in the kitchen making tea. Spanner pulled out Lulla's chair and pointed to a freshly opened bottle. 'Fill 'er up, Princess?' She noticed there was lemonade in Janet's glass. Had Kirk put his foot down after all?

Lemonade. She could not help the rush of quick resentment. A nice drink for a nice woman who does woman's work for woman's wages. A good girl. Pat your hand; or maybe your bum. Depending on the mood. She felt Spanner give her arm a gentle nudge with the cold bottle. 'Had enough?'

'Like fun, I have ...' She belched, tasting prawns and sour beer.

Kirk remarked that he had never seen Peggy so lit up. 'Saturday night at Luna Park.' Half in jest he offered a toast. 'Here's to young Scottie. And the Yank too, I suppose. May he—' Kirk stopped himself, laughing. 'No, we won't go into that. We know what sailors are. As for Yankee ones, well—'

Janet, returning from the kitchen, slapped a honey roll down before them. 'Yank or Aussie,' she shot back, 'what's the difference? Sexy-Rexys, the lot of you, given half the chance. But if I know Peggy Scott, she won't give any man a chance. Including Julian Ludwig!'

The contours of Julian's hand were stamped forever on her mind. Peggy locked her fingers into his, musing over a ridged scar that ran down the side of his palm almost to his wrist. A war wound? She didn't like to ask, but was certain that it had not been there before. She longed to press her lips against it, wishing that the crowded, jesting lounge would melt away; including the four who shared their alcove.

Julian squeezed back hard, his heavy graduation ring hurting. She willed the hurt to stay, like the feel of his kisses impressed on her lips. The shape of his kisses still tingled.

Gently, Julian released his grip and she panicked that her hand was too hot. Too damp. But he had only freed himself to run light fingers down her arm.

She wanted to stretch like a cat would, in warm sun. How could such a caress—the same that her mother had made a thousand times to soothe away headaches or a fever—set her heart pounding so? How could a heart swell with such tumultuous joy, yet keen in sorrow, knowing that each minute led to inevitable parting? A parting overshadowed by death. She had seen the death of a torpedoed ship in a film: the flame-stippled sea; men blackened by oil and terrible burns; the screams for help. That scene had haunted her for days. But not Julian—please God, not Julian ....

It was sweet anguish just to look at him.

Julian took her hand again, kissing the cupped palm. She shifted as much as possible away from him. 'Don't,' she whispered.

Julian moved along with her, murmuring. 'It's your lips I want to taste, Peggy girl. Right now.'

'Well'—hoping that no one heard him—'you're not tasting them here.'

'Where then? When?'

'I don't know, but not here. *Don't!*'

'Is that a dare?' She knew he was teasing, so was surprised when suddenly he shot to his feet and saluted; as did every other uniform in the room. Peggy followed the stares of the women focused on the entrance to the red lounge, and learnt the true meaning of Top Brass. But for one, the group standing there was rigid with braid, gold and protocol. Easy to tell that the respect and awe felt throughout the room was directed to the simply dressed man who led them.

Gold and braid were sidestepped by the casual open-necked shirt, and his cap, but for the U.S. Army badge, was modestly adorned. He returned the collective homage with a half-salute while his gaze swept over the hushed lounge as if searching for a face. Not finding it there, he motioned the men to be seated, then turned and made for the lifts, his entourage clustered to him.

Julian relaxed. Although seated as close to her as before, Peggy sensed with relief that the idea of public affection had been dropped.

'Who was that?' she asked.

He looked astonished. 'C'mon, honey. You have to be kidding.'

'Why should I be?'

'That's *him*. The big man himself. The General.'

'Which General?' Now she was teasing. But her pretended ignorance must have verged on insult by the expression on Julian's face. 'Just joking,' she said lightly, and could not resist a further dig. 'Yes, we know all about him.' She recalled factory talk. 'He just popped up from nowhere and soon took over the whole show.' She nodded wisely. 'Oh, yes—we know about the General all right.'

It was easy to tell that Julian had never thought of it that way, and she couldn't help feeling a little smug about it. The people next to them were leaving. Peggy looked at her watch. 'It's late, I'd better go too.'

Before she could make a move, Julian drew her to him. 'Don't go away, sweet Peg.' He cupped her face in his hand. 'And don't look so sad.' He would have kissed her then, but she drew back.

'I said not here.'

'Where? Where would you like to go?'

There was not a clear thought in her head. The night had begun like so many others, with early to bed the only prospect and Evie whinging that life was a bore. But from that heart-stopping moment when she'd heard his voice on the telephone, emotions had spun from one wild sensation to the next, leaving her breathless and utterly confused.

She didn't know where she wanted to go. Too late for the pictures. There was dancing upstairs, but she wasn't confident enough to go there with him; although Lulla insisted that apart from cutting the rug, a bumble-footed Betsy could follow any Yank's lead. 'A bit of dipping and diving, and they think they're making like Gene Kelly,' she'd said.

Peggy's voice now held the hint of a tremor. 'What would you like to do?'

'You can't guess?' Julian leaned back, assessing

her reaction, wondering what it would be if he mentioned the vacant room above them. The Colonel's lady and Judy O'Grady ... no, not Peggy. He held her trust and innocence in his hands. How far could he go? His loins told him to find out. He had dreamed of her strong, firm thighs strained against him; of smothering in the rich, heavy slide of her hair. Such a long time since his needs had pulsed so relentlessly and persistently, and even longer since he had reluctantly tried to ignore them. Peggy was unique among all the women he had met; she asked for nothing, and was content with an ice-cream in the park if he suggested it. He should not have lied to her over the letters, or lack of them. ('I wrote, honey, but you know how it is ...' Who was to check that he spoke the truth?) She need never know that he had decided against seeing her again. But the memory of her face had bewitched him into writing that one letter. One, that he regretted from the moment it had been posted. She need never know that *Tulsa* had been tied up in Brisbane for more than forty-eight hours.

A man could stand so much; even heavy petting was enough to make Peggy's eyes desperate, and her hands busy pushing him away. He had to get what he could get out of life before it was all too late; and there were plenty ready to give it. Smart, attractive women who knew how to take care of things. He would bet a million dollars that this grey-eyed girl, so eager to please, had never seen a rubber, let alone have one on stand-by in her pocket-book.

'Oh, Peggy girl. Only a few hours left.' He realised that he had said the words aloud.

'You're leaving tonight?'

''Fraid so.'

'But you've only just—'

'Special orders, sweetheart.'

Her face was tragic. 'Oh, Julian.' The break in her voice was hard to bear.

He made up his mind to ask her. Why not find out now? 'Look, sweetheart—' He paused, fearful that she might run away. But his tongue rambled on again, awkward, ungraceful as the youngest powder monkey above decks. 'There's a room—a private suite on the next level. A friend of mine works here, he's—'

'For Lennon's?'

'No—a Navy man. He's attached to headquarters and out of town at the moment. Do you understand?'

'I—I think so ...'

'It's ours for a while, if you want.' Before she could object he placed a finger on her lips. 'It's our one and only chance. To be alone. Really alone. There's always people, too many people. We've never been together, just we two.'

'I know, but—'

'Sh-h, my darling. Just for a little while. I swear ...' He stopped there, realizing that he was not prepared to swear anything.

Peggy was sadly, slowly, shaking her head. 'You know I can't, Julian.'

'Please.'

'It's not right. And I ...' Her voice trailed away. She felt as if they shared the same breath and there was not enough to spare. To be alone: to be quiet with him, free from the clamour of the red lounge, where the frenetic waiters, the laughter gusting from a nearby table ill-matched her despair: the notion churned and tugged at her, leaching away caution. She couldn't be sure if he loved her. He called her sweetheart, but did that count for anything? And did she love him? She felt an aching need to take his dear face and hold it close, as she had done with his letter.

Could that be love? His touch was a glory flowing through her. That she might never see him again was torment. Imagination fed the fears she concealed. The last time, perhaps.

The last chance ...

'All right, Julian,' she murmured, 'that's if no one minds we go there.'

'So who's to know?'

He guided her between the tables towards the lifts ....

The apartment was a disappointment—even if, she conceded, it did own a bathroom. It was nothing like the plush opulence of the floor below. A couch against one wall, a single bed opposite, and the other wall boasted a fireplace of simulated burning logs.

Reminiscent of her mother's boarding-house days, the room smelt of male; of shoe polish and shaving cream; stale underpants and stale dreams. Only the distinct spice-sweetness of the after-shave that all

Americans seemed to use made it any different.

Julian was the first to speak. 'Not your typical bridal suite,' he said ruefully, stepping aside for her to pass.

Commonsense urged her to leave. She brushed by the bed with averted eyes and plumped down on the sofa flatulent with ancient tobacco fumes.

Julian closed the door, hesitated, then locked it, half-apologising over his shoulder. 'Better this way, honey.'

She was incapable of speech and watched stiff-backed while he crossed to a dressing-table which held a collection of bottles and a few glasses. He held up a half-empty bottle to the light, unscrewed the cap and sniffed.

'The real stuff. Henry does himself proud.' He looked down at her. 'Bourbon?'

'No thanks. Yes! All right. I'm game if you are.' In for a penny in for a pound, she told herself, and felt shock to see that his hand trembled so. He rested the neck of the bottle against the edge of the glass to steady his pour. The discovery eased the mad chattering of her heart; and when he asked if she would prefer Coke, she found herself saying quite calmly that bourbon with a splash would do just fine.

Solemnly, half in jest, they toasted each other. The liquor trickling and spreading warm inside her was pleasant, and she swallowed a bolder mouthful. Side by side they drank in silence, until Julian, suddenly impatient, gulped down the rest of his drink, took Peggy's from her and placed both glasses on the floor.

'Later, sweetheart, later.'

Not giving her a chance to speak or object, he held her fast, nuzzling her neck, kissing her lips, her cheeks, the softness where her blouse had come apart; her mouth again, with a questing tongue.

'Not here, Peg, not here,' he urged, his lips whispering over her face. 'The bed—quickly!'

Already his hands were testing, demanding that she open to him, easing her up from the couch. Still holding her tightly, he half-carried her to the bed. A few paces only to get them there, but time enough for a wry *we're not dancin'* to flash across her numbed brain—and her sense of the ridiculous was restored as they lurched clumsily across the floor.

She caught back her breath, and some self-control.

But lost it again as Julian gently, persistently, eased her down, his body rhythmic as he moved against the exploding mass of her. So easy to follow him, to help with buttons and clips; to arch; to hold; to grip. Then, through the silent rush of pounding blood, a pinprick of cold reason. A diamond-hard brilliance that warned: too far, Peggy. *You're going too far!* Is this what it's like? Yes! Julian, I love you. Love you. But don't. I can't stop you—don't want to. It's so lovely. But Evie! Remember Evie—don't be like her—Mum worries—she trusts you—please, please, my love. No more! No more!

It took a powerful heave for Peggy to push him away. She struggled up from the bed, distraught. 'I can't!' Silently beseeching him to understand.

He did not move or look at her. He stayed facedown on the untidy bed.

As she pressed down her skirt with shaking hands, she could not believe what those hands had done. What instincts dredged up from where, to know how to touch him, guide him, to the brink of utter madness. She was no better than the women in Nott Street.

Was that love?

She remembered the bathroom and made it her refuge. The mirror above the washbasin told her that nothing had changed. She was a bit of a mess, but miraculously she still looked the same. No one would ever know.

Her hair needed combing, but there was only a jar of Brilliantine on the bathroom shelf. Comb and lipstick were in her purse on the sofa. Money, too.

Reluctantly, she tiptoed back to the room. Julian, still on the bed, faced the wall and gave no sign of hearing her. His aloneness stirred all the tenderness that lay just beneath the surface of willpower; there came a soft yearning to gentle him in her arms.

'I do love you, Julian. I know that now,' she whispered. 'Forgive me, my darling.' Without waiting to see if there was any response, she picked up her handbag and quietly unlocked the door, letting herself out.

Muted echoes from the ballroom accompanied Peggy along the deserted corridor. There came the sound of laughter, and voices singing. Vases of gladioli, standing stiff, bore witness to her pain; each step away from him a small victory. As she reached the stairway, the orchestra struck up the signature tune, its closing number for the night. Tendrils of the fading melody followed her. The dancing was over: a saxophone played, sweet and clear, the last notes of *Goodnight Sweetheart*.

17

*L*ULLA'S BLITZKRIEG OVER reduced wages presented the change room with a repast of delicious speculation. Every action, every word she had uttered was clucked over and pecked at until the bare bones of contention were all that remained. There were those who said it was a disgrace; especially in wartime. Others dismissed it as a 'bit of a giggle', and an uneasy few admitted to themselves that Lulla could be right. The easy cordiality between the annexe and the machine shop was marred by incipient distrust and timid prudence.

'What's wrong with a deputation, for crying out loud?' Lulla searched the ring of faces for some support. 'It's just a matter of sticking together. I'm telling you'—she thumped her chest—'I feel it here. There's more to come.'

'Like what?' This from one of the machinists.

'How do I know! Longer hours. Transfers. Take your pick!'

'And there's your trouble, lass,' Andy struck out. 'You can only guess.'

'Hear, hear!' Brave words from the new girl. She fidgeted with her sandwich, tucking errant lettuce leaves into place, before taking careful bites. 'Don't count me in.'

Lulla turned to Janet. 'Changed your mind?'

'Well, Kirk says—'

'Bugger Kirk!' Lulla railed. 'One night with him and you're soft as putty.'

Janet, not to be put off, continued: 'Kirk says you don't rock the bloody boat when it's sprung a leak. And I'm inclined to go along with that.'

Peggy remained silent. All morning she had cautiously picked her way between the verbal hazards that had littered the annexe.

'So I go it alone?' Lulla challenged the room. *They'd pee themselves if they got caught in a storm*, she thought, and seethed inwardly as a dumpling in overalls accused her of tainting the factory with 'commie talk'.

'You should be arrested,' she puffed.

'And you can kiss my bum!'

The siren snuffed out the dumpling's outrage. Andy, relieved, tightened overall buckles and said it was back to the benches, quick smart and lively.

Grateful to escape the sedition of Lulla Riddel's logic, the machinists hustled off. Distressed with communal guilt, the annexe followed slowly, deserting their mutinous workmate still seated at the trestle-table. Peggy motioned that she wanted to stay behind, taking Andy's helpless shrug as a sign of consent.

Unaware that Peggy lingered by the door, Lulla sat in lonely silence, overwhelmed by a hopeless situation that made MacIntyre's factory her prison and Manpower its warden. She mocked herself for a fool. How could one ex-barmaid with schooling enough to fit on a twopenny stamp alter the scheme of things? She wanted badly to cry; fat tears, big enough to rinse the bitterness away. But her eyes burned, anger-dry. There was nothing to do but knuckle down like the rest of them and accept whatever Mac's thought fit to offer.

'Lulla,' someone called softly. With flooding gratitude she realised that Peggy had stayed behind. 'Coming, Lulla?' The girl sounded almost timid.

'Nope. Just snatching a bit of time to think things out.'

Peggy straddled a nearby chair, making it clear that she'd not quit the change room without Lulla. 'You're asking for trouble, y'know.'

'Who bloody cares.'

'I do. We all do.'

'Great way of showing it.'

'Would Andy have given me the nod to stay with you if no one cared? Come on, Lulla, let's get back. We're miles behind. We *need* you.'

'Big joke!' A dry sort of chuckle which ended in a sigh gave notice that Lulla had given in. She began brushing crumbs off the table and wrapped up what remained of her lunch. 'I don't know—you and the rest of them—none of you can see beyond the next fart!' She rose to her feet, ready to leave, and was puzzled to see that Peggy showed no intentions of making a move. There was a sudden and definite change in the girl's mood.

'I want to ask you something,' she said gravely, 'I've been wanting to all morning.'

'What's the matter, love?' Lulla was immediately solicitous. 'Didn't things work out with you and Julian last night?'

'No, not that. Well, yes ... but it's—' Peggy kept her head down, picking and peeling back flakes of shellac that enamelled her nails.

'Come on, spit it out,' Lulla gentled her, convinced the problem must be Julian; and wasn't she the expert in matters of the heart? Like hell, she thought wryly. Snogging the night away with Spanner Larkin practically cancelled any good advice she could pass on to Peggy. Never mind, she'd do her best; she waited until the girl sorted out her thoughts.

As if to dive headlong into deep and untried waters, Peggy took a huge breath. 'Did you see Evie after I left last night?'

The question was so direct, so unexpected, that all Lulla's homilies held in readiness collapsed in confusion.

'Evie? Why, no. I—no! I didn't. Why?'

'You said you would. You said you'd keep an eye on her. You promised.'

Evie Scott had been the last thing on Lulla's mind after the party had broken up. And she was willing to bet that it had been the last thing on Janet's mind when Kirk had bundled her off to bed. Neither of them had given the brat a second thought. Regret was a dozen little knives nicking viciously at her conscience. She tried to sound convincing. 'She was asleep. Out to it when we—when I went to bed.'

'How do you know?'

'The flat was dead quiet. In darkness—and by that time Hilda must have been home anyway.'

'Mum missed the last tram,' Peggy said quietly. 'She stayed with Andy.'

'Oh, Gawd.' The little knives gouged deeper. Hurting. 'Peg, I'm sorry.'

'Bit late now, isn't it?'

'Is it?'

'Evie sneaked out. Well, I think she did.'

There was nothing, she told Lulla, she could put her finger on; nothing to go on, except for traces of powder and rouge caking Evie's hairline: although Evie, in Hilda's absence, often dipped into Hilda's things. No, it was more than that. It was the hint of derision in her sister's smile, her aura of excitement that had touched on secrets and illicit games.

For once, numbed by her own pain and feelings of guilt, she had not probed, but had slipped into the double bed they shared with Hilda, and pretended sleep.

Right up to this moment she had resented the fact that Janet and Lulla had not kept their word. Now, thinking it over, she was ready to take full blame for Evie's escapade—if one existed. Her friends were not her sister's keepers.

Then there was Julian. How she longed to question Lulla on her thoughts about men. Men like Julian. If you loved them above all else, how far could you go before they thought you cheap—too easy? Or had she let him down?

Would she ever see him again? 'Work things out for yourself, Peggy Scott. Everyone else has to,' she told herself, aware of Lulla's probing gaze.

It seemed to Lulla that Peggy's drive and sense of duty had lost ground to personal problems. By the look of it, she intended spending the rest of the afternoon glued solid to the chair. 'Who's snatching time now?' she teased; and was rewarded with the touch of a smile.

'We've let you down over the wage cut, Lulla. Especially me. We all should've—'

'Rats!' Huge relief that neglect of Evie was so easily forgiven. 'Up now, Peg, back to the salt mines!'

More with bravado than defiance, they sauntered across the factory grounds impaled by office disapproval. Management had its spies and Mrs Daniels stood in full view by the office door, frowning. She called out, but they pretended not to hear, a simple enough ploy, engulfed as they were by the screeching and banging coming from the factory floor.

'How do they stand it,' Lulla protested.

'Easy. At nine quid a week and overtime.'

'Don't remind me.'

Production was running high; crates of freshly

turned and moulded metal were stacked high at the far end of the breezeway. They caught sight of Daryl Missim busy with the hose. He waved them over.

'Thought he'd gone finish,' murmured Lulla. She had pictured him nattily suited, sporting that solitaire on his little finger. Daryl in his element, jossing and lording it over the girls at Missims' clothing factory. He waved to them again.

'He seems real upset,' said Peggy. 'Come to think of it, haven't seen him lately. Usually hangs around like a bad smell. Better see what he wants.'

It was Lulla's arm Daryl grabbed. 'We've got to talk.' At close quarters he looked seedy. There was a greenish tinge around his lips, and his forehead was greasy with the sheen of ill-health.

Lulla was shocked. 'You look terrible. What's wrong?'

'A touch of fever. Kept me in bed for a while. Nothing to worry about.'

'You could have fooled me ...'

Daryl turned to Peggy. 'Look, Peg, I've got to talk to Lulla. Mind leaving?'

'Ta, very much. But me and Lulla are late as it is. And Mrs Daniels is on to us.' Peggy made it clear that Daryl was holding up the war effort. 'C'mon, Lulla.'

Lulla shook her head. She sensed that something more than fever had sapped Daryl of his bounce and cheek. No need for a crystal ball to warn her that bad news was on the way. 'You go on, love. Tell Andy I won't be long.'

Peggy included them both in her scowl; thrusting

hands into overall pockets, she trudged off without another word.

Daryl waited until she was out of earshot. 'We're in trouble, Lulla.'

'What do you mean, *we*?'

Without answering he eased her further and deeper into a labyrinth of boxed grenades. She shivered, for it was wet underfoot, and complained that the place was as cheerful as a butcher's slab. 'What's this about *we*?' she wanted to know.

'I should have told you long ago. Before I took to the cot. But I didn't think they'd follow it up. Now, I'm not so sure.'

'What the hell are you talking about, Daryl? Hurry up, I'm freezing.'

'Ever heard of Harris and Doyle?'

'Sounds like a vaudeville act. No, I haven't.'

'They're the police, sod 'em—and nasty.'

Her heart lurched. 'What's that got to do with me?' Stupid question. A wardrobe of cocktail dresses and evening gowns scudded through her mind in a technicolour swirl; and cigarettes; and Scotch. Gawd—now what?

She listened carefully as Daryl described Ingram's duplicity, leading up to his brush with the Law, and then the final fiasco of the missing parcels and the fury of the duped Harris and Doyle. In spite of Daryl's warning and fears, Lulla's lips twitched at the idea of him scrabbling in the dust and dark in search of his precious stuff. Poor love. She sympathised but could not entirely believe, like him, that they had not heard the last of the detectives.

'C'mon, Daryl, they found nothing, they got nothing. They've more to do than waste time on a sprat like you.'

Daryl ignored her deliberate jibe. 'I'm telling you the snouts don't give up that easy.'

'I'd like to see them try their tactics on me. Anyway, it's been a long time—'

There was no point in going on. What she meant was well understood. Daryl nodded in agreement, remembering. 'Yeah. It's been a long time. Fun times, Lulla.'

Another shiver scuttled down her spine. Cold air? Or was it a trace of real fear? Damp and dribbling wood touched her skin in the confined space and the wet concrete smelled like a prison cell. She had to leave, but there was one more thing to ask him. Was Daryl still nibbling at the edges of the black market?

'You've given the game away, haven't you?' It sounded more like an order than a question.

'It seems I must. I tell you, those two are rotten to the core. Crims the pair of them.' She refrained from pointing out the irony of his accusations. Daryl's eyes had never looked so sombre-black. 'They've got connections, Lulla, and maybe I'm honing into "something belong them". They've got pals down south, y'know.'

'Hey, there!' She punched him lightly on the arm. 'You've been reading too many Dick Tracy comics.

And look, I'd better go. Thanks for the warning.' With her eyes half-closed she studied him. 'Like I said, you look shocking. This cops-and-robbers stuff is getting you down. And it just might be catching. You'd better keep your distance for a while, Missim.'

She began to leave, then with a change of heart and mind she stopped and turned, hands on hips. 'Bugger the lot of them, Daryl. Look here. Are you up to a night at the Greek Club?'

A spark of the old devilment flickered for a moment in Daryl's eyes. 'I'm feeling better already.'

She nodded approval. 'Good!' Clicking her fingers, arms outstretched: 'Oom-pah! Bring out the ouzo, Missim, and have all the Doyles, the Harrises, the Daniels and the Mac's do their damnedest. You can't keep a good pair down.'

She gave him a swift kiss on the lips, and hurried on to the annexe.

'So ye finally made it.' Andy jabbed at the air with her paintbrush. 'Tha'll be a guid hour's deduction off your pay, lass. After all that fuss, now you're lettin' down your own workmates, Lulla Riddel. Mebbe you don't care.'

Janet pulled a face behind Andy's back. The rest of the annexe kept their heads down and missed Lulla's grin.

'I'll make up for lost time, old dear. Just watch me.'

An empty trolley stood by the entrance to the

drying room, and she began loading up, working fast. When it was full she hurtled it down the aisles to where Micky, balanced on a platform, was building city blocks and canyons with the help of a newly installed hoist-and-pulley system.

'How's it going, Mick? Easier than the old extension ladders, eh?'

'Yeath, Lulla.' Sweat and dried mucus caked his upper lip as he willingly heaved and pushed, tireless in his enthusiasm to do the job well.

Lulla squinted upwards to gauge his efforts. 'Not too high, are they?'

'Nah. Daryl does. Not me.' He jumped off the platform, ready to assist with unloading her trolley.

With the little man working hard beside her, she realised that she felt relaxed, and surprisingly cheerful in spite of disagreements with the office and Daryl's fears. Could the prospect of a night out with him be so important? Or was it the night she'd spent with Spanner Larkin? There had been little time since daylight to give it much thought. Now she relished the thrill in remembering those few, good, satisfying hours. Not bad—and Mrs Kel, due in a day or two, made the timing right!

Micky stood back making a noise of brushing his hands. 'All done, Lulla.'

'And more where they've come from.' A thought struck her. 'Hey! We haven't heard the mouth organ lately.'

His eyes blinked up at her. They were inflamed and sore-looking. 'You don't danth no more, either.

You and Peggy.' He sounded so wistful that she made up her mind they would spend the next lunchbreak with him. Together they wheeled the trolley back to the lacquer room.

'As a matter of fact, young Mick, I'm dancing tonight.'

'Where, Lulla, where?' He sounded pleased for her.

'Back to the old Greek Club.'

Peggy, hunched over her quota of hand bombs, could not resist a vehement snort. She slammed the last grenade into place and humped the completed tray to the trolley.

'I thought Daryl was scratched off your list,' she accused, making a business of straightening the bombs in the tray.

'You could call this the last fling, ducks.' Lulla's eyes discouraged argument.

But Peggy pressed on. 'He's a piker. Everyone knows that.'

'Careful, Peg.'

'And I don't know what you see in him, anyway.' At the sullen sulk in her voice, Lulla's lips tightened. She pinned the girl down with a gaze as direct and level as Peggy's own. 'Now that's enough!' The annexe paused and stretched to listen. 'I'll tell you what I see in him. For starters, he's kind, and generous. And above all else, he's good for a laugh. And there's little enough of that around here!'

In spite of her brave words, Lulla knew that Peggy was right. Daryl was bad news—especially now. But no one would dictate to her how she should spend her time: and tonight she and Daryl Missim would be seen at the Greek Club. Come hell or high water. And let the rest of the world go hang!

18

$\mathcal{F}$RANKLIN STREET SLEPT. A distant cat yowled midnight. It yowled again, and found its echo in the feline pair beneath the Scotts' window. They spat their hatred at each other and howled in an orgasm of murderous intent.

Lulla groped for the blanket and snuggled into Janet's back, drowsily pleased that Kirk was at sea. The back room was cold and they were short on bed-nap. Her feet searched out the hot-water bottle; finding it nearly cool, she debated the worth of leaving a snug bed to boil up the kettle ...

She dozed while the cats muttered spite and curses, and Janet popped air in gentle snoring. Not like Janet to sleep so easily with Kirk on his way north. How far north, by now? How far to Thursday Island? T.I., Spanner calls it ... dry and brown most of the time, he says. Palms, and wongai trees. Eat wongai plums and you return. Wongais patching sand deep purple. He can be poetic sometimes, Spanner. Green seas, turquoise like Evie's eyes. Do she and Kirk ... No! He's bossy though, what man isn't? 'Time for bed, old girl.' Didn't like talk about strikes—and now they were one girl short and the quotas had gone up. Sod 'em, as Daryl says. Are the cops ...? Even at the Greek Club that night ....

She drifted between dreams. Forget about the hot-water bottle and the vague need for a pee. She'd hold on 'til morning ....

Another squall shredded the night. Lulla, wide-awake, sprang out of bed. 'That's it! Cold water for you lot!'

Toes curling on the icy congoleum of the kitchen, she scrabbled in a cupboard for a saucepan. But the Scotts beat her to it. She heard the splash, the alarm outside, and reached the window in time to see two cats, silent now, tails stiff in shock, speeding across the grass.

The lawn lay flat and bare beneath moonlight, silvered by heavy dew. From across the hall she heard Peggy laugh and Hilda scold. Their window slammed shut. The night so still, and in its quiet she felt the need for company.

'You awake, Jan?' she called out hopefully. No sound from the bedroom. Would Hilda and Peggy drink cocoa with her? But she dropped the idea, picturing Hilda's face on being dragged from a warm bed for a second time. Two a.m. by the kitchen clock, and any thought of sleep had vanished with the cats.

She poured milk into the saucepan and while it heated, took pad and pen from the kitchen drawer. Spanner had asked her to keep in touch. He had shown real interest in her clash with MacIntyre's; more than anyone else, he had understood her anger.

'I'm out on a limb,' she wrote. 'Only the Miscellaneous Workers Union will take me on, and no hope at the present of getting the others in the annexe to follow suit. Equal work for equal pay—what a joke, Spanner. They say we're not as good as men. Ha! Ha! It's a lot of bull.' Lulla's pen dug troughs in the paper, emphasising her disgust. Modesty prevented her from saying that menstruation was an accepted reason by employers for women's inferiority in the workplace. She did mention that Daryl, who worked beside them, received factory floor wages, 'and poor little Micky who works like a demon, gets even less than we do. The whole thing stinks!' She didn't add that she and Daryl had been to the Greek Club. She and Spanner were good mates, she reasoned, but there was no point in laying all your cards on the one table.

The smell of burning caramel caught her attention. The milk!

She flew to the stove, snatching up a tea-towel on the way. The sound of footsteps on the garden path made her pause. She put the puddle at her feet on hold. There were two of them. Men, by the heavy tread, making no effort to quieten their noise. Her heart leapt at the three solid raps on the door. Their door! Not Spanner. Not Kirk. Kirk never knocked.

News of death—or lost in action? Surely that could wait until business hours ....

By the time her hand was on the latch, Lulla had convinced herself that it must be—had to be—one of her friendly boys with a mate; half-drunk, flat-broke, in search of a spare bed.

At this hour?

She was ready to crack their thick heads together, and send them off to camp or ship when she opened the door.

'Well?' What else she had to say stuck fast in her throat.

She recognised them at once. Daryl had described them well. Detectives Harris and Doyle. Careful now, she cautioned herself, just a friendly visit.

'Lulla Riddel?' They knew her, all right.

'It is.'

'Police here. We want to ask a few questions.'

Her stomach curdled. She allowed herself to register cool enquiry. A gusting westerly flicked her ankles, and she pulled her dressing-gown more tightly around her, pleased that it was new, and that the scarf protecting her pincurls was freshly laundered and banner bright.

They were a tough-looking pair, as Daryl had said.

She decided to take them full on. 'You have something to ask me?' Eyebrows raised. Mrs Ritch-Bitch couldn't have done it better.

Harris remained unimpressed. 'It's about the factory. MacIntyre's. There's been a break-in.'

Lulla's relief was immense. She could have laughed

aloud. 'Anything taken?' Cool as you like.

'The strongbox. They were lucky.' The eyes probed deeply. 'Payday tomorrow. But of course you know that.'

A thought slammed through her. Daryl! But no. Robbing banks, let alone MacIntyre's, wasn't Daryl's long suit. She waited for what else they had to say.

'Just routine.' Wasn't that the usual approach?

Harris scratched and stroked his jawline, staring over her shoulder into the flat as if searching for clues. She half-closed the door, reluctant to stand alone with them in the hallway.

'Have you noticed strangers hanging around the factory? On your way to work? Coming home?' Harris asked.

'The streets are full of strangers.' She realised that no identification had been shown her. Be polite, she warned herself, but ask about it. 'As a matter of fact, Officer, how do I know you yourselves are the police?' Eyes round with innocence, she permitted herself a mere tilt of the lips. 'Haven't you a badge or something to show people?'

It was a reasonable request, but Harris narrowed his gaze, and instead of answering gave Doyle the nod to continue questioning. 'Americans,' Doyle said casually, ignoring her question, 'notice any hanging around?'

'No more than usual. Why?'

'One of their trucks has been seen parked near the works. More than once.'

'For goodness sake! Their hospital's not that far

away.' She couldn't help herself. 'Haven't you heard of Somerville House? They're crawling all over it.'

'But you know someone with a truck, don't you? An American Army truck. Right?'

'No! Why should I?'

'You've seen the safe, though. Haven't you?'

'The office safe.' Harris cut in.

'We've all seen it!' *What were they getting at?*

'But you more than others.'

'C'mon, Lulla,' Doyle carried on, 'you're a smart girl.'

Was this the way they interviewed people? God help you, if you were guilty! The tone of their voices; their questions spiked with innuendo nourished a growing anger hard to disguise. Already the Hickeys were taking in every word. From the dress-circle of the top landing, they watched goggle-eyed. Even the Scotts' door had opened a shade. It seemed as if Detectives Harris and Doyle were prepared to keep the whole house up, with Janet and the Scotts still to be questioned. They *would* be questioned, wouldn't they?

'You know,' she said, 'we're all on late shift tomorrow. Couldn't you come back in the morning?'

The scar signalled white beneath Harris's eye. 'We're not finished yet, Miss Riddel.' He nodded towards the flat. 'I'd suggest we go inside.' They still hadn't bothered to identify themselves. *Over my dead body*, Lulla thought, and jumped as Janet's voice snapped over her shoulder.

'No! You certainly may not come in.'

She had been concealed behind the half-closed door, and now she stood close to Lulla, determined to have her way.

'What do you mean by disturbing the household at such an hour. Frightening women out of their wits. Women unprotected by their menfolk.' Indignant as a bantam defending her one and only chick. 'When my husband's commanding officer hears of this, you'll have His Majesty's Navy to contend with. Be sure of that!'

Lulla could have hugged her.

Janet crossed her arms, wedding ring on full show. Deliberately? The thought crossed Lulla's mind. A wedding band carried a lot of weight. Earned respect. Harris noticed it. He even made a token gesture of tugging the brim of his hat. It hurt a little to see them listen to Janet when her own words had been ignored. As if on cue, both men dug into their vest pockets and produced badges of office.

That stung!

Lulla heard Harris apologise for the late intrusion; make excuses that they had to move fast, before the culprits disappeared and the safe and contents were forever lost. He signalled to Doyle that they should go 'and not upset the ladies', and that tomorrow would do for further enquiries.

As their footsteps faded down the street, Lulla thankfully closed the door. With her back pressed hard against cold timber, she gradually subsided to the floor. 'Phew! What was that really all about? And why only me?'

'What?' Janet, puzzled, squatted down beside her.

'Only me they got stuck into. Or didn't you notice?'

'But you were the one unlucky enough to open the door. And this *is* flat Number One,' Janet reasoned.

'I'm telling you, they singled me out.'

'Rubbish. You're a chump, Lulla Riddel, with an imagination to match. They finally realised that they'd get little sense from any of us at this ungodly hour.'

'You don't understand. Not after what Daryl told me the other day. I didn't pass it on ...' She gave a helpless shrug. 'You may as well know all about it.'

'All about what?'

Janet listened intently while Lulla described the fiasco at the Manpower office, the rage of Harris and Doyle, and Daryl's fears. Nothing was left out.

'All a bit too coincidental, I'd say.' Lulla was showing concern.

'Because MacIntyre's was broken into? What's that got to do with the price of eggs? You're as bad as Daryl.'

Another wind-blast swept along the hallway, finding its way under their door.

Janet scrambled to her feet. 'Come on, before we end up with piles.'

'It's cold all right.' Lulla managed a grin. 'Bums freezing tonight, and grilled out of our minds tomorrow. What a life!'

They agreed on a cup of cocoa, and as Janet led the way to the kitchen, her worried frown belied the assurances she had given Lulla. She missed the laughter and solid maleness of Kirk. He would have jollied their cares out of the window, and Harris and Doyle out of their lives.

She dreaded being quizzed by them. They had looked so threatening; so implacably in control. How would she be if they asked her about Daryl and his muddy little deals? About Lulla, for that matter. If only Lulla had not confided in her. Almost automatically, Janet began mopping up the boiled-over milk, miserably aware that she had never been good at telling lies, and almost wishing that Lulla Riddel had never stepped into her life.

19

THE ANNEXE COULD talk of nothing else. Overnight they became experts in deduction, crime, and punishment. A robbery! A break-in! Soon a person wouldn't be able to leave the house without locking the windows and bolting the doors. Oh, yes indeed, things had changed since the war began. They tingled with nervous anticipation at the thought of police interrogation—and could hardly wait their turn.

That the strongbox had been removed bodily was cause for awed comment; the amount it held was said to be a thousand pounds. It escalated by the hour to wilder figures that only princes dreamed about. All this was reported to the afternoon shift when they came on.

A policeman had arrived to stand outside the office door, followed later by two officers from the C.I.B. They were still poking about inside, consulting with the staff between interminable cups of tea—so the annexe said. A U.S. Army major and a corporal had been seen to join them.

It was true then, the excited whisper confirmed—the Americans were involved. Shades of Chicago gangsters! Speculation mixed with supposition was an effervescent tonic that purged the annexe of boredom, but kept production down to a dismal level.

Already Lulla and Janet had given vivid accounts of their collision with Doyle and Harris, and when Peggy reported those two were in charge of proceedings, no one was surprised.

It was the new girl who blinked in dismay. 'I'll die. Simply die when it's my turn to be asked things.' She produced a pocket mirror, adjusted her snood, and tidied the corners of her mouth. 'Simply die …'

'Isabel, ye canna' die more than once. For goodness sake g'on with your wor-rrk.' Andy strode to centre stage where everyone could see her. She rapped her clipboard with a pencil. 'Now listen, all of you. We'll be questioned by the police in their own sweet time. So what do we do? Stand around waiting, or do we get stuck into it? No use colly-wobbling.'

'It's hard to concentrate, Mrs Anderson, and my head's spinning already,' the new girl complained.

'Weel, ye don't use your head in this job, Isabel, just your hands and a wee bit of brawn.' Andy held up the clipboard. 'Just look at that tally. Disgraceful! And if ye're thinking of tea breaks, forget it. We'll work through this lot and more, till we catch up.

Now get to it!' Andy, relying heavily on the respect the team gave her, knew that she teetered with one foot over industrial quicksand. In the silence that followed she challenged Lulla's and Hilda's gaze with her own brand of steel.

Lulla was the first to give in. 'Okay, Andy, dinna' fash yersel. It's only a muckle we're behind, and we'll boost that tally sky-high before ye can sing *Annie Laurie.*'

Peggy and the new girl were the first of the annexe to be called into the office. They were back in ten minutes, chirpy and acting blasé about the supposed ordeal.

'Piece of cake,' said Peggy.

When she was asked about the Americans, and what they had to say, she reported that they had left. She brought back the impression that even the detectives had lost interest in the factory employees. 'You could see they were bored to sobs, and not getting nowhere. Wouldn't be surprised if after Mum and Andy, they shut up shop and go home.'

'What about Lulla and me?' asked Janet.

'They saw you two last night, didn't they.'

But a message came back with Andy that Harris and Doyle needed to have a word with the woman Lulla Riddel.

After the sun-bright factory yard, the office, by contrast, seemed gloomy. Mrs Daniels, looking pleased with herself, beckoned with a finger.

'Over here, Riddel. You've already met Detectives Harris and Doyle. Isn't that so?'

Lulla nodded briefly to the men. How much had they told the supervisor of their suspicions? For suspicious of her they must be. It explained the triumph in the old bat's eyes. Her stomach turned under the scrutiny of a cold and hostile enemy. Again she asked herself—why me?

Harris spoke. 'Can we use the other room, Mrs Daniels?' *Oh, very polite.* Mrs Daniels hurried to open the door for them.

'In here, Lulla.' Harris stood by the door and she managed to pass without touching him.

The inner room was a cubbyhole partitioned off from the main office by galvanised sheeting. The pay clerk, Simpson, worked there. His ledgers and lists half-filled the shelves lining the walls and a single chair and table were centred beneath the spotlight of a hundred-watt bulb. Although sunlight came through a window, the place was as bleak as a watch-house lobby. Harris closed the door and pointed out a space beside a filing cabinet.

'That's where it stood, Lulla.'

What was she expected to say? And did he call Hilda and the others by their first names when he questioned them? She doubted it.

Harris walked over to the spot, examined a fresh scar on the corrugated wall and strolled back, planting himself directly in front of her. In the silence she heard a clock ticking. The small, persistent noise was reassuring. She was alone with these two men; cut off from the office staff by factory noise and the clatter of typewriters.

'Well,' Harris said at last, 'we believe that you can help us in this business.'

'What do you mean by that?'

'I mean that you have a good idea who broke in last night?'

'No!'

Harris allowed the denial to hang between them, while Doyle circled the room, leafing through folders, opening filing cabinets and slamming them shut. He seemed morose, preoccupied, disinterested in what Harris was saying. The detective's tone now became confidential. Wheedling, almost.

'Getting your own back, eh, Lulla? We can understand that. Now tell us what happened.'

Bewildered, she took a step backward, crowded by his closeness and accusations. 'What are you talking about?'

'Don't act the innocent on us. We'll begin again. Now ... what do you know about last night.' Harris stressed each word carefully, as if she was hard of hearing.

'I—I don't know anything.'

'We say that you do!' The shouted words made her jump. 'You told them where the safe was kept!'

'I didn't know. I—'

'That's not what you said last night.'

What did she say? He thrust his face closer to hers. 'Don't lie.'

'I'm not. Please ...' how to keep the tremor from her voice. How to breathe!

Relentless, Harris carried on. 'You consort with Americans, don't you. Party with them. What else, eh? Come on, Lulla, own up.' His chuckle tripped her heart. 'I suppose you've never heard of the Snake Pit, either.'

'No. Yes!'

'Great pick-up spot, isn't it? You meet—what's his name?' Harris clicked his fingers. 'Ah yes ... Chuck something or other. You've met him there, haven't you?'

'I haven't seen him in months.'

'But you mentioned to him about the safe.'

'No!'

'And he supplied the truck.'

'No!' She screamed at him. 'No, he didn't.'

'Who did? COME ON, RIDDEL. WHY DON'T YOU ADMIT IT?'

She sobbed, losing control. Humiliated. Terrified. Now Doyle joined in, mouthing the same ugly phrases over and over again. They pounded her ears with their threats and implications. No longer did she wonder why they had singled her out from the others. It had gone beyond that. Now, mind and body focused on the one desperate denial that she was involved. Their assumption that she was guilty, made her guilty; their affirmation that she was a whore, made her a whore—no better than the lowest trollop who lay beneath the Story Bridge for shillings, nickels and dimes.

They shamed her.

But now the harassment veered off in another direction, and she caught a glimpse of what it might be all about. Why they were bullying her so? Harris had hinted of it at the very outset; she had been too dumb, too frightened to understand.

'*Getting your own back*' was what he'd said.

Doyle came at her again. 'You've been causing trouble.'

She kept quiet. Concentrating, while every nerve end quested out a hidden threat or verbal ambush that could shatter her self-esteem.

'You've been inciting the women to strike, haven't you,' said Doyle.

'You didn't like that pay cut,' said Harris. 'Thought you'd punish the boss—get your own back.'

'That's not true.'

'It was all your idea, wasn't it? WASN'T IT!'

Everything was clear now. She doubted they believed she had anything to do with the burgled safe. That was no more than an aside to keep her quiet. ('And while you're at it, Officer, frighten the be-jesus out of the Riddel girl. Nothing but trouble. Shut her up.')

Doyle was hammering at her again. 'You were narked the others weren't interested in your commie talk. You are a commie, aren't you?'

She kept her mouth shut and shook her head.

'Don't deny it,' cut in Harris. 'Illegal strikes—stirring up industrial unrest—I'd say you knew all about it.'

Industrial unrest! Her pitiful little protest. It was laughable.

Doyle removed a nail-file from a vest pocket and began cleaning his nails. 'It carries a jail sentence, you know. Not very nice ...' Slowly he shook his head, eyeing her over his fingers. 'But then for girls like you, Yankee lovers, those that deal with mongrels like Chuck and Missim, well—what else is there to say?'

'I'll have to give it to you, Lulla,' Harris cut in, 'you keep good company.'

By now, she was in control, the fear gone. She felt calm enough to say in a low, firm voice, 'I know nothing about this burglary, and you know it. I've done nothing to be ashamed of. Not here, or anywhere else. You can question me all day and all night. It won't make any difference to what I've told you already.'

She was surprised they had allowed her to have a say. Doyle smiled as he finished off his nails, tucking the file away. She loathed him more than she disliked Harris. Harris a bully; Doyle a viper.

The older detective studied her closely, his feet planted wide apart, belly thrust arrogantly forward. 'Remember this, Riddel, MacIntyre's wants no more trouble. Is that understood? You're where Manpower saw fit to put you. You belong to them. To MacIntyre's. You're theirs for the duration. Get that into your head, my girl.' The scar below his eye twitched whitely.

'We've got tabs on you, on Missim, and on that

P.X. boyfriend of yours. One word from your employers, one foot in the wrong direction, and it could be arrest and a jail sentence.' He poked air inches from her face. 'I mean that.' Then jerked a thumb towards the door. 'Now get out!'

No more mention of the safe. But what an opportunity to get at her! To keep her quiet.

She passed through the office ignoring the curious stares of the typists and gratefully stepped into the afternoon sunshine. The entire grenade team waited outside. The bush telegraph was at work and they understood what she had been put through. They escorted her back to the annexe loud with their sympathy and near-mutinous comments.

It was later, when things had settled down, that they told her of their unanimous decision. Hilda was their spokeswoman. In the future, no one, but no one, would listen ever again to Lulla's union talk. Leave well alone, they advised her. It's not all that bad working for MacIntyre's. Things could be worse.

20

'WOW! WHAT A DING.'

Lulla shoved a bottle of Coca-Cola into Peggy's hand. 'Drink up, there's more in the bathroom tub than Muckadilla got through at the Picnic Races and Show Week. Sure you wouldn't like a splash of Scotch?'

Peggy shook her head.

'Rum, then?' Lulla whistled a few bars of *Rum and Coca-Cola*, hips jiggling to the music from the radiogram. 'Glad you came?' she asked. Peggy took a few slow slips before answering.

'It's all right'—regretting in secret that she had been talked into it. Lulla could talk a brick into walking if she'd had a mind to it. Janet would have stayed home too, but Janet more than anyone needed cheering up these days.

The message tacked to the change room wall had intrigued them all:

GIRLS WANTED
PARTY TONITE!!
EVERYTHING LAID ON
SEE MADELINE AND
DO YOUR BIT FOR OUR
AMERICAN WAR HEROES

'If we stick together,' Lulla had urged, 'what's the harm? None of us have been laughing lately, and I'm ready to bust out.' When Evie set up a shrill cry to be included, they nearly didn't make it. It was Hilda who pushed them out the door. 'Leave Evie to me and go and have some fun. You could do with it for a change.'

Things had soured for Janet over the last weeks. No word from Kirk: she was convinced that her sailor husband had moved to some Pacific battle zone, and the strain was showing. As for Lulla, she was still in shock over the vicious bruising Harris and Doyle had given her, jumping at every unexpected knock at the door or ring of the telephone.

As Peggy had confided to Hilda, Flat Number One was not a happy place; the women were pecking at each other like eggbound chooks.

Although the empty strongbox had been found on a council dump and returned to its place in Simpson's office, the two detectives, on occasion, still poked about asking questions. Lulla they ignored, but their presence was enough to keep her tongue still and eyes down. The rumour that MacIntyre's might close shop had lost its credence, but the new work-to-silence rule emphasised the overall gloom and the stultifying monotony of the assembly line.

'If it wasn't for the occasional stomp and a good sweat-out at the Troc,' Lulla was heard to grumble, 'a person'd go bush and hang the consequence.'

Now the party had come as a godsend and Lulla was bouncing. 'Have you ever seen anything like it—the place, I mean? The whole damn street looks the same. Wooden palaces, every one of 'em. How the other half lives, eh?'

None of them had ever ventured beyond the Valley Baths. Clayfield was unexplored territory, and the mansion they found themselves in had Peggy doing sums on the number of boarders Hilda could have accommodated in such a place. 'All those rooms,' she said, her gaze fixed on the vaulted hand-pressed ceiling.

'Marry Julian,' advised Lulla, not taking her eyes off a large, good-looking G.I., 'then Hilda can forget about lodgers and you too could live in a joint like this; even on an Ensign's pay.' She gave Peggy a nudge. 'As for Handsome over there, I'll be dancing with him before the night is done.'

The house overflowed with Americans attached to a nearby airfield; for the duration, the house belonged to them. It seemed as if the full complement of MacIntyre's machine shop had answered the call to arms. For one carefree night, flower-garden silks had replaced the carapace of drab-worn dungarees.

'He's coming over,' Lulla sing-songed softly. 'You, or me?' Already Janet had been swooped up and was dancing on a crowded square of polished boards.

'You go,' Peggy whispered, 'I'll sit out for a while.'

As the soldier came closer, he held out his arms. 'Who'll take me?' From beneath heavy lids, onyx eyes glittered from one to the other. He wore a crew-cut, so dark and tufty that Peggy wondered if a Mexican must be like him. She longed to ask. His voice, a slow rumble, was easy on the ears. 'Wanna dance? Someone? Anyone?' Arms still outspread.

Lulla put down her Scotch. 'You're on, mate.'

'Pardon, ma'am?'

'Never mind. Let's make with the jive. Cut the rug. Let's dance!'

No sooner had they left than the music stopped; fascinated, Peggy watched the radiogram's arm and needle rise while another record fell into place. Six altogether, one after another it played; to witness such a marvel made the cross-city tram ride all worthwhile. No doubt about the Yanks, she had to admit, they were smart. It was common knowledge they could convert empty paddocks into airstrips overnight, and bush tracks into sealed highways quicker than you could turn out a batch of scones.

Beating time to the lively swing of Harry James's trumpet, her ear caught the rustle of wafer-thin paper tucked deep inside her bodice. Julian's letter—it was as if he'd touched her.

Six in a week!

It was hard to believe, when she had thought never to be near him again. Six letters: she hugged the thought close, her heart skipping and singing. Dear Julian. Not that she had seen him since that awful night at Lennon's. Not a word about it in his letters. All he talked about was his return to Brisbane and what they'd do together. He said he loved her, and that was enough.

Lulla was returning, followed closely by the American. She carried her shoes in her hand, and on reaching Peggy's chair dropped them and toed them out of sight. 'Those spikes are making scrimshaws of that lovely floor.'

'You're the only one who's caring, honey,' said the American cheerfully.

'Well, more shame on them.' She touched Peggy's head. 'You okay, love?'

'Yeah, why?'

'I want to see you up on that floor. Soon! And don't say you haven't been asked. Anyway ...' Lulla linked her arm into her partner's, pulling him forward, 'let me introduce you two.' She was grinning. Wickedly delighted. 'Peggy, meet Charlie Redwing. Yeah, that's right, Redwing. And he's a real live, honest-to-goodness Injun from the wild and woolly West.' She gave the soldier's arm a squeeze. 'You don't mind me saying that, do you?'

'Why should I, now? But not just a Redskin, honey. Add Cherokee to that.' Amiable humour framed splendid white teeth. 'And the closest I've ever come to a horse and saddle was on the merry-go-round at the country fair.' He made a half-bow to Peggy. 'Pleasure to meet you, Peggy—now that's a real pretty name. But if you'd excuse us, we have to go. The soles of my feet is gettin' real itchy!'

You had to laugh with him, and Peggy shooed them off.

The space between the rolled-back carpets was limited, and dancers spilled into an adjoining room. Lulla and Redwing followed. By its look, it could have been a library once. But now the empty shelves lining the panelled walls were littered with an accumulation of glasses and bottles, plates of peanuts and pretzels and ashtrays noisome with spent cigars and smouldering cigarettes.

Charlie Redwing pulled down his mouth, disgusted. 'Over here,' he said, and guided her through another door, into an alcove where a group of airmen squatted around a map of Queensland spread over the floor. Deep in discussion as to the whereabouts of Townsville and the Garbutt strip, they ignored the pair at first. It was Lulla's stockinged feet and legs that had them springing to attention. They set up a clamour of wolf howls and whistles, and demands for an introduction.

Redwing gripped her arm tightly and cheerfully ignored them, accepting with good grace talk of scalps and ravished conquests. He manoeuvred her through tall shutters wide-open to the breeze, onto a veranda, quiet enough to hear night crickets tick-tack across garden beds. There was a scatter of seagrass chairs, a lazyboy half-concealed by a wash of riotous allamanda, but before she could analyse the wisdom of leaving the lights and crowded rooms, the peace was ripped apart by clarinet and piano. Sound blasted from a loudspeaker wired to the record player inside, and its eight-to-the-bar beat had Redwing's fingers clicking.

'Come to Papa, baby.'

His grip was rock steady, his hand on her hip gauged her response and balance before spinning her to arm's length and coiling her back to him, slapping palm against palm. She gyrated dizzily around his stiffened, out-thrust arm. In. Out. In. Out. Legs scissoring in complicated triple-time to the frenetic crescendo of drum alone. The tempo increased. They flew: orbiting around each other oblivious to the night, the stars. No one watching. No one applauding. They danced only for themselves. Exhilaration pumped energy into extended muscles; drenched dress and shirt. He was tireless; she, rarely meeting her match, American-style, could have stomped with him to sun-up.

As suddenly as it had begun, the music stopped. They split and collapsed laughing and puffing against the veranda rail, the vacuum left by the extravaganza of Gene Krupa's sticks enough to hurt their ears. A cricket tested the silence with a cautious chirrup, another joined in and soon the darkness vibrated again to a chorus of nocturnal hallelujahs.

Charlie Redwing raked through hair as prickly as sagebrush and flicked sweat off his fingers. 'You're hep, girl. Very hep. Who taught you to move like that?'

'Just natural talent, Redwing. You don't mind me

calling you that, do you? It's too good a name to waste—and I know a dozen Charlies.'

'Go ahead. They all do, anyway.' He took cigarettes from his shirt pocket, flipped one up for her before taking his own. She could have used the hand holding out the lighter for a bread-and-butter plate.

'Anyway'—she returned his compliment—'you're pretty hep yourself. Anyone who can hurl me around like that has my undying admiration. Best fling—pardon the pun—I've had in ages.'

'You're welcome, honey, any time.'

They smoked, not speaking, sharing amusement at a couple floating by, swaying to a ghost tune, lips clinging, locked tight in a mating hold of mutual exploration. They smooched their way down the full length of the veranda and disappeared around the corner. Two more drifted past to where jacarandas kept one side of the house darkly secret. She wondered if it would give Redwing ideas. But Redwing excused himself, returning in minutes with a laden drink tray.

'What's your poison, Lulla? You Aussie girls sure have pretty names.'

She said that a Coke would be fine, and the American followed suit. They toasted each other with lifted bottles, sensing a friendship about to begin.

'What do you do, these days, Lulla? Work in an office?'

She was flattered by the assumption and wished that she could have answered, yes, or that she stood behind the counter of the exclusive and elusive Finney Isles store.

'It's munitions, Redwing. Hand grenades.' She made the war an excuse for being there. 'Just doing my bit for the boys.' Mocking herself, she blew on her fingernails and buffed them against her blouse. At least it sounded better than stitching tents. 'And what's your line of business? You a pilot? Air crew, maybe?'

He shook his head. 'Too dumb for that, honey. Nah ... I'm a driver. Staff car.'

'Oh.'

They were a pigeon pair, she thought wryly, one dumb broad and one dumb Joe. She gave him a sidelong glance. What a waste that a man such as Redwing should be nothing more than someone's chauffeur. 'You happy with that?' She couldn't help asking.

'Well ... me and the Colonel have been together for quite a while. Pago Pago. Pearl Harbour—'

'You were there?'

'Yep.'

'Must have been rough, eh?'

'You can say that again.'

She kept her thoughts to herself, recalling the relief when that distant island, Hawaii, had come under enemy attack. Charlie Redwing would hardly appreciate the collective heartskip of a nation when it realised that at long last, America would be called to do battle.

Curiosity overcame reticence: 'What was it really like, Redwing?'

'Bad, honey—we didn't know what hit us. Me and the Colonel finished up in a gun-pit made of packing cases and a heap of busted concrete, with nothing but a pistola between us and one mighty hangover a-piece. Hoo man, that was some party, and one helluva night.' He shook his head, actually smiling over a memory.

'You are talking about the bombing, aren't you? You could hardly call it a party. The pictures—'

'Nah. I'm talking about *the* party. Some buddies of mine belonged to a ship's band. Baby brother, too—he played trumpet. They'd won the base contest and were celebrating. The Colonel as well. As I said, it was some party. They were the champs, and the music was sweet ...' Intuition cautioned her to keep still, stay quiet. There was more to come. 'Y'know, honey, that was about the last thing they ever did. Got blowed up the next day. Everyone.'

'They were all killed? All of them?'

'Just about, I guess. They were the *Arizona* boys. Great bunch of kids.'

She gave his arm a sympathetic squeeze, wondering about the brother who had gone down with his ship. The feeling was strong that she was possibly the only woman—in Australia, at least—he had confided in; and wondered why.

Redwing finished off the Cola, swirling it around his mouth as if rinsing away a bitter hurt, and sprayed it into the dark.

'So be it ...' He turned to her, head on one side, eyes bright-black, inquisitive as a hunting magpie.

'Your turn, now. This factory—like it?' Half-guessing the answer, he carried on. 'We're putting on more women drivers at the motor pool. Now a smart-lookin' girl like yourself would be snapped up'—he clicked his fingers—'just like that. I could even put in a word for you. I told you the Colonel and me are buddies.'

Driving for the Yanks!

Her stomach flipped over. She had seen them around town. Classy women in smart uniforms. Women who would have driven their own cars before petrol rationing. Elation faded as quickly as it had flared. She shook her head. 'I'd give my right arm. But Manpower would never release me. Anyway, I can't drive.'

He looked surprised and told her that most of the girls he knew could handle wheels the day they stopped sucking dummies.

'Well, this is Australia, buster.'

'Sorry.' He looked contrite. 'I didn't mean it to sound like that.'

Lulla patted his arm. 'Forget it.'

A slower and quieter melody came through the loudspeaker and Redwing took her hand. 'Dance?'

She settled snugly into his arms, appreciating a sensation new to her: the protection she'd expect to find in an older brother. The irony was, that this large brown man was offering her excitement and a change of work that she, and hundreds of women like her, would never experience in a lifetime. Clean work; stylish uniforms; unbelievable wages; an entree into P.X. canteens and stores that beckoned like so many Aladdins' caves. Driving for the Yanks. Maybe he'd even have taught her to drive ... And here she was, tied hand and foot to MacIntyre's Munitions. Shit!

The tempo of the music suddenly came to life with Glenn Miller's bouncy *American Patrol*. Redwing swung her out. 'Okay, let's go!'

And go they did, fast and furious enough for the idea of smart uniforms and the classy jobs that went with them to be swept entirely from Lulla's mind. Halfway through a triple spin she heard Peggy's voice.

'Lulla!'

Peggy was standing at the door, Lulla's shoes and purse in her hands. 'It's nearly twelve! We'll miss that last tram, and I can't find Janet!' Peggy sounded desperate and Lulla called a halt.

'Sorry, Redwing. We've gotta go.'

Redwing volunteered to help find the missing Janet. Peggy was practically jumping on the spot, but Lulla refused to be concerned. 'The tram stop's only doors away, Peggy. Quieten down! Jan can't be far. Thanks all the same, Redwing. Peg's the panic merchant around here. Pounds to peanuts Jan's in the twink!'

Together, she and Peggy went back to the main room. It was crowded more than ever, but now most of the lights had been turned off and couples danced in semi-darkness. There was no sign of Janet.

'How'll we get home if we miss it?' Peggy said.

'Bum a ride, what else?'

'I'm not driving home with no Yankee stranger.'

'Gawd Aggie, you're the dizzy, Peg!'

They were now in a long hallway that led to a bathroom. Six doors, three on each side, opened into six bedrooms.

Peggy pulled back, dismayed. 'She can't be there.' Even Peggy was no innocent as to what could be going on.

'You want to find her, don't you?'

'Yes, but—'

'Well, come on! You take this side and I'll take the other.'

Lulla led off, Peggy still hesitating.

The first two rooms drew a blank. Lulla heard laughter and the sound of a glass breaking. She knocked. 'You there, Jan?'

'Get lost!' It was a woman's voice, but not Janet's. Out of the corner of her eye she saw Peggy knock, call, and, receiving no answer, open another door. She heard Peggy's gasp and the door slammed with a bang. Lulla had to grin: Peggy was learning about the seamy side of life, fast! Peg leaned against the wall, fanning herself with a hand. 'Phew!' she said, 'It's a rough time in the old town tonight!' Lulla wondered where the saying came from. Not like Peg at all.

There was a cosy foursome in the next room. Lulla couldn't resist a cheeky 'Time's up! Changey, changey!' and a chuckle. Then she opened the last door in the hallway. Peggy's face was comical with relief when they drew a total blank. Four minutes to twelve and there was nothing to do but go back to the main room. Janet was waiting there.

'Where have you been? I've searched and searched, and it's the—'

'We know,' they chorused together, 'it's the last tram! Run!'

21

THE LAST TRAM from Clayfield Junction lurched and rattled to a halt. The three friends scrambled aboard.

'Fares please!' The conductor's look was surly as he took Janet's ten shilling note. 'Nothing smaller?' He took revenge by dumping a fistful of coppers into her hand as change. They chose to sit in the empty open-sided section while he sulked in the front cabin, grumping loudly that decent women were already in their beds.

'Pardon us for living,' Lulla mocked, with looks droll enough to bring on the giggles. They were carried along on racketing wheels, belting through blacked-out suburbs, the tram crackling and spitting sparks in its midnight dash to the Light Street Depot; those city-bound, they were told triumphantly, would have to walk the rest of the way.

Dresses tucked between their knees against the wind, they agreed that the foray across the city had been a success. Lulla, sitting alone across the aisle, leaned over to nudge Peggy's knee.

'And who was making like Carmen Miranda, heading the conga line, no less?' She raised her voice above the clatter. 'So don't say you didn't enjoy yourself, young Scott.'

Peggy captured strands of hair blowing wild across her face, obviously enjoying the bucketing ride. 'Who's trying to,' she yelled, 'I had a ball!'

Janet sat neatly, her pageboy sleek in a snood, ankles crossed, and for the first time since their helter-skelter from the Clayfield house, Lulla noticed how pale she looked. She could do with a touch of rouge and lippy, she thought, then realised that Janet's lipstick had been thoroughly kissed off.

Janet of all people! So that's what she was up to!

As the shock subsided, Lulla reasoned that it was about time Janet let go a bit. All those lonely nights. Always waiting for mail, or worse, a telegram with black news. No wonder Jan indulged in a bit of kiss-and-never-tell-anyone, even if she was a married woman.

Married women, opinion judged, shouldn't go to parties, no matter how harmless; let alone have a cuddle on the dark side of a veranda. Lulla stared out at the rushing night. Wondering. Analysing.

Faint lights glimmered from a launch moored in the Creek, and she could make out the shadows of men fishing the tide. Were men so innocent? Like hell! She remembered nights of cosy fondling followed up by confessions that there was a wife—even kids—waiting in Dallas, or Toronto, Melbourne or Humpty Doo. Geography didn't come into it.

But Janet was a married woman. Married women stayed at home. They waited. They brought up the kids, knitted socks, made up comfort parcels. And knitted more socks.

Well, Jan, old pal—Lulla sent over a silent message of support—*Don't regret it, whatever happens. And never, but never, go soft and confess to that husband of yours. Don't let the left foot know what the right one is doing in a Pride of Erin. That's my philosophy anyway*—justifying herself as well as Janet. And then wondered what Spanner would make of Charlie Redwing.

Traces of the party still lingered. The hurtling ride to Light Street titillated their appetite for more adventure. They were reluctant to bring the night to its end.

Bundled off the tram, they blew kisses to the driver, and laughed away his warning to be careful passing through the Valley.

'Yank sailor was stabbed there, only yesterday. So keep your eyes peeled.'

Fortitude Valley was nearly deserted, and Queen Street, when they finally reached it, was much the same. At intersections the usual cluster of hopefuls waited for the odd taxi cab, and an occasional whistle echoed along the footpaths and silent shop-fronts. The town was theirs as they swung arm-in-arm towards the Quay.

Part of the way they were joined by roisterers in jungle-drabs, who belted out *Knees Up, Mother Brown* and *Roll Out the Barrel*, until an army truck appeared, scooping up the men and lumbering off to one of the somewhere-camps that ringed the entire city. A whiff of vanilla and sour milk from beneath the closed doors of the Pig 'n Whistle reminded Peggy that she had eaten little since leaving home, commenting that for a party the food had been 'light on'.

'Not a saveloy or a piece of sponge in sight,' she complained.

'Well, how about a pie and peas?' Lulla pointed out a light shining from a stall across the road. It stood wedged between a garage and motor works, an untidy, sprawling complex that swallowed up most of the corner.

'They never sleep,' Janet intoned, 'and they sell the best pies in town. Come on!'

They joined the stragglers—a shift worker and a mixture of uniforms—appreciating the stall's hospitality. An Australian sailor was demonstrating to his American counterparts the knack of eating a pie without spilling gravy. Just suck and bite at the same time he was saying—and between slurps they swapped information on ships, the war and lucky escapes; home, drydocks and refits.

Peggy's ears caught the word *Tulsa*.

'Did you hear that?' she whispered. Too shy to

ask questions, she agonised as Janet tapped a shoulder.

'Excuse me. Are you boys off the *Tulsa*?' She asked sweetly.

'No, ma'am.' His drawl was slow and soft. They had to concentrate to understand him. 'A'hm talking 'bout mah hometown, Tulsa. And mighty glad to make your acquaintance.' He edged closer, offering them a good time, but was given a cheerful toodle-pip as the three left the stall eating pies.

They took their time crossing the bridge, and halfway across paused to watch a ship, not large, but gun-spiked and quietly furtive, leave from a wharf downstream. A rope slapped water, stirring up fish smells that seeped from the nearby markets, and a spotlight momentarily speared the gloom.

Peggy tossed away the last piece of crust and licked her fingers one by one. She announced that as far as she was concerned that was the last party she'd go to. 'Not fair on Julian, and anyway—'

'But you had a ball. You said so yourself.' Lulla stared at her as if trying to make sense of it. 'He wouldn't expect you to sit at home, just waiting. For crying out loud, Peg, it could be weeks—months—before he's back. *If ever*,' she added under her breath. No one knew better than Lulla just how transient a brief encounter could be with a lonely, homesick serviceman.

But Peggy had made up her mind. 'You could be right,' she said stubbornly, 'but I intend being there if he does phone.'

'You're nuts!' Lulla appealed to Janet. 'Talk some sense into her, Jan.'

But Janet's buoyant mood had left her. She shrugged, her voice sounding almost disinterested. 'Maybe Peg's got the right idea.'

'Oh for Gawd's sake! What's got into the pair of you?' Exasperated, Lulla grasped Peggy's arm, ignoring Janet. 'Now listen to me, young Scott. Don't waste your time, and your life, waiting for maybe-phone calls. Get out and enjoy yourself. Soak up everything, every experience that comes your way. Make it count.' Intensely seriously, she forced Peggy to face her and listen. 'This war—this rotten war is giving us opportunities. Oh, hell. How can I explain myself?' Frustrated, she raked fingers through her hair, pins flying in all directions. 'Do you realise that you, me, all of us, are walking history and nothing, *nothing*, will ever be the same again!' She remembered her grip on Peggy's arm and let go. 'Crikey!' She gave a half-embarrassed laugh. 'Must be the night air. C'mon, let's get home.'

Even before they stepped through the gate, Peggy guessed that something was wrong. Her heart cramped at the sight of Hilda framed by the window, the light shining behind her. Hilda never waited up.

Her mother was already in the hall as she bounded up the stairs. 'What's happened?'

She was bundled into the flat, the door slammed shut behind her.

'Evie's gone,' Hilda rasped. 'She's gone!'

Peggy flinched. The news like a body-blow.

'You mean she's just sneaked out, don't you?'

Hilda shook her head. 'Her clothes—most of them—are gone too.'

Her mother's face seemed smaller, tighter; as if the underlying juices had been leached away by strain and fear.

'But you were here. Right here.' The girl's voice was shrill with disbelief. Then doubt crept in. 'You *were* here, weren't you?'

'Of course! I was in the shower. Getting ready for bed. There was time enough for mischief, I realise that now.' Hilda eased herself into a chair as if fragile bones might break. Eveleen had sulked through the evening, Peggy was told, alternating between damp silences and thundering tears. Finally the girl had gone to bed, crying herself to sleep.

'Or so I thought,' Hilda said.

'Oh, Mum. I knew I shouldn't have gone out.'

'Rubbish.' Hilda dug into her pocket, found a cigarette and lit up, eyes closed for the first deep intake of breath. 'It was bound to happen,' she stated flatly.

All the while Peggy had stood stiff-backed, buttressed against the shock-waves of Hilda's telling. She forced herself to take the few steps to the bedroom; with her own eyes she had to see the proof of Evie's folly.

Except for a crumpled and empty bed, everything appeared the same—the potpourri of familiar smells. Hilda's *Evening In Paris* mingled with the lingering bite of cigarette butts, and a damp, sweet smell of soap escaped through the partly open bathroom door.

She pulled back the curtain of the corner wardrobe she shared with Evie. Everything her sister called 'best', was missing; the few things remaining, rammed close together at the end of the rack, looked strangely abandoned.

Then Peggy noticed the empty vase on the dressing-table. The old vase, too crazed to hold water, had been a receptacle for all the loose change left over after the shopping had been done. The silver hoard had been looked on as special money, for birthday and Christmas spending. Evie had done well; the vase had been nearly full. There was no denying the reality of her sister's flight.

'You've been to the police?'

'A lot of good it did me.' Hilda stared down into her cupped hands, now idle on her lap, the cigarette spiralling smoke and forgotten in an ashtray. She chewed the skin inside her cheek.

'What did they say?' Peggy prompted her. 'What are they doing?'

'Nothing. Absolutely nothing.'

'I don't believe it.'

The mother managed a short, bitter laugh. 'Believe it. One man on duty when I got there, that's all. He said they were flat-out and from what I gathered runaway girls are a penny a dozen. Had the cheek to tell me that nine times out of ten they turn up the next morning. "A bit the worse for wear," he said, "but all in one piece." Nice, eh?'

'And that's it?'

'Oh, he took a few notes. Said they'd be in touch.'

All Peggy could think of was a group they had side-stepped on the way home. Four men, with a girl, stupid-drunk, preening and giggling as they argued over their share of her. Feeling helpless, swamped by a tidal wave of guilt, she heard Hilda describe her search for Evie. However unlikely, nothing in the district had been left out. Highgate Hill; the river flats behind the factory; Musgrave Park; as far as the railway station. Hilda had delved into every nook and cranny within walking distance of Franklin Street.

'I'm at my wits' end,' she said.

A soft tapping at the door. Janet whispering was everything all right.

Mother and daughter held still for a moment, reluctant to share their troubles even with good friends. Hilda was the first to speak. 'Let them in, Peg.'

Peggy showed them an anxious, frightened face, but it was Hilda's bleak and downturned look that shocked them. The night hours had aged her; lines cut deeply around her lips and between her brows.

Peggy, in a rush, blurted out the news. 'Evie's shot through—all her clothes are gone—and Mum's looked everywhere.' She went to her mother's side, an arm protective across her shoulders. 'She's just gone ...'

It hardly came as a surprise. Lulla guessed she was not the only one who felt relieved that Kirk was somewhere north, and Spanner—even Spanner—safely with him. There was no doubt in her mind that Evie would have taken the two of them on, given half the chance.

On hearing of Hilda's reception at the police station, Janet flared indignant, and insisted that they go back at once, and demand satisfaction. She found it hard to understand Hilda's refusal to go there the second time.

'It's useless,' Hilda said. 'I didn't want to go there in the first place.'

'Why ever not?'

For a while Hilda said nothing; her gaze seemed to bore into Janet. When she did speak she could not hide the break in her voice. 'It's all right for you, Jan, you've got a husband.'

'A husband? What's that got to do with it?'

'A lot. You can't understand … but a woman parted from her lawfully wedded isn't worth tuppence.'

'That's ridiculous.'

'It's true.'

Janet gave a helpless shrug. 'If you say so. But how would they—'

'Know? They know everything. And knowing puts the likes of us—me—in a different bracket. We're not *nice women*, Janet. It's a fact of life.'

There was no point in arguing. Hilda had made up her mind. No more police. She did say that with the help of Janet and Lulla they just might find Evie. She stopped short of admitting that serious harm could come to the girl. It was difficult to envision

Evie lying bruised and battered in bushland, or abandoned in some city lane. Lulla was inclined to think of her happily ensconced in a hotel double bed, gorging on Almond Rocca and smoking her head off.

Evie was no loser.

Plans were made that at first light, Peggy should remain in the flat just in case she returned, while Hilda would search once more the local streets and parks, as far as her legs could take her. It was up to Janet and Lulla to board every tram that terminated near a satellite camp. They could only do their best in the time they had to spare, one day only. A doctor's certificate had to be produced if they took more than one day off ... only Hilda would be exempt from that.

Sounds of morning slipped through the slatted blinds, and church bells pealed, announcing Sunday. Hilda insisted that before any of them left they must have a cup of something, and she put the kettle on. She worried about their lack of sleep, and, pouring tea, instructed Peggy to butter toast and put on jam. No one was going anywhere on an empty stomach, she decreed.

'If only we had a car,' she went on, 'it would save so much time.' She took hasty gulps of tea, anxious to leave.

Sunlight streamed through the window, highlighting the normality of the half-empty cups, toast crumbs and bread. It had a calming effect on Hilda; the sunshine, glowing yellow, thawed a little the heart-chill of night; new hope had arrived with the coming of friends.

As Hilda moved to the bedroom for her coat and hat, Lulla smacked a closed fist down on her other open palm and yelped. 'Daryl! Daryl Missim! He's got a car. Why didn't I think of it before!'

It was a thunderbolt of an idea that fused Hilda to the carpet.

'Daryl Missim! Oh, no! Oh, no, no!'

'Why not? He's always flush with petrol.'

'I'm not surprised.' Hilda sounded icy. 'If you think for one minute—if you think, I'd look for my daughter with blackmarket petrol ...'

'Come off it, Hilda.' Lulla was guiding the woman back to a chair. 'This is no time for standing on your dig. Daryl's the answer to our prayers.' With both hands she forced Hilda to sit. 'Daryl's no angel. He's no skinflint either and I know for a fact he'd use every drop of those ill-gotten gallons to find Eveleen.' She tapped the side of her nose, eyes sparkling. 'It pays to know the right people, remember? And Daryl does. I bet you he knows the whereabouts of every camp from here to the Birdsville Track. Headwaiters, night porters, you name 'em, he knows them. Now, how about I give him a ring?'

'He's got a tongue like a runaway bus.'

'So what? You've no choice, and every minute counts.'

Hilda was chewing her lips. Almost automatically she brushed up the table crumbs into one neat pile.

Her sigh was a surrender to Lulla's logic. 'All right, ring him. What difference will it make if the whole town knows I've a slut for a daughter. Why try to keep it quiet …'

22

$\mathcal{D}$USK HAD CAUGHT up with them. In a sunset shredded by saplings and bush, nothing had slipped by unnoticed as the Hillman tackled ruts and roots, gravel and slides leading to the army camp. Daryl stopped a short distance from a sentry post.

'This is it, Mrs Scott. Ekibin—the end of the line.'

He switched off the motor and waited for some response from the two guards on duty. By their lack of interest the car and its occupants might have been invisible. So far the day had been exhausting and utterly futile. This was the last camp, the last chance, and Daryl hoped, for Hilda's sake, it would prove a dry run, like all the others.

A small contingent, in full pack and battledress, swung into view, eyes straight ahead.

Hilda gasped. 'They're black—black as the ace of spades.'

'You said to try everywhere, and we have.' More as a sop to Hilda's concern, Daryl shook his head knowingly and said: 'Can't see her being here, Mrs Scott. Too far out of town and the rules for these boys—well, you know what I'm talking about—are tough. And who wants to be strung up by the—by the thumbs, eh? Not worth it.' He eased himself away from the steering wheel and stepped onto the road. 'I wouldn't worry too much, but I'll go and ask, just the same.'

Hilda's eyes missed nothing as Daryl strolled over and spoke to the guards. From the start she had left the questioning to him, having no heart or stomach for the job.

'Better that a man do it,' she'd told him.

It was the same scenario they had repeated throughout the day. Daryl talked. The men shook their heads, often grinning until they glimpsed the strained face peering at them through the car window.

The encampment was a clone of all the rest they had driven to, but with nightfall the brownout was ignored. Lights shone from windows and doorways, and arc lamps speared all movement with blazing accuracy. Hilda found it hard to imagine any intruder sneaking in unobserved, although the huts seemed to lead straight into bushland. She wondered if the back door was as stringently guarded as the front.

Daryl, with Hilda's implicit and silent consent, had kept exclusively to the American sites surrounding the city. They both knew that the shining, well-heeled Americans would fulfil all Evie's expectations.

He came back shaking his head. 'Well, that's that. She's not here.' He slid into his seat. 'Ready to call it a day?' Mutely, Hilda nodded her answer.

As the Hillman moved off, Daryl asked if it was a good idea to call in at the police station on the way.

'What's the use, Daryl. She's gone. I knew it would come to this—but not so soon, not so soon ...' she said wearily. Drained, she rested her head against the seat, eyes closed. Her head whirled with images of the day's events, beginning with an empty bed, and Peggy's face heavy with guilt, hating herself. Camp after camp washed over her brain in sepia monotone, as she recalled the pain endured under the impersonal gaze of strangers. She'd even got used to that, as the day had dragged on. How many hotels, as well? How many questions? Daryl seemed to know everyone who counted in that desperate, useless search.

She remembered with gratitude the touch of a major's hand when he insisted they eat in the hospital mess, before leaving for a shipyard city of cranes, slipways and tin sheds bright and white with oxy welding. Daryl had apologised, explaining that there were lucrative pickings for the women who hunted there—professionals, mostly, he'd said, avoiding her eyes. All she could think of was Evie's golden head close to the vigorous ebony of one of the Chinese workmen who clambered over the half-built ships.

They came from Hong Kong, Daryl told her, believing that one day the nine dragons of their city would rise again from the burning and the terror. Only then would they return to their island home.

Hilda thought of her husband, who had disappeared one night years ago. If Alf had stayed would a more pliable Evie be safe at home now? Who could tell? The anguish of his going returned to her.

She must have drifted off, to be awakened by a touch on her shoulder.

'Hilda, we're back.' Daryl was standing by the open door of the Hillman, his hand outstretched to help her. It was the first time he had called her Hilda, and she let it be.

Dead-log stiff, half-asleep, she struggled out of the car as Peggy hurried down the path. Behind her were Lulla and Janet. A quick look was enough to confirm what they had already guessed. No Evie.

Refusing an invitation to eat with them, Daryl placed two hands on Hilda's shoulders, forcing her to believe what he only half-believed himself.

'Don't give up yet. I'll dig up something. We'll find her,' were his last words before driving off.

As the four friends reached the front stairs, the Hickeys appeared and stood waiting by the door of Hilda's flat. Peggy whispered hastily that the police had been over after all and, by the look of it, that second visit was one too many for the Hickeys! Hilda braced herself, prepared for the worst. There could even be a notice to quit the premises. The landlord advanced to meet her.

'Mrs Scott—Mother and me are real sorry. You're

a good woman. A good mother. We've noticed, take my word—' He was cut short by the sight of Hilda crying. Silent tears sliding down her cheeks. All day she had faced up to her grief and worry, dry-eyed and steady. It was the old man's sympathy that caused the flow.

'Mrs Scott. Please ...' He put out his hand to comfort, then drew it back, awkward before her anguish. With a small cry Hilda brushed past him, running into the flat, Peggy close behind, leaving the Hickeys, Lulla and Janet standing helpless in the hallway. Peggy turned to face the landlord before going in.

'Mum appreciates that, Mr Hickey,' she said gravely. 'Thanks.'

'If we can help ...'

The girl nodded, then closed the door quietly behind her. They heard the key turning in the lock, shutting them out. Hickey took his wife's elbow, shepherding her to the attic stairs.

'Come, Mother—there's nothing more we can do here.'

Exhausted, yet wide-awake, Janet rolled over to a favoured side and hoped for rest. Quiet and still, Lulla's inert form lay cocooned in her share of bedsheet, pretending sleep.

Evie's disappearance had disturbed them more than they cared to confess. To admit concern to each other was to acknowledge that the girl might be in real peril. In spite of Lulla voicing 'good riddance to bad rubbish', she had jumped as much as anyone at the sound of a car turning into the street—not that many were heard in Franklin Street on a Sunday. Even the occasional army truck passing by had caused flurries of hope and a rush to the windows.

For Peggy, each passing hour meant heartache, and after midday there was worse to come .... Janet sighed and tried to turn over without disturbing Lulla. Peggy could have done without that phone call. It had come at midday, jangling nerve ends, and Peggy was the first to answer it.

'I can't,' they had heard her say. 'Not now—' her lips thinning into stubborn refusal as she whispered into the telephone. Before she had finished, they had guessed who it was.

Julian. He had talked himself onto a plane flying south. A snatched visit before returning the same afternoon to God knows where. Just a quick visit, that was all, Peggy said.

'Why didn't you invite him here?'

'You could have used the backroom,' Lulla had wailed.

But Peggy had shaken her head. 'It's the wrong time. It's all wrong—I couldn't—and—' Janet could hear again the despairing voice giving up. Trying to explain what they already knew. Who'd want her man to see the distraught mother; the defiant sister; and hear the eruption that was bound to follow when, if, Eveleen was brought home. Not Peggy Scott.

Thinking over the past weeks, Janet had to admit

that the brightest spot had been the Clayfield party. Perhaps that was why she had so easily been talked into going. No regrets there. It had been a feast of good things that had lightened her heart, eased the aloneness, sponged out the stains of dreary, loveless days.

She regretted nothing. Not the fever on the dark side of the veranda: now, remembering it, the excitement returned. She controlled her breathing, keeping it quiet in case Lulla heard, and allowed the slow surge of tidal blood swell from stomach-pit to groin, to thigh, to the soles of her very feet. She went with the flow; there were lazy half-thoughts behind closed eyes that one strong man's arms felt no different from the next one. Slowly the heat subsided and she starved for Kirk and wondered at herself, a little frightened. She snatched the pillow from beneath her head, clutching it tight. It gave her no comfort, this night.

Lulla stirred. Her hand touched the pillow between them.

'Feeling lonely, love?' Lightly she stroked and patted the arm hugging its pillow. 'Never mind. But it's been a long haul between letters, eh.'

'That it has.' Silence in the dark. 'Lulla, there's something—'

'Shush, kid. I don't want to know about it.'

'You don't know what I'm about to say.'

'Oh-ho, don't I just.' Lulla's chuckle wrapped them in secrets. 'But he was rather cute, wasn't he?'

'So you *do* know?'

'Nothing, ducks. Nothing.'

The trouble was that Kirk had been away too long. And where was he now? Thursday Island? The last letter had hinted there could be a change of course. That the milk run was nearing an end.

Surely he would come home soon. Didn't they always get leave before changing to another ship? Lulla was snoring gently and, nearing sleep herself, Janet's thoughts tumbled in her tired brain. Kirk home soon ... and a sudden feeling of relief swept over her, catching her unawares. Kirk home, and Evie gone! Perhaps for good!

Now it was out in the open.

She had tried to ignore Evie's fascination in Kirk, hardly believing Kirk's indifference to Evie. She had been so persistent. What man could ignore her? Lovely child. Wanton woman. And Hilda and Peggy possibly crying their eyes out, next door, wondering where she was. Shame pressed heavily on her heart for her lack of charity. 'Bring Eveleen home,' she said in prayer. 'Bring her home for Hilda's and Peggy's sakes.'

Evie could hardly believe that at long last she was standing on the platform of Sydney's Central Station. That she had been able to coax a ticket from a dour railway official in Brisbane had been a small miracle in itself. She had heard that the most desperate pleas, the most heart-rending reasons to make the ride, could be met with a flat refusal. 'No seats available,' was the standard reply.

But here she was, and she knew exactly where she was going. Kings Cross. Its fame had even reached the ears of the far North, from Cairns to Cooktown: a Mecca where the lighthearted, the greedy and the talented made pilgrimage. A magic place where life was lived to the full if you were clever enough, rich enough, good-looking enough. Evie felt the riches would come in due course: she had no qualms about the other two qualifications.

It took her just minutes to find out how to get there—not far, she was told. A brisk walk away. So Evie picked up her mother's scuffed suitcase, checked the time with Hilda's wristwatch and set out at a jaunty pace.

Evie had heard more than once that the Cross was crawling with crooks and molls, just like the pictures. But nothing could have looked brighter or prettier than Kings Cross the morning Evie arrived in Sydney Town. Nothing could have been further from her mind as to where she should sleep, or where she would go. To be there, was enough. She bounced along the freshly watered pavement with a light and careless heart.

A glimpse in a chemist window assured her that she looked all right; her dirndl skirt was a bit crumpled, but the new hat that Hilda had bought with precious coupons looked frumpy. It smacked of a country town in this street of smart boutiques, jewellers, and a spanking new Woolworths store. She pulled it off and would have dropped it where she stood, but a refuse bin stood close by. As if sloughing off the last constrictions of Franklin Street, she rammed it hard into the bin, out of sight.

'Say, you're out bright and early, baby ...' A seabee stood behind her, admiration shining from his eyes, sauce staining his jacket. Evie was not impressed. There were more attractive men on the move and there was plenty of time to pick and choose. She turned away from him, watching his reflection move on.

What had been noticeable on her walk up the long sloping street were the men in 'civvies' hurrying to work, filling the tramcars. More uniforms in Brisbane, she thought, but consoled herself that there were still enough around, even at that early hour, to liven the place up.

What impressed and delighted her was a feeling of ebullience that showed itself in the laughter and gaiety of a covey of girls in beach pyjamas and unbelievably high-heeled slippers; in the excited argument between a couple in full evening dress, oblivious of the hour or place to air their grievances: a barrow in full bloom with carnations; fruit glowing in another.

Evie was falling in love.

Not in any hurry, she passed one fascination after the other, until she came to a door open for business, its interior all chrome, polished wood and tiles. A standing sign on the footpath stated that a Hasty Tasty hamburger would not only satisfy the fastidious palate of Mr Wimpy, but would meet the approval of Popeye himself. As Evie gravitated to all things American, including hamburgers, the Hasty

Tasty Milkbar beckoned. She also found the smell of frying onions mesmeric.

'Nothing like it in Brisbane,' she concluded happily, stepping inside with the feeling that she had come home to roost.

Only one thing stopped her from lining up with the other early birds on the smart-looking stools. She was close to running out of funds. But the sizzling of fat, steak patties on the griddle behind the counter set up a belly-rumble impossible to ignore. She made up her mind to give it a try. More than one pair of eyes watched as she stepped up to the counter, easing herself onto a stool.

'What'll you have, Miss?'

'A hamburger, thanks.'

'With, or without?'

'With the lot.'

A plate was slapped down in front of her and the images that had enticed her inside lived up to expectations. 'The lot' meant just that and Evie's mouth watered at the sight of the golden bun with its laminations of beef, bacon and egg, tinted with slices of beetroot and tomato. She reached out to take it, but a hand grasped her wrist and a voice devoid of any humour demanded: 'That will be one-and-six, thank you, Miss.'

Her eyes were luminous, the soft mouth turned down. 'But I thought it was only sixpence.'

'The price list's up there for all to see, right?'

'I'm sorry, I didn't know—really. See, I've just got off the train. I'm supposed to meet my Dad somewhere. Here. He's just out of hospital, from New Guinea ...'

She could tell that he didn't believe her, but a lad not much older than herself, in dungarees and working boots, did.

'New Guinea, eh?' He asked her, face alight and interested. 'Was he hurt? Wounded or something?'

'That's right. A bullet with his name on it.'

The man behind the counter, realising that the hamburger would now be paid for, gave a dismissive shrug and went back to his griddle.

Already, the boy was offering to help out until she found her Dad. On the strength of it, Evie ordered a malted milk with a double serving of ice-cream.

His name was Bert. She found herself running out of answers to his many and varied questions about her father's bravery in combat: and about the perils endured by herself in the wilds of North Queensland. She was beginning to feel she had more than earned the price of a breakfast when Bert discovered that time was running out.

'Look—I hafta go. I start work soon, not far from here. You'll be all right?'

She toyed with the idea of asking for a loan, but the speculative disapproval from the man behind the counter discouraged her. 'I'll be okay.'

'Can I meet you here after work?'

'If my Dad will let me.' She made an attempt to sound hopeful.

Bert paid for the meal, beaming on his good luck. 'Beauty! Be here, at five. Promise!'

She watched him leave. If nothing better turned up, she'd be back. But something told Evie there was more to life at the Cross than a hamburger bun with 'The Lot'.

By eleven, and feeling peckish, Eveleen Scott had reached the reluctant conclusion that she should find herself a job. Nowhere but Kings Cross would do. For her, the rest of Sydney did not exist. She loved the tree-lined streets, the pervading aroma of coffee as shopkeepers took their morning break. She wandered up and down the avenues, delirious with the joy of being there. Totally free! Strolling around where none knew her. No one to nag her. No prissy Peggy to boss and fuss; no more lectures from a carping mother. No school! Franklin Street, and all that it meant, was in the past—over the border. There was hardly a thought or care for the two women she had left behind.

She would never forgive her mother for taking her away from Cairns; and even if Kirkland Hope did treat her like a baby, he had wanted *it*. She knew that. He'd made it clear enough. And how she hated that Lulla Riddel! But for her ....

From that moment, Evie dismissed them all from her mind. There was enough here to keep her happy for the rest of her life. She had also noticed, as the morning advanced, that the uniforms had multiplied—sufficient to inspire delicious speculation.

She was now resting in a minuscule park, deciding what to do, when a woman tripped by parading her poodle. Evie vowed that the day was not too far off when she, too, would have a little dog just like that; pink coat, pink bow and toenails painted to match. Two schoolgirls chattered on their way across the road. They were eating cream buns, which reminded Evie of a sign she had noticed in a cake shop, hardly bigger than a good-sized baker's oven. In a window lavish with cream cakes, eclairs, apple and custard tarts, there had been a card, no more than that, with GIRL WANTED written in purple ink. Such a small card, she had thought at the time, as if the one who had placed it there could not bear to hide the indulgence of the window display. With a card so small, maybe no one else had seen it, and the Daffodil Cake Shoppe (she remembered the name because of the way the word shop was spelled) was still in need of a girl.

Her good intentions to find out were nearly displaced by a wolf whistle of strength and purpose. She caught the wink that followed it, and much to her own surprise, discounted it by picking up her case and walking off.

THE DAFFODIL CAKE SHOPPE'S fussy gold lettering ill-matched the rotund, bustling bulk of its redbearded pastry cook and owner. An intimacy with hot ovens over the years had scorched his cheeks to crimson. It was a marvel that fingers like saveloys could coax butter and flour into the airy confections in the window.

At her query about the position, if it was filled, the baker rubbed his hands together, smiling and nodding his head at the same time.

'You're the first to ask and you're hired. References?' He brushed her hesitation aside. 'Never mind ...' He then said that with her around, those apple-pie-lovin' Yanks would flock to the door. 'And after that, dear girl, the sheer quality of the pastrycook's art will have them coming back—although, mind you, custard tarts are my speciality.'

He heard the same story that she had told the lad at the Hasty Tasty, embellished by the fact that her Dad had lost a leg on the Kokoda Trail. She had arrived in Sydney solely to look after him when he was discharged from the Army. She added that her purse had been snatched the moment she'd put her foot on the platform at Central, and would it be possible for him to advance her a part of her wages— 'for rent', she added.

Bently Smith (he asked her to call him Ben) gave the girl a long, steady look, the bounce in his smile fast fading.

'I'm no pushover, Eveleen—on the other hand, I don't like to see someone strapped for cash. Especially a kid.' He thought the matter over, pulling hairs out of his fiery beard. 'I tell you what ... that's a finelooking watch you have there. Leave it with me, find yourself a residential—that's what they call 'em here, and I'll see you at eight sharp tomorrow. Uniform provided.'

His hand dived under his apron and just as quickly he produced two notes and handed them over to the girl. 'Here!' He then opened the sliding door of the shop window and brought out two of his custard tarts, bagged them and gave them to her. 'Sample the goods. I won't dock them out of your wages.'

The day was ending for Evie as brightly as it had started. Two quid in her pocket, a job, and the afternoon sun on her back, a benediction. There was a coolness in the air quite different to what she was used to. Once she'd found rooms, it was only a matter of settling in and giving her face a quick wash before nipping out again to see what the rest of the day would bring.

Her search for a room took no time. One was waiting for her—and she had to thank the soldier who had given her the wolf-whistle in the park. As she came down the street, he appeared from a gate topping a flight of sun-dappled steps that led down to a curved beach and shaded water. She could see a house of matching stones nestled in gardens halfway down. It seemed the American had come from there.

'Hey! Haven't I seen you somewhere?' He blocked her path, confident, chewing gum.

'That's an old line, buddy' (she knew the word-play off pat) 'but as a matter of fact you're right, for once. In the park, remember?'

He snapped his fingers. 'Now that's what I call a real coincidence. Must be my lucky day. Hey! Hey!'

Evie could feel a mounting pleasure and she wasn't letting go. The American was tanned, as if he had spent many hours on the sand at the foot of the stairs. The hair would have been curly as her own, if it hadn't been so closely cropped. It was the same colour and she wondered if his body hair, like hers, was a similar shade of gold.

'Do you live round here?' he asked. But he was stealing glances at her travel-worn port. Wondering.

'No. I'm looking for rooms, but. I start work tomorrow.' She nodded towards the house. 'Do you know somebody there? Visiting?' She had to find out more about him. So cute …!

'Nope, I live there. Till tomorrow, anyway. It belongs to us G.I.'s for the duration. It's a rest house. Me and m'buddies are due to go—and the next lot move in tomorrow night. Hey!' He seemed to be struck with an illuminating idea. 'Saw a house with rooms to let, down the street a bit. Interested?'

Evie tossed back her hair, laughing up at him. 'Yes! Oh, yes!' Near a house full of soldiers? Compliments of Uncle Sam? Neighbours! Evie decided she would search no longer.

'Lead me to it,' she said.

He insisted on carrying her suitcase, although he commented on how light it felt. 'Not much in there, honey.' With his free arm, he took her elbow. 'This-a-way.'

Evie hoped the rooms were still up for rent. Not only was the stone house an attraction, but a beach at the foot of the stairs … too good to be true!

There was no problem in renting the two tiny rooms. To Evie's delight, they overlooked the cove below. Twenty-five shillings, the woman asked. There was a gas-ring for cooking—penny in the slot—and a shared bathroom. Rent in advance. The landlady, eyeing off the American waiting outside, warned Evie if there was any 'hanky panky', out she'd go! Evie found it politic to disown the legless father for a mother instead, poor soul, dying from a mysterious disease in St Vincent's. She thought the name gave her story a bit of class. She had noticed the stately grounds and buildings in her explorations and had no idea it was a school.

Hank, for that was his name, seemed anxious for her success. 'Get it okay?' He questioned her closely as if it was important to him. 'Sounds nice,' he said. 'Cost much?'

Evie dropped her gaze, biting her lip. 'Well, it's a bit more than I expected. Two pounds in advance. It just about skinned me.' She sighed, then brightened, her eyes aglow with hope and expectations. 'It's only till payday, but. The boss said I could take home the leftovers, anyway ...'

He looked shocked. 'The leftovers! Honey, that's real bad.' Already, he was pulling out his wallet. Evie pretended not to notice. He held up a five pound note. 'Will this be enough to see you through?' He cut off a protest. 'No—no, take it. I won't be needing it where I'm going.'

'Oh, thank you. I'll pay it back. Every penny.'

'Well, it's a nice excuse for writing me a letter.'

'Oh, I will. I will!'

At night, the Cross had a different face. A place of neon lights and flashing electric bulbs. There seemed little concern over brown outs—the Cross was a long way from the jungle and beaches of Pacific islands at war. The young and not so young massed on its pavements; humanity out on the town. On the move. Sly grog shops skulked behind coffee shops, and if the right word was given, sweet sherry was sold at a price. Two-up schools abounded in dusky lanes. Harlots, pimps, showgirls and singers; actors, good-time girls, factory workers; sailors, airmen, soldiers and marines; whatever the need, whatever the dream, most of the time the Cross could supply it.

Evie had found her level. She slid as easily into her groove as a bullet into a well-oiled barrel. She and Hank had dined well, and shared the flask he brought with him. Now they walked close together, arms entwined, down the street that led to both houses. For Evie the day had been one success after another. There had been the thrill of Hank's arms about her at the nightclub they had found themselves in. Cheek to cheek, they had moved to the slow rhythm of a jazz quartet, Hank's lips moving over her skin, taking chances in the dim twilight of the forty-watt globes.

'Ever heard of the "Y" dance?' he had murmured, as they threaded a dreamy path through other couples on a dinner-plate floor. Without waiting for an answer he had given her a gentle prod with his hips. 'See—why dance?'

Evie laughed. Keeping to the beat; feeling every part of him, she had envisioned how the night would end. Down on the sand? Certainly in his arms. Kisses and teasing; she knew all the steps that would lead her to the finale. Her body tingled in happy expectation. She shivered as Hank's fingers played along her back.

'Honey, I told you I'm leaving tomorrow.'

'I know.'

'Did I say that the others, my buddies, have already quit the place? I had some business to clear up. That's why I'm still here.'

'Yes?'

'Yeah ... Er—would you like some coffee to take back with you?' He was brightly pleased with the idea. 'There's a stack of it in the pantry. We could even have some before I walk you home. How about it?'

They were now standing at the top of his stairs. Dark shadows and moonglow on the way down and not a light in sight.

She snuggled against him. 'I'd like that.'

She felt him taut against her side, his body heat warming her like a blanket.

'Evie, you sure are some gal.'

Halfway down, he held back, hesitating. 'You sure, honey?' It seemed as he could not quite believe what was happening. Evie knew exactly what he was thinking. She kissed him full on the lips.

'What's wrong with a cup of coffee? Anyway, I want to see the house. It must be pretty looking over the water, and that.'

He laughed, held her tight for a moment, then released her. 'Come on, then, Sugar-sweet.' Making light of it 'Come with me to the Casbah'.* He took her hand, leading her on and down to the stone house.

Inside, the rooms were a strange mixture of army barracks and comfortable living. Some of the furniture had obviously been abandoned by the previous owners. It was a conglomerate of army bunks and single beds, placed around the walls with naked pillows and khaki blankets, folded with regulation precision for the next arrivals. There were deep leather chairs and occasional tables stacked with imported magazines, but the floors were bare. Yet the overhead light was enhanced by a shade of coloured glass pieces of intricate design.

As Hank had promised, the pantry was full. Evie's eyes widened at the variety and abundance stacked on the shelves: goods that had long disappeared from Brisbane's grocery list. She gasped, awed by the sight of tinned red salmon; asparagus; beautiful tins of biscuits, of ham and bacon and soups, some of which were completely unknown to her. There was sauerkraut, blueberries, cranberries, and enough Coca-cola to slake the thirst of a hundred Hanks and his buddies. Evie happily concluded there would be no shortages for her, from now on.

Hank boiled up coffee in a saucepan and before pouring, added to it the remaining bourbon from his hip flask.

---

* *a saying made famous by and credited to actor Charles Boyer in* Algiers *(1938)*

'Let's go to the other room.'

She took her cup to a window that overlooked a tumble of boulders and bracken, sand and sea, exquisite under moonlight. Everything so still and silent. She could hear his breathing, the only sound that told her she was not alone in the room. His footsteps came closer. She put her empty cup down on the windowsill as his hands slid around her waist. She felt the tension growing between them, her legs suddenly heavy as she leaned against him; desire growing slow and strong. That's how it always started. She felt him lift up her hair to cover the nape of her neck in kisses.

'Why only now,' he murmured, 'why only now?'

'What do you mean?'

'I've just met the most beautiful girl in the world, and I'm out tomorrow.' He tightened his grip around her. 'And I thought it was my lucky day. I don't want to go, Evie.'

His hands moved up to cup each breast as she nestled closer, to feel the full length of him from chest to thigh.

'You don't mind?' he whispered.

He should have known better by her heart quickening under his hand, submitting to his touch. Expert fingers freed the two buttons beneath her collar and finding an opening there, slipped inside and beneath the soft ripe curve, coaxing the satin-smooth nipple to bud in his palm.

She guided his other hand to her belly, still with her back against him, still looking down at the midnight sea. This was all Evie wished for, at this moment, all she wanted, delaying the final caress that would bring it all to an end. He made his move and began taking her with him towards the bed. He stopped only once. 'Take everything off, Evie. I want to see you. I want to remember every part of you.'

She obliged, smiling up at him. He allowed her to fall across one of the beds, his eyes devouring her, his quickening breath matching her own; in a hurry to remove his own hampering clothes.

'My God, you're beautiful.' Almost choking over the words.

She could see him clearly by moonlight, stocky of buttock, aggressively ready. But he lowered himself down almost gently, slotting hip to hip, thigh to thigh. As he moved, his gaze never left her face; enjoying the loveliness lying beneath him.

He stopped, half-rising from the bed and, slipping his hands under her knees, his breathing heavier, pulled her roughly up to meet him.

'Your legs, honey, your legs. Put 'em around me. A-ah ...'

She did what she was told and holding him tightly clung on for her very life. It was over. Too quickly for her, but there had been a hint of something marvellous if he had stayed there. Hank had left her; gasping and shuddering, he was on his knees beside the bed. He kissed her thighs.

'Thank you. Thank you.'

As she lay there, her body still awake, Hank's head heavy on her naked thighs, her thoughts for some reason turned to Kirkland Hope. Where was he now?

Brisbane? Cairns? Thursday Island? Who cared ....

She had worked it out long ago that why Kirk had kept his hands to himself, and off her, was her age. Under-age! As well as Lulla watching them like a hawk. 'Well, Kirkland Hope,' she thought, 'where-ever you are—you missed out on a good thing. Too scared, weren't you. You're the loser—not me!'

Hank stirred, lifting his head. 'Evie, will you be my girl? Will you write me? Stay with me here for tonight? Please.'

'No—I've got to go. First day at work tomorrow. If y'don't mind, take me home—' She bit back the last word. She had nearly called him Kirk!

23

*I*T WAS CAUSE for celebration on Thursday Island. With the appearance of the supply ship, the beer had arrived. The garrison town was wet again. All afternoon, thirsty men had supervised the landing. In fear that demand might exceed supply, anxious counts were made as every barrel hit the wharf. There had to be enough ....

There was never enough.

To create an illusion of plenty it was agreed that sessions should be staggered; hotels were honour-bound to open in turn, and play fair. With a bit of luck, some said, the amber should flow from mid-afternoon to T.I. closing time.

At the far end of the waterfront road the Federal Hotel was the last on roster to open up, and the last in line to close its doors.

Swept out with the Federal's sawdust, a lively

crowd cluttered the dusty footpath, reluctant to abandon what had been a pub crawl of immense satisfaction. A few hopefuls planned to try the Grand again. And some, like Kirkland Hope and Spanner Larkin, made for the beach no more than a stagger away. Those heading for the sand carried mudcrabs and bottled beer scrounged from the army wet canteen.

Still steaming from the pot, held fast by twine, the mudcrabs dangled puppet-like from Spanner's fingers. He held a hammer in the other hand. Kirk hitched the bottles tighter into the safe circle of his arms. He eyed off the hammer.

'Where did that come from?' The crabs were huge, and such an implement would be better than a rock.

'Just fell into my hand, mate.'

Kirk give a quick bark of mirth. 'Like pennies from heaven …'

They paused beside a stand of coconut palms to remove boots and socks, before rolling up their trouser legs and walking down to the water's edge.

'There it is.' Spanner nodded towards a large, flat rock that had been used on more than one occasion as a table and a place to sit. They nestled the bottles into wet sand, and at once began to dismember and clean the shellfish. Nothing like a good feed of muddies, they agreed.

Starlight was enough to see by and, with the last nipper and leg sucked dry, the companions smoked in content, the silence easy between them. Kirk broke it with a full-bodied belch that Spanner outclassed with one marvellous enough to set up complaints from nesting mynah birds. Not to be outdone, Kirk raised one buttock. His fart would have sent shock waves across to distant Murralug.

'Pick the bones out of that,' he challenged.

Laughing, Spanner gave in and reached for another bottle, cleaning it of sand. He took a long swallow before handing it over. 'Be good if the girls were here,' he said.

'Jan and Lulla?'

'Who else?'

'Dottie Lamour would go down real easy. All those coconut palms and things.'

'Mad bastard.'

'Better if we could take a few down with us—mudcrabs, I'm talking about—Jan likes a nice muddy now and then. And a fella can't afford to buy one in Brisbane.' He paused, thinking it over. 'Bloody Yanks—they've cornered the market in everything, eh? Including the women.'

'Not your Janet, lucky dog.'

'Yeah, well ... she's different. Now take Lulla—'

'Lulla's her own woman,' Spanner parried, his voice light with smiles. 'And what a woman.'

Each man to his thoughts. Starglow outlined the largest island bulking up from the channel, and a few lights blinked across from Horn.

Another bottle opened between them—Spanner said it was the last. 'So drink up, pal, and be merry, for tomorrow could be lights out.'

'Not bloody likely on this run. Still, there's that

whisper going about ... Reckon there's anything in it?'

Spanner shrugged aside all conjectures. 'They'll keep the old girl floating until she breaks up—or hits a reef, or a mine—and the betting would be one of our own, for true.'

Vague rumours had followed them up the coast, permeating the wardroom like the smell of a dirty bilge. You couldn't get away from it. Talk was that they were on the final haul, their last trip to Thursday Island.

Then where?

The two men spoke of ships and transfers and of sea manoeuvres yet to happen, and drifted on to what might be when the war was over, of dreams and schemes they shared: a fishing boat here in the Straits, with a base maybe in Cairns—or Townsville, even. Jan would be in that, Kirk believed, and Spanner wondered what woman would share his bed and fortune. If at all.

He thought of Lulla. Close his eyes and he could see her grin and Betty Grable curls. Phosphorus swirled and eddied around his ankles. The water was warm—nearly too warm. Close his eyes and he could smell her skin ... sweet ...

Kirk's growl broke into his reverie. 'Bloody waste.'

Spanner frowned. He swayed a little and the last soft wisp of memory faded.

Kirk's voice was slurred, but only just. 'Here we are in the thick of it, as I said. And where's the dancing girls? Come to me, Dottie.' Sucking air through his teeth in supposed ecstasy. 'Now there's a bit of skirt for you.' He squirmed, suddenly restless, and clutching himself, sprang up. 'O-ooh, it's jumpin' like a flour bag of cut snakes. Help!'

Spanner grinned. 'Dry up, you clown. You're making me nervous.'

Kirk relaxed. 'Only kidding.'

'And pigs can whistle.'

'Anyway, the beer's gone, all-finish. We'd better get back.'

A breeze lightened the night-heavy air. Spanner tilted his chin to it, thoughtful. 'Wind change.' In affirmation, a rising south-easterly, quick off the mark, flipped away his cap, and a second gust sent it rolling along the sand. He bolted after it. The cap, just out of reach, was picked up again by the wind and tossed, twirling, into the restive current of an outgoing tide.

'Bloody hell!'

There was nothing for it but to wade in shin-deep to the rescue. By the time he returned, Kirk was tying up shoelaces and about ready to go.

Spanner rammed the dripping cap back on his head. 'It could've ended up at the Point. It's building to a good eight knots out there.' He reached for his boots. 'Won't bother to put them on.'

'I would if I were you, mate. All them broken bottles.' Kirk toed aside jagged glass half-buried in the sand. 'T.I.'s secret weapon; a moral to slice the nuts off any Jap fool enough to belly ashore, eh?'

'On second thoughts ...' Spanner began pulling on

his socks. 'By the way, where's our empties?'

'Tossed 'em.' Kirk didn't say where.

Stitched to the curve of the island, the road led onto a jetty and further along to the wharf where ships were tied. They leaned against a wind gathering force, making the night crisply clear. It plucked and hissed its spite along the water's edge, flinging up saltspray, misting their cheeks. Surprisingly cool.

Kirk raised his voice to be heard. 'She's anchored out.'

Their ship had slipped its moorings and was well off-shore, companion to several pearl luggers and a naval vessel newly arrived. There was little cause for concern. Tied to the jetty, the ship's lighter waited for strays to be ferried back to their bunks.

Night and sea turned wild, and the jetty shuddered as dark waves clawed and slapped the pylons underneath. The few remaining fishermen who had defied the rushing night were losing heart and taking in their lines. They grinned a welcome at the sailors' approach, and said the wind was 'too much', and invited them to share a feast.

'Plenty here,' said one, showing a bucket full of flipping silver.

'Sorry, mate.' Regret tinged Spanner's voice. 'Leave's up for the night.'

Kirk was tempted. 'We could, y'know. For a while anyway. Nothing like a T.I. feast. Good tucker and plenty of it.'

'You go. I'm hitting the sack.'

Kirk toyed with the idea, but as Spanner moved on, he gave the nearest shoulder a friendly clap. 'Next time, mate.'

A soft voice answered. 'Sure, nex' time.'

Now the tide was falling fast and the lighter, a stride away from an iron ladder, salt-glazed and shining wet, bucked a good ten feet below them. Spanner was the first to reach the deck and stood by waiting for Kirk to come aboard.

Kirk gauged his distance, at the ready, then hesitated as a savage gust bulleted across the lighter's bow. He jumped.

And missed. A wild grab for the gunnel, and missed again.

Spanner already racing to the stern, snatching up a boat hook on the way.

Kirk swimming hard against the current—and losing. A lifebelt zings by Spanner's head and rope snakes out, hissing through the air, and slithers close to Kirk's outstretched fingers.

Shouts from the jetty and cheers as he grabs the rope tight. His grin of triumph under the blaze of spotlights as he's hauled closer to the boat. Now beneath the waves; now in view. He laughs sometimes. Coughs, and the slap of waves has him under again. He is closer to the boat and he lets one hand go and waves to the cheers from the jetty.

'Hang on, you mad bastard,' yells Spanner, relieved now. 'Hang on tight before you bloody drown.'

Kirk keeps on laughing and choking, no more than

a handclasp away. Spanner leans out, ready to help him aboard when a look of shocked surprise wipes out the spluttering bravado.

Kirk's eyes bug.

He heaves himself waist high, as if to fly bodily to the safety of the deck. One shout, then in a few seconds he vanishes from their sight. The rope sings and pings, vibrates with Kirk's dead weight still hanging on beneath the rushing surface. Spanner fights the tide to haul him in, but the rope slackens in his grasp, a limp and useless thing, easy enough to take on board.

Kirk gone. The current races on triumphant.

'Jesus!'

'What's happened?'

'Ki-rrrk!'

Words snatched away by the wind.

All night they searched, and all the next day. The day after that. And the day after that. Nothing found.

Kirk was gone; swallowed up by the swirl and savagery of the Strait's riptides.

24

'I DON'T KNOW what to do with her, Andy— it's got me beat.' Taut with concern, Lulla dragged deeply on the first cigarette of the day. 'She won't budge from the flat except for a bit of shopping.'

'Tha's an encouraging sign. It's a start.'

'Some start. She wouldn't do that if I wasn't around. By herself she'd starve to death. She's a mess, poor kid. She won't even come to the pictures with us. Cries all day and half the night. Talks about punishment, that it's all her fault. I tell you, I'm stumped.'

It was early morning, and the two women had the change room to themselves. Andy crossed to her locker and came back with a thermos flask and two mugs. 'Coffee? I'd say ye need it.' She was looking pleased with herself. 'It's the real stuff, too.'

'Well, now ... and who do *we* know?'

'Och! Ye're not the only one with connections, Miss Riddel.' Smiling, she poured out a good measure and handed it over. 'There—try that.'

'Perfect.' Lulla sniffed appreciatively, eyes closed. Six months ago, the forewoman wouldn't have known how to make a decent brew, let alone have Yankee coffee in her kitchen.

Andy blew into her cup before taking a mouthful. 'She'll be coming back to work, I hope?'

Lulla shook her head. 'I don't think so. I have the feeling she'll go home to her mum and dad. Bury herself in some hick town up north, and never be seen again.' She fell silent, thinking over the last sad weeks. After a few moments, she spoke again. 'I still can't believe it, Andy. He—he was so alive. And to drown, of all things. Kirk! Strong as a bull—Janet says he could've swum Sydney Harbour if he wanted to.'

'They're quite sure he is gone? You know, funny things can happen in wartime.'

'We're sure all right. He died a hero, Spanner said—not that that's any consolation.'

Spanner's letter had arrived a few days after the War Department's telegram. But nothing that Spanner said could ease the despair that settled on Janet's heart the night she learned of Kirkland's death.

Gawd, Lulla thought, she'd never want to go through *that* again.

They'd been on late shift, and old Hickey was waiting by the flat door, the telegram in his hand.

You'd have to die first, to forget the look on Jan's face. Pitiful. And not a word spoken until they were inside the flat.

'I can't—I can't,' Janet had whispered. 'Lulla, I can't open it.'

'You have to.' Lulla felt the chill again, and her throat tightened, as it had on that night when she'd stumbled over clumsy words. 'It might just say that he's been—been wounded. Something like that. Not badly, just a little bit ...' The memory of it was embedded in her soul. She could still see that telegram lying unopened on the table: a scrap of pale yellow paper, but enough to wrap Janet in grief and tears, and lost hopes.

Poor, darling Janet.

Then Spanner's letter came.

'... he died a hero, Janet,' Spanner wrote. 'He died to save a mate. Young Robbie. I don't think you knew him. Only a kid. Somehow or other, he got tangled up with the anchor chain. We were standing by to meet up with another ship, and letting out more chain as we were dragging a fair bit. To cut a long story short, Rob was whipped up and over before you could say Jack. Kirk went over after him. He followed the chain to the bottom. We could see them both, for it wasn't that deep, but the tide was running a beauty. We thought he was winning, but the cable started to run again, with the speed of a galloping train. Couldn't stop it for a while. It must have edged into a hole, for we were in wild territory. Currents every which way. They just disappeared ...'

His letter said more, and ended with a wish that when and if he got to Brisbane, would it be all right if he came to see her. Lulla never found out what Janet thought, but on reading Spanner's letter she decided she could do with a good dose of Larkin, any old time, day or night.

What a waste it all was. What a waste of all that love Janet had heaped on Kirk. What a waste of the glorious strength Kirk would have lavished on Janet to protect and provide for her.

Lulla could have wept thinking of it, but instead, finding her cup empty, she pushed it over to Andy. 'You wouldn't have more of that coffee, would you? I'll tell you what—we'll do a swap. Another cup for a packet of fags.' Life must go on!

Except for Peggy, they now all smoked, including Andy, the last to give in. She still viewed cigarettes with distrust, insisting on calling them coffin nails. Gratefully, she took the packet from Lulla, turning it over in her hand, stroking the cellophane as if it was silk.

'Chesterfields. The auld man will be pleased.' Reluctant to admit that the treat would be hers, she slipped them into a pocket, sealing the bargain by pouring coffee. 'Tell me,' she said, 'did they come from that nice Redwing lad?'

Everyone knew Charlie Redwing, and all approved of the genial American who often waited for Lulla after work. It prompted Andy to enquire about the driving lessons, how they were coming along.

Ah—the driving lessons.

Lulla warmed her hands around the coffee mug, breathing in the aromatic steam before giving an answer. 'The driving lessons? Not bad at all.'

She blessed Redwing for his undemanding friendship. Never had she experienced such lighthearted bliss as when driving Redwing's borrowed truck, a great lumbering machine that he had apologised for. It had terrified her at first, and she had tried every trick to avoid sitting behind the wheel: even to admitting that she had to wear glasses ... at a pinch!

'I'm short-sighted, you know. I have to wear glasses.'

'Put 'em on then.'

'Gawd ...' Feeling as if she was stripping herself bare, she obeyed. 'There! Just call me goggle-eyes from now on!'

'You look cute.' He popped a strip of gum into her mouth. 'Chew on that, honey. It helps.' And so the first lesson began. Lulla remembered the sweating and the panic, and Redwing's patience, and—she had to admit—his endurance. There had been some hairy moments.

All behind her, now; only yesterday, Redwing had settled back in the passenger seat, folded his arms, and closed his eyes. 'It's all yours, honey. Let's go to that crossing you showed me the other day. I've brought along the chow and we'll have a picnic.'

Oh, the freedom of it! To be in full charge, high up in the cabin, with a relaxed Redwing dozing off beside her. She could have gone on for ever, churning up the miles at a good fifty, the wind blowing through the window.

And some lucky beggars get paid for doing it, she mourned to herself.

Lulla had taken another sortie into the Manpower office, at the same time looking over her shoulder for Harris or Doyle. The outcome, as usual, had been disappointing. At least, Janet had comforted her, no one could take away her ability to drive a car. Although she couldn't really believe Lulla's boast that one day, she just might have a natty little sportster of her own.

'A red one,' Lulla opted for, already seeing herself behind the wheel, her hair blowing in the wind. 'Some sort of wild dream, eh? Especially for an ex-barmaid. But it could happen, after the war.'

Janet had only smiled.

By now the change room was filling with the rest of the morning shift. Cigarette smoke blue-rinsed the sunlight stream coming through the window. There was less fuss and hurry nowadays, for, like Lulla herself, most of the women came to the factory in overalls. Looking them over, Lulla felt a strange tenderness towards them. Pot bellies, droopy bums, all shapes and sizes, they braved the West End streets, taking pride in their workday garb. They strode to work with a navvy's gait, abandoning the tripping clip that came with high heels. She saluted them; but swore to Andy that she'd stick to stilts until the day she fell, breaking both ankles and wrists.

Andy had an office meeting to attend, and was

making ready to leave. 'I'm off—I'll not be the one keeping them waiting.'

'In your own time, I notice.' But Lulla bit her tongue at Andy's warning glance.

'Don't fash yoursel', lass. It's nothing.'

'That's just it. Nothing to them.' But Andy was striding off, refusing to listen. Lulla followed, happy to quit a room rapidly filling with cigarette smoke.

With Janet away, there were only the two of them left of the old team. Shifts had been changed around to accommodate Janet's absence. Hilda and Peggy now worked the opposite hours, while Andy coped with an influx of new hands. Isabel, no longer the new girl, still threatened 'to die' if the smell of change so much as tainted the annexe air.

Hilda found herself with a small pay rise, confirming that she had been promoted to forewoman. Peggy grumped that she couldn't wait to get back to the old team.

Much had changed at MacIntyre's munitions, with more women replacing the men who went away. There was talk that extensions were on the drawing board, to house a shipment of machinery waiting on the docks at Hamilton. It was partly confirmed, when the widow from the house near the works left with a lorry load of furniture, and the weeping figs in her garden were hacked down and carted away.

Isabel died many times.

The camaraderie—the cosy mateship that the annexe had enjoyed—was sacrificed to the demands of increased production, and Lulla accepted glumly that there was little to laugh about. Nothing to relieve the boredom of the assembly line. Working hours dragged, and the only bright spot was Charlie Redwing's army truck, compliments of the U.S. Wing Command.

As Andy went off to her meeting, Lulla caught sight of Daryl Missim and the boy Micky in the breezeway. Daryl was talking earnestly, gripping the little man's arm, shaking it now and then. There was doubt shadowing Micky's face. Not like him to be that way; Daryl was a hero in his eyes. What was Missim up to?

When Daryl released his hold, he put something into the pot-boy's hand before walking away. Flustered, Micky hurried into the annexe; by the time Lulla got there, he was busy topping up.

'Hello there, young Mick. What's new?'

''Lo, Lulla. Nothing new.'

'Everything all right?'

'Okay, Lulla. Hunky-dory.'

He kept to his task, carefully wiping up drips with a rag. He avoided her eyes—unusual for him.

'Hey, Micky.'

'Yeath?' Very cautious.

'What did Daryl want?' Immediately she regretted sounding so bossy.

Micky's head scrunched deeper into his shoulders. 'He didn't want nothin'.'

'Come on, you can tell me,' she coaxed, more gentle this time. 'Does he want you to do something bad? Something you don't want to do, maybe?'

Micky's head was shaking vigorously, his eyes blinking. He dug into his pocket, producing a small bar of chocolate. 'Look!' He knew she was not satisfied, and his agitation grew. She put out a hand, only to soothe, but Micky pulled back, spilling shellac over his boots and hers. Dismayed, he gave a small cry of distress, and before she could make light of it, scuttled off to the safety of the holding room.

Neither of them heard Andy come into the annexe, complaining that the meeting was cancelled. She arrived in time to see Micky disappear behind a cliff-face of crates. 'The wee man seems upset,' she said. Then she noticed Lulla's shoes. 'Och, and no wonder.'

'That's not all the trouble. Daryl's said something to upset him—and the way Micky was acting, it had nothing to do with the weather. Daryl's up to no good, and before the day's over, I intend finding out what it is!'

Andy raised a warning eyebrow. 'None of your business, lass. Daryl wouldn't put the lad to harm.'

'You're too trusting, Andy. I wouldn't ...' With the siren blasting off, Lulla snatched up her brush. She poked and prodded inside and around a grenade. Blast Missim! Just as he gets in sweet with us, he fouls things up. And if Micky's dragged into one of his nasty little deals, she thought grimly—so help me, I'll tear him apart.

Micky avoided her all that shift, and the shift after that. If she went to the holding room, he was out of her reach, high on a platform stacking boxes, pretending not to hear if she called him; staying put until she went away. As for Daryl, he was nowhere in sight. Nothing unusual in that: days could go by without a sign of him. Daryl was a troubleshooter, often assigned to some machine if production was flagging.

On her way home next afternoon, she saw them: Daryl, Micky, and an older man. They stood beside a car parked near the factory grounds, and as she drew closer, she could see Micky, this time in a calmer state, listening intently to what the stranger was saying.

The man's face was familiar, enough to make her stop and scrabble in her handbag for her glasses. She put them on, and when his features sharpened into view, she caught her breath. Her mind flew back to the Greek Club on the night when Daryl had left her waiting by the door. Daryl, deep in discussion with the man now talking to Micky ....

Micky was heading for big trouble.

Sudden anger sparked her into action and she began running. 'Micky! Mick-eee!'

But her voice was lost in the noise of a truck as it trundled past, and before she could yell again, the three men were in the car, driving away.

There was nothing she could do. She had no idea where Micky lived; ashamed, she realised for the first time that she didn't even know his last name. She vowed to make up for it, next time she saw him. And, come hell or high water, she was determined to wring the truth out of Daryl first thing in the morning.

Upset and worried, she was halfway along the street before she remembered to take off her glasses.

Now, without Janet and the Scotts for company, the once lighthearted trek from the factory to Franklin Street had become a test of endurance, a hike which capped a workday with exhaustion and heavy limbs. As Lulla trudged the last few blocks to the flat, she could not imagine things changing for the better. Her feet ached and toes itched, a reminder that she was out of tinea powder. She put aside the thought of going back to the chemist. Bi-carb would do.

Not that she was in a mad rush to get home, she reminded herself. There was little joy waiting there. Janet, as usual, would still be in her dressing-gown, her face swollen and damp with tears. Even the Scotts' flat was no place of refuge from her unkempt sadness. With the Scotts on different shifts, and all Hilda's spare time spent looking for Evie, Lulla hardly saw them.

Hilda was convinced that Eveleen was still about, in hiding.

Poor Hilda, Lulla sympathised, changing her loaded string-bag to the other hand. She was becoming an identity around the West End streets. Always on the same round of boarding-houses, hotels, dance halls and 'fancy houses' as she called them: the night people, the bartenders, madams and layabouts knew her well, and avoided her if they could. But Hilda was not giving up.

To Lulla's surprise, nor had Daryl Missim. Like the mother, he was certain the girl would turn up one day. Daryl could do no wrong in Hilda's eyes. Come Sunday, Lulla decided, she'd keep the woman company in her search. She changed hands again, and doubted that she had the energy for a fling at the Trocadero with Redwing. He would be on the lookout for her, and it *was* a good excuse to quit the flat. She'd see how she felt after tea-time.

Rounding the corner into Franklin Street, just one house away from home, Charlie Redwing and the dance hall were forgotten. There was a smell of roasting beef in the air. It mingled deliciously with the fragrance of the frangipanni tree dripping blossoms over next door's fence. Something told her that it came from Janet's kitchen. It could only mean one thing—Kirk had been found. He was here! She made a bolt for the gate; by the time it was unlatched, cold, common sense returned. Spanner's letter had sealed all hope in a leaden box. Hope lay dead—buried in the sands of the Strait.

But her heart tripped again, for, coming down the path to meet her, his grin a mile wide, was Spanner Larkin. Her eyes never left his face, as she carefully placed the string-bag at her feet. She needed both arms to hug him close. Miracles had happened while she had been at work. Standing at the top of the stairs, all frilled up in her best, was Janet. And—Glory be—she was smiling!

Spanner's arms were at the ready. 'How-de-do, Princess.'

She hurled herself at him. 'Larkin! Oh, am I glad to see you!' Breathless and laughing, she scattered kisses, not caring if Hickeys or the whole wide, mad world were watching. She clung to the lean, solid rock that was Spanner, their only link to the man Janet had loved.

Happy together, questions bubbling from Lulla's lips, they strode up the path to Janet, seemingly at peace with herself, at last.

There were near trips over dinner, snatches of memory that threatened to blight Janet's spirits and spoil the night and their gala meal together. Room enough around the table, now, Lulla noticed. She could not help remembering other nights and other feasts, elbow to elbow, knee to knee. Had Janet noticed also? She was sure of it.

So far, the perfectly cooked roast beef, the crisp potatoes and pumpkin, the apple-pie and heavenly tart, and the lighthearted hours were Janet's triumph. With Spanner there, she spoke of her missing husband, and the three drank to friendship, and the memory of able seaman Kirk Hope.

They didn't want him to go, and offered him the sofa for the night. But Spanner refused, saying the ship was catching the tide, and that anyway, his shore leave had been granted on sufferance.

'Sorry, girls, but it's a new Captain, new rules, and a new ship, and the crew in their normal place—on board! But when his nibs heard about Kirk, and Jan here, not a stone's throw away, he told me to shoot through and consider myself lucky.' He looked around. 'Now, where's m'cap?'

It was in the bedroom and Janet sprang up to get it. The sailor took Lulla's fingers, brushing them with his lips, raising an eyebrow in a way that she remembered off by heart.

'Know where I'd really like to spend the night, eh, Princess?'

'You never give up, do you Larkin ...' She recalled saying those exact words, way back when, and her bemused half-chuckle should have been enough of a reply.

Spanner nibbled a little finger. 'For a Princess, it's worth the battle.'

'Listen to it ...' But she didn't take her hand away.

He kept a strong grip on it, even when Janet returned with the cap. 'Here, Spanner. Don't go yet, I've got something for you.' She hurried off to the kitchen.

They could hear the rustle of paper and she was back in seconds, thrusting packages into his hands. 'Here's a fruit cake—and jam drops—Kirk used to love them. Share them around.' Her eyes were bright. Her lip trembled just a hint, but her smile was as generous as her gift.

Lulla took a guess that they'd be out of butter for the rest of the week.

Spanner held the young widow close. 'You're doing great, kiddo. Keep it up.' Over Janet's shoulder his eyes met Lulla's, compassion linking them solidly together. He gave Janet a few more pats before releasing her. 'Well, now ... must make tracks. Feel like stretching your legs for a bit, Lulla?' His look signalled that this was more than a casual invitation.

It was made quite clear that Spanner had something important to say. She nodded.

'There's the washing-up to do'—at the same time allowing Janet to bustle her outside the door. 'I could do with the exercise, but. Don't get much of it these days ... Ha! Ha! Big joke!'

'I'd be grateful for the company, Princess.'

Beneath the massive tangled branches of Musgrave Park, Spanner told Lulla the truth about his shipmate's drowning.

'I had to write that letter. I wanted her to believe that Kirk died like he lived—all the way go, and bugger the consequences.' He vindicated himself by saying that if someone else had fallen overboard, the mad bastard would have been the first to go after him, anyway.

'That was Kirk.'

Arm in arm, they strolled in darkness, careful to avoid bodies curved in love, scarcely hearing the promises made in whispers, and once a grunt of satisfaction that brought a grin to Spanner's lips. The soft, shadowed grass held no temptations to the sailor and the woman, on a night made solemn by such a sorry tale.

She could not imagine a sea made so rapacious by a wind blowing less than cyclonic. A sou'-easter, Spanner had called it, a trade wind that brought to mind pictures of balmy days and languid nights.

'I never dreamed it could be like that. So—so vicious. Dangerous.'

'It gets bouncy up there, sometimes. Cross-currents, rips going crazy, all at once.'

She shuddered at the description of those last moments in Kirk's life. His near rescue, then the sudden disappearance; the upthrust of his desperate body. She could see it all, and, in a way, felt surprise that Spanner had the need to share it with her. It was an act of trust and confidence she respected.

She asked him quietly, 'The search—it was thorough, wasn't it?'

'What do you think—of course it was.'

'But that's what I can't understand. Nothing washed up. No sign. Even an old boot finds shore eventually.' Then, half-apologetically, 'Well, so they all say.'

'And they know bugger-all.'

'Do you think—' This she hesitated to ask. 'Could a shark have taken him? The way you said he tried to clear the water ...'

Spanner shook his head. 'No. A shark bites, and tears off great chunks. Sorry, Lulla, but you asked. No, it wasn't a shark.' He seemed reluctant to carry on. But she felt his need to talk it out.

She squeezed his arm. 'Go on, I'm listening. I may as well hear the rest of it. What happened?'

'Well, we think a groper might have done it.'

'A groper!'

The shock sickened her. Somehow, she could have accepted a shark attack. Why, she couldn't tell. 'Oh, my God, that's horrible. I didn't think—oh, God—I don't know what to think.' She wanted to throw up.

Spanner was talking quickly now, as if words could expunge the memory of it all from his mind. 'Everyone knows he's there. The groper. Has been for years, and the jetty's his own personal territory. He's got more hooks in him than a butcher's shop ... and bullets ... the lot. He's a cunning old brute, with a mouth and gut the size of a railway tunnel.' He gave her a sidelong glance to see how she was taking it.

She nodded for him to keep going.

'We reckon he thought Kirk was bait. Just a lump of meat dangling off the end of a line, and like a hundred times before, he took it, not meaning any harm.' Spanner partly succeeded in controlling the shake in his voice. 'That's the rotten part of it. It was such a bloody stupid way to die.'

By now, they had crossed the park, a silence between them as thick and as heavy as the night air. There was nothing left to say. Earlier, light rain had fallen and puddles on the road reflected the hooded lights of a U.S. Army ambulance, its tyres hissing over the wet bitumen. Like the military police, they were a familiar sight around the southside streets. As its tail-light disappeared around a bend, Lulla mused over Redwing's words from a few days back. 'There's a motor pool, mostly ambulances, opening up not far from here. Just say the word, honey—they're waiting for you.'

An ambulance driver. Lulla liked the idea. She'd be in the thick of things in a job like that. But fat chance of getting it!

From the time they had left the flat, their steps had taken them in a wide loop and now they were heading for the tramline that would take Lulla back to West End. Spanner suggested that the night was young; he had a few hours of leave to go.

She stopped him from saying anything more. 'Sorry, Spanner, I'm dog-tired. And I'm anxious about Janet. It's the first time she's surfaced since Kirk died—thanks to you, and—and I—'

'Sure.' He seemed to understand. 'Seeing me, and all ...'

At the tramstop, she braced herself against the stop sign, suddenly aware of her aching legs and itching toes. The long street, even at that early hour, appeared asleep. No sign of life, not even a cat, strayed across their path.

Where had all the laughter gone?

She perked up as the faint strains of music from the distant Trocadero began. A roll of drums. The place would be jumping. Redwing would be there, popular, cutting up a storm, a sight to see. The floor always cleared when Redwing cut a neat and clever rug.

'Lulla, you're miles away.'

'Not so far. Just a block or two.'

He followed her gaze down the length of the street to where the lights splashed the footpath in front of the dance palace doors. 'I see what you mean.' He gave her a thoughtful look. 'Do you want to go there? Might cheer us both up a bit.'

'Thanks, Spanner, but no.'

Waiting side by side, yet in a way separated by the

secret they shared, the easy familiarity seemed to have gone. Suddenly, Spanner turned to face her full on. His hands rested lightly on her waist. His question came as a surprise.

'Ever thought what you might do when this is all over?'

'Plenty, I hope.'

'Ever been up north?'

'Don't know if I care to, after what I've heard tonight.'

'Don't let that put you off, Princess. It can be bloody lovely up there.'

'Yeah?'

'Might show it to you, one of these days.'

Thoughts of Redwing, ambulances and brightly lit dance halls were swept aside by the implication. It was the closest Lulla had ever been to a proposal of marriage—but she let it ride. She wasn't ready for anything like that. Not yet! And if she knew Spanner Larkin, neither was he! Before she could think up a ready quip, transport came clanging down the street at such a pace that Spanner risked his neck to slow it down. She leapt aboard.

The sight of him standing alone on the road, watching the distance between them lengthening, prompted a blow-away kiss.

'I just might take you up on that, sailor,' she called, but doubted that he heard as the tram rattled off towards West End junction.

• • •

She tiptoed into the darkened flat, through to the bathroom, careful not to disturb the sleeping figure curled up in bed. She closed the bathroom door before turning on the light.

Janet asleep already—now that was something.

As Lulla slathered cold cream over her face, Spanner's casual comment—it had seemed more of an afterthought, about taking her north—had set the wheels turning. In the many months she had known him, there had never been promises given, or taken. Spanner must be getting soft in his old age, she told the white, plastered face in the mirror. She tore a strip off the toilet roll, wrapped it around her fingers and began removing the cream from her throat. The long, steady strokes aided slow, careful thinking: a mulling over of things, a nightly ritual that she always enjoyed.

For Janet's sake, she decided against taking a shower. The gas heater, noisy and boisterous, was bound to wake her. Preparations for bed were easier now that her hair was short. No more pin curls. Lulla prided herself in being one step ahead of fashion, and, after seeing Ingrid Bergman's cropped curls in *For Whom The Bell Tolls*, had sworn never again to endure the clamps and weight of a Eugene Wave.

She turned off the light and was sneaking through to the front room when the bed lamp was switched on. Janet was propped on one elbow. 'Where are you going?'

'To the sofa. You were sound asleep.'

'Well, I'm awake now.'

Lulla's spirits sagged. Janet had been crying again. In a flash, she wished that she had accepted Spanner's invitation to go to the Troc.

Janet threw back the covers. 'Come on.'

Not wanting to, Lulla slid between the sheets to please her. Ignoring the tear-blotched cheeks, she gave Janet's arm a brief pat before turning over. She closed her eyes. Miserable, she had to admit that she'd had enough of tears and sadness; she was plagued with guilt for feeling so.

Drifting into sleep, she was alerted to soft movements on Janet's side of the bed; Janet's pillow would already be damp, and with a cry of pity, Lulla turned over quickly and gathered Janet into her arms.

'There, there, love. Don't cry so. This, too, will pass.'

She hardly knew what she was saying, she was out of comforting words, but she kept on making noises. It was a monologue that might bring some peace to the widow's bruised heart. She tried shushing Janet from accusing herself of unfaithfulness, of wicked thoughts. Kirk had been taken from her, it was a punishment, she said, for letting another man 'touch her'. And she missed him so. Oh, how she missed him.

Lulla was getting angry. 'Stop it, Jan! Stop it. You've done nothing. You were a good and faithful wife. One of the best. And Kirk bloody well knew it!'

'But you don't know—'

'I know everything! Now shut up! I thought you—

oh, never mind, what I thought. Go on—cry your eyes out.' Lulla's shoulders and arms ached, but still she stroked and petted the woman as a mother would a sobbing child.

Gradually, the weeping subsided and Janet's breath quietened. She gave little twitches, and Lulla realised—sweet miracle—that Janet had fallen asleep. Still holding her in her arms, she slowly eased herself down on the pillow. She lay there for a long time, with Janet's head on her breast. Then carefully, carefully, as if placing a sleeping baby back in its cradle, Lulla moved Janet to her own side of the bed.

Lulla lay staring into the dark, her thoughts on Spanner, the war, Redwing and all the men who had passed her way. News of some maimed, many already dead, like Kirk, and there must be many more to go down the same dread track.

But her thoughts always came back to Jan's golden sailor, and the bluster and joy that had swept through the tiny flat when he came ashore. That big, handsome lug gone for ever. It wasn't fair.

Goodbye, Kirk.

25

JANET WAS FIRST UP. She stood by the bed dressed, ready for work, a cup of tea in her hand. 'Rise and shine,' she carolled, all scrubbed and ready to go. 'It's a beautiful day and here's a cuppa to start it off.'

Feeling half-alive, Lulla sent up a silent thank-the-Lord, realising that Janet was finally over the hump.

Janet placed the cup on the dressing-table and made a fuss of plumping up pillows to support Lulla's sagging frame.

'Bacon and eggs for breakfast, believe it or not,' she chirruped. 'Spanner's gift, and I didn't ask from where.'

'Knowing Larkin, he possibly has a deal going with the cook.' Lulla took a grateful gulp of tea. 'He and Daryl would make a good pair.' Reminding herself that Daryl had some explaining to do.

The shadows had disappeared with the night's drizzle. Outside, the air sparkled fresh. Even at that early hour old Hickey could be heard mowing, and the sweet smell of grass drifted through the windows. As they ate their way through the unaccustomed eggs and bacon, Lulla foretold that it had to be some special day, a day of good surprise.

'Feel it in me bones ...'

It began the moment they walked down the front stairs. Daryl Missim was careering down the street in the Hillman. He braked outside the gate. Before Lulla could ask about Micky, Daryl bounded past them, took the steps in a few strides and was knocking at Hilda's door. They had to be satisfied with a hasty whisper: 'We've found Evie. She's all right!'

Hilda was still in bed. She had what she called 'The Wog', a battering onslaught of coughs, sneezes and aches. She nibbled at a teaspoon of sugar and kerosene to ease her hurting throat, and when Peggy answered the door, she tensed at the sound of Daryl's voice.

'Mum!' Peggy called excitedly, 'it's Daryl. He's—'

'Bring him in. In here!' she rasped. Her heart pounded as she struggled into a bed-jacket. Her hand trembled as she raked fingers through her hair to comb it.

Daryl bounced in, beaming. 'She's in Sydney, and okay.' He sat down at the foot of the bed, looking pleased with himself.

'Sydney ...' It was the end of the world to the

Scotts, who still called themselves Northerners. Sydney was *the South*, a warren of high buildings, rampant with high living and low morals. What was Evie doing there?

By all accounts, according to Daryl, she was making the most of it. He seemed unconcerned, or unaware of the implications of what he was saying. He was, in fact, grinning.

'Making the most of what?' He waited while Hilda sneezed violently into a square of torn bedsheet. She wiped her eyes. 'Well, give me the worst of it.'

He put up a placating hand. 'Now don't jump to conclusions. I said she was all right, didn't I?' Daryl seemed bent on spinning out his news. 'She's a showgirl in a nightclub at the Cross!' Hilda listened carefully as Daryl filled in the details, her eyes more wary than concerned as he outlined the facets of Eveleen's nights under spotlights. 'They don't ask questions down there,' Daryl told her, 'but she's doing fine, and I've got a couple of pals who are keeping half an eye on her.' He put up a finger. 'Wait a minute, I've an address here—' Producing a wallet, he fished out a piece of paper and handed it to her.

Hilda studied it with moving, silent lips, then without a word gave it to Peggy to read. As if playing for time, she slowly tore off a clean strip of the sheeting folded beside her. She blew her nose and tucked the rag under her pillow. 'Can't imagine Evie on the stage. I suppose you could call it a job,' she said tiredly.

Peggy shot her a startled look. 'Mum, you sound as if she's going to stay there!'

Hilda waved her exclamation aside. 'We'll talk about this later. Make Daryl a cup of something, love, and Daryl—I want to thank you.' She gazed into space, rubbing her forehead and ruminating over the end result of all their searching. 'I'll never be able to thank you enough.'

It was Daryl's turn to wonder, not quite believing the obvious. 'You *are* going to bring her home, aren't you? You've only got to give the police that address ...' His voice trailed off, silenced by the slow shaking of Hilda's head.

'What's the use. Now that I know she's all right— I suppose—she can stay there. Bring her back and she'd be off again first chance. She knows where her home is. The door's open.'

This was beyond Daryl's understanding. 'But Hilda, the way you've looked for her. Every spare minute you've had. You've walked to Burke and back again!'

'I had to find out what happened. Now I know.'

She turned her head away from him, closing her eyes, just as Peggy tiptoed back into the room. The girl looked down at her mother, not quite knowing what to do.

'Mum, I heard what you said to Daryl. We just can't leave her there.'

'Yes we can.' Hilda kept her eyes closed. 'We'll write. We'll keep in touch. Now go away, both of you.' Coughing racked her again.

. . .

Peggy, on late shift, was gone and Hilda, her headache easing, padded into the kitchen. She was feeling peckish; and Peggy, despite remonstrations over the decision to leave Evie be, had, as promised, left sandwiches and jelly and junket in the ice-chest.

It was the closest they'd ever been to a full-blown bust-up. The first time Peggy had banged out of the flat without a goodbye kiss. Hilda lifted the corner of a clean tea-towel covering something on the table, and smiled. Scones on a plate were proof that Peggy couldn't hold a grudge. Even the best china teapot had been brought into use. She decided such a dainty table warranted a shower and her hair tied back with a ribbon; and she'd refresh herself with the last of her *Evening In Paris*.

On the way back to the bedroom, she heard the squeak of the front gate. Taking a quick look, she saw an American, smartly uniformed, come up the path. As he reached the stairs she noticed that his face was vaguely familiar, and guessed that he was one of Lulla's boyfriends. Dry run for him, she thought. She wasn't prepared, in her soggy state, to enlighten him as to Lulla's whereabouts.

She did not expect to hear his knock on her own front door and was determined not to open it when he did. 'Yes?' She called through the keyhole.

'Hilda?'

Her mouth dropped open. The slight Yankee twang didn't fool her. There was nothing to do but get him inside quickly, before anyone noticed. Even so, from the corner of one eye she saw the Hickeys, faces hung over the banisters like twin full moons.

'What are you doing here?' was all she could say, her knees so weak she nearly sank to the floor. Running eyes, swollen nose, and that damned husband of hers picks a time like this to throw his hat through the door.

'Hello, Hilda. Must be a bit of a shock, eh? Been a long time.'

'Nine years to be exact.'

It looked as if everything was going all right for Alf. The droop of depression had disappeared, and his uniform sat on him snugly. If anything, Hilda thought sourly, the bastard's matured well. Her sneezes returned so vigorously that she wondered if she was allergic to him.

'How did you find me?' she spluttered, hating herself, and hating him for seeing her in such a pitiful mess.

'You've gotta hand it to the Yanks, Hilda. They can make anything happen once their minds are made up. They found you for me—well, where you work, anyway.'

'What the hell do you mean, "found *me* for *you*"? Who says I want to be found?'

'Now calm down, Mother—'

'Don't you "mother" me.'

It did little to damp down her growing resentment. His slight accent fuelled it, along with the neat moustache and the MacArthur glare glasses tucked into the pocket of his immaculately ironed shirt.

Without any encouragement, Alf seated himself on a chair. 'Sorry to see you have a cold. I've just the thing for that. But first things first. Now, Hilda, after all that's happened, I'm not here to insult you by asking to patch things up.'

'Thanks a million ...'

Ignoring her hostility, he carried on. 'But I've a favour to ask. A proposition, actually.'

'Oh yes? Tell me.' She was still standing, looking down at him, hand on the doorknob as if ready to show him out.

Alf's aplomb was slipping, along with his accent. 'Now, Hilda ...' His tongue did the circuit of his lips. 'Ah—you wouldn't make a cup of tea or something for a man, would you?'

'No, I wouldn't.' Her determination was scattered by three hard sneezes and, groping for a handkerchief, she wished that he would go away and leave her to the miseries. After she had blown her nose yet again, Alf gave a self-deprecating grin. 'I wouldn't bother you, but it's almost a matter of life and death. Well, my life, anyway.'

That old helpless feeling was returning. It was Alf again, half-pleading, sitting at some kitchen table, convincing her: 'You can't go wrong, Hilda, you just can't go wrong.' And at the end of it all, her paying the price for listening. But this time, it was a matter of pride that she look her best, before closing her ears and sending him off. Ordering him out of her life, for good.

'Alf, I'm not listening to another word until I freshen up. And I'm warning you that I'll not come into any of your pathetic schemes. Never again! However, as no man—or woman—leaves my kitchen without breaking bread, I'll make you that pot of tea. We could both do with one.' Under the circumstances, and with all the dignity that she could muster, Hilda made a business of swishing across the bedroom curtain, cutting off Alf's view of the crumpled, unmade bed.

The kettle was nearing the boil.

'Well,' said Hilda, buttering scones, 'what's this life and death business?' The kettle whistled, and after making tea, she refilled it with fresh water before coming back to the table.

'Still a four-cup girl, eh?' Alf commented approvingly. He jumped up, making a show of pulling out her chair.

She acknowledged the gesture by nothing more than a raised eyebrow. In silence, she poured out the tea. 'I'm waiting, Alf.'

'Ah, yes. As you can see, I'm working now for the Americans.'

'So I've noticed.'

'Have been for some time—small ships. Up and down the coast. In and out. All over the place.'

Almost by accident, Alf told her, it was discovered he had a way with ships' engines. In the past, bad luck and hard times had stultified an inventive brain. His brain, he boasted proudly. Under the influence of his new employers, an uncanny union between machines and Alf had developed.

'For once in my life, I'm onto something worthwhile. Just a gadget,' he pretended modesty; but embellished the word by saying it would make a big difference to fuel consumption—and, in turn, the war effort. 'That's all I can say at the moment.'

The Americans were keen to send him off to the States, where their expertise and superior equipment might bring to fruition the work he had begun in a ship's engine room.

'There's only one thing that stops me, Hilda ...'

'What's that?'

'You,' he said quietly. He smoothed and moulded his moustache with delicate fingers as he explained the necessity of obtaining Hilda's permission before he could set foot on American soil. Anxiety sharpened his voice. 'You wouldn't stop me, would you.'

'Give me time to think about it.' She concentrated on stirring her tea. Let him sweat a while. It was a temptation she couldn't resist.

'Hilda, I need to know soon. Very soon. There's a transport plane leaving day after tomorrow. We touch down in Sydney for a few days. Briefings—things like that,' he made it sound important. Which, Hilda admitted, it probably was; Alf straightened his shoulders, 'Then it's off, to the good ol' U.S. of A. You wouldn't deny me a chance like that, now, would you?'

'I said I'll think about it.' She could feel her lips

twitching and, to hide it, took sips from her cup. But her shoulders began shaking as laughter—strange laughter—stirred deep inside her. It was not at all a time for mirth, but the feeling grew stronger until it finally exploded into Alf's astonished face. Her belly shook as she put down her cup to avoid the hot tea spilling.

Alf was hurt. 'No cause to act like that, old girl.' His features settled into a pious mould. 'Refuse me on this and you could hold up the war effort, you know.'

Hilda gave a wild shriek of laughter. She held her sides; she choked and coughed. It seemed as if nothing could be done to stop her. The years of frustration and loneliness, the disappointments that had been held in check by rigid self-control, spilled over in a floodtide of hysterical braying. (She called it that herself, when she told Peggy all about it later.)

'You bloody hypocrite,' she gasped. 'You finally show up begging for favours. You act as if you walked out of this door no more than a few minutes ago. Not once have you asked about your daughters, or how we've managed over the years.' Now the laughter fizzled out, doused by scalding anger. 'Well let me tell you, Alf Scott'—she made an effort to keep her voice down—'Peggy and me are doing fine. But Evie, now—what about Evie? Maybe if you'd had the guts to tough things out with us, she'd be here now. Not whoring around in some sleazy nightclub down south. Yes, that's where she is, and that's about what she's doing.' She caught up with her breath. 'Aren't you proud of yourself as a father? Aren't you?'

'I'm sorry, Hilda. What else can I say?'

Subdued, Alf pulled and plucked at his moustache, then reached for the teapot as though from habit and poured her another cup, stirring in three spoons of sugar. He produced a hip flask from his pocket and poured a good amount into her cup. 'Best thing for a cold, and I could do with a drop myself.'

She only had the energy to nod, breathless with emotion and congested tubes. She drew back as he leaned over to touch her.

'Truly to God, Hilda, I'm sorry. But you know what it was like up there. No work, no money—a man can take so much. You must remember.'

She remembered, all right ... That which had been deliberately erased, more or less, now lay just outside the door. The familiar hall of the flat, the hatstand, the telephone, had vanished entirely, displaced by total recall. If she breathed deeply enough, the smell of dust and the sweet aroma of tobacco leaf was seeping under the door, invading the room. The flat across the hall was vanquished by rows of leaf, thirsty for water, vulnerable under a malicious sun. She heard again the derision of crows from the scraggle of bush at the end of an ochre paddock, and saw the three figures—a man, woman, a girl, bent low over those rows of ochre dirt, covering each tender shoot with slips of newspaper; and the three again, with pail and dipper, wetting the squares of shade under the newspaper tents. Row after row. All for what? For nothing.

Oh, yes. She remembered. But the anger, too, had now leached away, and she was ready to give him his answer. Alf was saying that he already knew about Eveleen. Peggy had told him at the factory. She had forgotten about that. Of course, Peggy would have mentioned it. Alf indicated the flask, asking if she wanted topping up. She was about to refuse, then nodded.

'Why not? It clears my head.'

He smiled with satisfaction, sensing that her mind was made up in his favour. He was generous with the whiskey. 'What's the verdict?'

'Before I tell you any which way, there's something you can do. I want your word on it.'

He looked and sounded very cautious. 'What's that, Hilda?'

'Don't look so dammed uncomfortable. All you have to do, for once in your life—'

'I'm listening.'

In answer, she pushed herself away from the table. 'Just wait there.' She went into the bedroom. On the dressing-table was a small box of inlaid wood. She opened it to remove the slip of paper Daryl had left with her. She smoothed out the creases and read again the Sydney address, before returning to Alf.

'Here.' She pressed it into his hand. 'Act like a father for once in your life. You're going to Sydney. I can't—whatever the reason, it's nearly impossible for a civilian to get there. So there's your daughter's address. See how she is. Who knows ...' A shuddering sigh escaped her. 'She might listen to you. One word from me and she does what she likes. See what you can do. Tell her I'll write. Tell her—tell her we miss her. I—we, want her home.'

'I will, Hilda. I'll do my best.'

'See that you do.' Then she held out her hand. 'Well, where are they? These papers I'm supposed to sign.'

'I'll bring them over tomorrow.'

In his delight, years slipped away from his features. To Hilda's disgust, he looked no older than the day he had deserted her. Envy flickered for a second—it's not bloody fair, she thought, aware of her own worn looks and the widow's hump from bending over too many washtubs, filled with other people's washing. But when was anything ever fair? Then, for Hilda, unsuspecting, there came reward: some sort of compensation for those lost, hard years. Alf had to pay a price for leaving Australian shores. He told her that the law said a portion of his salary must go to his wife—one Hilda Scott. A fine inducement to fall in with his plans—if she had known about it.

Alf managed to look sheepish. 'Should have mentioned it earlier, old girl. But there you are.' Pleased, as if the whole idea was one of his own inventions. He rose from the chair, settled the sunglasses on his nose, removed the cap that had sat snugly under an epaulet and jauntily angled it on to his head. His last words, as Hilda showed him the door, swaggered with confidence. 'With your factory wages and this little lot coming in regular, you'll soon have a tidy sum. It might make up for all the bad years.' As if he couldn't help himself, he gave her a wink, saying, 'You can't go wrong, Hilda. You just can't go wrong.'

Hilda sniffed, and her eyes watered so much that it was hard for Alf to judge if the cause was her cold, or something else.

26

As HILDA WAS giving Alf lessons in parental behaviour, their daughter, Eveleen Scott, was stretching and yawning into another day.

She eyed off the clock, surprised to find it was not yet midday. Usually she slept until well into the afternoon. Her days and nights had fallen into a loose but regular routine. Ever since the day that Evie had begun serving Ben's delicious pastries and pies to the habitués of the Cross, she had progressed, in her own eyes, from better to much better.

A mere two weeks had been played out in the Daffodil Cake Shoppe and then she was handing in her notice to a resigned but scarcely surprised Ben. Although Evie had been out on deliveries and did not see her, it began the day Cissy Gurney came in to order a birthday cake—three tiers high (four if possible) with thirty candles for the boyfriend—Buff Davies.

While Ben slathered chocolate fudge onto his masterpiece and scrolled fondant curlicues and arabesques, he told her all about Cissy. She was the owner of the Polka Dot nightclub. Swanky, Ben said: select, and noted for the most glamorous and beautiful showgirls in the business. Even the divine Belle de Rae had held court there for years.

'Quality, not quantity' was Cissy's boast.

She herself had been one of Florenz Ziegfeld's high-kickers. Love had brought her to Australia, and love had dumped her on a goldfield somewhere north of Capricorn. She had eventually arrived in Sydney, so gossip went, weighed down with an outsize handbag chock-a-block with nuggets, and a Colt automatic revolver which she'd used to end an unfortunate affaire. Some, over the years, claimed to have seen the nuggets, but none had seen the automatic.

Evie couldn't wait to set eyes on her.

On the day of the party, Cissy sent two of her 'boys' round with a wheelbarrow to pick up the cake. They left with Ben in tow, flinching over every bump and lurch, his fondant and forcing-bag at the ready for emergency repairs.

Cissy came in the next day to pay the bill. For the first time she noticed the girl behind the counter, and Ben gave a groan as she looked Evie up and down and asked: 'Can you sing?'

When Evie said 'no', Cissy flashed back: 'Well, dance ... jig ... do a Highland fling?'

Evie thought that jitterbugging would not count for much; she shook her head, for once awed by a presence that radiated a certain tawdry splendour: flowing scarves, rouged cheeks, a plethora of emeralds and diamonds, and a surprisingly wonderful smile.

'Well,' said Cissy, 'surely t'Gawd you can keep rock-still.'

Evie, not knowing what she meant by that, just stood silent, feeling that she was being stripped bare on the spot. Ben, meanwhile, was begging the night-club owner to go away.

'If you keep on hiring beauties to sell your lousy tarts, Ben, be prepared to lose them to me. If you want to keep 'em, hire a dame that's overweight, over fifty, and over the hill!' With that she gave the girl her startling smile once more and handed over a business card, tapping the counter with cigarette-stained fingers. Sunlight sparked off her diamond rings. 'Here, sweetie. When you get tired of selling custard tarts, come and see me at the Polka Dot.' With a swirl of scarves and a light clatter of brilliant-studded heels she was gone, leaving Evie gaping. Evie couldn't believe the heels might be diamond-capped!

The shop, despite the rococo enticement of Ben's window, seemed duller and quieter after Cissy had gone.

'She should hire me as her talent scout,' Ben had mourned, 'you'll be the third I've lost to her.'

Evie remembered the day so well; how her heart had thumped with excitement after Cissy had gone.

She still had the card with its gilt-edged border and sketch of a girl wearing nothing but a single polka-dot and long evening gloves.

'Of course you'll be going,' Ben had sadly surmised.

'I reckon ...'

She had gone to the Polka Dot nightclub that afternoon after work. Ben even told her how to get there. At first, she was not impressed by what she saw. The place looked dingy, dark and there was a musty smell of air trapped by too many velvet drapes. Tables and bentwood chairs were stacked around the walls, for workmen were doing something to the floor. In Evie's eyes the stage was disappointingly small. Nothing like the glorious ivory staircase that Lana Turner had descended in *Ziegfeld Girl*. It was nothing like what she had imagined; even the few girls rehearsing on the stage seemed very ordinary; not much different from Lulla Riddel with her hair up in pin curls before going to bed. They hadn't even noticed her standing there, and she was about to leave when a voice from a dim corner sealed off her escape.

'You took y'time getting here.' There was no mistaking Cissy's voice.

'I came straight after work,' Evie flared.

'Only joking, sweetie.' Cissy's hoydenish rasp was lightened by underlying humour. 'Come here!' she ordered.

Evie found herself doing what she was told. She crossed the floor, skirting the workmen replacing floorboards, nearly tripped over a brace and bit and, feeling more clumsy than she'd ever done before, approached the two people sitting at a table. Evie guessed the man with Cissy must be the Birthday Boy, Buff Davies. She would have taken him for her son if Ben hadn't put her in the picture.

Again her imagination had cheated her. Somehow she had cast Buff Davies with the looks of a Victor Mature. But the man lounging back at ease in the chair was fair and freckled, with candid blue eyes and a crop of nearly straight carrot hair.

'Evie, this is my nephew, Buff.' He could have been, with the fair skin and the freckles that Cissy probably hid beneath the heavy powder and rouge on her face. During the introductions, she was aware of the woman's penetrating gaze. It relaxed and softened only after Buff had casually nodded, still at ease, in his chair.

'Howdy do,' was all he'd said.

'Well, Evie, know anything at all about the business?' Cissy waved her diamonds around the room indicating the balconies, the curtains and finally the stage.

'Only what I've seen in the pictures.'

'H'mm ... that's not going to help much. Now stand back there.' Evie took a backward step. 'No! Further than that.' When she had moved far enough, Cissy put up her hand. 'Right! Now walk towards us—not so fast!' She paced the girl by tapping on the table. 'Yeah ... better ... what d'you think, Buff?'

Buff, with half-closed eyes, nodded slowly. 'Bit

rough around the edges, but she's got the looks.' He could have been analysing a side of lamb. Evie, still walking, came near to trampling Cissy's peep-toe shoes.

Cissy eased her back gently with both hands. 'Okay. Now let's see those gams.'

Eveleen knew exactly what she meant and lifted her skirt, posing like the pin-ups she'd seen of Betty Grable. Suddenly it was all too easy and she fell into the part, posing and strutting, encouraged by a low whistle of appreciation, not from Buff but from the lips of another of Cissy's boys who had strolled into view.

Buff remained silent, blue eyes expressionless. And that was all right by Evie. There was something about him that gave her the creeps.

'Think we should take her on, Buff?'

He shrugged. 'You're the boss.'

By the tone of Cissy's voice, Evie knew she was already employed. She couldn't believe her luck.

'Give Ben your notice, kid, and in no time we'll turn you into a showgirl. With those legs, you're halfway there—Mac!'

The Nightclub Queen had beckoned to the other man, still half-concealed by shadows, who had whistled. As he strolled over, she introduced him. 'Meet Evie.'

Here was the Victor Mature she had imagined!

'She's coming tonight to see the show, Mac; so introduce her to the girls. Give her an idea what it's all about. Buff and me will be in later.' She patted

the girl's hand, dismissing her. 'Be back by nine—
Oh, Mac! Give the kid something decent to wear.'

Between afternoon and nightfall, as Evie had discovered, magic transformed the Polka Dot nightclub. As arranged, Mac had met her outside, and as she walked through the doors an involuntary gasp escaped her lips; any doubts she may have had of a future tied up with Cissy, fled.

The place sparkled under bright chandeliers, and the balconies, that had crouched overhead in darkness, were as gilt-bright and decorative as one of Ben's Gâteau St Honorés. Tables had lost their afternoon nudity and were dressed to kill with linen, goblets and candlelight, while the crimson drapes glowed richly. There wasn't a polka dot to be seen; it crossed Evie's mind that Cissy could have picked a better name for her nightclub.

Evie, powder-blue satin clinging to every delightful curve, matched the glitter. She had found her niche at last.

She soon learned that Cissy's stage shows were as extravagant and as colourful as the nightclub itself. The whole parade was an extension of Cissy—smutchy by day, glorious by night. And Evie found out that under light bulbs Cissy's diamonds came into their own!

It was a night that the girl from North Queensland would never forget. Just the fact that she sat with Mac was enough to tell the regulars that Cissy had found another beauty. Speculative eyes looked her over ... she knew she met with their full approval. Evie, in that powder-blue dress and a sparkling paste choker, was a stunner!

Next afternoon, after the Daffodil Cake Shoppe had closed, Evie was around at the Polka Dot again. A week after that, she was on stage and already her long, smooth legs were becoming famous. She had never been so happy. Cissy, taking a special fancy to her, put her to the test. Worked her hard. Showed her how to walk—stalk, as she called it, or else not move a muscle when a G-string and feathers were Evie's sole adornments. 'That dab of sequins on your tits don't count as a costume, sweetie. The law says y'gotta keep still. No swingin' them about like a mad witch's piss—get it? Do just what I tell you, and you'll be the toast of the Cross in a month.'

There were two hard and fast rules Evie had to learn, even before she was taught to 'stalk'. Cissy made no bones about it.

'Keep off the liquor before and during the show—so that means most of the time! Ruins y'looks, anyhow.'

It was Mac who told her the second and even more important rule. 'Lay off the boyfriend, Evie,' Mac warned. 'Don't give him the glad eye, I'm warning you. You'll be kicked straight out of that door—or worse.' She soon noticed that no one broke the rules, even the first one. They were all too well paid for that.

Yes, in Evie's own words and thoughts, since meeting Ben and Cissy, she had gone from better to much better.

Evie yawned and stretched again, dislodging the poodle from the end of the bed. It gave a yelp but still hung around for its morning chocolate. She left the bed and, as always, crossed the room to look out of the window. The novelty of seeing sand and water at the end of a garden path had not worn off. A swim, weather permitting, was an integral part of her day: an important segment of the routine that kept her body in tune and a glowing suntan that looked marvellous under the spotlight at night. She then slipped off the nightie to study herself in the full-length mirror; partly to admire, partly to see if a spot, pimple, or blackhead marred the perfection of her skin. Finding nothing to worry over, she put on a bathing suit, and on the way out, satisfied hunger with a pear from a basket filled to overflowing with the choicest fruit—a regular gift found outside the dressing-room, often before she had the chance to finish the last offering. The full cast benefited from Evie's besotted unknown.

The tiny cove was smooth and virginal after a full night tide. No one around. It was the one place where Evie could tolerate solitude. She enjoyed swimming alone and diving deep, as much at home beneath the water, cool silk on the flesh, as on top. When she'd had enough she began the ritual of lying down to toast herself. Coconut oil smoothed onto arms and legs, the top of her costume pulled down as far as she dared, giving herself up to the sun.

She dozed ... then wondered if she dreamed when

a voice whispered in her ear: 'A pearl for a mermaid true. Wear it tonight for me.'

Something cool and sleek was dropped into her half-opened palm. She rolled over, opening her eyes. Her heart lurched as much in fear as surprise. 'What the hell are you doing here!'

Hot blue eyes stared down at her; his body, not used to sun, was already turning pink.

Buff Davies!

She could hardly believe his audacity. He knew the rules as well as she did. All the warnings she had heard backstage raced through her mind ... 'Leave him alone. Don't even look at him.'—'Cissy will skin you alive, and serve up his balls for your breakfast!'—'She's the best boss in the world, Evie, but stir her up over lover boy, and she'd rage like a bushfire out of control.'—'Leave him alone!'

Evie had no desire to string Buff along in any shape or form. She felt a prickle pass over her, a chill as when a breeze touches a sunburned back. He stood there, the hard light behind him; his hair afire.

'What are you doing here?' she asked again.

'It's a free country, Evie. Anyway, it happens to be one of my favourite watering holes, too.'

And you're a bloody liar! She thought to herself.

Casual and unconcerned, he settled down beside her as if they met each other every day at the same spot. She shifted away from him and then realised that she still clutched whatever he had dropped into her hand. She uncurled her fingers. It was a teardrop pearl—baroque, flushed pink and of some size, set in gold with a fine gold chain. Although she found it hard, she placed the piece carefully on the strip of towel between them, feigning disinterest.

'You're mad, Buff Davies, and I don't want your pearl. *Thanks* very much.' Her voice flat with rejection.

Buff hunched his shoulders. 'Give it away, then.'

Evie looked about her to see if they were being observed. The cove still appeared deserted, but it was rumoured that if Cissy wasn't around, someone else was; usually Mac, to keep an eye on Buff no matter what.

He looked innocent enough as he trickled sand through his fingers, not attempting to touch her, behaving like any sun-lover on a day off. She wasn't happy.

'Take that damned thing and go! Scram! If you don't, I will.'

Even if his body was as white as the driven snow, it was well proportioned, and any guesswork was removed by the light silk of his bathing trunks. She'd seen the style only once before, on Bondi Beach. She'd been surfing with Claire, her counterpart onstage, who had pointed out a couple posturing and doing handstands, only a few yards away. 'They're reffos ...' she'd whispered. 'You can tell by those trunks—if they can be called that. Made of sheer silk, I reckon ... shows off "the lot".' Claire had giggled.

Evie could not help but notice that Buff's 'lot' was more than adequate. She understood why Cissy held a tight rein, seeing she was old enough to be his mother! For once in her life, she was not tempted. Pale skin and freckles, combined with Cissy's reputation, held little appeal.

She glared at him. 'Are you going? Or me?'

Buff turned to her, innocent as a two-year old. 'I'll go ...' Taking his time, he got to his feet, stretching. A shock stabbed through Evie as he arched his back, looking down with blatant invitation. She wondered what would have happened if by chance they'd touched.

'Don't forget,' he said, indicating the pear-shaped pendant. 'Wear it for me—and I'll know what to do, eh?'

One second he was there, then he was gone, hidden by one of the boulders that held the cove together.

On her beach towel, the sea jewel lay warmed by the sun. Evie picked it up, stroking the long, slender drop with her thumb. What to do with it? She couldn't leave it behind. Almost absently, she let the gem drop down the front of her costume feeling its warmth, almost burning, between her breasts. She stood up, gathered her towel, and looked about her again. No one ... Slowly she walked back up the path leading to the house.

He had never so much as looked at her before ... so she thought. The cunning bugger!

When Evie came in for rehearsal that afternoon, she was relieved that Buff was nowhere to be seen. Her nerves flared when Cissy called her over. They *had* been seen! Probably by that greasy tyke, Mac. Cissy motioned her to sit down. Evie's stomach churned into solid lard.

'You been swimmin', kid ...'

'Yeah, Cissy ... why?' She held her breath.

'Just your hair's a bit wet. That's all. See that it's dry by tonight. Noticed it damp the other night. Never swim at twilight, sweetie. The sharks love it!'

Evie had never given the sharks a thought. Sweet relief swept over her. She could kill that Buff Davies.

'Oh, there's another thing, kid'—Was Cissy playing with her? But the nightclub owner was smiling at her. 'You're doing a great job. As I told Buff, you're a natural. A bee sting your arse? Not a move out of you. Just keep on the good work, sweetie. I love ya!'

27

BUFF DIDN'T TURN up at the cove the next day, or the day after, and Evie relaxed. The encounter had shaken her. She hadn't realised just how important the Polka Dot was to her. Buff Davies fouling things up was the last thing she wanted to happen. As for the pearl, *'Wear it for me'* ... Like hell she would!

The pendant went into the bottom of her shoebox. It contained most of the bits and pieces she'd collected, bowerbird fashion, over the weeks. She found Woolworth's junk jewellery irresistible—the shoebox held little of value.

No more than a few nights later, Cissy came into the dressing-room behind the scenes. There was a bemused look to her face as she called Evie to her side. 'I thought you said that your Dad was wounded and died, and that your Mom went too, not long after,' she said quietly.

'That's right. Why?'

'Well—there's a gent out there who says he's your old man. A Mr Alf Scott.' Cissy raised questioning eyebrows.

'I told you he's dead.'

With a blood-red nail, Cissy removed a smidgen of steak from between her teeth, studying it thoughtfully before looking up. 'He says he's got a letter for you ... from your Mom. What gives, Evie?'

'I'm not going home! And he's not my father!'

'I think you better talk to him, kid. Let him see that you're all right. He don't seem the demanding type to me. But this has to be settled. Okay?'

She told the agitated but defiant Evie to settle down, that there was a show going on out there, and that she'd put the gent at one of the best tables, with everything on the house.

Before leaving, she looked Evie up and down. 'No tits tonight, kiddo! And that goes for you too, Claire! So cover up!'

She refused to meet him until most of the customers had left. Already she had scrutinised him from the stage and through a chink between the curtains. As far as she could remember, it was him. But what was he doing wearing a Yankee uniform?

Alf Scott jumped to attention and pulled out a chair at her approach. She drew back as he went to kiss her cheek. 'Well, Eveleen—you've sure grown into a beauty. Always knew you would. Sit down, sit down!'

She could tell he was nervous, and his accent intrigued; but she kept silent, not wanting to put him at ease. It was better that way. She didn't want him acting the heavy father bit with her.

'What do you want?'

'Is that the way to talk to your old Dad? C'mon, give us a smile.'

Evie, her stomach taut with misgivings, was not in the mood for smiling. 'I'm not going home. If you take me back, I'll—'

'Now, Evie ... who said anything about doing that? I'm here because your mother—'

'How does she know where I am?'

Alf shrugged helplessly. He had the look of a man who knew that he was beaten even before he got started. Alf had never been one for a fight. 'How should I know?' He lifted his shoulders, his hands weighing air. 'She just gave me the address and a letter for you. I'm off to America day after tomorrow. I thought maybe we might spend the day together. Father and daughter, like.'

'Huh! Not on your life. Since when have you been a father to me? So don't start acting like one now!'

Alf could see he was getting nowhere, but he kept on trying. 'Well, girlie, I know I deserve it; but listen to me. You've made your mother very unhappy. She really would like you to come home.'

'No,' she said sullenly, the schoolgirl once again.

'We could make you, you know.'

'Try! Don't forget I'm nearly eighteen—old enough to join up if I wanted to.'

As if suddenly remembering, Alf dived into a breast-pocket and brought out Hilda's letter. Evie scanned the writing and gave a slight nod of recognition before dropping it down on the table. Alf shot her a startled look. 'Aren't you going to read it?'

'I will ... after.'

Alf shook his head about to give up. 'I have to say, I enjoyed the show. I got to say I was proud of you Evie. Er—you won't change your mind, eh? About spending the day together.'

She looked him up and down. 'You've got a cheek. I can't understand Mum even talking to you.'

'Things change, Evie.'

'Not for me, they don't.' She looked down at a dainty gold watch, 'And it's time I went.'

'Well, I'll see you home.'

Evie had no intentions of disclosing her address to her father. 'No thanks, Mac'll take me. He always does.' She knew that he was hanging around somewhere. Cissy had arranged it.

She sat stiff and silent as Alf made to go. 'Would you like me to bring you something back from the States? Something pretty, maybe.'

'No thanks.'

'Well, I'll write and tell your mother I've seen you. Keep in touch with her, eh?'

Evie pursed her lips and shrugged. 'I suppose.'

She never lifted her eyes off the table until he was gone. Then she picked up the envelope, scanned the writing again and slipped it into her kimono pocket. There were things she wanted to collect back at the dressing-room, as well as getting dressed. Mac seemed to be nowhere about; she'd find him later.

The nightclub's change room could have been larger, Cissy admitted. But there was a decent mirror, good lighting, and one wall jammed with an assortment of sequinned gowns, ostrich feathers in every rainbow colour, trains and capes of velvet and chiffon, taffeta and silk. No expense spared for her famous costumes to adorn on her famous girls. Evie had discovered to her delight that even the marvellous furs were real. Sometimes she dressed up in them just for fun.

There was one thing the Nightclub Queen insisted on, and that was skin care. 'Get that greasepaint off before you hit the sack, that's what that cold cream's all about. All right for the spotlight, but outside with it on you look like a slut. So get it off!' They all took her advice. Now Evie sat before the mirror wiping away the last traces of cream, patting her skin with rosewater just as Cissy had shown her.

In the mirror she saw the doorknob turn. It would be Mac, although he knocked before he entered ... always. Ready to chip him, instead, she caught her breath.

Buff Davies was standing there.

'Hello there, Mermaid.'

Again that stab of fear. 'Don't you know Mac's waiting for me? I don't want trouble, Buff. Go away!'

All he did was close the door behind him. 'Mac isn't here. Sometimes he and I make a small deal. Only sometimes ...'

She couldn't help feeling interested, watching him in the mirror as he sauntered towards her. She surmised that what he said about a deal with Mac must be true. No one could act so cool if it wasn't so. She found herself thinking of that morning down at the cove and enjoyed a new sensation that was spiced with danger. If Cissy only knew he was here ... her heart hammered at the thought of it.

He came right up to the stool she was sitting on, pressing himself close to her. His hands dropped on her shoulders. 'You're not wearing that pearl I gave you.'

She could barely answer him. 'I told you I don't want it.'

'Don't kid yourself, Evie. You want everything—we know that, don't we.'

Slowly he removed the kimono from her shoulders, kissing them, all the while gazing at her in the mirror. She made a belated attempt to cover herself but Buff's light grip stopped her.

'Why so coy, Mermaid? Every Tom, Dick and Harry has glommed on those gorgeous baps since day one ... I correct myself: since night one. True?' He kissed the top of her head. 'Do you know what I'd really like to do with them? Slather 'em with Ben's whipped cream, then lick every skerrick off.' He smacked his lips. 'H'mmm ... wonderful!'

'Don't be silly.' She was grinning, but still not at ease, even if Buff had fixed it up with Mac, as he said. 'Anyway, you'd better go.'

He pushed hard into her back and for one moment

she responded. But ... 'No, Buff—Cissy would kill us.' She was thinking of that automatic revolver. There was no doubt in her mind that Cissy was capable of using it.

Buff gave an easy laugh. 'You shouldn't believe everything you hear, Mermaid. She lets me have my little treats on the side—you didn't know that, did you? As a commission, sort of, you might say.' Already, he had her half off the stool. 'So come on, how about it?'

She allowed him to push her towards the satins and silks and feathers on their hangers. He pinned her against the wall and she suddenly realised what was happening. 'Not here! We can't do it here!' To her, it seemed sacrilegious, smothered as they were by such exotica. Already his knee was forcing her legs apart. 'No!'

'Why not?' His magnificent prod demanding entry.

Evie forgot about being nervous, for the first time in her life feeling the delicious shock of it. Every touch, every move added to the roiling pleasure building up inside her. She began to gasp. 'Don't—don't stop!' she begged, 'ohhh ...' Nothing existed for her now except that mounting pleasure fast overtaking her body. They burrowed into the feathers and satins like two happy bees in a bed of honeyed clover. Cissy, Mac, the entire cast of the Polka Dot could have charged through the door ... nothing could stop her now. She clutched him tightly to her as a joyous spasm burst into a full climax of pounding blood and heartbeats. 'Oh Buff—yes! Oh yes!'

When it was all over, all Evie could do was murmur: 'Well ... so that's what it's all about.'

Buff gave a grunt of satisfaction as he buttoned up. 'Any time, kiddo, any time at all. Not bad for a knee-trembler, ay?'

It seemed as though he had given her the favour when she heard the words she had so often used herself: 'I've gotta go now.' He kissed her on the nose.

She looked at him, bewildered. 'How'll I get home, but?'

'Mac will pick you up.'

'Oh.' She didn't like that idea at all—but Buff had gone before she could object. She went back to the dressing-table. Everything looked the same as before. Her hairbrush where she had dropped it; the jars of cold cream; a set of false eyelashes someone had left behind. Just the same ... and yet because of those few passionate moments nothing would be the same again.

She reached for the shoebox she took everywhere with her and lifted the lid. She took out some of the gee-gaws, buried her hand beneath the rest. She found a small velvet pouch and untied the drawstring, removing the baroque pearl from its secret cave. She stroked the smooth and lustrous surface with one thumb. It must be true that Cissy allowed Buff to have his 'little treats', as he called them. He'd seemed so sure, so confident ... Slowly, almost dreamily, Evie clasped the pendant around her neck. Admiring it in the mirror, feeling it there between her breasts.

28

Andy took up a hand grenade, stuck two fingers inside the cavity, and with a deft twirl of wrist and brush, grey metal came up gleaming caramel. She gave it a quick once-over for spots her brush might have missed and finding none, slammed it back into its place. She picked up another before speaking.

'So—she's letting that husband of hers off the hook, eh? Och, she'd be a daft one if she didn't. With what she'll get from him, she'll be set up in life. Good for Hilda!'

Hilda, feeling much better and looking ten years younger (so the annexe agreed), had wasted no time in telling her news to both shifts. The women were agog with it. By Hilda's reckoning, they'd always known the worst, so they may as well know the best. She said it made for a nice story—and now, with

Janet back, there seemed to be a more cheerful lift in the day.

Not to spoil things, and with one eye out for Daryl, Lulla kept her worries over Micky to herself. But Micky seemed completely at ease and whistled a funny, lopsided tune through gappy, drifting teeth. Only once had she asked him what he and Daryl were up to, but Micky had tapped his nose, eyes merry, and, looking strangely like Daryl, left her open-mouthed but none the wiser.

If anything, a subtle change had come over the pot-boy. As he filled his pots, the careful concentration was missing. His 'whoops' when he spilled a few drops held the touch of a light and happy heart. When he topped up her own pot, he gave a wink then strutted off to the caverns of the holding room without saying a word.

It was during the lunch break that Lulla bumped into Daryl Missim. She caught him by the arm. 'Just the one I'm looking for.'

Daryl struck a pose. 'My God—she's mad for me.'

'Mad *at* you, more like it. What's between you and Micky?' It was better to get it out quick. To startle him into some admission. But his eyes narrowed, their usual brilliance dulled with caution. 'What's it to you, Lulla?' He took a backward step to study her better, prepared not to give anything away.

She gave a satisfied nod. 'I thought so ...'

'You thought what?'

'I don't quite know. But you're dropping Micky right into it. I saw the three of you—you, Mick and that—that black marketeering crook. You know who I mean. It's despicable—it's rotten—'

'You're interpreting, Lulla.'

'Don't fob me off with smart-alec words, Missim. What's going on?' Her probing was stirring up anger, but she pressed on, her heart racing. 'I can't get one word out of Micky.'

'Because I told him not to say anything.'

'You bastard! I've a fair idea what you're up to.'

'You know bugger-all, Lulla! Now shut up! Shut your noise and let me think!' He had finally silenced her.

Daryl looked around to see if they had been overheard. But, as often happened between siren whistles and the few moments before a rest break ended, the grounds were empty. He massaged cheek and jowl, weighing up the necessity for saying anything, while she changed gears ready to put up a fight; to protect Micky any way she could. Her eyes never left his face, and, at the end of it, hunching a shoulder, he gave in.

'Anything for peace.' But he gunned her with an index finger. 'You're way off track, sister. Way off track.' He took her arm, not so gently. 'Let's get out of sight'—indicating, as he had done over the Harris and Doyle affair, the stacked grenades that waited in the breezeway to be hosed. 'In there.'

The grenades surrounding them could have been so many ears, for Daryl kept his voice low. 'That black marketeer, as you called him, happens to be a doctor—a damned good one, too. He owes me a few, and I'm calling in the bill.'

'What's that got to do with Micky?' Suspicious. Ready to pounce.

'Plenty. He's going to fix up that snotty nose of his. Joseph reckons it's a simple enough job.'

For the second time, he succeeded in robbing her of speech. 'You've got to understand,' he said, 'the poor little sod has never seen a doctor in his life—just had to make the best of things. His Mum's not much better. She's already got one foot in the grave.' He apologised for them. 'They do their best. They thought that filthy nose of Mick's was just a fact of life. And frankly, Micky took some persuading even to talk about it to Joseph.'

'But why the secrecy?' she asked. 'It's wonderful! We—we could have pitched in and helped you to make him—'

'Ah—well ...' He scratched his chin as if it itched. There was a sheepish, almost furtive look about him she didn't like at all. 'There's a bit of a hitch there. You see, Joseph's not quite legit. Not registered. Yet—'

Stunned, she drew back from him. 'You're putting our Mick into the hands of a backyard quack!'

'No! No, no! Nothing like that. He's a good doctor, well thought of back in his own country. He's family, Lulla. But his English—' Daryl shrugged. 'His English is not so good. You know what it's like here. Einstein himself couldn't crack it for a job if he couldn't speak-a da Eeenglish.' Daryl was half-joking, but Lulla wasn't smiling. He grabbed her hand, holding on tight. 'Look, trust me. I know what

I'm doing. Joseph knows what he's doing. Don't say anything to put Micky off. Please!'

She now wished she hadn't forced Daryl to speak about it. It was wrong—dangerous, even. This doctor, this quack—she couldn't let go of the damning word—could be a fraud. He had looked too prosperous for an out-of-work doctor; Lulla bet herself pounds to pennies that he fixed more than runny noses.

On the one hand, she feared for Micky, but she was reluctant to betray Daryl on the other. She had never, Lulla once told a friend, been a 'dobber', and she held a hearty contempt for those who did. To her, the whole business over Micky was sickly grey around the edges. She didn't know what to do about it.

'I have to think this one out, Daryl. That's all I can say for the moment. I realise you had a time talking Micky into it. Well, friend, it's just as likely that I'll have a good try talking him out of it. Whatever I decide, you'll be the first to know.'

Daryl released her hand. 'That's up to you.'

When Daryl walked into the annexe, the mid-afternoon tally was going strong. He looked over Lulla's way but she avoided his gaze.

'They want a final count of the holding room, Andy,' he tapped the clipboard he carried. 'The Army moves in tonight, to clear it out.'

'About time, too.' Andy wiped sticky fingers down the sides of her overalls. 'It's chock-a-block in there.

But why should we do the counting? We're flat-out and knock-off time is coming up.'

'That's what I'm here for.' He made a pretence of spitting on his hands, rubbing them briskly together. 'Finish that little lot you're doing, then we can take a row each, work fast. The last shift can do the rest.' Passing Lulla on his way to the holding room, he stopped and gave her a light flick on the backside. 'Still friends?'

'And do you want your face slapped!'

He chuckled softly, moving on.

The annexe could hear him laughing over a joke shared with Micky. They could hear the squeak of pulley and ropes as Micky lowered the platform to the floor. If they turned their heads, they could see what was going on—Micky taking on another load and Daryl advising to leave it; the stacks were more than high enough.

'In fact, I might just take a few off the top,' they heard him say. 'You've been a bit on the enthusiastic side, young Mick. Stack the rest in the drying room, and we'll take it from there.'

Micky trundled back to the women with the empty trolley, and when Lulla saw his cheerful face and heard again the toneless whistle, her concern for his welfare intensified. The impending operation, if it went ahead, filled her with a fluttering of black moths, a dread that it all could go wrong. Daryl Missim, as go-between, was in deep enough, and she took a guess that it was not the first time he had arranged such matters with the doctor. Both of them could end up behind bars and the pot boy, the innocent, with them ... or worse. Micky, with an aged mother, was even now only one step away from an asylum; she shuddered at the idea.

Micky, delighted to have Daryl sharing the workload, toiled tirelessly, eager to show his friend how efficiently he worked. The annexe, nearing the end of their quota, gave him a hand, and when it was finished, he pelted back to the holding room before they could stop him. They heard Daryl say, 'No, not here, Mick. The drying room. Remember? Remember what I said?'

They saw Daryl high above him, with boxes in his arms, a dozen or more stacked beside him on the platform. Micky looking up, nodding and grinning. Then they saw the expression change on Micky's face, and heard a thin, high wail, hardly human, stream from the pot boy's lips and ricochet from side to side: a sound that iced their hearts.

They saw a crate, just one at first, teeter; then, like the one rock that starts an avalanche, it began to fall. It was followed by another. And another. Daryl tried to stop them, but as one hit the platform, he lost balance and instinct made him reach out, lunge to make contact with his fingers. Another tray unseated—and Daryl fell. He smacked the platform once before crashing to the floor.

Hand bombs, promiscuous as hail, bounced down and over the narrow passageway, while Micky darted about and around in a desperate attempt to reach Daryl, lying somewhere behind a barrier of crates and grenades.

Shock waves of disaster imploded in the women's ears, and, when the noise ended, the shrieking from one of the new girls carried on without pause: her screaming in tandem with the siren wailing of accident. As Lulla, with Andy close behind, tore down the corridor, she wondered how the workshop already knew. Not more than a minute had passed since the first crate had fallen.

They could see Micky burrowing in and hurling crates aside. But that was all they could see, for their way was blocked by the debris of the collapsed tier.

'Try the next one!' Andy called out.

They did a turnabout, running fast, and found that the parallel passage, except for the end of it, was clear. Hoping their side was as solid as it looked, they raced on to Daryl and Micky.

More trays and bombs had fallen than they first believed. Two back rows had caved in as if attacked by termites. They climbed over a rubble of splintered wood and caught their first sight of Daryl. It appeared that the bulk of the collapsed tiers had missed him but, as they got closer, they could see that one leg and hip were pinned under the pile. There were now more footsteps racing down the corridors as the others from the main floor came over to help.

Micky, sobbing and incoherent, tore crates aside with the frenzy of a terrier after rats. They joined him. Cursing and straining, the annexe and factory floor worked as one to rescue the unconscious man.

Someone called out that an ambulance was on the way and, that once the leg and hip were clear, they were not to move him. When Daryl was freed, a silence fell as they looked down at what was left of his leg.

It was a nightmare puzzle of jagged bone and seeping flesh. Those who saw it felt relief that Daryl was still unconscious. Still alive. There came a sound of crying and the voice of Mrs Daniels ordering that room be made for a stretcher coming through.

'And the rest of you,' she demanded, 'get back to work. There happens to be a war on!'

Still in shock, the annexe returned to the lacquer room. It was past knock-off time by now, but none wanted to leave.

Lulla, with Andy, waited beside the injured man. She was determined to stay there as long as she was allowed. Micky came over. He was trembling, his face wet and mucky with mucus and tears. She put her arm around him. 'Stop it, love. Don't cry. You've done a mighty job. You helped more than anyone.' She gave him a squeeze. 'And for Lord's sake, wipe that nose.'

'Lulla?' He begged for her attention. 'They were stacked too high. Weren't they?' The trembling increased.

'Now none of that, young Mick.' She swung him around to face her. 'I've had enough of people feeling sorry for themselves.' She gave him a little shake. 'And if you want to make Daryl real happy, you just have that operation. I know how badly he wants it to happen. And when it's over we'll go to the hospital and visit him. Okay?'

'Okay, Lulla.'

She walked beside the stretcher into sunshine. Daryl opened his eyes. He took her outstretched hand, his grip surprisingly firm. Lulla asked one of the bearers if she could go with them to the hospital, but the ambulanceman shook his head.

'Sorry, miss—but you can come as far as the van.' He noticed the clasped hands. 'Boyfriend, eh?'

'You could say that.'

She asked Daryl about the pain.

'Not feeling a thing.' She put it down to shock and hoped that it would last. Once in care he'd be put under, for sure.

'Lulla?'

'Yes?'

'You saw it. How does it look?' His grip tightened. 'Now don't bullshit me, Princess.'

Lulla's throat tightened. 'Well, you won't be dancing for a while.' She swallowed. 'It's bad, Daryl. Real bad.'

He nodded, closing his eyes, and stayed like that for a while. She thought he'd fainted again. He lay quite still. She kept close by the stretcher, reluctant to leave him; the factory gate and waiting ambulance were not so far away.

But he then looked up at her; unbelieving, she saw the fleeting ghost of a wicked smile light up his face. 'I told you I'd beat 'em somehow. Now let's see what the bloody Manpower can do, eh? I'm off the hook!'

29

*M*ALE PAVS, IT was called by the medical staff; to outsiders it was known as Ward 15. The Male Pavilion—Urology, its official name—was under canvas; a circus tent of men attached by rubber tubes to their bottles of urine, blood and pus. Sunshine days found the sides rolled up like window blinds. The old men, and the convalescing with their umbilical tubes and bottles, were then wheeled outside to soak up their share of Vitamin D. On a sunny day, Male Pavs had a cheerful look.

It was raining the day Lulla and Janet were finally permitted to visit. Phenyl and damp canvas did little to erase the smell of urine that permeated the ward. The sides were rolled down tightly, blocking out fresh air and light.

They had expected to find him pale and still suffering, but Daryl waved them in cheerfully, with an aside to his neighbour that brought on a nod and hoot of laughter.

Daryl looked tanned and practically normal, and gave the appearance that all was under control. Going his way. Bearing gifts of flowers and sweets, they ran the gauntlet of beds and inquisitive eyes, suspecting that already the ward knew everything about them. There was a distinct impression that they were considered the exclusive property of one Daryl Missim.

The difficulty was in ignoring the sheet, flat and neat on the bed where Daryl's leg should have been. He forced their acceptance of the missing limb by patting the bed and inviting Lulla to sit beside him.

'Fill the space, Lulla, it makes me nervous. There's room enough,' he added gallantly. It was a cruel jibe against himself, an act of bravado that wrung their hearts.

'Always the clown, Missim. But what I'm after now is a jar of water for these zinnias. Hilda sent them.' Lulla held them up to be admired: medallions of captured sunsets were splashed against the sombre khaki of the canvas walls. Finding her tongue tied in knots, and with her excuse not to sit near him left intact, Lulla hurried off. It was left to Janet to cope with the first awkward moments between grounded patient and agile visitor. She felt a need to explain why they had not visited him before.

'Only family, they told us, Daryl. We wanted to come, but rules are rules.'

'I know.' His grin was contagious. 'And haven't I

missed the lot of you! Believe it. Now tell me all the news.'

'Later. First things first. Are you all right? Really all right? And the leg—I mean—is it hurting? Do they give you enough to stop the pain?'

He waved aside her concern. 'Sure they do. A bloke can put up with it.'

'You won't be back at work, I imagine.'

'Try and catch me! What's been happening down there?'

Janet reported that MacIntyre's was rushing headlong into further expansion. Extensions all over the place, she said. Another house in the street gone, and with it three grand old weeping figs, and a rainforest of tree ferns and staghorns. Demolished in a matter of days.

In exchange, Daryl spoke of Missims' plans. Now that his return to the family nest was guaranteed, new contracts had been accepted and signed for.

'Never mind about the houses, Jan,' Daryl enthused. 'West End is set to be the industrial hub of the city. And we're right there in the thick of it! Shame you and Lulla can't come in with us. Good wages and conditions. Any chance?' Janet knew what Lulla would have said to that. As far as Lulla was concerned, to work for Missims'—or any other clothing factory for that matter—was one more step to hell. As Janet started to wonder what was holding her up, she returned, the zinnias in a pickle jar, her eyelids puffy, her nose shiny and red. She fussed over the flowers.

'I came here one night, you know. But that prune of a sister would have none of it. All I got was a dressing-down for my trouble.'

'And serve you right,' Janet said almost severely.

Daryl shifted position with a grunt of pain, exposing the catheter linking his penis to the jar below. It was half-full of urine and pink from damaged kidneys. Lulla kept her eyes away from it. It seemed like spying on his most private parts: not so Janet. Unperturbed, she straightened his sheet, lightly adjusted the catheter so that it would not pull or hurt. For her it seemed the natural thing to do.

It was easier for them to talk now, and Daryl listened, delighted, while they told him about the night Julian Ludwig had dinner with the Scotts. It was the sort of gossip Lulla told so well. Her eyes sparked off blue splinters, her talking hands framed the words that captured Daryl's lively imagination.

'It was a scream,' she chortled, 'when Peggy found out that he'd phoned, and that Hilda had invited him to eat with them. She had kittens five times over. Peg had always avoided bringing him into the house, as you can imagine.'

'I can't. Why?'

'Well, who would, with Evie around? Guess she got into the habit of keeping him out of sight.' Lulla reached for the box of chocolates they had brought him, tested them out for hard centres and popped one into her mouth. 'Compliments of Redwing,' she beamed. 'But back to young Scottie. Their flat was turned upside-down. She would've spring-cleaned the hall and stairs, if they'd let her. It was a gas. Peggy running around like a chook with no feathers, Hilda, calm as you like in the kitchen, cooking up everything she could lay her hands on.'

Janet swooped in when Lulla paused for breath. 'And she needn't have bothered—all that cooking, I mean. Julian turned up with a turkey and all the trimmings—cranberry sauce, a huge bucket of ice-cream—'

'You've never seen such a feed,' Lulla chortled. 'Hilda divvied it up between us. So we stayed. It was a treat to see those two budgies together.' She gave a happy sigh. 'Bloody lovely, it was.'

A nurse seemed to spring up from nowhere, and thrust a thermometer between Daryl's lips. When they made a move to leave she smiled for them to stay. 'O—ooh, chocs. May I?' Searching for a soft centre, she pounced on one with satisfaction. 'Mr Missim always has lovely grub. You should see what his Mum brings for him.'

An excitement of voices at the ward sister's desk attracted the nurse's attention. She whipped out the thermometer, saying brightly, 'And speak of the devil—' Hurriedly, she plumped up pillows, pinched another chocolate 'for afters', and dashed off. 'You might have to leave after all,' she called out over her shoulder, 'he's only allowed three visitors at a time!'

Janet was already pulling on her raincoat. Daryl looked disappointed. 'Just as things were pepping up,' he said.

'Never mind, we'll come again,' Janet murmured,

giving his cheek a quick brush of her lips.

A man and a woman, bolstered by confidence and fine living, swept down the aisle of hospital beds. They were followed by a young girl who had almost the appearance of a Biblical handmaiden, bearing something wrapped in a serviette as starched and sterile-looking as the ward sister's veil. A rich savoury smell preceded the three of them.

Was this Daryl's bethrothed, Lulla wondered. The girl had a look of unblemished innocence with her plump, smooth cheeks, lustrous curly hair, downcast eyes. Well, sometimes those arranged marriages proved successful. Perhaps this sacrificial lamb would prove the ideal wife for Daryl Missim.

The mother brushed Lulla and the proffered chair aside and swarmed over Daryl with kisses and an outpouring of love, sympathy and questions that repulsed any hope of a sensible answer.

Janet and Lulla, outgunned by such parental solicitude, tiptoed off.

They were already whispering a polite goodbye to the sister when Daryl called Lulla back. He waved a sealed envelope—she assumed he had a letter to post. He thrust it into her hand.

'My mate across the road there'—nodding to a patient on the other side—'is an old union battler from way back.' He indicated the envelope. 'For you—something in there that might come in handy.'

His mother was busy straightening his locker. She sniffed at the sight of the chocolates. Lulla caught a clear message that she should disappear as quietly and as quickly as possible, in spite of Daryl's attempts at introductions.

He gave up with a helpless shrug and a smile. 'Let me know your ideas on that.' She studied the envelope in her hand before dropping it into a raincoat pocket. Its blank face told her nothing.

'It can wait till I get home.' She leaned over, deliberately kissing him full on the mouth. 'See you soon, honey-chile.' Spike heels clicked-clacked a win, as she swung with cheeky hips towards the waiting Janet.

Put that in your pipe and smoke it, you old trout!

It was not until they were back home, seated at the kitchen table eating fingers of toast and drinking tea, that Daryl's note was read and discussed.

'I can't believe it,' Lulla chortled. 'It's all too simple.' Mainly to reassure herself her eyes were not deceiving her, she read aloud the words Daryl had written down. The note contained several reasons why conscripted workers, women—or a female already employed in a protected industry—might be withdrawn from the workplace.

' "Unsuitable type." Surely I'm unsuitable enough.' She couldn't help a giggle. 'Just ask Madame Daniels that one.'

'No, you're not,' said Janet firmly. 'You're too good at the job for a start. And too honest to be otherwise.'

'Well, what about "sub-standard health"?'

'You've said yourself that you're as strong as Riley's bull.'

'Don't remind me. Poor eyesight, but'—hopefully.

'MacIntyre's wouldn't accept that. Look at Andy. Blind as a bat without glasses.'

'Okay. On to the next one. "Married, engaged or about to be married".' Lulla pondered over that. 'Now—there's a thought. Who can I get engaged to? Redwing? No. He might think I'm serious. Daryl's spoken for, and hoo—just imagine having *her* for a mother-in-law. Did y'see the looks she gave us? Forget Daryl!'

'Spanner?' Janet gently prodded.

'He's not serious enough!' But with a pencil she underlined the clause. 'I'll keep that one in mind.' She carried on. 'Now, here's a beauty. Wonder what Peggy and Julian would think of this? "Employment refused if applicant is of German parentage." Does that count for in-laws as well? And what about the Japs? No mention of Japs ...'

She tapped the paper with a finger. 'It looked so hopeful at first, but thinking it over ... Well, at least it's a straw to clutch onto; who knows?'

Lulla squeezed the last of the tea from the pot, her thoughts turning over the information Daryl had passed on. Surely, she told herself, she could make that piece of paper work for her. Given time, she would. Even if it meant spending her last penny on an engagement ring!

With the first hurdle of hospital visiting over, the flatmates arranged to see Daryl on alternate days. One at a time, they reasoned, would give variety to the daily boredom of ward routine. The amputation was a matter of resigned acceptance; taking their cue from Daryl, they sometimes joked about it. 'Missim's war wound', they called it. Lulla said that if he'd been a Yank, he'd be up for a Purple Heart.

Peggy brought Julian along one afternoon, with an order to get better quickly or he'd miss out on the wedding. She wore his graduation ring.

'Julian thought diamonds would be nice, but this—' she stroked the heavy gold with loving fingers, 'this is the first thing I really saw when he gave me back Lulla's hat. His hand, and this. Wasn't game to look anywhere else,' she confessed, blushing.

They all tried to avoid the Missim family. Any female under thirty was viewed by the mother as a threat. Daryl's intended (as Janet called her) was often on display, and if Lulla showed up alone, the family drawbridge was drawn up tight, targeting her with arrows of speculative suspicion.

Lulla fought back bravely but gave up in the end. The fight, as she told Janet, wasn't 'valid the sufferment'. She sent, through Janet, fruit salad, flowers, notes and a promise that the first night he could make it, they'd toast his health in retsina at the Greek Club.

Before Male Pavs discharged Daryl, the first stage of MacIntyre's proposed expansions had been completed. Manpower went to work. Application forms were posted out to women, and the few men who still worked in what was called non-essential industries. A new edict pronounced that all childless women between the ages of eighteen and forty-five were to register with the Manpower Committee and be prepared for immediate call-up.

'That's put paid to any ideas I might have had,' Lulla despaired.

A trickle of new hands began filing through the factory gates. It soon turned into a sizeable flood. Most were assigned to the expanded machine-shop. A few showed up in the annexe, to Andy's relief. Brushes and lacquer pots were pressed into their hands while Mrs Daniels counted heads, well pleased with the result.

30

*J*ANET'S ANNOUNCEMENT WAS the first shock in what turned out, as far as Lulla was concerned, a lousy-rotten sod of a day. She was amazed Janet could be so calm as she shattered the morning's content with a disclosure which left Lulla in a disarray of futile argument.

'You can't,' Lulla spluttered. 'I won't let you!'

'I've applied, been interviewed and accepted.' Janet mashed curry powder into a bowl of hard-boiled eggs. She licked a modicum of the mixture off the fork and added a dash of tomato sauce. 'I'm lucky. There's a new crop going in next week. And I'm one of them.'

'A nurse! All that blood! And worse than that—' Lulla slapped careless gobbets of butter on squares of bread. 'You never told me. You kept it all to yourself!'

'What was the point until I was sure? It was touch and go, I can tell you. At first Matron put up a hundred reasons why I shouldn't. Too old, and of course, I'm married ... or was,' she corrected herself. 'Marrieds aren't welcome as student nurses. Not used to the discipline, she said. They like them fresh out of the schoolroom.' Janet took over the buttered slices and cemented them together with curried egg.

'It'll tie you down for years,' Lulla protested.

'Only three.'

'Long enough! You're mad, Janet, absolutely mad.' Lulla snatched up a tea-towel, twisted it around her head, and struck a pose that closely resembled the stance of the sister-in-charge of Male Pavs. 'Make sure you're in by ten sharp, Nurse. And hands behind your back when you address me, thank you! Clean up that vomit, Nurse!—Gawd Aggie, it never ends! Jan, you won't make rissoles because you hate putting your hands in mince!'

Unperturbed, Janet continued preparing their lunch. 'Finished?' Very polite. Trying to hide her amusement.

'Not quite. How will you manage on that pittance they pay you?'

'I'll manage.' Janet pointed out that it was Lulla who advocated independence for women, that sitting at home waiting for things to happen was strictly for the birds. She spoke of Daryl and all those like him, cheerfully tended by a handful of nurses, competent, caring, and run off their legs. She might be on the far side of twenty, but that left a good thirty years of service in her.

'Oh, so you intend staying single for the rest of your life.' Lulla was irritated that Janet was effectually blocking every objection put up to her.

'And look who's talking,' Janet teased. 'Wasn't it you who told me there's more to living than a husband and a bunch of kids?'

'I was talking about me,' Lulla snapped. 'I'll give you six months before you quit!'

But Lulla knew in her heart that Janet had found her niche. She remembered how comfortable she was on that first visit to Ward 15. She'd seemed right at home even then; had appeared not to notice the stomach-churning rankness of pee and pus. As a matter of fact, she couldn't imagine Janet being anything else but a good and tender nurse. It was hard not to feel that already she was losing a friend.

The second jolt came when Lulla arrived at the factory gate. She was greeted by the watchman, who said that Mrs Daniels wanted her in the office before the shift began.

Now what?

Janet, immediately concerned, offered to wait outside, but Lulla waved her on. 'You go ahead, Jan. Can't think of anything I've done to tread on her toes.' She attempted to joke it aside. 'Unless the safe's vanished again.'

In spite of the flippancy, a vice-like doubt squeezed her stomach to the size of a pea. Harris and Doyle could be ready to pounce again—this time, maybe over Micky. He'd been absent for days. Had Daryl's misguided scheming been uncovered? If so, Lordy, keep her out of it!

She stood outside the office door, taking deep breaths; with the slow emission of air through half-closed lips, the fright gradually subsided. It was only then she went inside.

The relief was sickening. Detectives Harris and Doyle were nowhere to be seen. Mrs Daniels was waiting with the foreman from the workshop.

'Ah, Riddel. At last'—looking vastly pleased about something. Lulla braced herself, relief subsiding. Knowing Daniels, she was not about to hand out medals.

The foreman was smiling. 'How would you like to join us in the main shop, Miss Riddel?'

Overwhelming dismay as she listened to the foreman babble on. So that's why the old bat had looked so smug. Lulla Riddel had made it clear often enough that if she must work in munitions, the annexe suited her style.

'You'll have a wage increase, of course,' Mrs Daniels purred.

And boils, maybe, and busted eardrums, protested a silent Lulla. But there was nothing to be said. By the look on Mrs Daniels' face, there was no choice but to follow the foreman out of the office away from the annexe.

Work had begun when Lulla stepped into the whirl, the whine, the crash and clash of MacIntyre's workshop. It was a cavernous collage of industry, clangorous with the sounds of lathes and surface grinders, spindles and indomitable drills. The cut, the slice of metal shrieked through the slap of overhead belts, and already the sun was clamping down on corrugated iron. Heat pulsed through the roof with sullen intensity. Sweat started to trickle down her neck.

He led her through a battery of machines, over a floor greased with oil and slopped with water, stopping before a lathe. To her, a mystery; a bewilderment of handwheels, faceplates, belts and cutters. Lulla, who could not replace a light bulb without incident, was told that the silent monster hunched before her was to be her partner—her other self for the duration.

Oh, Gawd. Oh Gawd—bloody—Aggie.

She never knew how she got through that first awful week. Every night, a splitting headache, and, even wearing safety boots, the mix of oil and water seeped through socks, greasing toes until they itched enough to drive her nearly mad.

To Lulla's consternation, and to the foreman's satisfaction, she proved to have an affinity with her nemesis that was hard to ignore. After a few near-misses, the lathe had been mastered before the break for morning tea.

Lulla was not pleased. Her ability became her jailer; glumly she faced a future of no escape.

'I can kiss goodbye to any hope of driving for Uncle Sam,' she wailed to Redwing. 'I'm too bloody good, and the foreman's a creep!'

. . .

One Sunday afternoon Lulla slumped on the bed, watching Janet pack. Black lisle stockings, neatly rolled, were placed inside sensible shoes. Shoe polish and a pocket watch were crossed off Janet's list. For the umpteenth time, she felt Lulla's pulse and shoved the bathroom thermometer into her mouth. She giggled, and hugged her arms. 'You know, Lulla, I'm actually excited. You should see my class. Babies, every one of them. They're calling me Gran already!'

Her smile faded as Lulla, frowning, got up and went to the bathroom. She returned with Aspros and a glass of water.

Janet bit her lip, worried. 'You're not getting used to it—the machine shop—are you?'

'Nope.'

'What about ... I know!' The words tumbled out before Lulla could object. 'They'll give you a release for nursing. It's true!'

'Come off it, Jan. I nearly puked every time I walked into that ward. Me a nurse? I wouldn't last a week.'

'But you want to work for the Ambulance Corps.'

'As a driver. Nothing else. Drop it, Jan.'

Restless, Lulla left the room. Janet heard the kitchen door open, heard her stomp down the stairs. Lately, Lulla had been taking her headaches up to the back room. Janet felt partly to blame for her friend's depression. Dear Lulla—her constant love and cheerful presence had meant so much during those first dreadful weeks after Kirk's death. Normally Lulla would have bounced off the news of her nursing ambitions: a phone call to Redwing, a night on the town and she would have come up smiling. But Lulla wasn't smiling these days.

As Janet closed down the lid of her port, her eyes came to rest on the rucked bedspread where her flatmate had been sitting. She straightened it and was filled with a vast sadness that a chapter in her life was drawing to a close. She saw the husband lying there, replete and well content. Love-making had been an act of pure joy; she touched a sudden mourning heart, remembering. The flat still echoed sometimes with his teasing and laughter.

Dearest lover ... goodbye.

Now a new beginning—a new challenge ... and a single bed.

Easter was close; over the factory fence errant cassias scattered gold across the grey-rust of corrugated iron. In the fragrance of the morning, blossoms audaciously challenged the brilliance of autumn skies. Head down, intent on some errand, Micky trotted along the breezeway. He would have passed Lulla by if she hadn't pulled him up.

'Micky! Long time no see,' she feinted a punch on his shoulder. 'Hey, hey! Something's different here.' She stepped back, head to one side, while Micky stood straight to attention. He was grinning in anticipation and huge satisfaction.

Lulla scratched her head in pretended puzzlement,

then snapped her fingers. 'Got it! It's the glasses. They look great. Bet you see a lot better now.'

He nodded eagerly. 'Yeth.' Peacock proud. 'Something elthe, Lulla. Look hard.' He stayed motionless while she carefully looked him over, but nearly broke rank when she clapped her hands.

'Your blow-rag. It's gone!' She patted the bib where it had always been pinned. 'I can't believe it,' she hammed, delighted for him. Micky dug into his trouser pocket and brought out a clean white handkerchief still in its folds. 'Daryl gave me six. Not used yet,' he announced proudly.

'You've seen Daryl, eh?'

'Not in the hospital, now.'

'I know.'

'He takes that leg off sometimes. It doesn't hurt much, either.'

'That's good.' Lulla found that there was nothing left for her to say. She looked at her watch. 'Have to go, Micky. My boss wants to see me, worse luck. Says it's important.'

Micky looked at her, hesitant; wistful. 'You coming back soon?'

She tousled his short spiky hair. 'Sure. Sometime ... give my love to the girls, won't you.'

She hurried off to the main shop, where the foreman, Keith, waited. Ten minutes to spare before the siren sounded for another day.

His office was a partitioned nook in one corner of the machine-shop. He sat behind a work-stained table with a clutter of papers and, to Lulla, the unrecognisable bits and pieces of factory dross. Behind him was a calendar featuring a lovely Chinese girl wearing a chrysanthemum. The month before, Lulla recalled, she was in a cheong-sam split up to the armpits. 'A Chink give it to me', he'd bragged to her, and offered at the same time to take her to a place in George Street for Chinee kai. Lulla had refused. She had no liking for the foreman.

Now he invited her to sit down, leaning back in a swivel chair, his look speculative, assessing her. 'You like it here, Lulla?'

'Not much.' She tensed, waiting for the rest of it.

'Would you like it better as a leading hand?'

That surprised her. There were others out there just as good, if not better; certainly they had been at the benches longer than she. Lulla pointed this out to him and then said: 'Thanks very much, but no thanks.' It was the last thing in the world she wanted. She sensed a need to convince him of it. 'To begin with, I don't like bossing others around, and for another, I'd be stepping on too many toes.'

The foreman pursed his lips, appraising her refusal. He was far from happy. 'I could make you one, you know.'

'I wouldn't if I were you, Keith,' she warned him. 'I'm telling you, I'm not cut out for it.'

'It's more money.' His glance was sly. 'You've got a reputation for wanting more wages, Lulla. Team up with me and you'll get all you need.'

She felt the gorge swelling and her face settled into the flat planes of dislike. It wasn't the first time he had slipped in with his double-edged remarks.

Even so, like all foremen he was keen to get the most out of his shift, and there was no denying that Lulla Riddel was top-class in the production line. Lulla was also aware of it, but being a leading hand would entrench her more deeply into the MacIntyre fold. She made a point of noting the time from a clock on the wall, hoping he'd take notice. There was movement in the workshop as hands took their places beside their machines. Voices chiacking across the aisles, an overture to another clamorous day.

The foreman made for one more try. 'With your talents, Lulla—the women get on well with you, you know—we could jump production sky-high. We could be the premier team. Not to mention the boost to the war effort.'

Lulla allowed herself a short bark of laughter. 'Who're you trying to kid, Keith? You've a half-dozen girls out there who'd bring you the same results.'

'Not quite.'

'Well, sorry. Count me out.' She stood up ready to leave. 'Is that all?'

'For the time being.' His smile, greasy as the factory floor, slid over her. 'Think about it, and give me your answer tomorrow.'

Without answering, she turned on her heel, glad to escape him. By the time she reached her lathe, the factory was geared up and going. She was aware of covert glances and curious speculation about the early morning interview. Proof she was a tart, to the ones who had witnessed Keith's straying hands, in spite of her protests. She took solace from those who said that, knowing Keith, all she had to do was stick to her guns until another looker came along for Keith to perv on.

Lulla adjusted her safety goggles and switched on. No response. She switched off, then tried again. The lathe remained static, emitting strange clicking noises. She switched off while she made careful checks, going through each phase of procedure as she had been taught. The stutter continued each time she flipped the switch, but the machine remained stubbornly inert. Another check of wheels, levers and spindles: finding nothing, she turned on the power, loath to ask the foreman's help. He stood nearby, deep in discussion with one of the few men left on the factory floor.

Success! This time the lathe moved smoothly ... for a full five minutes before it stopped again. It happened that the foreman was passing. He frowned, coming over.

'What's up?'

'It's stopped.'

'I can see that.'

'Well,' she snapped back, 'it clicks!'

'Clicks?' He smirked at her incompetence while he checked a few sundry pieces. 'Looks all right to me.' And threw the switch.

The machine purred to life. He tested it again. On-off. On-off. 'You've imagined it, Riddel.' Giving her a curt nod, he moved on, saying she should call him immediately if anything went wrong. Nothing did.

For an hour, Lulla worked steadily, a rhythm flowing between woman and machine, scarcely noted until that rhythm was bludgeoned into screeching silence. It happened so quickly. A rasp of stripping metal; a noise that pierced her eardrums. She jumped back in fright; before she could make another move, metal carnage flew in all directions. Pieces catapulted past her face as the carriage slid along its bed and fouled the chuck.

The lathe's shrill protest was clearly heard above the factory din. A sliver of metal thwacked Lulla's glasses, miraculously bouncing off and embedding itself in a nearby crate. In those first chaotic moments she seemed unable to move or dodge away as, horrified, she saw the lathe fall apart before her eyes.

The unthinkable had happened. The fear of it happening, the cardinal sin that it had happened, brought the shop floor to a standstill.

'*Jesus Christ*!'—This from the foreman as he raced over. Lulla, still incapable of moving, yelped as a small explosion of twisted metal whizzed by her ear.

He pushed her out of the way. 'You bloody, stupid bitch!' he yelled, switching off the power. 'What have you done?'

Lulla found her voice. 'Nothing!'

'Couldn't you tell something was wrong?' His eyes were bulging in their fury.

'You said it was all right. You saw it!' she screamed at him.

'I know I did—that was an hour ago. But what's

happened now? What did you do?'

'How the hell do I know. The whole rotten thing just went crazy.'

He was standing close, his breath hot in her face. 'No brains—no fuckin' brains. Get back to the annexe where you don't fuckin' need them.'

'I won't, you bastard! I bloody won't!' Words were not enough. She attacked him with her fists. His contemptuous dismissal, his failure to admit the part he had played in the breakdown goaded her on. Hatred for him, her anger at the bad and sad events that had happened to all of them—to Janet, Daryl, Kirk, herself—filled her with a wild black fury. The tears were a relief when they came, but she kept hitting out, and when one of the male hands joined the foreman to try to pin down her flailing arms, he was rewarded with a bloodied nose.

The foreman backed off for just a second. Enraged, she sprang like a cat at him, claws extended. Both man and woman hit the floor: writhing and rolling in a hate match, as her workmates, alarmed by her frenzy, tried to drag her away from him. They succeeded at last and attempted to pull her up, but she pushed them off.

'Leave me be.'

She was left alone, sobbing, her back against the mangled lathe, her mind going back over the scene— and in a strange way she found herself glad that it had happened. In a flash she saw a way of quitting Mac's. Already she was halfway there!

'Unsuitable'—that's what it said. She knew those

damned clauses off by heart. 'Sub-standard health'—
'poor eyesight'—'German parentage'—'*Unsuitable
type*'. Her thoughts, calculating data beneath the hullabaloo
of sobs and bellows, had found a solution.

Deemed unsuitable ... oh yes, she could be as
unsuitable as all get out.

Her shoulders heaved and she gave full-bodied
voice to the frustrations, the back-biting, the hurts
and shame that life and the rotten police had dealt
her.

'Christ! She's gone mad!'

'Wimmen,' a voice answered, and suggested that
a bucket of cold water might do the trick.

She was getting tired by now, and when she heard
Andy demanding to be let through and felt the firm
hand clasp hers, she staggered up and buried her
head in Andy's chest. Arms held her tight, hands
patted and comforted. 'What are they trying to do,
ye poor wee love?'

She allowed the forewoman to lead her away to
the first-aid room. A wet cloth was placed over her
eyes, smelling salts waved under her nose. It all
helped. Then she was left alone. Exhausted. She
dozed and drifted in and out of dreams, and wondered
if the foreman and management had been sufficiently
impressed. If not, she promised hazily, she'd
do it all over again.

Stack on a turn, Lulla Riddel, she advised her
sleepy self. If this lot hasn't worked, do it again ...
and again. One after another, until they give you the
golden handshake—the royal push!

EPILOGUE

DAWN BREAKS AT the Archerfield airstrip. The Dakotas are running late. For two hours the hooded ambulances have waited, lined up in convoy mode like a chain of caterpillars, sluggish in the early chill, waiting for a given signal.

Not a sign of the drivers or their orderlies. They stay snug inside the vans, windows shut, drinking coffee, eating chocolate, smoking, creating their own illusion of warmth in a temperature a fraction below zero.

Lord of some suburban henhouse stridently challenges the sound of a distant humming. The noise evolves into a persistent drone, sensed rather than heard.

It is enough.

Doors open. In pairs, the women step down to front the cold and watch the planes come in. One driver, smart and splendid in uniform, adjusts her forage cap to an angle that perkily defies gravity. She snuggles deeper into her windjacket, tugging the collar tightly around her chin and cheeks.

'Here they come. And about time.' Lulla speaks to an older woman who checks out the contents of the miniature first-aid station beneath the canopy of the van, set up for any emergency. Today, the wounded from some Pacific war zone will occupy the four tiered beds that line the canvas walls.

'Everything okay in there?' Lulla asks. 'Not that you'll be doing much. They'll be sewn up and tidied by the time we get them.'

'You're right there. Give me a good old stand-by anytime. Day or night, with nothing more serious than a broken bone or three!'

Lulla laughs. 'That was some rough-house if you're thinking about the other night. Thank God Aussies use their fists, not knives!'

By now the aerodrome has come to life. Men hasten from hangars and the canteen, ready to shepherd the Dakotas in. The air comes alive with shouted commands, roaring engines; it vibrates with an underlay of excited tension as the machines land one by one.

Lulla counts them. 'Only six, so far. There must be more to come.' She runs her eye over the waiting ambulances. 'Can't be many left in the motor pools. They've brought in every clapped-out Tin Lizzie they could lay hands on. Biggest convoy yet!'

A staff car drives slowly by, brakes, and backs up

to where Lulla is standing. A copper-tanned face beams out at her. Leaving the engine running, Charlie Redwing unfolds out of the car.

'Hi there, honey. Long time—'

'It surely is.' Lulla is delighted to see him; more so, as he steps back to admire, with a low wolf-whistle. 'Say, you're looking great. That uniform suits you real good.' Black eyebrows raised. 'Happy?'

'As a lady pig in mud, Redwing. All thanks to you.' She introduces him to the orderly, who looks the large American over with unabashed interest. 'Meet Marcia, Redwing.'

The soldier flashes Marcia a grin. 'You Aussie girls sure have pretty names.'

Lulla hollows her cheeks. 'Seems I've heard that line before.' Suddenly thinking of Peggy and the night of the Clayfield party.

Redwing remembers too. 'How is Peggy?' he asks.

'Getting ready to leave us. You Yankees aren't waiting till war's end to send the brides over to the folk back home. We'll miss her. Every one of us.'

Now the first two planes, heavily pregnant with wounded, are disgorging stretchers. Lulla takes note. 'Better start up,' she tells Marcia as the lead vehicle peels off to take on its load.

Redwing nods. 'Before you go. How about tonight? We could have dinner someplace, and then the Grove.'

Lulla, stepping high into the cabin with a show of long legs, nylons and polished, sensible shoes, waits until she's settled in before giving her answer. She adjusts the spectacles on her nose.

'Sorry, Redwing. Can't. Already have a date for tonight. That's if we get back in time.'

Redwing is disappointed. 'Lucky fella. Anyone I know?' He feels he can ask. They *are* buddies.

'Don't think so. Oh, maybe you did meet him once. Goes by the name of Larkin. Spanner Larkin. Know him?'

Redwing shakes his head. He studies Lulla's face. She stares back at him, revealing nothing.

'Spanner Larkin.' Redwing muses over the name. 'Is it serious, maybe?'

Lulla smiles. Pensive. 'Who knows, Redwing— who knows?'

AND AFTERWARDS ...

*A*T THE END of hostilities, *Lulla* and *Hilda* pooled their savings and headed north. Even in those early days, Hilda guessed rightly that the North was the place 'to make ends meet'. She and Lulla opened a first-class guesthouse for tourists escaping southern winters and invading the towns north of Capricorn. They never looked back.

Janet stayed in her profession right through to retirement. By choice, she never went beyond the role of nursing sister; she was content to be a good nurse, and as she once told Lulla, the administrative side of hospital life for her held little charm or appeal.

Peggy never returned to Australia, but happily followed her man to where his ship and promotion took him. She and Julian agreed that a family of three was quite enough, but that didn't stop them from having three more offspring in three different parts of the world.

Eveleen married an officer in the Australian Army and proceeded to drive him to distraction and an early retirement, treating every officers' mess as her own personal hunting ground in a never-ending search for the enticing prey.

Daryl only got richer, an opportunist to the very end of his post-war political career.

Spanner Larkin. There was enough deferred pay when he left the Navy, to buy a small fishing boat. Outside of Cairns, he fished the reefs and beyond. Always the sailor, sometimes the fisherman, he made just enough to keep himself and the boat afloat. And Hilda and Lulla's guesthouse never lacked its famous servings of Coral Trout, Barramundi and fried potato chips.

Judy Nunn
Araluen

From the South Australian vineyards of the 1850s to mega-budget movie-making in modern-day New York, Araluen tells the compelling story of one man's quest for wealth and position and its shattering effect on succeeding generations.

Turn-of-the-century Sydney gaming houses ... the opulence and corruption of Hollywood's golden age ... the colour and excitement of the America's Cup ... the relentless loneliness of the outback .. Judy Nunn, best-selling author of *The Glitter Game* and *Centre Stage*, weaves an intricate web of characters and locations in this spellbinding saga of the Ross family and its inescapable legacy of greed and power.

Fran Kendall
To Touch The Earth

Christine Florey has everything. But her pampered life on the broad acres of Aijal station comes to an abrupt end when her husband dies.

Aijal is heavily in debt, and Christine must swallow her grief and guilt and dedicate herself to saving the property. But high a price must she pay to realise her dream?

Flamboyant Laila Schulz is Christine's sister-in-law, and her best friend—until her own life is also marked by tragedy. Laila leaves Aijal to lose herself in the glitz and glamour of city life. But the past can never be left behind completely . . .

Spanning the years 1922 to 1940, *To Touch The Earth* is an unforgettable saga of family secrets, love, betrayal and retribution.

Di Morrissey
The Last Mile Home

FROM ONE OF AUSTRALIA'S FINEST STORYTELLERS COMES A CLASSIC LOVE STORY THAT WILL REMAIN IN YOUR HEART FOREVER . . .

It is 1953 in a small country town in Australia, a time of postwar prosperity and hope.

The Holtens are wealthy austere graziers who have lived on the land for generations. The McBrides are a large and loving shearer's family who are new arrivals in the district.

When the McBrides' eldest daughter falls in love with the Holtens' only son and heir, the barriers to their love seem overwhelming.

But in the end, their love triumphs even over tragedy . . . and hope and joy are their enduring legacy.